English Connection

English Connection

by

Keith Hoare

Publish by: Ragged Cover Publishing

ISBN - 978-1908090-45-4

June 2015

www.keithhoare.com

Chapter 1

"Come on Larisa, come to Ricky," Ricky Strong mocked, gripping a kitchen knife in his right hand.

The terror in Larisa's eyes said it all, as she gazed transfixed at the knife glinting in the single central light of the small bedsit. Except his words had also shocked her into self-preservation. Desperately backing away, she looked around the room for something, anything she could use as a weapon for protection, but could see nothing. Her movement backwards came to an abrupt stop as she finally hit the wall of the room, and she began to raise her hands in the forlorn hope that action may protect her.

As the knife touched her skin, before penetration, Ricky's face inches from hers, with a supercilious grin written across it, summed up her pitiful attempt at escape. He knew she was dead.

Determined to at least wipe the grin from his face, before she died, Larisa brought her hands up even higher, then sinking the long manicured nails deep into his face, ripping her nails down, turning his mocking look into a distortion of agony. He pulled the knife from her body, slashing it at her as he backed away, blood blinding him, the pain intense.

Larisa stumbled away, through the door and down narrow stairs. The room was on the first floor of a building, the stairs leading to a single door between two shops in Gerrard Street, London. With her hands covered in blood, the wound in her side had already part-soaked her blouse. Her head felt light, her vision was going, she fell down the last three steps, sprawling in the short hallway leading to the front door. Larisa could hear Ricky screaming at the top of his voice, his words filled with abuse and threats, as he stumbled down after her. Drawing herself up, in a final effort to escape, Larisa tore open the door, falling through and out onto the narrow pavement.

At first, because she was face down, and her cries for help sounded pathetic and more like whimpering, passers-by believed she was drunk, taking wide berths, carrying on with their own business, until, that is, the tell-tale crimson blood began to trickle away from her body.

A woman screamed, people ran towards her, mobiles were used to call the emergency services. CCTV cameras moved around to see why there were increasing crowds, zooming in on her. A cruising police van had now stopped. First aid, at last, was being given to the badly injured girl.

***

Colonel Karen Harris, aged thirty-two and commander of Unit T, an EU military force drawn together by all the member countries to combat people trafficking, entered the hospital. She was accompanied by two of her soldiers, both wearing civilian clothing, the same as her. Except all of them were armed, the vehicle they arrived in bulletproof and left guarded by another soldier.

Detective Inspector Morris, from New Scotland Yard, approached. "Colonel, it is good of you to arrive so quickly."

"We were local, Inspector. Is the girl awake?"

"Yes, the doctors wanted to sedate her, but she wouldn't have it until she'd spoken to you. Sir Peter Parker was able to get a message through to your office. They confirmed you were in the area and you would make your way to the hospital."

"Then I should see her immediately, so the medical staff can get on with their job?"

As they went up in the lift, Karen asked the inspector what he had found out about her.

"Her full name is Larisa Vance. She is a known prostitute, but doesn't have a room above the shops. Why she was there, she's not saying, but it's not unusual for girls who rent the rooms to share with another working girl, it helps with the rent. We've checked the room, which is now a crime scene. The blood on the wall and floor is being tested to see if the other person in the room was injured. CCTV camera recordings are also being checked for sightings of anyone else coming out of the entrance before, or after her. There is, however, a back door leading into a yard, that shares its back wall with the property directly opposite, and the side boundary walls are low enough to scale, so we could be out of luck. I believe whoever was in the room left that way. I'm of the opinion Larisa had taken a client to the room, he turned out violent and fortunately she was able to escape."

Karen shrugged. "It sounds feasible, but we shall see. Often what looks simple, turns out to be far more complicated. After all, how many clients try to kill the pro, apart from serial killers?"

He smiled inwardly, how was it these people always had to complicate what to him seemed logical? "Maybe you're right, but this is the West End, it attracts quite a mix of people, and often with them, violence comes in the extreme. We, the police, see it every night."

Nothing more could be said, they'd arrived at the private room Larisa was in. A policeman was standing outside. He looked at Karen's warrant card, even though she was with the inspector.

When Karen went inside, the room was cleared to

leave her alone with the girl.

"You know who I am, Larisa?" Karen asked.

"Yes, you're Karen Harris. The police told me you were on your way. I didn't want then to sedate me until I talked to you."

"Why me?"

"I met Stacy. She and I talked a lot and she told me about you. How you'd often go covert, become one of us, to get at traffickers and take them down. She didn't really need to tell me, all the girls trust you, Karen. You're one of us and have helped so many. Besides, when you come, you often bring violence. For the traffickers, the pimps, it's the only law they respect."

"Thank you for your confidence in me. Where is Stacy?"

Larisa looked down. "She's dead."

A cold shiver ran down Karen's back at her answer. Stacy was one of her girls. "How did she die?"

"Her pimp I knew as Ricky, had taken us both to a house out in the country. He'd arranged a weekend for us with good money. We'd been there for one day, but the next day Stacy got a violent one and was beaten up very badly. When I say badly, it was life-threatening. I was with her in her last moments. It was then she told me that she worked at times for you and had found out about a group of men who were extremely violent and had actually killed. She wanted me to go to her bedsit on Gerrard Street. If I took the metal bed knob off the bed head, there was, hidden inside the tube of the headboard, a mobile SIM card, with a piece of paper wrapped around. That paper had your contact number. She said it was very important and I must promise to get it, and call you using the number and no one else. What could I do, but agree. The girl was dying and all she could think of was to get that bloody SIM card to you."

"You found the SIM card?"

She shook her head. "I didn't have time, it's still there. Back at the house, I was shocked by Stacy's death, realised I could be next, after all, I'd witnessed it. So I didn't wait around and climbed out the bathroom window." She hesitated, reliving those moments. "I'd never been so scared. How far I ran, god knows, but I ended up on a main road. Wearing a short skirt and high stiletto boots, it wasn't very difficult to get a lift. Mind you, it took three rides to get me to London, then a tube to Gerrard Street. I'd hoped, if I could find the SIM, you'd help me."

"So what went wrong?"

"They must have known Stacy and I talked. Ricky was waiting at the bedsit. We had a fight, I escaped by digging my nails into his face, well, more his eyes really, he'd pulled back in pain. It was enough to get out, even though he'd cut me."

"You did well, Larisa, I also know you have refused a sedative, to help with the pain and give you some much-needed rest. I appreciate you doing that. But we're after one of the most vicious gangs that have ever operated in the UK. They prey on children's homes and the naivety of young girls seeking a career in modelling and theatre, besides the runaways and homeless. You're the only girl who has survived following one of their attacks. In fact, you're so important to our investigation, I intend to move you to our unit in France as soon as possible. There you will be safe. Then, with the help of my charity, you can start to rebuild your life; you will never be alone, I promise."

"I'd like that, my life's been a nightmare over the last year. Once you're taken by one of their pimps, there is no escape, they never leave you alone. You don't know just how much I wanted to die, laid out on the pavement. I'd kill myself rather than walk out of here on my own. They will be waiting for me."

"You say they will be waiting, why do you believe that?" Karen asked with interest. Although she knew, she wanted to hear why Larisa thought they would.

"I've been to loads of parties, been used in sex games, taken to bed by two and three men at the same time. I was on occasions afraid to even look at myself in the mirror, I was so ashamed at what I'd been doing. But this party was different. Apart from girls like me, they had very young children, not even old enough to have been on the game. They had them running around naked, giving blowjobs and sometimes held down by men while they raped them. The men I was servicing were household names, politicians, TV personalities, besides senior police inspectors. These people are powerful, have good connections and think they can do as they like with you. Even as far as murder to satisfy their perversions. They will already know I'm here, will want to shut me up, after I saw Stacy killed. For me, without your help, I'm dead."

Karen walked to the window and looked out, then turned. "They may believe they are immune. They're not, and up against me this time. I'm just as powerful and will meet them head-on. If they have any ideas I'm soft, they will soon learn, I'm not and can be just as violent. From you, I will want names, times, dates, full descriptions of your experiences, Larisa. We will not be able to pull them in with your evidence, they would shoot us to pieces, claiming you were a prostitute and there voluntarily. However, these people don't give up, they're addicted to such depravity and because of that, with names, we watch and wait. Then when we do strike, we'll bring them all down, like a pack of cards."

"I understand. For me just to be able to tell someone means so much. I, like you, will watch and wait, they will slip up, even I can see that. I agree, for such people it is an addiction. When you see the raping of a ten-year-old by three of them. The screams, the terror in that little girl's face will live with me forever. How I wish I could be with you, when you fire your gun."

Chapter 2

Sedrick Main, a man in his forties, six foot three, who hired himself out as a bodyguard for the rich, was driving. Alongside him, Ricky Strong. A man in his early twenties, small, muscular, with a passion for kick boxing. He had also been Stacy's pimp.

Ricky turned the rear-view mirror to look at his face for the second time. The deep scratches down his face looked angry, infected. "I'll kill that Larisa when I find her, rip her fucking heart out while it still beats," he muttered.

Sedrick laughed. "You should have done that when you had her, rather than let her escape, ending up worried that she may have spoiled your looks for the women. As it is, I'm told Unit T has Larisa, so you'll not get near her now."

"Fucking Unit T, they're wimps, pansies. They'll not stop me," he retorted bravely.

"I see, then you want me to turn around and drop you off at the hospital to complete your botched job? I understand their commander is there. Are you sure you want to take on a hardened killer, like her? Because that's what she is."

"You think I'm stupid enough to walk into the hospital looking like this, besides, the Harris woman is never alone. I'm not facing a trigger-happy psychopath like her. But once you know where they have Larisa holed up, then I'll complete the job."

Sedrick sighed inwardly; why did he have to work with such idiots? Killing Larisa now was academic and would only be for revenge. He knew with Unit T's commander having already seen the girl, it was too late. All they could do now was close up the routes that Larisa knew about. That included Ricky here. Before that happened, he'd a job for him.

Coming off the motorway in Slough, Sedrick turned into the drive of a pre-war semi-detached. A woman looked out of the front window and had already opened the door for them, by the time they'd climbed out of the car.

"What happened to you?" she asked Ricky.

Sedrick gave a laugh. "He finally met his match with a girl who wouldn't let him shag her. How about bacon and eggs, Janet, I'm bloody starving?"

"No problems, I'll get on with it. Musowa's in the cellar."

Sedrick ran down the cellar steps, Ricky followed.

"All right, Musowa?" Sedrick asked.

Musowa was from Pakistan, had been in the UK for over six years. He'd come as a student, but overstayed his visa after teaming up with Sedrick. He now ran a grooming business for him.

"I'm good. Janet and I are really busy at the moment, we've got close to forty kids online at any time."

Sedrick leaned forward and using the mouse on the computer, he clicked through the latest 'selfie' photos the kids had sent, stopping on one showing a young girl completely exposed, sitting on her bed.

"She's ready for the next step. Lives in London and thinks I'm the same age as her," Musowa told him. "I've also got a fifteen-year-old who lives in Sunderland who has agreed to meet after school next Wednesday. Here's her photo."

Musowa clicked on a file named 'autumn' and a girl's photo came up. She was wearing a bikini, obviously taken on holiday.

"Pretty girl, why did she agree to meet?"

"She's really into the band 'Wild Things' and I told

9

her I knew them all really well. She asked if I could get signed photos. That was easy, all I did was drop their public signatures on a photo, after I added a bit extra that made it personal for her. A week or so later I asked if she'd be interested in meeting them backstage, but she had to keep it to herself, or it couldn't happen. She's been mailing every day, since then, wanting to know how she could meet them and promised she'd tell no one else, including her parents."

"So how did you handle that?"

"I told her in a month they'd be at the Leeds Arena and I'd set it up for her. Then I mailed her an even better opportunity to be with the band for her summer holidays. That the band are looking for a few girls to act as groupies in a movie they're making. I've promised to take her to meet them backstage when they are in Leeds. Maybe if they like her they'd offer her a part in the film, but she must keep it secret, or everyone else would want the part and she'd not get a look in."

"She fell for it?"

"Completely, she's not even telling her parents, that's how scared she is of losing the opportunity."

"Good, once you have her, I'll make arrangements for the sale. How about the live cam programme, have you got it working?"

"Perfectly, I've already six online all the time. Four of those are in the kid's bedrooms, they have no idea we have control of their computer and are watching them. The other two computers are notebooks. Those kids often close the notebook up when they finish on line."

"Can't the police online protection unit track you?" Ricky asked.

Musowa laughed. "You wouldn't understand, Ricky, but we use remote servers in different parts of the world to access the kid's computers and deal with the emails. Nothing comes directly into here, from any of the kids we're in touch with. We could have the police agency in the next room and they'd not know it was us talking to the kids from in here."

"It's time you learned how to groom the kids, Ricky," Sedrick cut in. "I want you here for the next month. Apart from allowing the scratches to heal on your face, which are a dead giveaway to the police looking for the person who attacked Larisa, I want you off the streets, in case they come looking for you, from her description."

"What! Me having to spend all day chatting to naive snotty-nosed kids?" he came back at him.

"It's that, or you take your chances on the street. So you can make use of your so-called smooth tongue and get the kids to strip in front of a camera, then send you the photos."

"For what reason?"

"That's not any of your business. Help out here, do everything Musowa wants of you, or you fuck off."

At that moment Janet shouted down the food was ready.

***

Later, Janet was sitting with Sedrick. Musowa and Ricky were down in the cellar.

"So how's the model agency going?" Sedrick asked.

"It's getting there. After the flyers, which were handed out to girls in the shopping centre, we've had quite a few come in. Most with parents, but a few just off the street with their friends. I've earmarked five that are suitable."

"That's good, for the moment keep it all above board, do the test shoots and follow up the potentials with the offer

11

of our three-day residential training course."

"How much can I discount the package, to pull them in?"

"Thirty per cent and sell the portfolio as an extra; once they have done the first day and been enthused over by the photographer, they will have the belief they could be the next supermodel."

She laughed. "Some hope, but many will do well on the glamour side, with a few going on to prostituting, once we convince them that's their only route to success."

"Well push as hard as you can, we've lost two good girls after the party at Macgregor's got out of hand."

"How long's Ricky here for, I don't like that man?"

"Not long, we have plans for him. Just keep him on the low-grade contacts."

Chapter 3

Karen was in her flat located above the London branch of the charity, Lost but Never Forgotten, which she was the director of. Normally her friend Sherry Malloy would be with her, except Sherry, being part of the unit's Dark Angel strike force, was on a compulsory annual assessment course. The girl was twenty-two, and had worked hard training for this assessment, wanting desperately to remain part of the group.

Karen was glad Sherry wasn't with her, she'd a date with a man called Howard Driver. They had first met at a fundraising party she'd attended, put on in aid of her charity. He was a businessman running a small but profitable company in the pharmaceutical industry and was very wealthy. In fact, he'd donated ten thousand pounds that night. A month later, Karen met Howard, quite by chance again, when they were both queuing up to be served in a coffee house off Kensington Road. After collecting their drinks, both of them ended up sharing a table. The coffee house was absolutely packed and they were the only seats available. They'd talked more and Howard had asked her out. Karen wasn't sure, after all he was in his forties and in her view a little old for her, but she was lonely and desperately wanted company away from the operations she was involved in. So she'd agreed to meet him at a restaurant in Knightsbridge. However, although Karen had agreed to go out, she wasn't a believer in chance meetings, they always worried her and she told Stanley, the senior man in her intelligence unit, of the date.

"I'd like you to look into Howard's business and associates," she'd told him.

"Very wise, Karen, it would be the height of stupidity not to. I also think you should have protection until we're certain of Howard's intention. You must carry your tracker, besides wear your watch. I'd be more comfortable, when you are with this man, that by pressing the watcher's winder you could summon help."

Karen had no option but to agree, except it had put a dampener on her date, knowing she was under surveillance.

***

Wearing a black dress, finishing three inches above the knee, five inch heels and a light coat, Karen climbed out of a taxi, owned by the unit and driven by one of her soldiers, at the restaurant where she'd arranged to meet Howard.

The head waiter came up to her as she entered the foyer. "You have a reservation, madam?" he asked.

"Yes, the name's Lady Harris." Karen rarely used her official civilian title, but on occasions she'd use it for devilment, to see the reaction. "I'm joining a Mr Driver for dinner, I believe he's booked a table?"

By telling him her name, he'd suddenly realised just who she was. "Yes of course, Lady Harris, Mr Driver is already waiting for you at the bar, may we take your coat?" he asked, snapping his fingers, and another waiter approached them to take the item.

"Karen, you had me worried that you'd changed your mind?" A man, tall, thin and dressed in an expensive suit said as he kissed her on each cheek, when Karen entered the bar.

"Sorry, Howard, the traffic was really bad. But I'm here now. This is a lovely place, do you come here a lot?"

He shook his head. "Not as often as I'd like. I'm

abroad a great deal. Anyway, how about a drink, while we look at the menu?"

Dinner was good, the waiters attentive, the conversation light and general. Now they were left with a glass of brandy each in front of them.

"You have told me little about yourself, Karen. Of course I know your public persona and all about your charity, but what do you to do for relaxation, when you're not working?"

Karen shrugged. "Anything really. I ski, dance, ride at times and have even done a little skydiving. That was to raise money for my charity and pretty scary. I also like to swim. What about you?"

"I like to walk, often before breakfast. I too ski, you should come to my lodge in Switzerland. There's still nearly a month of good skiing left."

She smiled. "I'd love to, but I warn you, I'm not very good, so you'll need to stick close by me."

"Then it is agreed, I'll arrange flights."

"There's no need to do that, Howard. I'll need my aircraft with me, so we can use that. My work is 24-7, so I may have to leave at very short notice."

"I understand completely. Then, I assume with the way you're talking, you'll join me?"

"Why not, it's been a long time since I skied, I'm already looking forward to it."

"I intended leaving this coming Friday, would that be convenient for you?"

"Where's your lodge?"

"St Moritz. I always fly to Zurich, it's around four hours drive from there."

Karen sat quietly for a moment, not sure if she should be doing this. Then she made a decision: even if he changed his mind, she wouldn't. "I'll log a flight plan, we'll go from Gatwick. There is one more thing, Howard. I cannot go without protection, well, cannot is untrue. More to the point, I won't travel alone these days; for me, it's far too dangerous and if you're with me, for you as well."

"That sounds very ominous, Karen. At the same time intriguing. Tell me, are you alone tonight?"

"Do you want me to be, alone?"

"Of course, a man would be very foolish to want to share you. Although I now suspect you're not and haven't been since you arrived. That also begs the question if you've looked into my affairs before even turning up tonight?"

Karen picked her brandy up and sipped it slowly, all the time looking at him. "I live in a very dangerous world. It's a world that exists in every town and city, Howard. How many attempts have been made on my life, I've lost count. But my work is vitally important for thousands of victims caught up in trafficking. I'd love us to be friends, spend time together, but you must understand to be with me, you also risk a great deal. I'd not ask any man to do that, without them being very aware."

Howard put his hand across the table, grasping hers. Karen didn't pull back. "I've a confession to make. You made a great impression on me at the charity dinner. Your speech was frightening for a man when most things that happen to me, don't hold a candle to your life. And yet it obviously showed the passion and commitment you had in helping these victims. That is why I gave as I did, to help in my own small way. Then I couldn't believe it when I saw you in the coffee house and I confess I joined the queue deliberately to strike up a conversation. When we found ourselves at the same table, it was the perfect chance to ask you out. So in answer to your question. Bring the entire unit with you, but please come."

Karen smiled. "Then how can a girl refuse? Two will be more than sufficient, I promise you'll never see them."

Chapter 4

"Why aren't you coming with us, Autumn?" her best friend Rose asked. "You always come to the bowling alley on Wednesday afternoons."

"Well, I can't today, I'm with mum," she lied.

Rose said no more, just shrugged and walked away with three other girls.

Autumn looked at her watch, it was a quarter past twelve and she'd told him twelve. She began to run, hoping he'd not decided she wasn't coming and left. As she rounded the bend she recognised the registration number, texted to her that morning: he was still waiting.

Musowa wound the window down as she came alongside, she was breathing heavily.

"You're Autumn?" he asked with a smile.

"Yes, I'm really sorry I kept you waiting, I couldn't get away from the other girls."

"It happens, get in and we'll be off."

Once in the car, he looked her over. The photo she'd sent hadn't done her justice. She was a very pretty girl, with long auburn hair. "You didn't tell your friends you were meeting me?"

"God, no, they'd want to come, or tell mum and she'd be grilling me on how we met and then stop me coming."

"So how long can you stay out?"

"I've to be in for nine on schooldays. Mum has forgotten I've got the afternoon off and thinks I'm having my tea at Rose's. I told her we had to finish a project." Autumn shrugged indifferently. "She's cool with that, I often have tea there when mum's working overtime, which she is tonight. So long as I'm home for nine, she'll not be bothered."

"We meet the group at six and it's only an hour and a half back to your home, so you'll have a good hour with them and be back in plenty of time. Have you brought a change of clothes with you? You can hardly meet them in your school uniform."

Autumn opened her bag and pulled out jeans and a jumper. "I've got these and really sexy underwear I borrowed out of mum's drawer. I could hardly wear school knickers under my jeans," she added with a laugh.

"I don't know, are they really naff then?" he ribbed.

She scrunched her nose. "Believe me, they are. We'll have to stop, so I can get changed. I also need the toilet."

"We'll stop at a service station for the toilet, but I don't want you walking through in your uniform. People are funny these days and dead suspicious. A girl out of school during school hours, besides being at a service station in school clothes, might be stopped by the police. You can change in the car."

"I never thought of that. I could tell them you're my brother."

He laughed. "Do I look like your brother?"

She shook her head. "I suppose not. But you could be as far as they were concerned."

"Maybe, but we don't take the risk, get yourself changed and stop delaying."

Autumn said no more and began to remove her cardigan and blouse. Pulling the jumper over her head, she let it drop down, covering her arms, while she changed her bra, embarrassed with him at her side.

He looked across as she removed her shoes, then pulled her knickers off, keeping herself covered by the skirt. "I can see your point about the knickers, Autumn, what are the others like?"

She showed them to him. They were, as she'd said, sexy, flimsy and virtually see-through. "Do you think they're okay and not too revealing?"

"Why not, you're hardly going to stand around with nothing else on. But if they make you feel better, rather than the school knickers, wear them."

Autumn grinned and slipped them on quickly, followed by the jeans, before she released the skirt and replaced her shoes. Then tying her hair back, she put a little make-up on, with eyeshadow. Already she was becoming excited as they came closer to Leeds.

They pulled into a service station. Musowa nodded to the back seat. "Put the leather jacket on and the peak cap, not your school coat, it's cold outside. Then you can also pick up a burger for each of us from the takeaway," he told her, at the same time taking a ten pound note from his pocket, pushing it into her hand.

"Are you coming?"

"No, I want a smoke and you can't smoke inside. Just don't hang around. Forget a drink, I've got bottles of coke in the boot, I'll get them out."

Autumn ran off, while Musowa took two bottles of coke from the boot and opened one. Drinking a little, he took a small bottle from the dash glove compartment, emptying a little of the contents into the coke bottle he'd drunk from. Then replacing the lid he turned it over and over carefully, in order to mix the liquids, but not let the pressure increase much. Once mixed, he released the cap slightly, allowing the gas to come out. Finally, he tightened the cap and placed the bottle in the cup holder on the passenger side.

He was leaning on the side of the car when Autumn returned, carrying a paper bag. "I got fries as well, I hope you don't mind?" she said, handing him the change.

"That's fine. No one stopped you, did they?"

She shook her head. "No, even the toilets were empty and the lad in McDonalds didn't say anything."

"That's good, now into the car, we'll have ten minutes while I finish my cigarette, then we set off again. We'll be there in plenty of time."

Musowa watched Autumn finish off the coke. Now he was happy, it was all slotting into his plan for her.

"So do you have a boyfriend then?"

"No, I've been asked out once, but he didn't turn up. Something about he had to do work at home. But he never re-arranged our date. I was a bit upset, I'd spent all my pocket money on make-up and a necklace to go with my top." Then she turned to look at him. "But you're my boyfriend now, aren't you?"

"If you want me to be, then yes. Except people of my age expect more from their girlfriend than just holding hands."

"You mean like sex?"

"Yes."

She hesitated, biting her lip, nervously. "I can do that, but you'll have to teach me, I've never done it before. Then I'd have no chance in getting the pill from the school nurse, she only gives those out to the older girls, so we'd have to use condoms. Even those you'd need to get, I'd die going into a shop to buy some."

He laughed, glancing at the car clock. "We've got at least three hours to spare. We'll go to my place."

Autumn's stomach churned, she'd not realised he lived in Leeds. Now he was suggesting they go there. "You're not expecting me to have sex, are you? I don't want that yet, until I get to know you better."

"Of course I'm not. If you're going to be my

21

girlfriend, we both need to trust each other. I want you to see where I live, we'll have a couple of drinks in comfort, rather than sitting in a car till six."

***

By the time they arrived at the so-called flat of his, Autumn was very sleepy. Most of the time he spoke to her after leaving the service station, she'd not even answered. The drug he'd put in her drink was taking its time to work, but it was working. Although, when they arrived, she was still awake. Except she needed helping out of the car and into a lift.

Sedrick was inside the flat when Autumn was brought in.

"I need to lie down, Musowa, I really don't feel well," she said, her voice low and virtually a mumble.

"Come on, let's get your shoes off, then you can lie on the bed. After a couple of hours you'll be fine," he told her, urging her through and into the bedroom.

A little later Sedrick came into the bedroom and looked down at the sleeping Autumn. "She's a good-looking girl, you did well," he told him, with obvious satisfaction. "I've already got a sale for her, so she could be with her new owner by the weekend. You get back to London and keep an eye on Ricky."

Chapter 5

Kay Grove stood for a moment in the hall at home, confused. Why were all the lights off? Where was Autumn? Picking up the telephone, she dialed Rose's number.

"Jane, it's Kay, is Autumn with you?"

"No, Rose told me she was with you today. I'd asked where she was when Rose came back from the bowling alley, she's usually with her when you work late. Rose was a bit put out, because she said she was coming last week. Has Autumn been home at all?"

"I don't think so, the place was in darkness when I got in. Jake's on the 2:10 shift today, so he's not back. I'll call him, check if he saw her before he left for work. Thanks Jane, sorry to have disturbed you."

"No problems, call me later, let me know she's safe. I'll be worried all night now."

"Will do, bye."

***

The time was just after eleven the same night. Jake was pacing the room, Kay had telephoned every person she could think of looking for Autumn. Now they had finally called the police and reported her missing. There was a knock on the door. Both looked at each other and Jake headed for the door. It was the police.

"Have you found Autumn?" Jake burst out, as soon as he opened the door.

The man shook his head. "I'm sorry, Sir, I've just had the call and made my way here to take all the girl's details. I'm Detective Inspector Walsh, the man with me is Detective

Hammond. May we come in?"

Once in the lounge he pulled out his notebook. "I will need the time she was last seen, contact numbers of who you have called and a recent photo. Also, does your daughter have a laptop, or tablet. I will need to have them checked for recent communications on any of the social sites."

"That's all very well Inspector, but shouldn't you be out looking for her?" Kay asked.

"We already have a general missing persons out Mrs Grove, but we require a recent photo to circulate, with a description of what she was wearing. I know you reported to the desk that she was in her school clothes, but you need to make sure she'd not been planning this and taken other clothes, or even come home and changed. Perhaps we could go to her bedroom?"

"Autumn wouldn't just walk out of the house, Inspector. That's not her way, I can assure you," Kay retorted.

"You misinterpret me. We have to be sure. I'm not judging the girl in any way, most who go missing seem perfectly sensible, yet later we often find it was planned to some degree, even if it's just to go to a concert, or whatever. So please check her drawers, make sure and give us an alternative description of what she might be wearing."

While Detective Hammond checked the computer, Kay was going through the drawers. Then she turned to look at DI Walsh. "I'm sorry, you're right. Her best jeans are missing, so is her favourite top. Her going was planned, but where and with whom, I've no idea."

"Think nothing of it, Mrs Grove. At least this is not pointing to an opportunist, as she knew she was going. I'll circulate an alternative description of what she may be wearing now. Let's hope wherever she's gone, it's just the matter of a late bus, or a car breakdown."

***

Two days after Autumn had been reported missing. DI Walsh was making a report. Already, hundreds of volunteers along with the police had searched local areas, resulting in nothing. The national papers were making a big thing as well, with the girl's photo on the front page and a clever overlay showing what she might be wearing now.

"Call for you on five," another Inspector shouted over.

DI Walsh picked up the receiver, he'd had so many calls they had been shifted towards other detectives, only the most promising sightings came to him.

"This is the manager of a service station on the A1. Am I talking to the detective looking for the missing fifteen-year-old, Autumn Grove?" a woman asked.

"You are, how can I help?"

"We have the girl on CCTV. One of the lads in McDonald's said he recognised her. We've gone back on the recordings and he pointed her out in the queue. It certainly looks like Autumn. We also have the same girl leaving the complex and getting into a car. You'll need to send people down to look at it."

"I'll be down myself, can you give me the exact address?"

An hour and a half later DI Walsh, with Detective Hammond, was standing watching the recordings.

"How about recordings from the petrol station, would it have picked up the car leaving the service area, even if it didn't go in for fuel?" DI Walsh asked.

The manager shook her head. "No, only if the car

went into the petrol station area. It didn't, we've already checked at that time and up to an hour beyond. This is all we have, I'm afraid."

"That's fine, what you have is fantastic, congratulations on your employee being so keen-eyed and remembering her."

The manager grinned. "She was a good-looking girl, young yes, but didn't look that young. I think he fancied her, between you and me. I'll have him come in and give you a statement. If we can help any more, just ask."

Later, DI Walsh and Detective Hammond were sitting in their car.

"It's time I spoke to the chief constable. With what's been found in the transcripts of the chat line she used and seeing her casually buy food, the girl's been groomed. I think she's also been trafficked, that is something that needs to go to our specialist unit in London."

Detective Hammond's eyes lit up. "Does that mean Karen Harris will come to see us? You know she's really famous and mega-rich. She deals with traffickers."

He shook his head. "Very unlikely, we have our own unit in Scotland Yard, run by a Sir Peter Parker. She's international and wouldn't be interested in one girl, believe me, she goes after the gangs."

"Well, at least someone who has experience in the way girls are groomed should be looking at that chat site. What little I read was obviously directed towards fishing for girls such as Autumn."

"You can believe they already are, the child protection unit in the police are not so stupid they'd miss that site, believe me. But now we can show a possible link, they may be able to track back and find out who this guy she was talking with is and hopefully get an address."

Chapter 6

Howard and Karen were in St Moritz. They had arrived the day before. Already Howard had arranged for Karen to have a refresher lesson with an instructor, to bring her up to speed. While she was with the instructor, Howard had made his way to a ski shop for a replacement strap for one of his skis.

"Howard, I heard you were here," came a male voice from behind him.

Howard turned to see Sir Samuel French standing there. "Samuel, what a surprise, is your good lady with you?" he asked.

He shook his head. "No, she's not well and decided to stay home. Come, join me for coffee, we should talk."

Howard glanced at his watch. "Delighted, except I can only stay a short time. I need to collect someone from the bottom slopes shortly."

Samuel urged him out of the shop towards a cafe. "Yes, Howard, I've been told you're with Lady Harris. I didn't know you were friends with her."

"We met at a charity do, and later, after bumping into Karen in a coffee house, we went out for dinner. Do you know her?"

Samuel didn't answer immediately, as by now they had entered a small cafe. Asking for coffee to be brought, Samuel urged Howard to a corner table.

"You ask if I know Lady Harris. I don't personally, but of course she's a well-known figure in the social world, as well as the press seeming to follow her around like lap dogs."

"That's unfair, she's really a very nice young lady. You should meet her socially."

"Why shouldn't she be, after all, the girl has had the world at her feet since she was abducted, besides getting very rich on it. As for meeting her, I intend to, in fact, you'll bring her to the casino tonight."

Howard frowned. "Excuse me, I already have plans and intend to stay in tonight. Maybe later in the week."

Coffee was brought, the conversation was curtailed until the girl left them alone.

"I'm not interested in waiting around for you to get into her pants. From what I hear, she'll give you no problems on that score, Harris often spends her time away from her unit, working as an escort, which as you know is a posh word for a prostitute. So forget wasting your time cuddling up with her in front of the fire, like some lovesick child, drag her into the bedroom, have her strip for you, she's good at that, then fuck her hard, that's what she's here for and would be expecting you to do. It's all she understands."

"I'm not liking your tone, Samuel, perhaps it would be better if we avoided each other," Howard retorted.

He smiled. "I couldn't care less if you like it, or don't. I know your pharmaceutical business is a front to sell marijuana, besides at times, class A drugs to the rich. As for your potential lover, you realise I presume, her intelligence unit will already know everything there is to know about you, which means she will also know you deal. So is she here with protection, like she normally has, or hasn't she mentioned that small point?"

"Yes, she did mention it. But I've not seen anyone. Although it's understandable she does have protection, considering her role as commander of Unit T."

Samuel nodded his understanding. "They'll be here, count on it. They could even be sitting watching us, you'd never know. But I come back to asking myself, just why is an attractive, rich and eligible women messing about with you? I'll tell you why, you're probably now part of one of her covert operations and she's here to bring you down big time. Keep in mind, in the EU, under her mandate, it's ten years for dealing and all your assets taken. How do you think she is as rich as she is? Even the aircraft you were in she purchased for a fraction of its worth. It originally belonged to a trafficking cartel she took down. That woman doesn't bugger about with people like you, believe me. So make sure you're at the casino tonight. Don't have me sending Clout to fetch you, he's more of an action man, rather than inclined to stand there and ask you nicely, like I'm doing." Samuel said no more, finished his coffee and left.

Howard remained there for a time. He knew Samuel was right, women like Karen wouldn't waste their time with him. Her aircraft was more valuable than all his assets, and then, the flat where he dropped her off after dinner was obviously expensive, in the area it was located. As for Samuel's assessment that she'd willingly jump into bed with him, he very much doubted that. Even last night, she'd just made the excuse she was tired and went to her own room. Now, with Samuel laying the facts bare, he was nervous, in fact, frightened that she'd come for him.

***

"How did you get on then?" Howard asked Karen, when he picked her up from the practice slopes.

"I did well, in fact it all came back pretty quickly, so tomorrow we're out on the main slopes."

"That's good news. I was thinking, would you like to visit the casino tonight?"

Karen looked at him for a moment. "If you want, but

I thought tonight was going to be a stay-in night?"

He shrugged. "Well, we're only here for a few days, it's a nice night and not snowing, so we should get out and see what the nightlife has to offer."

"I'm cool with that, what should I wear?"

"A long dress, if you have one, would be good."

Chapter 7

Following dinner and coming up to nine the same night Howard, accompanied by Karen, left for the casino. Once inside Karen was impressed. It was smart, contemporary and already buzzing, with most tables full.

Collecting a few chips, she was soon standing at a roulette table, Howard at her side.

"So how do you suggest I play my chips?" she asked.

"I usually use the side odds, I'm hopeless at hitting the right number. Most of the time I'm lucky to get the red or black right."

"That doesn't sound very good as a ploy, I think I'll just do the numbers. You never know, it could win and it's less hassle to keep up with the game," she said, after watching what everyone else was doing.

Of course Karen was not winning, and as she was just about to place her last chip on the table, she was addressed using her title, by a man behind her. She dropped the chip on the table and turned to see who it was. A man, she assumed in his sixties, was standing there. "Excuse me, do I know you?" she asked.

"The name's Sir Samuel French, Lady Harris, please, would you and Howard like to join me for a drink?" he asked, holding out his hand to her.

She shook it and smiled. "Why not, I'm not doing very well at the table, in fact I'm down to my shirt, so to speak," she answered, moving away from the table for other players to get close.

They all walked over to the bar area, taking seats around a low coffee table. Drinks were brought and soon only Karen, Howard and Samuel were left.

"It's very nice of you to invite me for a drink, Sir Samuel, have you known Howard for long?"

"For quite some time, haven't we Howard? Although, these days, we only seem to bump into each other here in St Moritz. I'd prefer that you call me Samuel, Lady Harris."

Karen did not reply immediately, but was sipping her drink, looking at him for a moment. "Then you must call me Karen. Except, I've a feeling I've heard your name before," she eventually said. "My memory is not too good these days, but names that come across my desk are usually not of particularly nice people. I hope you're not one of them, otherwise calling me by my Christian name may not be appropriate."

He smiled. "Then I will call you Karen and hope my name hasn't crossed your desk by way of being a villain, shall I?"

They talked for a short time, generally, before Karen stood. "If you will excuse me, I'll be back shortly."

Both men stood until she left, then sat down again.

"That was very sudden," Howard commented.

Samuel sighed. "You're so naive. She no more wanted the ladies than you or I want the gents. Karen may be wired, if so her intelligence unit would have picked up my name and found out all about me, so she's going to call them and ask what they have."

Howard laughed. "You read too many Bond books. Karen's on holiday, she's come to the casino for a night out. Why in god's name would she be wired? That's ridiculous. Besides, with the dress she's wearing, how would she hide it. Her unit's in France, it would have to be very powerful to get that far."

Samuel shook his head. "It's immaterial how she does it, if she has protection with her, they will be listening to every word that is said and could relay it on. Believe me, this is how Karen lives, how she survives, by being one step ahead. Now make yourself scarce, before she comes back. I'll tell her you've gone to use your chips up. I need to talk to her in private. After that you're welcome to take her home and carry on with your planned seduction in front of the fire, or just take my advice and go directly to the bedroom and fuck her. She'd appreciate that more, believe me."

Howard stood. "I wish you wouldn't be so coarse at times. It makes me sick."

"Me! Coarse? I can be worse, much worse, so fuck off, Howard, I'll send her to find you, so don't come back."

**

"Where's Howard?" Karen asked, after returning from the toilet and sitting down once more, taking a sip of her drink.

"He's back on the tables, addicted you see. Not like you, who walks away once you've blown your float. I presume you know Howard's into drugs?"

"I do know he deals in pharmaceuticals. Are you implying there is a problem?"

"Deals is certainly the correct word, Karen, after all, he supplies most of the users' personal needs around here, if you know what I mean."

Karen's mood changed. "I thought he was your friend - should you be telling someone like me?"

Samuel raised his hands slightly in a gesture. "Friend, no. Acquaintance maybe. But you must have known, he not only deals marijuana, but all the Class A drugs too?"

"I didn't know," she answered, except that was a partial lie, she did know of his dealings in marijuana.

Samuel tried to look shocked. "Come off it, Karen,

this attempt to play down what he does, won't wash. But it does beg the question as to why you're with a known drug dealer, who's obviously far too old for you, unless you're investigating his operation. If that's the case, I can understand why you're sharing his bed, the same as you've done many times with men, who shall we say, sit on the opposite side of the fence."

Karen didn't reply at first, but when she did her tone was more threatening. "You seem to have a thing in wanting to pull people down, Samuel, even interfere in their private lives. I should warn you, carry on talking about me the way you are, and expect your life to come to an abrupt end. I've killed people for less."

He looked directly at her, their eyes met. Hers cold and lifeless, the same as most professional killers passing sentence on their victim. He shuddered inwardly; Karen might seem naive, even passive, but she was far from that, and he knew it. He, however, showed nothing of his thoughts, and gave a slight smile. "Hit a raw nerve, did I? Is that how you sort out people who make you feel uncomfortable, by killing them? As it is, your visit to the toilet, I presume, helped with your conveniently bad memory and you've been given my background?"

"You mean, do I know you were accused of being mixed up in a paedophile ring and are still suspected of being associated with one, then yes I do."

Samuel waved to the waiter, who immediately brought more drinks, falling silent until he left them.

"It is good that you have been given that information, it saves lots of talk. As it is, I want you to do a job for me. Before you say anything, hear me out. There's a group in the UK, run by a man who can only be described as a psychopath. In the past you dealt with such a ring, one that gutted their victims after a bizarre auction, to see who would pay the most to do it. This man's actions make that operation seem like a kindergarten."

Karen thought back for a moment. "I remember the operation, we got most of them, but some evaded capture."

He laughed. "Evaded capture maybe, but not justice. I seem to recall those were the ones who died later under, shall we say, peculiar circumstances, like jumping from the top of a multi-storey car park, accidentally drowning in their bath, one in this country was even shot by a sniper while he and his friends enjoyed an after-dinner drink by the side of their pool. Need I go on?"

Karen shrugged. "It happens, many people commit suicide in those ways. As for the one shot, he may have had a very jealous lover."

"Whatever," he shrugged. "But to business. Have you heard of a man called Kenneth Parker, he was mentioned in the papers as running a private school in the north of England, that, it transpired, had a particularly bad record as far as looking after the children in its care? Or to put it more crudely, some of the staff were fiddling with the children's private parts."

"I read of the case, but he was never convicted of being a party in the abuse, in fact, wasn't he the one who blew the whistle?"

"That is true and shows just how stupid the law can be, or more to the point, how many powerful friends he'd lined up. Parker was the ringleader. The ones convicted were very scared of him and so they should have been. He's vicious, threatened harm to their families if they blabbed. Except the threat was very real, as some found out to their cost, when they tried to implicate him."

"So the reason you want me to get rid of this Parker

for you, is that you're in a power struggle with him and want to take over?"

He smiled. "I deserve that, but let me tell you this. Yes, I like the young, naive girls. But they are always over sixteen, give their consent and go home with money in their pocket. Parker is a sadist of the worst kind. Children, both girls and boys, are subject to appalling abuse, skinned while they still live. He's been known to chop bits off a child to see just how long they live, or go insane."

Karen sat silent for a time, taking another sip of her drink. "This is not for me, Samuel, it's a matter for the UK police. Parker's actions are that of a serial killer, not a trafficker. I mainly deal with trafficking cartels. It's true, as in all aspects of trafficking there is abuse of the victims, that goes without saying, but we will not go in just to pull them out, unless it means bringing down a significant operation. That is Unit T's mandate from Europe. But I will give you the name of someone in Scotland Yard who will act on your information. As for me, I won't, or rather can't. Murder is not part of my remit."

"I can accept that. However, if I told you his gang, working out of the UK, has already trafficked two hundred children this year, some snatched off the street, but not all... others brought into the UK, many of them to end up on the slab to be butchered... you'd still not be interested?"

"If that's true, of course I would, it's now sounding more like a trafficker operation, maybe even internationally connected with other rings. With so many victims, I would be interested."

"Very well, give me a number I can call you on and we'll talk again very soon."

Karen handed him a card with just a mobile number printed on it. "You can get me any time on this. If it goes to answer, I'll call back, so don't withhold the number. Although I'd be interested to know why you're telling me all this and what you're expecting out of it?"

"Your communication with the lads protecting you, switch it off before we discuss that."

Karen opened her bag and pulled out a mobile phone, with a thin wire plugged into it. "It's part of my mobile. If I pull the wire, then the microphone is cut off."

"No, I want to be certain, you also take the battery out."

She took it out and placed both on the table.

"That's good, now we talk more. The prostitute Larisa that you have under your protection, I want you to lose her statement, implicating a number of powerful men at a party that got a little out of hand."

"I'm not sure that you can call murder getting a little out of hand. Although you again are talking to the wrong person. The Metropolitan Police would be the ones to talk to on that."

"We can handle them, it's with you we want the reports wiped out."

Karen shrugged. "Then give me Parker and providing your group is not involved in trafficking, I will delete Larisa's statement from our records. Like I say, I'm only interested in trafficking."

"Very well, I can assure you we aren't. You can even come and see for yourself what we get up to."

She smiled. "I think I'll decline. Old men running around naked, believing they're super studs and wanting to prove it to me, doesn't turn me on."

Samuel glanced at his watch. "I should go, it's been interesting meeting you, Karen. One little point, I will know if you have removed the statement and any reports pertaining to our group. So don't believe for one moment you can say one thing and do something else." Then he stood and walked away.

Karen watched him go, at the same time replacing her mobile battery. She could understand him wanting Larisa's statement removed, after all, it contained a number of prominent names. What worried her was his statement that 'he would know'. That pointed to an informer within the unit. Something she'd suspected over the last few months, when operations seemed to be going wrong, although she'd been no closer to finding out just who it was. Finishing her drink, she wandered off; joining Howard at the roulette table, she touched his shoulder. "Hi, I'm back. Are you winning?"

He turned. "I was beginning to wonder when you'd come and find me. I'm glad you've come to take me away, my luck's on the floor, but you must be the luckiest woman in this room?"

"Why?" she asked, frowning.

"That last chip you left on the table was on a number that came up, you've got yourself thirty-five to one and your money back. What was the chip valued at?"

Karen smiled. "That's for me to know, Howard. I wouldn't have asked how much your chips were worth, or how much you have lost."

Chapter 8

Karen left St Moritz the following day. She couldn't see the point of staying, as already the information on Howard had been passed to the local police. The advice coming from them, via Karen's intelligence unit, was to leave immediately, before the press got wind of his imminent arrest.

"You're back, I didn't expect you till the end of the week," Sherry said, when Karen walked into the lounge of her chateau in France.

"Well, you shouldn't be here either. Why are you not on refresher training getting ready for your assessment?"

"If you'd not heard, until like yesterday, half the bloody camp was down with some stomach thing. They were throwing up everywhere, besides keeping bloody close to a toilet for the other end. Now everyone is better, it's put them behind, so I go next week."

"I didn't know. But you're right, I should have been told."

"So did you get any skiing in then?"

"A bit, but circumstances dictated I needed to bail fast." Then her eyes lit up. "I did win at the casino."

"You! Gamble in a casino, since when?"

"I gone there socially with a man, bought a few chips and down to the last one. Leaving the table while I got a drink from the bar. Me being me, apparently left it on part of a number and the man who ran the table thought I'd made a bet, pulling it completely over the number. I've got myself a banker's cheque for nine hundred euros," she told her, at the same time pulling it from her bag and waving it proudly. "I've never won anything in my life before."

Sherry grinned. "That's great, where are we going?"

"We're not, I've a load of work to catch up on. You can help if you've nothing to do?"

"That's fair enough, except I'm not working Saturday, I'm out partying that night. Which means you don't rope me into anything that includes the weekend. I'll be in no condition on the Sunday."

"What's so important about Saturday?"

"It's my birthday, don't say you'd forgotten?" she asked, then hesitated. "You had, hadn't you. You weren't coming back till Sunday."

Karen had no intention of admitting she had forgotten, so she just sighed. "No, I hadn't, except if you'd been on training, you'd not have been here to celebrate anyway. I was waiting until you were back next week."

"Oh!" she said, realising what Karen said would have been correct if she'd gone on her assessment. "Anyway, where are we going, now it's back to the actual day?"

"We should use the unit's clubhouse. It'd be unfair not to let all your friends in the camp share in your birthday."

Sherry's mouth dropped open. "Are you suggesting you'll also be at the club and will party with us?"

"Yes, why shouldn't I, I'm not that old?

She just looked at Karen. "I've got to see this, the great Karen Harris comes to the club. I'll even bring my camera." Then she left the room.

Karen sighed, had she drifted so far away from them all? Picking up the telephone, she called Stanley, her intelligence man. "Stanley, we need to get together. When are you free?"

"How about over lunch at my house, Karen?"

"That's fine, I'll be there at one."

***

After a particularly good lunch with Stanley and his wife, Karen was now sitting in their conservatory with a cup of coffee. Stanley's wife had gone to the shops.

"Right, what have we got, Stanley?" Karen asked.

"Where do I start? Stacy's SIM that we retrieved from her bedsit was full of pictures she'd taken with her mobile phone. On top of that she'd also overlaid small movie clips with her talking, giving the names of the people. Most I might add, had masks on, hiding their identity. I've had them all categorised and added notes. There are some quite high-up people among the names she gave, others are particularly wealthy. Unfortunately that's as far as we can go, with no true visual identities. Larisa's statement also mentions most of the names Stacy had, which is understandable since they were at the same sort of get-together. One name that did come up with both of them, was the man you met in Switzerland, Sir Samuel French."

"Interesting, particularly now he wants to help us in capturing Parker."

"Yes, we must ask ourselves why he wants to help. The problem we have now Stacy is dead and Larisa is out, is we have no way into these so-called parties. To close it all up, we need a girl inside, who can carry on where Stacy left off. How we're going to achieve that is not clear. You found Stacy, what's the chance of finding another girl?"

"I'll look into it, but the parties are only one outlet for Parker. What have we got on him?"

"Very little, we don't even know where he operates from. We have a London address, but he's not there much. We also know he travels to Germany a great deal. Whether he stays in the country or goes on to another, there again we have no details. All we can do is see if this Samuel French comes good on his promise."

Karen sighed. "Right, I'd better start talking to some of my informers. In the meantime, we need round-the-clock surveillance on names that keep coming up in Stacy's report. They could be the regulars and may lead us to the next venue. Ask Sir Peter if he can help out on that. I don't have an issue with him knowing what we're up to, except leave Parker's name out for the time being. Let him believe it's a paedophile ring using underage girls for the moment."

"No problems. Will you be around, or leaving the area?"

"I'm staying until Sunday at least, before I head to my London flat and work from there. You know it's Sherry's birthday on Saturday?"

"I do, why do you ask?"

"I think it's time we had a party to include all the camp. Don't let her know just how big it will be, she'll think it's just a few friends at the club."

Stanley frowned. "Then you're going to be there as well?"

"Yes, why does everyone think I'm some party-pooper? I'm not, just bogged down with so much work these days."

"Very well, I'll arrange it all. You just keep her away on the Saturday, until you both come to the club."

"I will, maybe we'll fly down to the coast and find her a present. That will keep us well away."

"It sounds like the old days are back, Karen. It'll do the morale of the camp good, particularly with you being there."

After she left, Stanley called Lieutenant Foster, her second in command, to tell him what she wanted for Sherry.

He in turn arranged a meeting with the other officers, for later the same day. Now they were all in the meeting room, Lieutenant Foster opened the meeting.

"It's Sergeant Malloy's birthday on Saturday. Normally she'd have a few drinks with the lads, end up drunk and be put to bed. Except our Commander has stepped in. She wants more than that, she wants it to be a camp party and like Stanley said, to boost morale."

"That's a turn-up for the books," one officer commented. "Karen never gets involved any more. Thinks she's too good for us these days."

Lieutenant Foster glared at him. "It's that sort of comment and attitude which can get you court marshalled, Lieutenant Ryan, and never do you, as a second lieutenant, refer to your commander by her Christian name in front of me. The unit is fortunate to have such a professional and highly decorated soldier in command. She is not only involved with unit operations, but runs covert and surveillance teams. Then, if you add in the charity she runs and public engagements, she has little time for social activities and very rarely gets a day off. Except, on this occasion, she has made it known to Stanley that she intends to attend. That means I want to see no jeans and T-shirts. I want trousers and open-neck shirts. Commander Harris may expect everyone to let their hair down, but every soldier will conduct themselves accordingly, as they would in front of an army colonel, so it won't be an excuse for the party to become a drunken binge, not on my watch. You will all make it very clear to everyone attending, step out of line and they do so at their peril. Also, Sherry is not to know."

Chapter 9

Sedrick came into the back room of a remote farmhouse outside Manchester with another man in his early fifties. His name was Donald Troop; he was a self-made millionaire who had made his money on the stock market and was now reaping the rewards. Sitting on a wooden chair in the middle of the otherwise empty room was Autumn. Her head was slumped forward, she had a headache and felt sick, both effects caused by the drug she'd been given, which was making her responses slow, and laborious. To make matters worse for her, she wanted to rub her eyes, blow her nose, but could do neither, with her hands secured behind her back.

Grasping her hair, and yanking her head back, Sedrick shouted at her to stand.

Autumn stood; her legs felt like jelly, her head was spinning.

"Is she alright, she looks drunk?" Donald commented.

"We had to add drugs to her food, she was going hysterical. Anyway, do you want her or not? I've already three other clients who want to see her."

Donald looked over her more carefully. "She's a good-looking girl, I'll take her. Can you deliver to Belgium?"

"The price includes delivery anywhere in Europe, but it won't be until the end of next week at the earliest."

"Then we have a deal."

Autumn, although still coming out of sedation, could understand what was being said. "Why am I not going home? Why am I going to Belgium?" she slurred.

Sedrick forced her back down on the chair, his face inches from hers. "Get this into your thick head. You're never going home. I own you and I've just sold you to my friend

Donald here. So from now on you don't speak, unless asked a question, or you'll feel my whip across your bare bottom."

She stared at him, obviously in shock, tears beginning to trickle down her cheeks, frightened at his threat.

"I see you're already keeping that mouth of yours shut. Remain this way and we'll get on. Otherwise, you'll see another side of me. Do you understand?"

"Yes," she muttered.

He said no more, then left the room with Donald.

"It's a hundred and seventy pounds to have her sterilised, if you want it done before she's delivered?" Sedrick asked Donald.

"Can they do girls of her age then?"

"At her age, she'll already be ovulating, so yes, it's pretty easy, half an hour and she'll be sorted."

"Then get her done, it saves us messing about. Can she still be with us next week?"

"No problem, as I said, she won't be leaving till the end of the week. I'll have the doctor do her in the morning. He's already coming to do two others."

***

A man, all the traffickers knew as Cropper, who had been a doctor before being struck off, after being caught fiddling with children while examining them, knocked on the door of the farmhouse.

Sedrick pulled it open and let him in. "You are sober aren't you?" he asked, as they walked through to the back kitchen.

"At this time of the morning, of course," he replied indignantly.

"Yes, well, you'd better not have a hangover from

last night. You've three girls now and the first one is worth sixty grand, fuck her up and I'll not be too pleased."

He shrugged indifferently. "She's only to be sterilised, it's hardly major surgery. Has she been washed and shaved?"

"We know what we're doing. She's already laid out and prepared in the cellar. So come on, or she'll wake up."

Cropper, along with Sedrick, entered a room in the cellar. In the centre of an otherwise empty room was a table, Autumn already laid on top, a sheet covering her naked body. She was asleep. Alongside the table was a trolley on wheels.

Cropper placed his bag on the floor before opening it. Then he took out a case containing his instruments, laying them on the trolley. Removing gloves from a sterile bag, he pulled them on.

"Take the sheet off her," he said to Sedrick who was standing watching. At the same time, he took out a small bottle and a cloth from another sterile bag.

Looking at Autumn for a second, he looked back at Sedrick. "How old is she?"

"Fifteen, why?"

He shrugged. "She's very young to be sterilised, that's all."

"Yeah, well, her life from now on is servicing clients, so it's best for her."

Cropper said no more, just began to massage the lower part of her stomach, feeling her intestines through the skin, working them up towards her belly button. Once satisfied, he wiped her skin with liquid from the bottle he'd soaked the cloth in. Then quickly made a small incision below the belly button, forcing the opening to remain open by inserting a shallow metal tube. Following that it was just a case of pushing a hooked rod through the metal tube, drawing out her Fallopian tubes one at a time, looping each one and tying it off, before cutting the loop away. Finally, after pushing them back into her, he removed the metal tube and closed the incision with two stitches.

"She's done, tell the owner not to shag her without a condom until her second period, just in case there's an egg already in the tubes beyond the tied part. You can get the next one in now, while I clean the instruments."

Chapter 10

Karen and Sherry had arrived back at the camp Saturday afternoon, after staying overnight in Cannes. Sherry was in her room changing. It was then that the mobile phone that Karen used for taking calls from her informers rang.

"Karen here," was all she said.

"It's Samuel, can you talk?"

"Yes."

"Parker has five children coming in at the end of the month. Already they're being offered for sale. We need to meet."

"The sooner the better, if I've to set an operation up."

"Of course. Except I don't have the details yet. I've a gathering in two weeks in the UK. I'll call you."

"That's good, I'll also be in London from next week."

"Then you should come and join us."

"I think not, Samuel, like I said, I'm not into old men chasing me around."

"Have it your way, I'll call when I've more."

***

Sherry stood rigid, her eyes wide. The entire club had been decked out in balloons, bunting and a huge banner wishing her a happy birthday. Apart from the decorations, the room was packed, all of them clapping and whistling as she came in.

"Come on party girl, let's get you a drink shall we?" Karen said, urging her forward.

"God, Karen, you knew about this?"

"Well, I might have suggested we widen your birthday

celebration to include more from the camp. Although, I didn't expect this."

Lieutenant Foster came up to them. "It's good of you to attend, Commander. We have reserved a table close to the dance floor for you and our party girl here."

"It looks quite spectacular, Lieutenant. Can you arrange a five hundred pound float behind the bar, to give everyone a drink on me? Also tonight, as I am out of uniform, my name is Karen. That is for everyone."

"Very well, Karen, if that's what you want, I'm more than happy to make both the announcements. Come on Sherry, let's get you to the front and then you can open your presents contributed by everyone."

Later that night, Karen was driven home. She was alone, Sherry had decided to stay at the camp. The girl had a brilliant time, never off the dance floor and by the end of the night had been really taken by a soldier not belonging to Dark Angel. As for her own night, Karen had been on the dance floor a number of times, besides meeting lots of people working in the camp she'd never normally come into contact with. So for her it had also been a productive night, socially that is.

**

The following morning, after breakfast, which Sherry didn't turn up for, Karen returned to the camp and her office.

Ten minutes after she arrived, Larisa was brought in.

"So how are you settling?" Karen asked, once they were alone.

"Really well, thank you. I'm working in the camp store, but Phyllis, who's looking after me, said I will soon be going to a more permanent flat in Spain, sharing with another girl. I'm looking forward to my new life. I don't know how to thank you."

"No problems, it's what my charity does. But I've asked you here to talk a little about your statement."

Larisa frowned. "Have I done something wrong?"

"No, not at all. I'd like clarification on a few points, that's all."

"Oh, what do you want to know?"

"The Fairmont club, you said you'd been asked to go to the parties. Who asked you and how did it come about?"

"The owner, Stubbs, knew I was on the game. He didn't bother much about me meeting clients at the club, after all it was really a drinking club, so there was just the odd stripper as entertainment and two lap dancers who'd come some nights and take his customers into the back room. Those were the only busy nights. At twenty pounds a pop they did well, but had to pay five of that to Stubbs. They'd never spend longer than a couple of hours there to get through twenty dances each and go home with three hundred quid. It also turned the customers on, so I got a few jobs on the back of it, especially when the customers found the lap dancers didn't do extra services and buggered off. Mind you, looking at the place, you'd wonder how it actually made money. I never saw over forty people there. Anyway, as for the parties, I'd come into the club one night, it was virtually empty. Stubbs was with another man at the bar and he called me over. Asked if I wanted to go to a private party and earn a bit of money," she sighed. "When you live like me, you take anything, especially if you find the place empty and you need money just to live."

"Yes, I can understand that. So how often did you go?"

"As I put in my statement, there were parties most

weekends. The problem for me was they were at my busiest time of the week, so I could earn more on the street. I only did one weekend. From the moment I got there till I left on Sunday, I never had my clothes on. It was a bloody orgy, everyone fucking everyone else. I was expected to service man after man and got two hundred quid for the whole weekend. I worked it out and I got less than a fiver per shag. I'm not working for that."

"I wouldn't have either," Karen commented. "So you were offered week long sessions?"

"Yes, you wouldn't get them that often, but you'd earn two grand for the week. It was hard and you'd often spend all night with not one but two clients. But they fed you, and you had the mornings off, clients would come and go every day. That worked for me, especially the money at the end of the week, besides a few tips off some of the clients."

"But it all went sour?"

"It did. They were bringing in girls far younger. Some as young as fourteen. They suffered terrible abuse; as for me, I was just a plaything - when the clients got turned on with the young girls and couldn't pay the fees demanded to use them, I was the next best thing. Anyway, I decided it wasn't for me and stopped going. That was until Stacy's pimp convinced me to join her on that weekend she died. I'd earned very little money that week and was desperate, the two hundred pounds for the weekend would pay my rent, if I didn't pay I'd have been out with nowhere to work from. You know the rest."

Karen pulled out a photo from a file in front of her. "Tell me, did you ever see this man?"

Larisa's face changed. Karen could see the fear the photo of this man instilled in the girl. "He called himself the

Master. He'd come dressed in his regalia and would beat and abuse the young girls. The more they screamed, the more he relished it, urged on by everyone else. I don't know his real name but he's a man you should find and castrate, so he could experience just a little of what he put others through."

"We'll see what we can do. One other thing. The Fairmont, did the women go in there on their own?"

"You mean, like, to drink, or score?"

"Either really."

"On the two days they had strippers and lap dancers, no. But the other nights, you'd see a few women around, not all were on the game. Most of them were pretty rough, I can tell you. Then you'd get a few coming in looking for work as a dancer or stripper. Stubbs liked that sort. He'd take them into his office for an interview. Some interview, they'd not leave for at least an hour. Everyone knew what he was up to, then no-one ever got a job that I saw. Maybe some went to the parties, but I don't know."

"Right, I think I've filled some of the gaps."

"Are you going to close the Fairmont?"

"No, they're not doing anything illegal. Maybe allowing soliciting on their premises, but that would only hurt the girls trying to make a living. It's this man who calls himself the Master I want to take down. That will take time, but I will get him."

"Well, if I can help further you only need to ask."

"Thank you. Have they given you a date when you're to be moved to Spain yet?"

"Not an exact one, the lady from your charity told me about five weeks. I've met the girl I'm sharing a flat with and I'm also going to language lessons. There's even a job waiting for me. I can't thank you enough, Karen, for getting me out of the life I lived."

"I'm glad we could help. Tell them at the shop you've been with me, if they ask, but not why."

Larisa stood. "Okay, I'll see you around," she replied, then left.

***

After returning to her house, Karen was packing when Sherry came into her room.

"Hi, I've just got back. Where are you going?" Sherry asked.

"London, I've a few things to do there. So who's the lad then?"

"James, we got on well. He's a chef in his second year."

"You're seeing him again then?"

"Hopefully, after my assessment next week." While she spoke, Sherry was looking at what Karen was packing. She lifted up the lap dancing outfit, laid on the bed. "This is gorgeous, why are you taking this?"

Karen shrugged. "I was going to sell it in London. It's unused and like you say, really nice."

Sherry looked directly at Karen. "I'm not completely stupid, Karen. Maybe I'd have believed you if you'd left out the suspenders and matching underwear, but you haven't. That means you're intending to wear it on a covert operation. I want to come."

"You're on assessment, so you can't. But you're right, although it holds bad memories, I love the outfit and will never sell it. As for going covert, I've a few ideas, so I may need to use it."

"I'm coming, stuff the assessment. With one phone call, you can have that postponed easily. As it is, Karen, if you're lap dancing, what else are you getting up to? You could need my help."

"We've talked in the past about covert operations, Sherry. You told me then you just wanted to remain in Dark Angel, following the last time you were covert and they tortured you."

"Yes, well, I lied. I like the excitement and pitting my wits against them."

Karen stood for a moment, looking at her, then sighed. "Come on, let's get coffee and sit down."

"If this is to talk me out of coming, Karen, it won't work, I'm coming with you."

She smiled. "No, I'd love you to be with me, Sherry, we're a good team, you and I. I'm only going to give you the background as to why I'm going."

Shortly afterwards, they were sitting in the conservatory. Karen took a sip of her coffee. "A little while back, I was abducted, or rather, it was an attempted abduction."

"I never heard about that."

"No, you wouldn't have done, it wasn't made general knowledge. I was snatched by a man called Hans. You know about him I presume?"

"Yes, wasn't he with a man called Jarek? A sort of heavy for him?"

"Yes, but he was also so full of himself, he wanted to prove he was the best and determined to take me down, to show how important he was. Anyway, he failed and ended up going down for twenty years."

"So what's he got to do with it?"

"He abducted me, not for himself, but because he was paid by others. He was supposed to take me to a so-called party. There, I'd have been subjected to abuse and then they intended to hang me on the Sunday. All of it was to be filmed and the result sent to the EU committee, to show how easily I could be taken."

Sherry shook her head slowly. "These people, they must be sick in the head? That, or they're so terrified of you, they would do anything to take you down."

"Maybe, but it's how we live, so I'd not lose sleep over it. As it is a man called Sir Samuel French made sure he could talk to me in Switzerland. Some cock and bull story about a man called Parker, who was not only a trafficker, but some sort of serial killer of children. He told me the man had needed to be stopped and he was prepared to help do it."

"Sounds strange, why not go to the police?"

"Because he claimed he ran parties for the rich and this Parker was bringing in young children for them. He was frightened that Parker's actions would bring him down too."

"He'd be right, Karen."

"He would, but I think it's all a con. He said he wanted to prove to me that his parties were a harmless bit of fun and I should come. They are not fun, they abuse children, commit murder and more. I believe this is where Hans was going to take me, so when he failed, Samuel came up with a new excuse as to why I should be involved. Particularly when he said I should see for myself and spend time at one of these parties. I can tell you this, Sherry, if I'd been stupid enough to accept, I'd not have come out alive."

"If it is the same people, then I agree. So what makes you believe it is?"

Karen stopped and sipped her coffee. "I can't be a hundred per cent sure, so first things first. I intend to go and see Hans in prison."

Sherry grinned. "You think he'll see you?"

"He will. I've already made the request and he's

accepted. You forget, he and I are the same. We are both professional killers and talk the same language."

"When do we leave?"

"The flight plans are already logged with air traffic control. We leave in three hours."

Chapter 11

Karen's ID had been checked four times before she was allowed to sit with Hans in a small room at the prison. Between them was a table. He was also secured from getting at her by handcuffs, with the coupling chain threaded through a steel loop on the table.

Hans was a big man, born in Germany, but he had spent time in the British army, before moving back to his home country and becoming an elite soldier in one of their anti-terrorist units. After leaving, he had become a minder for the rich, but supplemented that income working with traffickers, in particular a man called Jarek, who brought children in Europe from Asia and Africa, as well as the Baltic States.

"You were the last person who'd I'd have expected to visit me, Karen. Why are you here?"

Karen didn't tell him immediately. "I was surprised the injury didn't manage to kill you, I must be slipping. I presume you're upset about that, after all, we're the same, you and I. We live and die by the gun; to be locked up for many years must be very frustrating?"

He nodded his head up and down slowly. "You're correct, I'd rather have died in the wood. You proved at the time to be a formidable opponent and for me, it was demeaning to lose. I was also annoyed with myself, I'd underestimated just how well you'd been trained."

"No, Hans, that wasn't the real reason I won. I'd been trained in unarmed combat, yes, the same as you. Your problem was you hadn't kept the fitness part of it up. You didn't have the speed, the agility I had, besides, I'm ten years your junior. But I respect you and your word, when you threw your gun away and placed us on an equal footing. Most men, knowing there was half a million in the boot of the car and all that prevented them taking it was me still being alive, would have just shot me and walked away."

He shrugged indifferently. "Perhaps, but I was there to prove a point, not just kill you. But we digress, I presume this isn't a social visit and you need something from me?"

"I do. It's a lot to ask I know and you could just tell me to go away. Except, you and I are professionals in our own way. We hold no allegiance to anyone but ourselves. Those people are still out there who want me dead."

"That's true, just because I failed does not mean you're safe, you're not. But if you're here to ask the location that I intended to take you, I will not tell you that. Although I believe you know it already. So what is it that you want, Karen?"

"I'd like you to tell me if Sir Samuel French would have been in the place you intended to take me?"

Hans sat silent, then smiled. "Tell me, Karen, has he approached you?"

"He has."

"Then all I'll say is, step very carefully."

"Thank you, Hans. One more question, again, nothing to do with this place I was to be taken to."

"And that is?"

"Kenneth Parker, is he into trafficking?"

"There again, Karen, that is a man who you should deal very carefully with. I will tell you this, he's had dealings with Jarek in the past. But even Jarek refused to deal with him, later on."

Karen stood to leave. "I'll leave you now, we may never meet again. You really did pick the wrong side and are now paying for it. I could have offered you so much more."

He looked up at her. "Maybe, but you make your own bed in this world, sometimes you get it wrong. Look after yourself, Karen. There are a great many people out there wanting to take you down. Me, I respect a girl who does what you do, even though I tried to kill you. But you proved on the day, you are more than capable of making sure that whoever tries will not find you a pushover, and will have a real fight on their hands."

Leaving the prison, Karen joined Sherry in the car.

"Well, did he talk to you?" Sherry asked, as Karen climbed into the passenger seat.

"He did, in fact we left with a good understanding and respect between us. The important thing is, he confirmed that Samuel French is not to be trusted, and out to get me. It would seem by attempting to have me go to one of his so-called parties, he may have thought I'd go and tell no-one, being the sort of party it was. Also, Parker is into trafficking, but not taking from the usual channels, they won't deal with him. For them to refuse, the man could be more than a trafficker and as Samuel claimed, a psychopath. That means we have to get into Parker's operation, besides bring Samuel French and his cronies down."

"God, Karen, he seems to have told you such a lot. Are you sure he can be trusted?"

"It's not what he said, Sherry, it's what he didn't. Now let's get back to the flat and plan our next move."

Chapter 12

Ricky Strong sauntered into the Fairmont club at just after eleven at night. This for him was a regular haunt.

"Alright Ricky? We've not seen you around lately," the barman responded, at the same time pouring his usual pint of lager.

"Been away, on a little business. So who's stripping tonight?"

"None tonight, it should have been Sinartra, but she was arrested yesterday for dealing. Stubbs tried to get her bail, but the pigs are having none of it. She had a kilo of the stuff in her car and could go down for five years."

"Fucking hell, it couldn't have been hers, that would be worth a fortune."

"That's what Stubbs said, but she isn't saying whose it was."

Ricky was watching two girls come in; they looked in their twenties, both blonde, tall, slim and particularly good-looking.

"The club's coming up in the world, are they hookers?" Ricky asked.

The barman shook his head. "No, lap dancers and only around for the month. Apparently working the hotels locally and staying at the Calton."

"Fucking Calton, can they get any lower? So how do you know?"

"They've been in a couple of times on their nights off. Stubbs was trying to tap them up last night. He didn't get anywhere, I think they're lesbian."

By now one girl had sat down in the corner, the younger one had come to the bar.

"Hi, can I have two Becks, both still in the bottles?" she asked the barman.

He pulled two out from the cool tray behind him, then after opening them placed them on the bar. "You want a tab?"

She nodded. "Yes, we're here for the rest of the night."

"I've not seen you around, are you on holiday?" Ricky asked the girl.

She looked at him. "No, working locally."

"The name's Ricky."

"Charlie." Then, not waiting to talk longer, she took the two bottles and returned to the seats.

"Give me two Becks," Ricky told the barman, a few minutes later.

He opened the two bottles, placing them on the bar. "If Stubbs couldn't pull them, you've no fucking chance. They're obviously high-class lap dancers and probably very expensive."

He grinned. "If you don't try, you never know. Besides, imagine having those two in bed, I've a hard-on already at the thought."

The barman laughed, then began to serve another customer.

Grabbing the bottles, Ricky walked over. "Hi, Charlie, I heard you tell the barman you were here for the night, so I bought you and your friend a top-up."

Charlie looked at him standing there for a moment, then smiled. "This is Ricky, he was the one at the bar who spoke to me."

The other girl had been watching him approach and smiled. "Thank's for the drink. I'm Tori."

"No problems, can I join you?"

"If you want," Tori answered.

He hurried back to the bar, grabbed his drink and returned, sitting down opposite them. Already he was taken by Charlie, but now he was closer, he could see just how attractive Tori was, her long blonde hair and deep blue eyes were captivating. These were some girls.

"So what do you do for a living Ricky?" Tori asked.

He gave a light shrug. "You know, this and that. There's always work around the West End. How about you two?"

"We do private lap dances in hotel bedrooms. Sometimes followed by a performance between us both, on the client's bed," Tori answered.

"Sounds good, I've never seen you around here before."

"You wouldn't, we were working in Spain. Now the season's over, we've come back to the UK and will move from city to city. The hotels would soon catch on if you hung around too long."

"Stubbs, who runs the club, is always looking for girls to work here, you should see him."

Charlie laughed. "You're too late, he collared us last night. Wanted us to give him a performance in his office to show what we do."

"Yes, I've heard he does that, did you fall for it?"

Charlie shook her head. "We would have done, it's what we do. Until he told us it would be fifteen pounds a dance. We charge far more and extra if you want a performance by us on the bed. So his job offer was a non-starter."

"Then you do parties, or singles?"

"Both," Charlie answered. "Providing the lads are not too drunk, that is."

He shook his head slowly. "Risky, have they ever

tried to take you?"

Tori smiled. "What do you think?"

"Say no more, anyway, why are you not at one of the clubs where you can dance, this is the pits for girls like you two."

"It's close to our hotel, cheap and we've done ten dances tonight, now we're just out for a drink," Tori answered.

"Ten, you don't hang around. How much would that have earned you?"

"This job you do, Ricky, do you earn good money?" Tori asked.

He grinned. "I understand, it's none of my business."

They talked generally about nothing in particular. Ricky really did fancy Charlie, but could see no way to separate her from Tori.

Tori pulled out her mobile. "Can you take a photo for us?" she asked Ricky.

"Sure," he replied, taking the phone.

"How about one of you with me, Ricky?" Charlie asked, after he'd taken the photo.

He jumped at the chance and this time Tori took it, in fact, she took another, more of a close-up of him. Ricky never noticed. He was more interested in putting his arm around Charlie.

Collecting more drinks, Ricky was back. Tori had been fiddling with her phone while he'd been gone and sent a photo text.

Ten minutes later she left Ricky with Charlie, heading for the toilet. She wanted to look at a text which had just come in.

'This man meets the description. Will contact tomorrow after showing the photo to Larisa. Take care!'

63

Tori returned to the table.

Ricky looked up at her. "I've just been saying to Charlie. Rather than go from city to city, I've a friend, he arranges long weekends. Two lap dancers like you would go down well. You could make a grand at least over the weekend."

Tori shook her head. "We did one like that once. Most were old men wanting us to join them on the bed. We don't prostitute, in fact don't need to, we do well dancing."

"You have me wrong. They already have girls who look after that side. You'd be part of the entertainment, on the poles, to keep the night going."

Charlie glanced at Tori, who nodded. "We'll talk to him, but won't promise anything."

"I'll get him to come and see you, when are you around again?"

"Wednesday, we're booked solid till three tomorrow night."

"Wow, you're really in demand. How much for me as a friend?"

Tori smiled. "Good effort, but we don't do friends, we like to perform for people we don't see again." Then she looked at her watch. "Right, I'm calling it a day, are you coming, Charlie?"

"I'm with you. I'm knackered and going to be in bed till lunchtime at least. Thanks for a great night, Ricky, we'll see you again, yes?"

"You'd better believe it. I'll bring my friend to the club on Wednesday at around eleven, will you be here?"

Tori shrugged indifferently. "We will, don't hold us to an exact time, it depends on the clients."

After they left, Ricky returned to the bar. "How much?"

"Fifty-five quid," the barman told him. "Then you never got a shag. I did warn you. Those girls are expensive, don't you think?"

"I will, you can be certain. They're back on Wednesday."

The barman laughed. "Then you'd better bring plenty of money."

Chapter 13

Karen turned over, then stretched when Sherry came through from the adjoining room and pulled open the curtains.

"Come on, sleepy, I want breakfast, I'm starving."

"You're always eating," Karen commented, as she dragged herself up and went through to the bathroom.

"I'm not, we haven't eaten since yesterday afternoon," she shouted after her.

Karen returned, pulling on a jumper and jeans.

"You never said last night, when we came back to the hotel," Sherry began. "Was this Ricky the one who tried to kill Larisa?"

"I'll not know till later today. It was a bit much to expect them to go and wake Larisa at one in the morning to ask her. Not that it matters, he's besotted with you and will be back Wednesday, you can believe it."

"I noticed. He's horrible and slimy, but he'll get his come-uppance once we take him down. Just the right age and the small bottom they like in a prison."

"That's a catty thing to say, Sherry," Karen came back at her, as she combed her hair.

Sherry didn't comment, watching Karen while she readied herself. "You know, Karen, you should have gone blonde a long time ago, it really suits your eyes. Besides, you look so different, even I hardly recognise you."

"That's the idea, Sherry. But I did go blonde once. In fact, after I returned from the Lebanon the first time, I joined the army and went blonde as part of my disguise. I liked it then and believe me, I had a queue of lads wanting to take me out." Then she shrugged slightly. "Mind you, I was only eighteen, and had no trouble getting dates when I had my natural colour. It will be interesting to see if going blonde now I'm older has the same effect."

Sherry laughed. "I can't see you having any trouble. But I'll be glad if they confirm this Ricky is the man we're looking for, I hate that club. Your feet stick to the carpet as you walk, it's so dirty."

"Yes it's a bit downmarket, but it looks as if we could be moving on. We'll collect your clothes later for lap dancing, then you need to practice. I'm not saying you'll have to do the dance, we could well have pulled them all in by then, but you can't afford to break cover."

"I'm looking forward to it. The long slinky dress I chose could be used to go clubing in as well."

Karen laughed. "What, virtually open to the crotch and fastened with one button, I don't think I would. Anyway, let's go down, shall we, and see if the chef's eggs are any softer. The ones yesterday you could have used as weapons, they were so hard."

***

Later the same day, Karen and Sherry went out together. After collecting Sherry's lap dancing clothes from a shop, they were on the way to another hotel, where they'd booked a room. They used this as a retreat away from the Carlton Hotel, as if they were out working. Now Karen was sitting in a chair, in the middle of the room. Music was playing and Sherry was stripping slowly.

"No, stop," Karen told her. "You'll be naked far too soon. You've eight items, each item is removed in sequence and under strict timing. You're only to be naked for fifteen seconds before you go astride the client, then fifteen seconds simulated intercourse, after that you finish."

"Sorry, I lost my timing. What were you like the first time?"

"If I forget the ones I was forced to do, when I was first abducted, before they raped me. In France, when I learnt to do it properly, I was as bad as you. I just wanted to get it over with, finding myself standing naked for half the bloody dance. Apart from being freezing standing there, all the girls were laughing at my pathetic attempts. At least there's only you and me here."

"So do you always use nine items, I've only eight?"

"Yes, unlike you, I prefer the short separate skirt and the jacket. I've done it so many times now, I couldn't do it with eight, I'd be out of sequence. Right, again. I'll watch the time and count from one to eight. At each number I shout out, you take an item off."

By the time Karen's mobile rang, Sherry had dressed and undressed close to thirty times. Now, she was happy just to flop on the bed, wearing her dressing gown, while Karen took the call.

"What have we got, Stanley?" Karen asked.

"Ricky Strong, the man you photographed, has been confirmed by Larisa as the man who tried to kill her. The police are also looking for him, having identified him as the possible assailant from Larisa's description. He disappeared from his usual haunts for a time. The police believe he was lying low because of his facial injuries. Incidentally, when we alter the photo with enhancing computer software, it's showing up the scratches that, although healed visually, still have a slight difference in skin colour, so we have him."

"That's good. But the police must stay away for the next week. He's introducing another man to us on Wednesday, this man could be our route to the weekends Samuel has told me about."

"I'll talk to Sir Peter. You take care Karen, these people are not nice. Also, make sure you or Sherry don't lose your back-up teams. They may be the only ones who can help you, if you're in trouble."

"I understand. I'm not a one-girl army these days, Stanley."

Chapter 14

"Why are you blabbing to strangers about our weekends?" Musowa wanted to know, after Ricky had told him about Sherry and Karen, except Ricky knew them as Charlie and Tori.

"Call Stubbs, ask him about them. The girls are stunning, I can tell you. They worked in Spain and are back in the UK until the new season begins. They're really busy doing the hotels, we should look into doing the same."

"So how much do they charge?" Musowa asked, ignoring Ricky's suggestion to work the hotels.

He gave a light shrug. "They wouldn't tell me, but they were interested when I talked about a grand for the weekend."

"What! Just for lap dancing? They'd have to be offering extra services for that sort of money. Sedrick wouldn't wear that."

"Then talk to them. They're working tonight, but will be at the Fairmont around eleven tomorrow night."

"I'll think about it. Anyway, the girl called Ally, when did you say you'd meet her?"

"She'll meet me anytime. Why?"

"Autumn's not well. Cropper's fucked up the operation, so she can't be used. Now the client wants his money back."

"So offer him Ally. She's fifteen, the same as Autumn," Ricky surgested.

"We're ahead of you on that. Sedrick's shown Ally's photo to the client and he's agreed to take her instead."

"You need her quick then?"

"We do."

"What will happen to Autumn?"

"Parker's using her in one of his performances. It's best for the girl, she's fucked anyway, so ten minutes on his table, before she passes out, while he skins her alive, is far better than her being in constant pain and unable to hold anything down, like she is at the moment."

"That's a bit harsh on the girl, can't Cropper do anything?"

"He was the one who told me to sell her to Parker."

Ricky shook his head in despair. "Some fucking doctor, when his only cure is to have the patient butchered, because he can't be arsed to help her. It's no wonder they struck him off. How about we dump her outside a hospital."

"Are you fucking stupid? If she survives, she could describe Sedrick and Donald, besides me. No, Parker will take her on Saturday and our problem is finished. Anyway, what about Ally?"

"I'll make contact tonight. What's your deadline for her?"

"Like today, except I need to change the travel arrangements, so that won't happen till at least next Monday. You try to arrange to meet her this weekend. I'll give you a small bottle of coke that will knock her out."

After Ricky left the room to mail Ally, Musowa called Stubbs.

"All right, Musowa? We've not seen you at the club lately, got a new watering hole then?"

"No, been a bit busy. Ricky told me about two lap dancers coming to the club."

"You mean Tori and Charlie? They're only around for about a month, before moving on. Fucking smart those two. I tried to get them to do a night at my club, but they work as a pair and charge seventy-five. They laughed at fifteen quid each."

"I'm not surprised, the women have got to be a bit desperate to do it for fifteen quid. Ricky told me they also offer a lesbian act for the client as well?"

"Yes, apparently. It costs an extra fifty. They said most clients wanted this after the lap dance. I think I would, just to see what they get up to."

"So you think it's worth my while to see them and offer a couple of weekends?"

"Let just say it's rare to get two attractive and sexy girls together. But they're doing at least ten a day, with extras that's over a grand, so you'd need to better that, or they'll turn you down like they did me."

"I'll come over tomorrow night."

"Yeah, okay, look forward to seeing you."

Musowa then called Sedrick.

"Sedrick, it's Musowa. I might have two lap dancers, that also perform a lesbian act. Are you still short this coming weekend?"

"I am, they're not any of Stubbs' girls are they? If so, forget it."

"No, two girls from Spain and here till the season opens up again. They aren't cheap."

"Money's no object, if they're good."

"I'll see what I can arrange and call you."

Chapter 15

Ricky was with Musowa in the Fairmont, it was coming up to twelve. The club was full, with two big stag parties on. Because of that, Stubbs had brought in two strippers earlier, which went down well and kept the parties drinking.

"You said the girls would be here tonight," Musowa said to Ricky, with obvious annoyance in his voice. "I've better things to do than sit around here."

"They're working girls and said they could be late."

"I'll give them till one, then I'm out of here."

Stubbs came up to them. "What do you reckon, we're buzzing? I've got this guy who arranges these stag nights. I pay him a hundred and he guarantees at least two stag parties."

"You need them, Stubbs, that's for certain. But to keep them drinking in the club all night, you'll have to attract the women," Musowa commented.

"Yes, I know, how about you direct some working girls here for me?"

Musowa laughed. "I wasn't thinking working girls, but if you can do a deal with the guy who arranges the nights, like including a good shagging for the groom and best man on the night, I'll provide them."

At that moment Charlie and Tori came into the club. Stubbs' eyes lit up when he saw them. "It's a deal, if you get lookers like those two?" Stubbs replied.

"What did I say?" Ricky cut in. "I said they'd come. Charlie's the younger of the two with the short blonde hair. The other, and really sexy in the way she walks, with the longer blonde hair and deep blue eyes to die for, is Tori."

Musowa looked at them. Neither were in jeans, but

short dresses and very high heels, showing off their long, slim legs. Already he could see most of the men in the room were looking at them. "Fucking hell, you and Stubbs were right, they are lookers. You're sure they're lesbians, I could fuck either, maybe both? Introduce me," he muttered.

"I didn't say they were, only that they do a routine together, but don't include the client," Ricky came back at him.

"Call them over."

"Charlie, Tori, come and join us," Ricky called.

Charlie smiled. "Hi, Ricky. Sorry we're late, work you know?"

"No problems, this is Musowa. Musowa, Charlie and Tori."

"Drink girls?" Musowa asked.

"Becks, please, in the bottle, we don't do glasses. In Spain they tend to drop drugs in a glass, for laughs. Bottles you hold onto, with a finger over the top, so they have less of a chance," Tori replied.

"Sensible. Ricky here tells me you lap dance? Are you getting plenty of clients?"

"It's quiet for us, we often do twenty to thirty a day in Spain. Here we're down to ten, maybe twelve at weekends. What do you do?" Tori asked.

"I've a few bedsits I let out to working girls. But if you're short of work, I could find you plenty."

Tori smiled. "Yes, Stubbs offered us a couple of nights here. But we don't dance for fifteen pounds, besides, a hotel room is far more intimate."

"Understandable. I'm told you offer clients a lesbian act to follow?"

"Not exactly lesbian, we just play around with each other. Nothing heavy, but the clients like to see two girls simulating sex," Charlie cut in.

"Then you're not lesbians?"

Tori shook her head slightly. "No, Charlie here has a boyfriend. I'm between boyfriends at the moment. We do it to make the clients think we are. That way they don't come on to us all the time, or ask for extra services, believing we're prostitutes. It works for us."

They carried on talking for a while. By now they had all found seats. Musowa had slipped in alongside Tori, while Ricky, although with them, was a little put out to find Charlie had a boyfriend.

"Smile," Charlie said, pointing her mobile phone at Tori and Musowa. Musowa put his arm around Tori, pulling her close. Tori didn't object. They needed a photo of this man, this way it was casual. Although, as Tori had with Charlie and Ricky, she took a more close-up one of Musowa, as well as one of the two of them.

"What do you think, Tori?" Charlie asked, showing the one of her and Musowa together.

"I like it, what about you Musowa?"

"Yes, it's good. You two like taking photos then?"

Tori scrunched her nose. "Not really, we only use the phone camera for fun and maybe have a laugh later when we look back. Charlie's the one for selfies. Me, I think they look awful, with distorted faces and things."

Charlie looked at her watch. It was coming up to two in the morning. "I'm off, Tori, are you coming?"

"Yes. Thanks for a great end to the night, Musowa."

"No problems. I was going to ask if you'd do me a favour?"

"Like what?" Tori asked.

"I run weekends, like from Friday afternoon till Sunday afternoon. I'd really like to use you both for entertainment in the lounge."

"You want us to lap dance in front of a load of men, not one to one?" Tori asked.

"No, I want you on the pole in the lounge and occasionally taking one off to give him a private show."

"We don't do sex," Charlie reminded him.

"No problem, we've working girls there for that. They're useless on the pole and a lot of the men like to see a private strip, it turns them on for later, when they take a girl for the night."

"How much do you pay?" Tori asked.

"We'd only want you from Saturday till two. So you'd not be there Friday or Sunday. I'll pay for twenty dances at your usual rate."

"Can we call you tomorrow? I'll have to check what we've booked and if we can move the times?"

"So long as I know before twelve, otherwise I'll have to offer the job to other girls."

"I'll definitely call by twelve, with a yes or no."

Musowa wrote his number down and the two girls left.

"I'm fucking gutted, now I know Charlie's got a boyfriend," Ricky commented, after they had gone.

"What did you expect? Those sort of girls are never without, unless by choice. You should have chatted Tori up."

"I've no chance with her, she's older, more sensible. Besides, you didn't get far with Tori and still a bloody long way to getting into her pants."

"I wasn't trying, plenty of time now I know she's not a lesbian."

"So what do you think, do you belive they'll do the weekend?" Ricky asked.

"Course they will. Their need to check bookings is

an excuse, they'd already know and not have to look at any book."

"Then why delay agreeing to go?"

"To make it sound as if they're in demand. That Tori's a smart girl. She'd be suspecting I may lower their rate by immediately accepting, and showing they had no work on."

"Sneaky. Why are you not having them Friday and Sunday?"

"Parker's on Sunday, with his skinning of Autumn. A great many have paid advance money to be there and see him do it. So I don't want girls who aren't under our control to be anywhere near the place on Sunday. As for Friday, I'd struggle to keep the clients from wanting to take them to bed and fuck them. Most have paid good money, with the understanding all the girls are available. They'd be well pissed off if a girl refused and believe me, Charlie and Tori would refuse. They're not there for that. This way I get the entertainment and will spirit them away well before clients begin looking for a girl to take to their beds. I'm not risking wrecking the entertainment by them walking out. Maybe if they go down well, I've another coming up in two weeks. Then, I may try the full weekend and see if they really are celibate."

Chapter 16

"Karen, the photograph Sherry sent last night is of a man called Musowa Raja. He's suspected of trafficking, but the British police cannot get any solid evidence, only hearsay. An interesting part of the report over the Autumn Grove abduction lists him as a suspect. Mainly because of a poor video shot of someone who looks very much like him in a service station car park, where Autumn was caught on security cameras in McDonald's."

Karen sighed. "It's all beginning to fit together, Stanley. I intend to accept the invitation for Sherry and myself to attend on Saturday. My only concern is, do I mobilise Dark Angel? Is this gathering, that runs from Friday to Sunday, so important that we cannot let it run its course, without the capacity to be able to bring it to an abrupt end?"

"Personally, I'd be happier if Dark Angel was there, Karen. If these are the same people Hans was supposed to be taking you to, you're going in without weapons. Even if they're not, with knowing what happened to Stacy, you owe it to Sherry to keep her as safe as possible. I know she will stand by you, no matter what, but she's still a girl that needs your protection, she has no one else."

Karen said nothing for a moment. Stanley didn't push her. He knew when she was weighing up all the options.

"You're correct, Stanley. I'm really concerned with what we may be faced with. At the end of the day I, like Sherry, am part of a military strike force, and should use it. If this Parker turns up, I have to believe what Samuel said about him and have the muscle to take him down. So if I find children there, I intend not to let him go anywhere near them. I'm issuing the order to mobilise Dark Angel as at," she looked at her watch, "O-nine-hundred hours."

"I concur, Karen. I've logged your order, Unit T is now in lockdown. I'll arrange a video conference as soon as possible. If you can get a location, that would be ideal, if not, then surveillance will be critical. You and Sherry must activate your telephone trackers immediately and wear your watches. Then, before you set off to the venue, you must activate your secondary tracker system. You take no chances. We need to know exactly where you are at any given moment."

"This time, it goes without saying, I will follow unit protocol to the letter. Can you send me the time of the conference and I'll make sure I'm in a place where I can join in."

After Karen went off the phone to Stanley, she joined Sherry in the breakfast room, collecting cornflakes and orange juice from the side table.

"Everything okay, Karen?" Sherry asked, at the same time buttering a slice of toast.

"It's fine. I'll call Musowa shortly and agree to go to the party."

Following breakfast, they returned to the room. Karen shut the door and turned on the television, taking Sherry into the bathroom. "I've mobilised Dark Angel, we're now in lockdown, no personal calls, Sherry, from now on."

She nodded. "I understand. I've a bad feeling over this weekend and not just for us. I'll feel a lot safer with the lads close by."

"I agree. Activate your telephone tracker. Also, wear your watch all the time. We will transfer to the covert trackers once on the way to the venue."

"I was going to ask you something, now you're going to call Musowa."

"Like what?"

"I'm okay with the lap dancing. But what if one of the clients wants us to do the lesbian bit?"

Karan shrugged. "Then we do it, our cover has to be perfect in what we say we can do. Although I suspect one of us will always be on the pole downstairs, I can't see both of us going with a client."

"Maybe, but we need to be prepared, it'd be very obvious we'd never done it before. That means we'll have to spend time going through a routine. Any ideas?"

"No, I was hoping you had?"

"Me, what do I know?" Sherry asked, a little taken aback. "The closest I've got was on that ship from America, trying to teach girls to be prostitutes. That was well embarrassing."

Karen gave a sigh. "I'm the same, you know. Now I'm thinking I shouldn't have said we do that…should I?"

"No, but it's a great idea on how we've avoided selling extra services to clients and why we go to hotel rooms together. Personally, Karen. I'm glad it's with you and not under duress with other girls."

"Me too. It looks like the next few hours are going to be an interesting experience, for us both? It also means a visit to a sex shop."

Sherry grinned. "It does. Do you think they might stock instruction videos?"

Karen laughed. "Maybe, but there's always the internet."

Chapter 17

It was the Friday morning. Kenneth Parker, a tall, thin man in his forties, leaned back in his chair, holding a glass containing brandy. Sedrick had met him when he arrived at the country house, to be used for the weekend when Karen and Sherry were joining them on the Saturday.

Kenneth was the man who ran both the weekends and trafficking operation, although as far as guests and many of his workers, such as Musowa and the ones working for him were concerned, it was Sedrick who fronted it. Looking down at the list of people attending, Kenneth was happy. In all there were forty-five. Thirty-two had paid extra to stay later on Sunday for his performance. "It's a good attendance, have the two children arrived yet?"

"The boy has, the girl we've left behind. For her I've an alternative, and she's on her way as we speak. She's white and will go down well with the clients. She caught some sort of infection after a bodged sterilisation by Cropper. Musowa wants her gone, he can't risk her being seen by a registered doctor. If she was, then that doctor could insist an ambulance was called."

"Very wise. Mind you, why you used Cropper, I've no idea, he's completely useless and half the time under the influence. How much have we lost on her?"

"Sixty grand. But we should be collecting a replacement on Saturday. So the deal's still on."

Kenneth shook his head in despair. "From now on, Cropper is out. I'll find a doctor who will do a good job. Musowa has no idea I'm running the operation, does he?"

"No, he believes I sold the girl to you, for your part of the entertainment. He's on a need-to-know basis and has no need to know you are involved."

"When does Samuel arrive?"

"He'll be here just after lunch."

"I don't trust that man. He has some fixation over the Harris woman and paid Hans a great deal of money to snatch her."

"He's a fool and always has been. Blabbing around all that weekend she'd be brought and executed in front of them on Sunday. He was left with egg on his face, when she didn't arrive."

"Oddly enough, he very nearly did succeed. Although, for Hans, his capture of Harris was not for Samuel, but because of a personal vendeta between them both. He wanted to prove he was better than her in combat and had no intention in bringing her, alive that is, to Samuel."

Sedrick frowned, confused. "I knew he had her, we were expecting them by lunchtime. So it wasn't what was being said in the papers, that there had been a car crash?"

"No, there was no car crash, apart from Bill, Hans's partner, trying to get away. Hans stupidly tried to take her on in combat. I think he still believed he was a fit special forces soldier. She ran rings around him and he ended up in hospital with knife wounds, not wounds as a result of an accident. Samuel was out of his mind to believe she could be taken so easily. Cartels have tried in the past, with all their resources, and she still walks free. I notice he's not on the list for the Sunday event?"

"He's not; when I asked him why, he said he'd got another appointment he couldn't break."

Kenneth looked at Sedrick for a minute, alarm bells were ringing. "I'm not happy with that, Sedrick. Samuel's not one to miss a live show for anything, particularly a double one. You know he met Harris in Switzerland. Howard called me in a panic. He told me Harris had suddenly bailed the next day, after meeting Samuel."

"You're sure of that?"

"I am. In fact, he believed that whatever Samuel told Harris, brought the police to his house with a search warrant. Bit of a coincidence, don't you think, now Samuel's avoiding being here on Sunday?"

Kenneth pulled out his telephone and began going through the messages he'd received while travelling. "This is interesting. I've a text from a contact, who has an informer in Unit T. He's saying they mobilised yesterday and are now in lockdown. That means they have a target."

"Can your contact find out where?"

He shook his head. "Maybe, but it's not very likely. Once Harris issues that order, all communication in and out of the unit is suspended. Even if the police tried to communicate with them, they wouldn't respond."

They fell silent, sipping their brandies. Then Kenneth suddenly slammed his glass onto the coffee table. "Fuck, I bet we're the bloody target. Samuel's sold us out."

Sedrick shook his head. "He'd not be so stupid, he'd be caught as well."

"Not if he's told them Sunday would be the time to move in. He'd be long gone."

"The cunning bastard. What do you suggest? We abandon the live show?"

"I need to think," Kenneth replied. "How about if we brought it forward to Saturday?" he eventually said. "Then we'd be gone if Unit T moves in on Sunday?"

"Why not? If Samuel has done a deal with Harris, he'd be in a panic and want to get out."

"Yes, he would. He'd also want to get in touch with them and give the new show time. Bug his room and see what he does, after we tell him it's been brought forward. If he's out to get me, he'll need to call Harris, besides make sure he'd not be arrested as well."

"Good idea, I'll go and get it sorted, before he arrives."

***

Samuel French arrived later than he'd anticipated. With delays leaving the office, then heavy traffic, he was already worked up.

"Samuel, it's good to see you again?" Sedrick said, when Samuel came into the large entrance hall of the house, carrying a small overnight case.

"You too, Sedrick. I'm in my usual room, I presume?"

"But of course. When you've unpacked, there's drinks in the back lounge with nibbles. Dinner is at eight as ever."

Samuel was soon back down, he wanted a drink. Going through to the back lounge, he grabbed one and began chatting to others already in the room.

Sedrick approached him, taking him to one side. "I know you can't do Sunday, Samuel, but I've some good news on that front."

Samuel frowned. "In what way?"

"We've moved the Master's performance to Saturday. He won't be here Sunday; similar to you, he has another session at a different venue. So rather than upset everyone who's paid, I agreed Saturday. Can I book you in?"

"What time? I'm hoping to get a few good sessions on Saturday."

"Five, when the girls go off the floor for their own break before the night session."

"Then book me in, by all means. I'm on the special rate as usual?"

"Yes, I'll need the fee in advance."

"Very well, I'll call in the office before dinner."

Leaving Sedrick, Samuel joined a group of three men, chatting to them generally.

"Have you picked your partner for the night, Samuel?" a man asked who'd just joined the group.

"No, not yet, I've not seen the list."

"Well, little Rose is back. Also, Hanna is still available. You should see Sedrick and claim her, before she's taken."

"Hanna, you say. I think I will." Then he wandered off.

***

Before dinner, Samuel was back in his room, changing into a smart dinner jacket and bow tie. He was now looking forward to the events in the main lounge following dinner, when it would already have been set up with plenty of large cushions scattered about and semi-naked girls dancing among them, offering personal services.

Pulling his mobile out, he keyed in a number and waited.

"Samuel, you want me?" Karen asked.

"There's been a change of plan. Sunday is off, it's Saturday at five. I'll not be able to get out of here. You can ensure I'll be allowed to leave without charge?"

"Yes, leave it to me. I'm only interested in Parker." Then she cut off.

Chapter 18

Sherry opened her eyes, glancing over to the clock at the side of the bed. It was just before eight in the morning. She could hear the sound of the kettle coming to the boil.

At that moment Karen came out of the bathroom, wearing silk pyjamas; going to the kettle, she poured the water into two cups with instant coffee in them. Adding milk, she took hold of the cups and returned to the bed.

"I see you're awake," she said, placing a cup on Sherry's side and going around to the other. "Move over, I'm bloody freezing. How this place can be so cold when it's not even winter, God knows."

"I'm knackered, what time do they pick us up?"

"Nine thirty," Karen replied, sipping her coffee.

"You're not embarrassed at what we did together last night, to get ready for our performance, are you?"

"No, why should I be? You're my best friend, and besides, what we are forced to do as part of our job, I just accept, as you should."

"So you don't think it makes us lesbian then?"

Karen smiled. "It's possible, to the outside world that is. As it is, do you really want to exchange James, the new love of your life, for me? It'd be a turn-up if you do, Sherry. I'd feel flattered."

Her eyes went big. "You mean you really do want me as a lover?"

Karen touched her own lips with a finger, then briefly touched Sherry's lips with it. "We're covert, Sherry. Doing what's necessary to try to bring down a particularly bad trafficker and by the sounds of it, a psychopath. Discussions like that need to happen away from these sorts of pressures and never be taken lightly."

"You're right, I didn't think. Are you nervous?"

"In what way? Doing the dancing, or being in a house with this Parker guy?"

"Both I suppose. I am."

Karen placed her cup on the bedside table, turned to her, and put her arm around Sherry, pulling her close. "This is what I do, Sherry, and have done since I was abducted. I don't have a problem with the dancing, or anything else. Am I apprehensive at being around Parker, yes, who wouldn't be? But I have my watch, so I can call for assistance at any time. As for you, if you're having second thoughts about being back on covert operations, just tell me. I'd understand, believe me, it's not for everyone. You could remain here and join the lads waiting to go in. I'd say you're down with food poisoning, after a bad curry last night, or whatever. I'm only there till two in the morning anyway and would just have to work a little harder."

"No, I'm coming with you. I want to do it, Karen. In Afghanistan I was told it was okay to be a little scared, it keeps you focused. To tell you the truth, this time we've been together has been the best for ages. Although I've realised how high-risk these covert operations are, it could all so easily go wrong."

"Anything's possible, Sherry. Even in a shop or office, there're risks."

"You're right, let's do it. The first risk is the breakfast here, do we take it on, or chicken out and find something edible?"

"We'll go out, I want something substantial, who knows what will be on offer later."

***

At nine twenty-five, Karen called her control. "We have activated the trackers, Stanley, are they coming through?"

"Yes, they're fine, Karen. Can you press your watch winder once, then get Sherry to do the same?"

Both girls did as he asked.

"That's working, now three times to check the change of signal."

Again, they pressed the winders.

"That's okay, we're ready at our end. Take care and don't take risks. We'll be very close."

"Then Sherry and I are going dark, as at," she hesitated, "o-nine-twenty-seven."

After breaking off with Stanley, they both went down to the reception, taking seats close to the door, so they could see when the minibus arrived to collect them. All they had with them was a small bag containing the clothes they intended to wear that day. Also in the bag were a number of sex toys, which both girls hoped they wouldn't have to use, with men standing around watching.

"It's here, let's go," Karen said, after seeing a minibus draw up. As they made to leave, Karen stopped Sherry, her voice low. "We talk of nothing, on the bus, in the house when we arrive, about anything beyond our work from now on. Not even the slightest of comments, even when we think we are alone. Our lives could depend on us only doing what they're expecting from us."

"I understand."

***

The journey took over an hour and a half. They were sharing the minibus with six other girls. By the way they were talking, they were going to stay there overnight. The minibus drew up behind a typical country house, of a design that would date it to the Edwardian period, with its very large and high windows.

A man poked his head into the bus. "Hi girls, I'm Arnold, I'm here to look after you. The ones here overnight follow me. Richie, who's waiting at the door; will look after the lap dancers."

"Which of you are Tori and Charlie?" Richie asked, as all the girls followed Arnold into the house.

"I'm Tori, this is Charlie."

"After a bite to eat, Tori you're first to dance. Charlie, you're on the pole. Every half hour, change over. There's an hour's break at half-four and half an hour at ten. You've around forty men to potentially dance for up to the ten o'clock break. After your break at ten, I understand you also offer a lesbian act for a client. I've got six of those booked already."

He took them through to a small room off the main hall.

"This is the room you bring the guests to for your dance. During the break at ten, I'll have a bed brought in, with a few chairs. I presume you're used to performing in front of a number of clients, if you're already doing the hotels as a pair?"

"Yes, that's fine with us. Do we have a minder to call on? I expect most will be a little worse for wear by that time?" Tori asked.

"We don't call them minders, they're waiters, serving drinks, or whatever. They're also there to make sure no guest gets out of hand, you call on them. Right, there's a buffet in the back kitchen for all the workers, you begin in an hour."

Chapter 19

It was coming up to half-past four. Already the gathering was in full swing. In the large lounge, some of the guests were sitting around with the girls; most were naked, or semi-naked. Sherry was up on the pole, wearing just knickers, since Richie had told her to get rid of her top. Already she'd lap danced for ten men; Karen took the brunt, with twenty men. Ten of Karen's being the same men who Sherry danced for.

The man Karen was dancing for now, being particularly drunk, had for most of the dance been slumped back in his chair, eyes closed. Karen, as usual, had lost herself in the dance, ignoring the client, and would have finished it anyway, except now he was snoring. She only gave up once she was down to her bra and knickers; it was pointless going any further, besides the danger of ending up naked, sat astride a drunk, with all the risks that entailed.

Dressing, she gave him a shake. "Come on, I've finished, it's time you were out."

He opened his eyes. "What time is it?" he slurred.

She glanced at her watch. "Half-four, why?"

"I shouldn't be here, I've paid for the entertainment?"

"What are you talking about, I'm your entertainment, or I would have been, if you'd stayed awake."

"You, you don't call what you do entertainment, you're a fucking stripper and not very good at that. The Master's entertainment is beginning at five," he stammered. Then grinned. "He's got a white girl, and is promising to hack off limbs, while she still lives." He burped, the smell caught Karen's throat, making her feel sick. "You should see it? Proving she still lives by opening her up and pulling her beating heart out."

"I can see now why you say my striptease is no contest. Where is it being held, I'll help you there? Maybe they will let me watch as well?"

"I don't know, out the back somewhere. I need to get to it, help me up."

Karen helped him up and with him holding onto her, he stumbled into the main hall and headed towards the back of the house.

At a far door, a waiter came up to them both. "Where are you going with Alex?" he demanded.

Karen looked at him. "He said he was late for some entertainment by a man called Master. I'm just helping him there, he can't even stand up on his own."

The man pulled out a list and looked down, to check Alex's name was on it. "Help him through to the back door. He's supposed to be in the barn at the back of the house. Someone will take him from there, then you get back working."

"It's my break now."

"Then go on your break after you take him."

As they got outside, quite a number of the guests were standing around smoking; the barn door was currently closed.

Karen stood for a moment by the side of Alex. It seemed Samuel's call was genuine and Parker really had brought his act forward. The barn must be the location.

"I see you've brought Alex," Richie said, coming up to them both. "I'll take him from here."

Karen just nodded and went back inside.

Going over to Sherry, she picked up her robe and handed it her. "Come on, it's our break. Get this on quick," Karen urged.

"You look stressed, Karen, do you want me to take over the dancing?" Sherry asked, as they left the lounge.

"Not here, let's go to the dance room, so you can dress."

Once inside, she told Sherry what Alex had said. "I'm bringing it to an end, Sherry. Where I thought we'd be here till late tonight and among them, with the time to really get into just what has been happening during these weekends, it's not going to happen. I'm sorry about what you've been through for nothing, but it cannot continue. If we can belive Alex and with the waiter looking at some list, which could be the ones who have paid, they intend to kill a child as entertainment, we can't let it happen no matter what."

"I agree. We tried, Karen, that's all. Bring the lads in."

Karen pressed her watch winder three times. "We failed, Sherry, all we can do is wait." Then she sat down on the chair.

Sherry was leaning against the wall looking at Karen. "No, we didn't fail. If we'd not come here, we'd never have found the place."

"We would, Sherry, Samuel had given me the location."

"But you couldn't trust him. You said that yourself. As it is we're still covert, and won't be suspected. We go back to the Fairmont and follow up with Musowa and Ricky."

Karen smiled. "You have the same enthusiasm I used to have, Sherry, you'll make a good covert operator, believe me. You won't accept failure. As it is, you're right, we must go back to the Fairmont and see if we can pick up the thread once more."

Sherry gave her a hug. "I did enjoy the lap dancing

and can understand why you do it. Although I'm glad it's finished; I didn't relish what was going to happen later."

Karen looked at her. "I see, so you and I are finished as potential lovers, then, before we even started. You're back with James?"

Sherry had no time to answer, all hell had broken loose outside in the hall. She opened the door to see Unit T soldiers, dressed in black, with bulletproof jackets, helmets and carrying M4 carbines, entering through the front door, quickly spreading out.

Karen and Sherry watched quietly. Then Lieutenant Foster approached, joining them in the small room and shutting the door.

"You need to check the barn behind, Lieutenant, they were about to dismember a child at five, according to a guest called Alex. I couldn't wait any longer, the risk was too high for that child."

"I understand, Colonel. We'll check it out. As it is, it's time you were both put with the other girls."

***

Five minutes later, Karen and Sherry were led into one of the lounges where the other girls were being held. Their names taken, they were left to find somewhere to sit down.

Shortly a soldier came into the room and spoke quietly to a guard.

"Which one of you calls herself Tori?" he shouted.

"Me, what do you want?"

"You're first to be interviewed. Follow me."

She was taken outside and around the back, out of sight and into the command vehicle. Once inside the soldier took Karen to one side. "Sorry about that, but the lieutenant wants you in the barn immediately, Colonel. To keep your identity secret, he suggests you change into your combat uniform."

Karen quickly changed and tied her hair back. With her helmet on, the visor down, carrying an M4 carbine, she followed the soldier round to the barn.

It was empty of guests, but in the centre of the room was a rope; attached to it, and hung by the neck, was Samuel. A large sheet of paper was pinned to him, with the wording: *'This is what we do to informers, Harris. Your turn will come very soon, believe it.'*

"They knew we were coming, Colonel. As to them intending to kill a child, are you sure this guest who told you about the child, wasn't put up to do just that? If he was, your cover is blown."

"No, he was really drunk and completely out of it. Why do you ask?"

"We stopped a vehicle leaving around an hour back. Surveillance reported what looked like a child was being carried out of the house and put into the back. So if you are certain the guest was genuine. There was never any intention of killing the girl tonight. The barn was set up for you. "

Karen sighed. "It's a mess, Lieutenant. Is everyone now in the lounges?"

"They are. But you shouldn't blame yourself, Colonel. You did the right thing, and were working on information given to you that indicated a child was in serious trouble. These people live in a different world, believe they can do what they want. We only dismantle, we will never win."

"You're right, of course. But who do we arrest for this murder, or the abduction of the child?"

"That isn't our problem, it's up to the British police.

Although you and I know, there's always another day. We're on to them and won't let go, until they're dead, or in custody."

"That's very deep, Lieutenant. We will pursue and yes, we'll bring them to justice one day. Shall we go and see who's been caught in the net and more importantly, if they recognise me?"

They entered the lounge where the men were being kept separate to the girls, Karen still with her visor down. The guests were sitting on the floor along one side, in various states of undress, their hands behind their heads and guarded by four soldiers.

A soldier came up to Karen as she entered and saluted. She saluted back. "We're secure, Colonel."

She nodded and walked down the centre of the lounge. Most, if not all, were watching her. They all knew who she was. Except none had put together that this was the girl who'd been among them for the last few hours.

"You're Colonel Harris, commander of Unit T?" one man asked.

She stopped and looked at him. This was a man she'd not seen in the lounges. "I am, who are you?"

"Kenneth Parker. I've just arrived, what's the meaning of holding all of us? We are doing nothing illegal? All the girls are over sixteen."

"At present the girls are being interviewed, to confirm their age and that they are here on their own volition. As for this get-together, it's over. A murder has been committed, this is now a crime scene. We will go as soon as the British police arrive. They will answer your questions, not me."

"I see, I'd not realised there had been a fatality. Although you're not the police, so why are you here?"

"It is not my place to answer your questions. Again, you must talk to the police." Then she carried on down the line, noticing Alex, who had told her about the child, was now completely out of it, leaning against the back wall asleep. Satisfied that her cover was not compromised, she left.

Kenneth turned and looked at Sedrick sitting by the side of him. "So that is the great Karen Harris. I can't see why so many are frightened of her, she seems a wimp to me, hiding behind all these soldiers of hers."

"That's not what I've heard, she's no wimp. But you're right, she'd be better joining the orgy, rather than playing at soldiers."

"Yes, I like that idea. Mind you, she must have egg on her face now. Moving her unit across Europe, just to gatecrash a party," he said, before beginning to laugh.

After Karen left, she changed and returned to the lounge. Already, more girls had been taken to be interviewed. Making Tori's absence just part of the interview process.

Chapter 20

Ricky had parked in the cinema car park, close to a fire exit. It was the same Saturday that Karen and Sherry had gone to the party. He was here to collect Ally. Coming out onto the High Street, he made his way into the foyer of the cinema. Ally was standing inside the entrance, alone. She was wearing jeans, trainers and anorak. Her long hair was tied back in a ponytail. Ricky was taken aback slightly, she looked much younger than she did in her photos.

"Ally?"

She turned and smiled. "Yes, you're Ricky?"

"I am, shall we go in?" He looked down at the bag she was carrying. "What's in the bag?"

"My clothes. I couldn't leave the house dressed up, mum would want to know where I was going. As it is, she thinks, I'm going to meet my mates. I wasn't sure if you'd turn up, now you have I'll get changed."

While Ricky bought the tickets, Ally ran to the toilets. She came out minutes later, dressed in a crop top and a very short, flared skirt and high heels, had let her hair down and put a little makeup on.

"Will I do?"

"You would have done the way you were, Ally, but I love your clothes, they suit you."

She grinned as he took her hand and they went into the cinema, taking a seat at the back, in the darkest corner they could find. Soon he had his arm around her and was kissing her long and hard. At first she was hesitant, unsure how to respond, but in minutes she relaxed and allowed him to explore with his tongue.

"You're my first real boyfriend," she whispered.

"I'm flattered. We should see a lot of each other, can you get out?"

"Up to nine or half past. Then there are nights Dad's shop is open late, which means I can stay out a little later. I'll soon be sixteen and allowed out more," she hesitated. "Is that alright?"

"Course it is, Ally. I do know how old you are and wouldn't expect your parents to let you out very late."

She snuggled closer, he dropped his arm down, his hand on her bare skin, between her top and skirt. Ally didn't object, she had a boyfriend, that's all she wanted. Again he kissed her. "This is a crap film, shall we find somewhere better than this?"

"Yes, I'm happy with anything you want to do."

Ricky and Ally left through a fire exit. Parked directly outside was his car.

"I love the car," she said, climbing in and fastening her seat belt. "What is it?"

"Golf GTI, it really moves, I can tell you." He pulled two small plastic bottles of coke from the door pocket on his side and handed her one, before opening his own and taking a long drink.

"Haven't you got anything stronger?" she asked, opening it and taking a sip.

He laughed. "There's vodka in yours, can't you taste it?"

Ally looked at the bottle and gave it a sniff. "I've never had vodka before. Although I must admit the coke has a strange taste. But I'm cool with that."

He started the car and left the car park, heading out of the town. Two miles out, he turned into a lay-by, which had really been the existing road before it was straightened. Cars parked in this lay-by were hidden from the road by a row of shrubs and it was popular with locals who took their girlfriends there. He came to a halt away from two other parked cars.

"You've not told anyone about me, have you, Ally?"

She shook her head. "No, not even my best friend. She'd be dead jealous. She fancies a lad who's eighteen, but he just ignores her."

"Shall we get into the back?" he asked.

"If you want," Ally answered, at the same time releasing the seat belt, climbing out of the car and into the back.

Ricky leaned over to the front passenger seat and released it, pushing it forward, then once he was out of the car did the same to his own, giving far more room in the back. He climbed in alongside Ally, slipping his arm around her.

"You're not drinking the vodka and coke, don't you like it? I may have another coke in the boot, without vodka."

"No, I love it, besides you shouldn't waste alcohol, it's really expensive," she said, opening her bottle and taking a large drink.

Ricky watched the level, she'd only drunk half the bottle, she needed to drink more.

He opened his own and began drinking. Ally carried on with her own bottle. Already she was feeling a little strange, light-headed and more relaxed.

"I think this is really strong, I'm feeling a little tipsy," she told him, at the same time giggling a little.

Ricky said nothing, slipping his arm around her back he pulled her close, kissing her long and hard, before he broke away and again drank some of his coke.

"God, I've never been kissed like you kiss," she said, at the same time taking another swig of her drink.

99

"Are you complaining?"

She shook her head fervently. "No, I love it." Then she looked at the bottle. "Oops, I seem to have drunk it all."

"There's plenty more, I'll get you a refill in a short while, now kiss me again."

This time he was more passionate, Ally responded with equal passion, mainly because of the drink she'd begun to lose her initial shyness.

"I seem to have known you for ages," Ally said when she pulled away, at the same time pulling her short skirt down. For the second time, it had ridden up, exposing her knickers.

"Yes, I'm the same. You're having trouble with your skirt I notice."

She grinned. "I don't think they were designed to wear in the back of a car."

He laughed. "You could be right there, but I am your boyfriend, so it's alright and you shouldn't be embarrassed."

"Yes, I never thought of that, not that I'm embarrassed, I just don't like showing my knickers. I've been really excited all week, after I got your email. But you've never told me where you live and what you do. Me, I'm an open book, got the next four years either at school or college. Really boring, don't you think?"

"So you'd like to bail and perhaps go backpacking across the world."

She looked up at him, her eyes sparkling. "God, yes, that would be cool. Will you take me one day? Maybe even America, or better still the Borneo rain forest. I own a bit of land there," she said, scrunching her nose. "Well, not a lot, more a postage stamp. All the girls in our class have a bit, but it's big enough between us all, to grow one tree and they send us a photo every now and again to show us how big it's grown."

"Sounds fun. I think I'll buy a bit of land. As it is, I live in London and work in the nightclubs. You should come sometime."

Ally laughed. "At my age, they'd never let me in. But it sounds really cool, do you meet like, stars and things?"

"Things, what are things?" he asked, confused.

"You know, like dead famous people," she added.

"Sometimes. I'll get you signed photos if you want?"

As they talked, Ally was beginning to feel progressively more tired, now she was even struggling to keep her eyes open. His words had begun to sound distant. She snuggled closer to Ricky, feeling more secure, even indifferent that her dress had ridden up again, exposing her knickers. "I'd like that," she said quietly.

"Like what, Ally?" But Ally didn't answer, her eyes were closed, her breathing steady. To be sure she was not just relaxing, Ricky had moved his hand down to her knickers, pushing them off her bottom, then began rubbing and massaging her cheeks gently, knowing if the drug hadn't done its work, she'd object, but she didn't.

Sitting her up, he slapped her face a number of times. "Come on, Ally, don't go to sleep on me," he shouted at her.

She never responded.

"Oh, I see, can't take your drink then?" he mocked, pulling away from Ally, laying her back on the seat. Taking a large plastic tie wrap from his pocket, he secured her wrists together. Then, with a strip from a roll of duck tape, he put a piece over her mouth. This was followed by a cloth bag over her head, secured around her neck with two plastic tie wraps, joined together. Finally, he removed her shoes, before using more duck tape to bind her ankles together. Climbing out of the car, he leaned in and covered her with a car blanket. Then adjusting the front seats, he set off for London. He had no real idea how long the drug would keep her unconscious, so if she woke, she had to be secure.

***

By the time Ricky arrived at the address he'd been given to deliver Ally, she was awake. For a time she had struggled, but she was now still, after realising there was no escape. Climbing out of the car, he knocked on the door of the house.

A woman opened it. "Yes?"

"I'm from Musowa, I've got the girl, Ally."

She gave a hint of a smile. "I'll open the garage, drive straight in. We take her out when the door is closed."

Once inside the garage, Ricky released Ally's ankles and keeping the cover over her head, he helped her out of the car and guided her through into the house.

"Follow me," the woman said, making her way upstairs.

Now they were in a bedroom. There was only a single bed, with a Portaloo at the side. Two blankets were folded up at the end of the bed.

"Keep her stood up, while I get her clothes off," the woman told him while she released Ally's hands.

"Why are you stripping her?"

"It's easier than searching, in case she carries anything that she could use to self-harm, or even harm me. I've got a nightdress she can wear."

Once Ally was naked, the woman sat her on the side of the bed, picked up an ankle iron left under the bed, which was already attached to a chain secured to a large ring set in the floor, and fitted it to one of her ankles. Finally, she released the cover still over Ally's head and removed the duck tape from across her mouth.

"There's a nightdress under the blankets at the end of your bed. Put it on, then sit on the side of the bed," the woman demanded.

Ally, embarrassed at Ricky seeing her naked, soon had the nightdress and pulled it over her head. Then she sat down, she was shivering and very frightened. "Ricky, why am I here, what have I done?" was all she could think of saying.

The woman suddenly slapped her face, hard. "Shut up, speak when you're spoken to, or you'll feel my stick on your backside, till you do shut up."

Ally said nothing more, tears were trickling down her face, her cheek stinging.

The woman looked at Ricky. "You go now. Leave the car in the garage and take the tube."

He nodded, glancing at Ally. "You said school was boring, welcome to a new life, Ally. Soon you'll begin those travels we talked about, to a new country." Then he left the room.

Chapter 21

Karen and Sherry were back at the Carlton Hotel. It was Sunday, Karen was talking to Stanley.

"It didn't go as I planned, Stanley."

"Sometimes it doesn't, but we have Autumn and also very strong links between this Parker and what's been going on."

"How is Autumn, Lieutenant Foster said she wasn't well."

"They tried to sterilise the girl. Whatever instruments they used, can't have been clean, as it caused an infection, so yes, she's very ill. At the moment she's in intensive care, but they don't believe her condition is life-threatening, they just need to get control of the infection."

"I should talk to her as soon as possible."

"I agree, Sir Peter has taken charge and fully understands the urgency. He'll be in touch as soon as she's able to talk to you. What are your plans now?"

"We believe we're still in a good position to continue the covert operation. I'm going in hard for our money. It's the logical thing two working girls would do, they'd think it strange if we didn't. Then we'll see where it takes us."

"I agree, we must milk the operation for all we can. I'll need regular daily reports, Karen. I'll also keep you abreast of anything that comes through that could have a bearing. Take care and we'll talk soon."

***

Later, the same day, Sir Peter called Karen. "Can you talk, Karen?"

"Yes."

"I've been informed that you can see Autumn on Monday. She's responded well to the drugs they have used and although still very weak, her talk is becoming more lucid."

"That's good, I'll make my way over and meet you there. What time do you suggest?"

"In the afternoon I think. Shall we say three?"

"Yes, fine. Has there been any progress in Samuel's murder?"

"No, we're still waiting on forensics. Everyone was so drunk, it's virtually impossible to get any coherent statements as to who did what and where everyone was. On a different issue, there has been another abduction. The circumstances are similar to how Autumn was taken. The local police are gathering everything they can together and will forward their findings to me."

"How old is the girl, Peter?"

"Fifteen, her name is Ally. The last sighting of her was at a local multiplex cinema. The woman in the ticket office said she was with a man in his twenties, who bought the tickets. They didn't come out through the foyer. Currently local police are working with her for a photofit. They're also going through CCTV of the area as we speak."

Karen had a thought. "Is it possible she's a replacement for Autumn? After all Autumn was taken to sell, not kill. She'd have been worth up to sixty thousand, you don't kill such girls. Although I'm certain if we hadn't intervened, they would have done, after the operation went wrong, she'd have had no value."

"I'm of the same opinion, that is why I've asked for details, except it's early days and I could be wrong. But you're in the best position to progress that possibility.

We're a good ninety per cent certain Autumn was taken by Musowa. Autumn should be able to confirm that when we show her photos."

"Okay, we'll talk further tomorrow. "

"Very well, Karen, look after yourself."

Sherry looked up from a magazine she'd been reading, after Karen came off the phone. "From what I could glean, it's not getting any better, if another girl has been taken."

"No, it's not, Sherry. But this is how it goes. With the club closed tonight, I was thinking of going back to my flat for a decent bath. How does that sound?"

"Brilliant, apart from actually being able to watch a television that isn't tiny and flickering all the time. Are we coming back here later?"

"We'll have to, to keep up the pretence. Disappearing in the day and early evening is okay, we could be working, but we still need to sleep here."

"Then let's go, shall we? Every hour out of here is a bonus."

Chapter 22

Kenneth Parker was in London. Everyone who had been at the house where Samuel French was murdered had been interviewed and told they were still part of the investigation and to make themselves available. In the room with him was Sedrick. Kenneth had just come off the telephone.

"It seems Autumn was picked up after the car was stopped by Unit T forces, as it left the house. She's in hospital and by all accounts getting better. Soon she'll talk, which means Musowa is now a clear risk and a direct link back to us."

"You want me to make a call?"

"Yes, make it a matter of urgency, before he's picked up."

"No problems. I've had a few of the girls call earlier, asking if they were going to get any money."

"We should pay them, we've two more weekends coming up and we don't want them bailing. What happened to the lap dancers?"

"They were interviewed like the other girls and allowed to leave."

Kenneth frowned. "It will be interesting to see if they turn up to be paid as well. While we knew about French, I can't help thinking someone gave Unit T the heads up to come in when they did. I also can't believe they would have relied just on an informer, they'd want someone inside."

"Anything's possible I suppose. As it was, while the dancers were there, they didn't stop working. Richie told me Tori had brought Alex, who was as drunk as a skunk, to the yard. Told him Alex was babbling on about some different entertainment, but had no idea what he was talking about.

She didn't stay and Richie sent her on a break."

"Interesting. What we don't know is what Alex really told her? Call Stubbs, get him to call us if they turn up looking for Musowa or Ricky. If they're genuine, they will, like the other girls, want their money. Besides, they went down well and kept the guests buzzing. We'll use them again."

"What of Ricky? I still consider him, like Musowa, to be a risk, after he allowed Larisa to escape."

"Yes, so do I. Did he deliver Ally on Saturday?"

"He did. She's leaving in two days."

"Then, his work is done. Get rid of him,the same as Musowa."

Sedrick began to laugh. "We seriously need more people, at this rate of loss."

"We do, and I've already two possibles lined up. Both are ex-commandos and worked as mercenaries in Africa. We can't have idiots like Ricky and Musowa, who fail to take simple precautions."

"I don't have an issue, but these ex-commandos you talk about would not have been able to pull Autumn, or Ally. They would have been far too old."

"I agree, I'm looking into just how we do that from now on. Snatching young girls by befriending them, is getting very difficult, because you can hardly turn without a CCTV camera watching. Particularly in public places. I'm of the opinion, once we have agreed a sale with photos, we should snatch them from their own house, while the family sleeps. What's it matter to us if anyone in the house gets in our way, they just get eliminated. As far as I can see, after a child is taken, he or she no longer has a family, so why worry if they're dead or alive?"

"Looking at it that way, you have a point. Hence the

use of mercenaries then?" Sedrick commented.

"Precisely. I may even send them after Karen Harris. If she's so lax that Hans could get close, they would have little problem."

Sedrick gave a hint of a smile. "I like that idea. But they kill her. It seems to me the major error everyone makes is not killing her there and then, but taking her somewhere else, putting her to work, or imprisoning her. Doing that always leaves it open for her to escape; she can't if she's dead."

Chapter 23

Karen didn't dye her hair back just yet, she wanted to leave it blonde, and remain as Tori. To this end she'd had a wig made, that was precisely her natural colour and style. So, dressed in a smart black trouser suit and blouse, and wearing the wig, she arrived at the hospital where Autumn was a patient. Going directly to the girl's private room, she showed the police her pass and soon she was alone with her.

"My name's Karen Harris, Autumn. It was my unit that rescued you from the traffickers."

"I know, the police told me."

"You were a very stupid girl, ignoring all the warnings given you at school. But when we're young, we all do stupid things. I was the same."

She looked down, preferring not to look directly at Karen. "I've paid for it. Now mum and dad are on their way, I'm dreading that. I'll be grounded till I'm eighteen at least."

"You'll certainly have to eat humble pie, like I had to, but I think your parents will be so relieved you're safe, they won't be that hard. For a lot of families going through this experience, it's a wake-up call for all of you. But I think in future it won't take a no from your parents, you yourself will be saying no."

She nodded. "I can believe that. I read your book on your abduction over a year back, it was terrifying. I'd have fallen to pieces and let them do anything they wanted of me, faced with what you had to go through."

"You think I didn't? Believe me I did, Autumn. I cried my eyes out in the hold of a ship, every night. Then, given the alternative of being thrown overboard as food for the sharks, or stripping in front of men, I grasped the straw being offered to me, stripped and got raped for my efforts."

"I never knew," she gasped.

"No, very few do. My book was written to sell and help others with its profits. They made me out to be a super girl, a one-girl army. I wasn't, I was hiding behind a gun. Never asking, just pulling the trigger if anyone stood in my way." Karen hesitated. "I've paid for that so many times in my life since, believe me. So when your parents come, understand what they have gone through, believing they had lost the daughter they spent fifteen years bringing up and, like I say, eat humble pie and learn."

They both remained silent for a short time.

"Right, although you and I need to talk about your abduction, it can wait till another day and you feel a little better. All I want you to do now, is to look at a few photographs and tell me if you've seen any of these men before. This information is to help others, not you. You're free, there are many out there who are not."

"I understand, and will do anything I can to help you."

Karen pulled a folder from her bag and gave Autumn a number of photographs. "First look at them and say nothing. This isn't spot the criminal, look at them carefully and try to tell me first if you ever met them and second, when and under what conditions."

After Autumn had gone through the photos she'd put three in one pile, the rest in another. "Those three men I've never seen. These four I have." Lifting the first one in the pile, she showed it to Karen. "That's Musowa, who met me outside school and took me to Leeds." Putting it down and taking the next, Autumn sighed, thinking back. "This man, I don't know his name, brought another man to see me. They agreed my sale between them, I was to go to Belgium. That's where he lived, I think." Putting it down, she picked up the next. "He came to see me when I was ill, I think he was a doctor by the way he was examining me, but I don't know." Autumn never touched the last photo, just stared down at it, her voice changed to one of fear. "He came to see me in that house, before I was picked up by your soldiers. I was naked, laid out on a table, my hair tied up." She shuddered as she remembered. "He ran his hands over me, made marks on my body, around my breasts and hips, with a felt tip pen, before turning me over and doing the same. It was as if I was being marked for some bizarre operation. Even though I was ill, he terrified me."

Karen was relieved. Autumn had identified not only Musowa, but Sedrick and a doctor they suspected was still practising, called Cropper. But more importantly, she had implicated Parker. It would seem by him visiting her at the house, he'd every intention at that time to butcher the girl. "Tell me, Autumn, this man who came to see you at the house, did he see you as soon as you arrived?"

"I think so. I was a bit spaced out, but I was still awake when he came. After he'd gone, I must have slept because the next thing I knew was being helped out of the room, before being pushed into the back of a van. Is it important?"

"Yes and no. It's more to get a complete picture, so even tiny bits of information can be vital to piece everything together." Karen was satisfied with what Autumn had said. Now she was convinced that Parker must have heard Samuel call her, when Samuel told her of the change of day that Parker intended to dismember Autumn; so that was why Parker had abandoned this show.

Autumn collected the photos and handed them to Karen. "Will I ever see you again?"

"You will. I'll visit you at your home shortly and also introduce you to your contact in my charity. We will never abandon you, Autumn, remember that. You will go through a difficult time coming to terms with your ordeal, have no doubts. Sometimes you may not want to discuss your thoughts, your feelings with mum or dad, that's where we come in. You can tell us anything, there is nothing we haven't heard before and won't understand. We don't judge, or treat you like a little girl. We're like a big family, not so-called do-gooders, many of us were victims, the same as you. The help and advice we give is built up from a great deal of personal experiences, so take it on board. I've told you things about me that are not generally known. I'll expect you to keep them to yourself, the same as you'd expect us to do for you."

"I understand and will keep your confidence. Thank you for getting me out. I really believed no-one would come for me, then when I fell ill, I just wanted to die. I had no future, or rather, I had a future I didn't want."

Karen gave the girl a big hug. "We would never have given up looking for you while we still believed you were alive, Autumn. Think how I felt, when I was forced to listen to a news report that said I'd drowned. When you know no one is coming, that's when you feel alone, believe me."

***

As Karen left the hospital a lady stopped her. "Excuse me, are you Karen Harris?"

"I am, you are?"

"We're Autumn's parents. We just wanted to thank you for bringing our little girl home?"

Karen smiled. "It's what we do, but it's nice to see

a successful outcome." Then she changed her tone a little. "Your daughter has been through a great deal, she still has no idea what they have done to her. Don't judge her, at the same time don't be overprotective of her. She's learned a harsh lesson, she will protect herself from now on, believe me, I did."

"We were all young once, but we will take your advice, Karen. We're just happy she is safe and will be coming home."

"I'm glad you see it that way, but I must go. I'll come and visit you all very soon," she said, then she walked away.

Chapter 24

Ally was lying on the bed. It had been two days since she'd been brought to the house. The first night she'd cried herself to sleep. Now that had gone, leaving her annoyed with herself at being so stupid. She always believed what was said at school to be just talk. She'd never known anyone who had been abducted, and then, most of her friends had loads of lads on social media sites, some had actually met them, so why did she end up with a weirdo?

For Ally, the reality of her dilemma had still not sunk in. She remembered reading a book about when Karen Marshall had been taken, later changing her name to Harris. She thought back on how Karen had to fight for her freedom, how she'd taken on her abductors, the chase across a foreign country, the fights and final escape. Nearly every girl in her class had read the book, mostly in awe that a girl could have done what Karen had done. Now she was reaping the rewards, with a multimillionaire lifestyle, jetting around the world, which to any girl was a fairy tale. Already Ally's thoughts had drifted to her own abduction; she too would escape, fight her way across the country to be finally rescued by really fit soldiers as Karen had been and more importantly, she'd become really rich.

The woman looking after Ally came into the room, carrying a short, stubby-handled whip. "You're leaving later today, so you'll wash, then get dressed into more suitable clothes for travelling. When we go through to the bathroom, I'll be watching you all the time. Refuse to obey my orders, and I'll lay into you with this whip. Do you understand?"

"That's not very difficult to understand, where am I supposed to be going?"

"You're not here to ask questions."

"Why shouldn't I? I'm entitled to know what's going to happen to me?"

"You want to know, do you? Believe you're entitled? Very well, you're going to work in a brothel, let's see how cocky you are after you've worked your first fifteen-hour day, servicing no less than twenty men. So now you know what awaits you, no more questions, or delays; remove your nightdress and lie face down, your hands gripping the rails of the bedhead."

Ally reluctantly did as she was told, not sure what else she could do at this moment, with the woman brandishing the whip. The next moment the whip came down on her back, her bottom and the top of her legs in quick succession. The woman hadn't been gentle, putting her full weight behind the whipping. Ally screamed in pain and was soon sobbing her heart out.

"Such a child aren't we?" she mocked. "I hardly touched you, compared to what you'd get off your new owner, if you refuse what he wants from you." The woman came closer and unfastened the ankle iron. "Get yourself up and out onto the landing. All the doors of the house are locked, the double glazed windows are also locked. So scream as much as you want, no one will hear. Now move."

The bathroom was at the end of the landing. Inside were clothes for her to wear. Knickers, jeans, shoes and a t-shirt. Ally went under the shower, watched all the time by the woman, as she washed herself down, followed by her hair. It felt good, just to get under the water and feel clean, after not even being able to wash her hands when she'd gone to the toilet.

"Hurry up, I've not got all day," the woman urged.

With rushing, Ally, while washing her hair, had got

liquid soap in her eyes, it was stinging. At home, they used shampoo that didn't sting the eyes, so she'd not expected it. After shutting the shower off, she glanced at the woman. She had her back to her, taking a towel off the radiator. Ally thought for a second, the prospect of being with one man revolted her, but twenty, she'd rather die. As far as she could see, there was only the two of them in the house. When she left, there were bound to be more people around, if only the ones who were taking her. As it was, this might not be as she'd imagined her escape would be. Ally had imagined it to be like Karen's escape - brandishing guns, standing beside really cool soldiers - but if she wanted her freedom, she had to at least try. Squirting a large amount of the liquid soap into her hand, before closing it, she stood there for a moment, her heart beating at an alarming rate; Ally was scared, her body shivering, but at the same time she was excited about the prospect of taking this woman on.

"Don't just stand there, get yourself out and dressed," the woman demanded.

Ally came out. Then, just as the woman handed her the towel, Ally moved like lightning towards her. Her hand full of liquid soap, she slapped it directly into the woman's face, moving her palm over the woman's eyes.

Like Ally had experienced, the stinging pain in the eyes as the soap got in made the woman scream, temporarily blinding her. She dropped the whip, and was trying desperately to get the soap out of her eyes, using the towel she still held. Ally grabbed the whip, beginning to hit the woman relentlessly, until she'd fallen to the floor, still blinded by the soap.

"Crawl on your hands and knees into the room you kept me in. Try to get up and I'll hit you again with this whip," Ally screamed at her.

Soon the woman was on top of Ally's bed, her ankle firmly fixed by the ankle iron she had used on Ally.

"Where are my clothes?" Ally demanded.

"In the next bedroom. But you're wasting your time, you're dead child, they will come for you, believe me, you will never be free."

"I'll take my chance, anything is better than being raped every day."

The woman began to laugh. "Then run girl, run for your life, it won't help," she mocked.

"Shut up, or I'll hit you again with the whip. Where's the keys for the doors?"

"In my pocket."

"Pull them out and throw them onto the floor."

The woman did as Ally asked, allowing a slight smile to cross her face. "We know where you live, Ally. Do you want to risk your parents, even your little sister's life, after the trafficker finds you're gone? Just release me, get yourself dressed and ready to go. I'll say nothing about what you've done, you'll not even get a beating for attacking me."

"Yes, I can see you doing that for me, after all, you were quick enough to punish me just for a few words," she replied, at the same time picking up the keys. "But thanks for warning me, I'll be sure to tell the police what you said." Then she left the room, locking it after her.

Going into the next bedroom, Ally found her clothes and quickly dressed.

Once dressed, Ally cautiously went down the stairs, the whip gripped firmly in her hand. Checking that there was no one else in the house, she opened the front door, using a key from the bunch she'd taken off the woman. Not hesitating and still holding the whip, she ran like she'd never run before. The words of the woman were still ringing in her ears. She felt scared, but relieved to be out of that house.

Eventually Ally came out into a main shopping area. There she hesitated, looking around hoping to see a policeman. There were none, so she made her way into a large store, going up to the customer service counter.

The girl stood behind came up to her. "Can I help?"

"Will you call the police, I was abducted and escaped, they could still be after me?" she asked, with surprising calm in her voice.

The girl grinned. "Excuse me, you've been abducted?" she asked, obviously disbelieving Ally.

"Call the fucking police," Ally shouted, her initial composure completely gone, because of the attitude of the girl.

A man came up to them. "What seems to be the matter?"

"This girl claims she's been abducted and has escaped, Mr Ross."

He looked at Ally. "Where's your mother, child?"

"For god's sake, someone call the police, I need help," she screamed at them both, then Ally looked around, not knowing what to do. She saw a large display of cans, ran over to them and pushed them over, then began throwing the cans at the man and girl, desperate that they would now call the police.

They did, and minutes later, with customers running out of the store, thinking the girl was drunk or on drugs, finally the police arrived. Ally was arrested and taken away.

Chapter 25

Ally was initially taken to the local police station, given a hot mug of tea and a biscuit, while they confirmed she actually was who she claimed to be. Then, with her description of the house and how far she had run, police were on their way to arrest the woman. While she drank her tea, they took her statement, sending a copy to the special department in New Scotland Yard run by Sir Peter that dealt with trafficking.

The station sergeant came into the room Ally was in. "Have you finished your tea, Ally?"

"Yes, thank you. I'm sorry I wrecked the shop, will I have to pay?"

He smiled. "What, for knocking down a display?"

"Yes, but I did throw a few cans."

"You did, although under the circumstances, it was understandable. But no, they're not pressing charges, it was obvious you were in a great deal of distress. As it is, we're moving you to New Scotland Yard. They have better facilities there. Beyond cells here, we only have this interview room. Hardly suitable."

***

When Ally arrived at New Scotland Yard, she was taken directly to Sir Peter's office.

"My name's Sir Peter Parker, Ally. You're a very brave and plucky young lady. I understand the police have already been to the house you were being held in, the woman has been arrested."

She shrugged, perhaps a little too indifferently. "I watch movies, they make escapes like that all the time. So it was cool. Have you called mum and dad?"

"We have, they're on their way. I've been told you've declined going to the hospital for a check-up?"

"I'm not ill, or anything. I could do with some decent food, I got a biscuit at the police station earlier, but have had very little over the last days and I'm starving."

"You will soon be going down to the canteen, I promise. Have you ever heard of Karen Harris, commander of Unit T?"

"Course I have, she's dead famous and really popular at our school. Why do you ask?"

"She's on her way here as we speak. Karen needs to talk to you urgently. That's why I'm delaying taking you to the canteen, she will take you down. In the meantime, I can have coffee, tea or even a coke brought."

"No thank you, I'm fine and will wait for Karen. I was gobsmacked when you mentioned her name, but to say she's coming to see me, I can't believe it. She's dead rich, isn't she?"

He frowned. "Why do you ask that?"

"They featured her in a magazine. They said she lives the life of a millionaire, owns and flies her own jet and has property all over the world. My mates will be so jealous when I tell them we've met, besides had dinner together."

He smiled. "Karen is not as they portray in magazines, Ally. She's very down to earth, comes from Lancashire and was brought up in a semi-detached with her mum and dad. She also has a sister."

"I know all that, but she now lives in the South of France in a big house."

Sir Peter said no more. He was satisfied Ally wasn't in shock, in fact she seemed very level-headed and outwardly none the worse for her experience. In lots of ways she reminded him of Karen. When he had first met her, she displayed the same cockiness and self-confidence. But Karen had been eighteen, Ally was fifteen. This was remarkable.

At that moment his secretary buzzed him. He picked up the handset.

"Lady Harris has arrived, Sir Peter. Would you like me to bring her up?"

"No, I'll come down." He looked at Ally. "Karen has arrived. I'll collect her, then you can join her for lunch." Then he left the office, going down to the reception.

"Karen, it's good to meet you," Sir Peter said, giving her a hug and kissing her on each cheek.

"It's good to see you also, Peter. I read the initial police report on Ally, while I travelled here. She seems a smart girl?"

"Oh, she is, very much so. I think you will be surprised, for fifteen, she's you Karen, through and through. She also knows all about you, apparently you were featured in a magazine."

"Magazines are always doing that. Much of the information about me is made-up, to sell copies. But if it makes the kids aware how dangerous it is out there, I'm all right with that."

"Perhaps. I'll leave you with her and we'll talk later."

***

"Was that good? Apparently they made the pizza especially for you," Karen asked Ally.

"Brilliant, it really was. You didn't eat much?"

"I eat at night usually. I read the initial report as to how you escaped? Except it didn't say what made you decide to have a go."

"That woman said I was going to be with twenty men a day. It made me feel sick inside at the thought of being touched by even one, let alone twenty. Then I thought back to the book you wrote. You faced the same, but made your escape. So I thought, if you could, so could I?"

"That's true, I did," Karen answered, "but it was full of risk. What made you attempt it at that moment, after all, you had no idea if there were other people in the house?"

"I suppose," Ally said thoughtfully. "I really didn't think if anyone else was there. It was the liquid soap in the shower that gave me an idea. It stung my eyes, ours at home doesn't do that. So I knew it would do the same to that woman. Besides, she'd hit me with the whip. I was really mad and wanted to get my own back."

Karen smiled. "I can understand you were mad, I would have been too."

Ally was fiddling with her glass of coke. "I was very scared, Karen. Except, unlike me, who just took a chance, you were clever and used people around you, besides skills gained from those mock army exercise weekends you went on. You also carried guns and grenades. If I had them, rather than a whip, I'd have shot her like you did."

Karen couldn't believe just how much this girl knew about her. She was getting the impression Ally had aligned herself to her, based on the book and reports in the papers she'd read. Although Ally was fifteen, where she had been seventeen and was already well versed in survival techniques, with experience of melting into the landscape. Deciding to play down Ally's obvious fixation on her, Karen changed the subject to why she was here. "I've come to see you, Ally, because I believe you're still in danger. You see, the papers will have a field day telling the world how a fifteen-year-old girl made traffickers look like fools. Many papers, like they did with me, will make big offers for your story."

"You mean I'll get as rich as you by selling my story?" she asked with big eyes.

"I didn't get rich, all my payments from the papers went to setting up my charity. The problem we have with you, Ally, is the traffickers themselves. Traffickers rule and control victims with fear and intimidation. They cannot let it lie like this. Once you're back home, alone and vulnerable, they will come and collect you; after all, in their eyes you're already sold and your home, your family offer little protection."

She nodded her head up and down slightly. "That woman said they would come. Trying to frighten me, I think. But now I'm beginning to believe her. So what do I do and will mum and dad be at risk?"

"Don't be so despondent. The advantage you have within the world of trafficking, is they all operate separately - actually, in competition. That means if I can haul in the gang who took you, then the risk goes away and you can get on with your life. The only problem in that, until I do, you need to be kept safe. I'm suggesting that you come back to France with me, there you will be protected, believe me."

Her eyes lit up. "You mean, come to stay with you at your house?"

"Of course. But would you want to come?"

"God, yes, I'd love to. You're my hero, to actually be with you now, I could never have dreamed it would ever happen, but to go to France with you, that's so cool." Then she suddenly had a thought. "Except mum and dad would never let me go."

"They have no option, Ally, we need to keep you safe. The alternative is for you to be virtually a prisoner in a house with twenty-four hour guards. In France I can offer

124

that, without you being confined."

"I'm not sitting in a house all day, I want a life," she said indignantly. "I'm coming with you. Will we go in your aircraft?"

Karen laughed. "You could, and it would probably work out right in my schedule. You couldn't leave imediatly. Sir Peter will want time with you to go through your statement, identify the woman at the house besides look through photographs to try to identify your abductors."

"Then I'm definitely coming."

Chapter 26

"How the fucking hell can a kid of fifteen just walk out of one of our holding houses?" Kenneth Parker demanded of Sedrick. "She's made us a laughing stock. Have you seen the headlines in all the papers?"

"I have, but it beats me, it just can't happen. Adah has been arrested, so we can't even talk to her. That woman has over the last few months looked after and shifted close to twenty children; somehow she made a grave error of judgement, we need to know what went wrong so it can never happen again."

"We do, I've sent our solicitor to find out the story. I'm also not prepared to lose sixty thousand. This is an ideal job for our two new associates. I want her back by the end of next week. It will also show we won't be made fools of and there is no escape, no matter what."

Sedrick didn't say anything, but went over to the side table and poured two straight whiskies, bringing them back to where they were both sitting.

"On another issue, Kenneth, all the girls have been paid off and agreed to go on the next weekend. The two lap dancers were in last night, looking for their money. Stubbs called me and I told him to tell them they would be paid tonight. I'm meeting them at half-eleven, do you want them booked for the next one?"

"In your opinion, were they an asset, or a waste of money?"

"They went down well and certainly broke the ice at a time when most would have been drinking to excess, with problems later. For what they cost, I'd book them. Maybe this time we'll incorporate the lesbian act earlier, by first having them both in the room stripping at the same time, for two lucky guests before others joining them when the girls perform on the bed."

"I like that plan. It should really loosen the guests up, and make them more willing to pay for the extras offered during the weekend. But you don't tell the girls of our change of plan. You also only pay them for what they did, not for the entire night. They need to learn they have to work to be paid."

***

Later that night, Sedrick was at the Fairmont club. He was sitting with Stubbs.

"I was expecting Musowa, Sedrick, not you. He was supposed to pay Tori and Charlie tonight. I told them he was coming after I called you."

"He's off the books, I'm looking after his contacts until we replace him. I'll sort the two dancers out."

Stubbs looked put out. "If he's not coming back, that leaves me with another problem. He said he'd supply me with a couple of prostitutes, for my new stag nights. I was relying on them to keep punters in my club by giving the groom and best man a good shagging, before opening themselves up for the rest of the party. It should stop the party moving on."

"We'll supply girls for you, that's no problem. You give me a list of the nights and I'll make sure they are there."

Stubbs sighed with relief. "Thanks, Sedrick. Things are a bit tight at the moment, the stag groups are a life saver."

Sedrick smiled. "We can't have you going down the tubes for the sake of a few girls, Stubbs," he said, then looked at his watch. "Are you sure they said they'd be here by half eleven, it's after that already?"

"They're always here before twelve, it depends on their last client. Some decide after the lap dance they want their lesbian act and it delays them. At least it shows the girls are in demand."

"Yes, I suppose it does. Although, talk of the devil, look who's walked in, Tori, and she's alone?"

Tori came directly over to Stubbs. "Hi, can I have a Becks? Is Musowa here yet?"

"He's not coming, Tori, I'm here instead," Sedrick cut in. "You should remember me from the weekend you and Charlie went to?"

Tori looked at Sedrick and smiled. "Of course I remember you. Is Musowa ill?"

"Sort of, anyway, sit down, I want to talk to you. Where's Charlie?"

"She's gone to bed early. It's the end of the month, she has it bad sometimes."

Stubbs gave Tori the Becks and left them alone.

"Tell me, why didn't you wait for the minibus?" Sedrick asked.

"Everything just seemed a little bit up in the air. We'd both had a right grilling by a soldier and then the police. The other girls sitting around waiting for their interview told us some had already left. So we changed into our normal clothes, walked to the main road, thumbed a lift to the railway station. Then we took a train to London."

"Well, so long as you got back alright. Right, to business. You earned seven-fifty," he told her, handing her an envelope.

"That's not right, we did a total of thirty dances. We get seventy five pounds a session . Musowa told us he'd give us our going rate which amounts to over a thousand."

He shook his head. "No way, Tori. You may get that when you both perform at the same time, but not on your own. We give twenty-five pounds a dance, you'd have got another fifty between you if you'd done the lesbian act."

Tori looked put out, saying nothing, preferring to take a swig of her Becks.

"You don't look too happy, Tori?"

"Would you? We could have earned more working around here on a Saturday night. I'll bloody kill that Musowa when I see him. He's ripped us off good and proper, leaving you to make the true payment."

"Yes, well he does that sort of thing, that's why we got rid of him. We can perhaps make it up by offering you another weekend. We'd want you from Friday lunch till the Sunday afternoon. But rather than a payment per dance, how about I offer you fifteen hundred each?"

"We'd want it in advance, I'm not coming cap in hand again and only getting part paid. Also, even though we would stay over Friday and Saturday, neither of us are prepared to share a bed with any of the guests, we're not prostitutes."

"So you two really are lesbians then?"

"Why shouldn't we be? We spend most of our life together, although Charlie tries to pretend we are not, and claims she has a boyfriend if anyone asks."

"It's not me to comment on your sexuality. Personally, it seems a shame, two good-looking girls like you deciding you prefer each other. You'd have no shortage of men wanting to take you out."

Tori smiled. "You mean wanting to fuck us? I can assure you, we have no shortage of offers on that front. Except men don't take lap dancers out, or if they do, it's only for one thing."

"Possibly, but isn't that what a relationship is for? Anyway, I digress. Are you prepared to work a long weekend for the money on offer, if we give you a room away from the house to sleep in?"

"Yes, so long as it's in advance. And not deducted from if you get raided again."

"We've never been raided in the past. It also won't happen again. I'll call you in a few days with details, including where we will collect you from. Once you have a date, come and see Stubbs for your money." Then he hesitated for a moment, his tone changed. "Take our money, you come and work, no matter what. Don't turn up, we'll send people to find you both. Believe me girl, when they do, you and Charlie will never work again. You won't be capable. Do you understand?"

Tori shrugged indifferently. "We'll be there, this is work for us and neither of us is looking to retire, particularly for a paltry fifteen hundred, we earn more than that a week."

"It's good we understand each other. I'm off, there's another Becks waiting behind the bar for you."

Chapter 27

Karen stood for a short time, looking at Musowa and Ricky in the morgue. Sir Peter was at her side.

"It looks like they decided these two were now liabilities after Autumn and Ally got out, Karen."

"It does. The point is, Peter, who's replaced them? For us, it's starting all over again. Although we do have Sedrick identified by Autumn. Not that it would stand up in court."

"So what are your plans now?"

"Sherry and I will need to go in again. To tell you the truth, I didn't want to. Last time gained us very little, other than demeaning ourselves."

"I beg to differ. I believe in doing that, you saved Autumn's life. She may have been a foolish girl, but she didn't deserve to die in the way Parker had in mind for her."

Karen sighed. "You're right of course, no child should be left to die. Anyway, I'll call when I have the date."

"Very well. Have Ally's parents agreed she goes with you?"

"Yes. They understand the risks, preferring it to Ally being kept off the streets. I've also arranged she should attend the camp school, so she won't lose out on her education. We leave tonight. I'll be back by the end of the week." Karen looked at her watch. "I have to go. I'm meeting Sherry in less than half an hour as Tori."

Sir Peter gave her a hug and watched her climb into her car, relieved Karen was working this operation. Her contacts and ability to get right into a trafficker group always proved to be fruitful. His route would have been long and cumbersome. Even if he could get someone into Parker's operation, which he doubted. Now, if she was meeting Sherry as Tori, then she had another possible lead.

Five minutes later his own car drew up.

***

Dressed in jeans and top with a small waistcoat and the wig removed, Karen was now looking like Tori. Karen entered a hotel in central London, carrying a small case, and went through to the bar. She could see Sherry, dressed as Charlie, sitting on a bar stool talking to a man.

Sedrick had called earlier. He'd told her he'd an important visitor in London and he and his friend wanted entertainment that afternoon. Karen had a mind to decline, to become regular lap dancers, just for an afternoons entertainment was not part of her plan for her and Sherry. Even so, against her better judgment Karen accepted. She was interested to find out who this man was. She knew Sedrick worked with Parker and Parker would need a supplier working in Europe. It was just possible the man they were meeting was the supplier, or his agent. Either way, she intended to have a photo of him and possibly a name.

Charlie saw her as she entered the bar. "Tori, come and join us," she called.

She approached them. The man looked Scandinavian, he was around six foot three, of muscular build, with short-cropped blond hair.

"Hi, sorry I'm a little late, the traffic was pretty bad."

"No problems, we've been chatting. This is Yannick."

He nodded, then stood. "I should go. In ten minutes, no sooner, take the lift to the fourth floor, room 406. Expect to be searched. If you've any drugs on you, for personal use or not, flush them away before coming. If I find any, you'll be going home in an ambulance," he said, then walked away.

"Nice guy, don't you think? I'm glad you came. He was obnoxious. It's bloody difficult to keep smiling with a man like him."

Tori ordered a drink, taking the stool alongside Charlie. "Yes, he's doesn't seem a very nice man. Did he say who we're supposed to be dancing for?"

"He told me he worked for a Belgian called Luca. Said he and three of his friends were in the room and they wanted us not only to dance, but expected us to perform on the bed together afterwards." Charlie hesitated. "I know we've practiced a little, but this is the first time we're doing it in front of strangers. I'm really nervous," she hesitated. "Our practice was very intimate and personal between us, more like we were actually lovers. This time people are watching. I'm not sure now that I want our intimate relationship pulled down to a performance."

Tori grasped her hand, squeezing it gently. "There was always a chance this would happen, Charlie. Look at it as the better option than the men insisting we finish our dance in bed with them. Just lose yourself, as you do in the dance, pretend there's only you and I in the room. I'm not immune you know, I found our practices to be just as intimate and private between us. On a more practical point, have you remembered the toys and lubrication?"

She nodded. "Yes, I've even got the harness, not intentionally, it was just in my bag, from taking it to the party in case we had to do it there."

"That's good. Don't forget, as I told you after my meeting with Sedrick, we're lesbian, but don't like to admit it, especially you. We also don't like men to touch us."

"I understand. But I've had to prostitute many times, although not by choice, always under duress. Even so, I'd rather have done that, then share our intimate times together with strangers."

"You must remove the doubts, Charlie and just get on with the job. All my times acting as a prostitute were like you, under duress, or from the need to get deeper into an operation. If we went upstairs prepared to do that, we could find ourselves ending up with more than one man in the bed with us; do you really want to take the chance? I don't," Tori told her curtly, then downed her drink. "Come on, let's get it over with. We leave for France tonight."

***

As Yannick said, immediately they entered the hotel suite, he searched them both very carefully, besides their bags. Tori wasn't so sure this was just for drugs. She had the belief they were making certain they were as they claimed and not there with recording devices, or even weapons. Satisfied, he took them directly through to the bedroom, where two chairs, back to back, had already been arranged in the centre of the room.

"Your clients will return from their lunch shortly. Use the bathroom to change for your dance. There are four of them, you dance in a pair, doing two at a time. Then after a short break, you perform on top of the bed for them all."

"That's fine, who pays us?" Tori asked.

"I will. You will receive two hundred pounds. Is that what was agreed?"

"That's more than our fee, we charge seventy-five to strip as a pair and fifty pounds for a lesbian act."

"Then you perform longer on the bed and give them a good show. Do a good performance, and we will use you both on Saturday night as part of the entertainment for a private dinner we're holding, before we leave the country, if you are available?"

Tori shrugged. "Depends on the time and how long you want us for. We are always very busy weekends and can do at least ten sessions on Saturday night."

"I understand. If we use you, we will not let you be out of pocket. What do you charge for an all-night session with a client, as a pair or separately?"

Tori shook her head. "We don't prostitute. If you want girls for entertaining the guests all night, we're not your girls."

"Very well, get yourselves ready."

A short time later, after they were both dressed for the first dance, they hugged each other. "This is the time when we should have gadgets like James Bond, Charlie. Relying on a fifty pound pen with a recording camera built in, laid on the dressing table by the side of my handbag, doesn't seem that hi-tech."

"I agree, let's hope it gets some really good pictures. The only thing we should do, before that lot in the camp get hold of it, is crop out the bits where it catches us. I'd be well embarrassed knowing others were watching."

Tori laughed. "You're shy then? But I'm with you on that."

At that moment there was a knock on the bathroom door and Yannick came through. "Your first two clients are ready, you have set up your music?"

"Yes, it's all ready," Tori answered.

Following the dances for the clients, Tori and Charlie were both back in the bathroom, making ready for their next part of the entertainment, on the bed.

"The dances went well and they all seemed to enjoy it," Charlie said, handing Tori a jar of lubricant, after she'd

135

applied some.

"Yes, they did. I hope the camera worked. I'm sure I recognised one of the men from our files."

A knock came at the door, to tell them the men were ready. Both Tori and Charlie were wearing tiny knickers, and a see-through nightie that ended just below their bottoms. Tori took Charlie's hand, kissed her gently on the lips, and saying nothing they went into the bedroom.

The men were sitting on chairs a short distance from either side of the bed. Tori went to one side of the bed, Charlie the other. They looked at each other for a moment, then climbed onto the bed, kneeling down opposite each other. Then they began their routine, first kissing and holding each other, before Tori removed Charlie's nightie and pushed her down on the bed, drawing her knickers down, caressing her body as she went. Soon they were both naked, their simulated lovemaking becoming more intense, before using vibrators on each other to enhance their performance. Much to the delight of the men watching.

The man who introduced himself as Luca Desmet, turned out to be a man of around fifty, Tori's height and overweight. Tori had danced for him and he liked her. Now he wanted more. Grabbing the harness off the bedside table and the largest penis out of three sat alongside that could be attached to it, he held it out. "Come on, Tori, put the harness on and finish off your performance by showing us how you really fuck Charlie, when you're alone together. What do you say lads, do you want to see young Charlie here squirm with a ten-inch penis up her fanny?"

"Yes," they all shouted. "Fuck her, Tori! Fuck her, Tori!" they all began chanting.

Tori had no option, so she quickly attached the harness, while Charlie positioned herself on her hands and knees close to the end of the bed. Tori came around to the back of the bed, grasping Charlie's hips, preventing her moving as she entered. Neither of them wanted this, Charlie just gritted her teeth and accepted it.

Later, after settling up with Yannick, they caught a taxi to take them back to their own hotel. Neither had said much, just dressed and left as soon as they could.

Once sitting in the taxi, Sherry looked at Karen. "I hope our efforts were worth it Karen? I believed I could lose myself, like you told me too, and I did, imagining it was just you and I in that room. That was before that man Desmet piped up demanding you use the harness. I've never felt so embarrassed and disgusted, as at those men shouting you weren't working me hard enough, and to work me harder, ending up with me having a real orgasm in front of them watching."

Karen sighed. "You're right, how do you think I felt having to do it? Let's hope after that, what's on the camera can allow us to identify these people and where they fit in the organisation."

"What about Saturday, will you be agreeing to go?"

"I'll have to, but only if it's absolutely necessary, after I look into what we have." Then she took Sherry's hand, squeezing it gently. "I'll go on my own, say we've split up, whatever, you don't need to come any more. I've already got an in, thanks to you being with me. So your work is done."

"You mean you'd do the same again, if they wanted you to?"

"What alternative is there? Providing it has value and moves the investigation forward."

The taxi travelled on, with both girls silent.

Eventually Sherry turned to look at Karen. "No, we'll both see it through to the end. The first time I was abducted and taken to work in a brothel and shagged by ten men, one after another, I felt the same. But like you, finally you accept it, learn to be detached as if it's not actually happening. If you didn't, you'd go insane, or I would anyway."

Karen placed her arm around Sherry, pulled her close and hugged her. "I'm glad it was with you, Sherry. I really mean that. We're good together and look after each other."

She looked up at Karen. "Then we need more practice, to get it right. Maybe if we have a routine that will hold them to the finish, we're in control, not them."

Karen didn't answer. She was concerned that they were going down a route she wasn't comfortable with. What began as a talk in the Fairmont to discourage having to prostitute by claiming they were lesbians had led to something else, and with Sherry suggesting they continue the practice, it could easily become a way of life, no longer needing anyone else in their relationship. Very aware as to how much Sherry clung to her, Karen wasn't sure if this was the right thing to be doing. But she nodded. "You're right, if we want to pull this off and give them no cause to doubt this is what we do, normally, we'll need a slicker act."

Chapter 28

"Come on Ally, you can sit in the co-pilot's seat," Karen told her when she came aboard.

"Wow, this is so cool, when do we leave?" she asked, looking around at all the instruments.

"Not long now, I've just been talking to the control tower and we've been given permission to move to join the queue ready for take-off," Karen replied, flicking switches and starting the engines up.

Minutes later they were on the move, following two other aircraft, coming to a halt before the main runway.

Karen glanced at Ally, after the other two aircraft had departed, and she'd received an all-clear from the control tower. "It's time we left the UK, Ally," she said, moving onto the main runway for take-off. "Hold on, this is the best bit."

Opening the throttles, the aircraft began surging forward, building speed, until in seconds they were up, banking sharply as they climbed.

"That was so weird," Ally said, "To see the ground suddenly disappear, ending up staring into the sky. Nothing like going on holiday and sitting in a passenger seat."

"Yes, it always hits me the same."

Very shortly, Karen flicked a few switches, then leaned back.

"That's it, we just sit around twiddling our thumbs, while she takes us home. She's done it so many times, without my help, I just leave her to it these days."

"You mean that's all there is to flying an aeroplane? I've got to get myself one someday, this is really cool, my mates will be dead envious."

"Then in the meantime, make yourself useful as co-pilot, and pour me a coffee, from the machine behind the bar, will you?"

"We have a bar as well?" Ally gasped. "What about a bedroom, have you one of those?"

"Come on, Ally, even large aircraft don't have beds. You get a seat that tilts back and like it."

Ally grinned. "Just wondering," she commented, unfastening her seat belt and going through to the cabin.

Sherry looked up from her book. "Are you winding our pilot up?" she asked with a grin.

"Me! Would I do that? You should learn to fly Sherry, it's really easy and dead cool."

"I can, but rather than this toy of Karen's, I fly real aircraft. I'm also doing helicopters now."

"God, how the other side lives. I'm definitely joining you lot, I suppose you have a cool car, the same as Karen?"

"We don't talk about that. Karen had me buy a car, said I couldn't pose in an army Land Rover, so I ended up with a Cayman. Which she keeps pinching, because her Jag's in London. I hardly get a look-in."

Ally was confused. "What's a Cayman? Sounds like some weird perfume."

"It's a Porsche, don't you know anything?"

"You've got a Porsche?" she stuttered. "Now I know you two are winding me up. I bet when we arrive, I'm in a dormitory, your Porsche is like twenty years old and this aircraft is hired."

Sherry smiled. "Yes, Ally, something like that. But you'd better fetch Karen her drink, she doesn't like waiting, she'll put you on a charge."

"She can't, I'm not in the army," Ally said haughtily, at the same time going down to the bar and pressing a button on the coffee machine.

"That means nothing, once we get you in the camp," Sherry called back at her. "And while you're there, I'll have one as well please, otherwise you can do some of my chores, like scrubbing the dormitory floor."

***

Once they landed at the camp, Karen left Sherry to take Ally to her house, while she went directly to see Stanley. Soon she was sitting in his office.

"The photos and names you managed to get at the hotel, Karen, have proved to be very useful. Luca Desmet is Belgian and according to the Belgian authorities is suspected of trafficking. They have some information on him. An official request from Unit T will release to us what they have. I've already sent that request. Yannick Smets is also Belgian. He was in the military for a number of years. Once he came out, he spent some time as a mercenary in Iraq, following the war, and now works with Luca. He has quite a criminal record and is suspected of being involved in a number of gangland killings, but like I said, it's only suspected, there is no evidence."

"What of the others?"

"The photos haven't come up with any positive IDs. We need names, Karen, if that's possible?"

"Maybe, I'll possibly meet them again and with a few more on Saturday night. Luca is hosting a private dinner, before he leaves the country. I think we should get surveillance teams in, find out who his guests are."

"I agree, they're hardly likely to be of no consequence, even if they are financiers, or maybe purchasers. What are your plans for the rest of the week, will you be at home?"

"I will. I need time to go through all I've done over

the last weeks. Try to get it into perspective. Then, with Ally expected to be here for at least a month, I'm intending to have her enrolled in the camp school, then she can meet others of her own age and not lose out on her education. I don't want her hanging about doing nothing."

***

Making her way home, Karen found Ally and Sherry lounging by the side of the pool, both in bikinis.

"I see, while I'm working you two are skiving."

"No, Ally offered to help in the kitchen, but your housekeeper threw her out, told her 'guests do not work in the kitchen'. Me, it's my day off. I do work a five day week, you know, well, sort of."

Karen shrugged. "I knew you'd have excuses, just admit it Sherry, you prefer posing by the pool? Anyway, Ally, can you swim?"

"Course I can, I'm really good actually. I also love my room, thank you for letting me come and stay with you."

"No problems. I'm having a swim, let's see if you can keep up with me," she said, going to a changing cubicle.

Ally looked at Sherry. "Is she for real? If I can't beat a thirty-year-old, I'll give up."

Sherry smiled to herself, this girl had a lot to learn about Karen. It would be interesting to see if she could keep up the twenty lengths Karen swam, let alone beat her.

Karen was soon out. "Right, come on, twenty lengths, Sherry will be the judge."

Ally stood, a little aghast. "Twenty, I was thinking more like five."

"That's for wimps, so stop whining, we've not long to lunch. Then the loser can wash the cars this afternoon."

Chapter 29

Luca, with Kenneth Parker, was in a coffee bar a short distance away from the hotel Luca was staying in.

"It's not good being shown up like you were with this girl Ally," Luca began. "The papers are full of it, suggesting traffickers are idiots. Have you sorted out what went wrong?"

"The girl overcame Adah in the bathroom. At that stage she wasn't secured, just getting dressed to leave, after showering. Ally was a brighter kid than we thought and quick-witted, blinding Adah with shampoo, with enough about her to secure her, so she couldn't raise the alarm."

"So where was Musowa, he was supposed to be there, during that time, just in case."

"He'd been compromised, had to go. Adah waited, then decided to carry on when he didn't arrive, believing he was held up in traffic."

"What are the chances of getting this girl back?"

"Unit T has her. According to a contact who knows someone in Unit T's camp, Ally arrived with Harris, on her aircraft, yesterday. We won't get near the girl now."

Luca sipped his coffee in thought. "Then, if she's lost, someone has to pay. There's a need to save face in all this, besides showing the papers they can't publicly mock us without a public backlash against them."

"I could send Shaun and Liam to fire the house, with the family in it. They may get out, or may not. Either way, it will stick a finger up to the press for mocking us."

Luca gave a slight smile. "It would be ironic if a family member did die and Ally went to the funeral, then you can snatch her back from there."

"It would. I'll see what can be done. As it is, I've a

waiting list not being fulfilled for fifteen- to sixteen-year-olds and can't really snatch more just yet. What have you got coming in?"

"Couple of fifteen-year-old Russian girls, both very attractive and one Scandinavian girl. She's stunning, sixteen, blonde hair, slim and can speak three languages. I'd want fifty thou for the Russians and a hundred for the Scandinavian."

"Your prices are top end."

"Maybe, but demand is outstripping supply. You may have a waiting list, but I get close to twenty bidders for every girl I put up, that's how busy I am. I'll make a good twenty-five thou profit on any one of these girls once they put up for bids. Such girls, for a pimp supplying to the richer clients, can command at least ten grand a week for their services; a bloody good investment, don't you think?"

"It is, if you can keep the girl working at that level. We earn around seven thou a week off the girl's pimped out and want our investment in her back in two months. As it is I'm after girl's for direct sell to private clients." He hesitated, then nodded. "I'll take a flyer with the Scandinavian girl with an offer of ninety, I need a margin."

Luca delayed a decision by drinking more of his coffee. Kenneth also took the opportunity to finish his drink.

"I'll tell you what," Luca finally said. "Two Russians for ninety the pair and you can have the Scandinavian for ninety. That my friend, is a very good price, these girls are the best, believe me."

Kenneth shrugged. "Why not, we'll move them, that's for certain."

"Then we have a deal. Will you be joining me and the backers on Saturday night?"

"Yes, I understand Sedrick is supplying girls for you all?"

"He is, I've also asked if he can get the lap dancers he brought the other day, to start the night off. I like the one called Tori, I think with a little persuasion she'd stay all night."

Kenneth shook his head slowly. "She's lesbian, you'd have to take the two of them, if they'd agree that is."

"Hmm, I've never had two lesbians in my bed before. It sounds like it could be an interesting night."

"Then I wish you luck. I should go, I've a few problems that need sorting."

"I'll see you Saturday. Don't forget, before I leave the country, I'd very much like to see headlines on a resolved Ally situation. Remember the backers are here to talk about funding our biggest deal ever, we can't show weakness."

Chapter 30

Shaun O'Dockerty and Liam Sharp were in the cafe of a service area on the M1 motorway. Shaun's thoughts went back to their meeting with Kenneth only that morning.

"You say we couldn't get near her, how do you know?" He'd asked Kenneth.

"Believe me, the military unit Karen Harris commands is second to none. Many have tried to take them on and failed. Ally will be kept very secure, we'd need an army to get her out. As it is, I've already got comments coming from people we deal with, as to our competence, when a fifteen-year- old can walk out of one of our houses so easily."

"Well, she wouldn't have, if we'd been looking after her," Liam added.

"That maybe," Kenneth had replied. But she has. So you Shaun get down to the family house and burn the fucker down. You do it at two to three in the morning, if her family are injured or die, all the better."

Shaun leaned back, watching the comings and goings of travellers coming into the cafe. "The bloody idea of no smoking is stupid, you come into the cafe to relax after a long drive and you can only stand outside in the rain to have a drag. Do you want a refill, I'm getting one."

Liam shook his head. "I've had enough. How far have we to go now?"

Shaun looked at the satellite navigation on his smartphone. "An estimated two hours. That would get us there around eleven, far too early. But we shouldn't hang around inside the service area for that length of time. We'll settle down in the car."

***

By two in the morning Shaun and Liam had parked up a distance from Ally's home. That was after they had stopped, attached false number plates to the car and driven down the street the house was on. They had been looking for any street cameras, the type of street lighting and the general layout of the area. Now satisfied, they were on foot. Liam was carrying a plastic petrol can with a long spout.

Meeting no one, they turned up an open drive three houses from their target. Making their way down to the garden, both of them slipped thick plastic bags over their shoes, pulled their hoods up and put their leather gloves on.

It was easy, going between the gardens, with their low boundary fences. They were well tended, and had large lawns with narrow borders. In minutes, they were in the garden where Ally's parents lived.

Shaun moved swiftly to the side gate between the front and the back of the house, pulling it open, carefully making his way to the front. He stopped dead, a police car was parked outside on the road, already two police were climbing out, one was female. They had not been there earlier. Moving quickly back, he shut the side gate.

"What's the problem?" Shaun asked.

"We've company, two cops, probably on a scheduled perimeter check. Let's hope they're just checking the house."

He nodded and they both moved deeper into the garden, squatting behind shrubs.

Minutes later the policeman came through the side gate and carefully checked the back door and windows. Then he headed down into the garden, along the path. His torch was not flashing around, but facing the ground, to see his way.

Liam glanced at Shaun, he just nodded. Both knew that if the policeman passed them and began to return, they'd be seen. If he didn't they would be okay.

As it was the policeman came level, then passed them. Liam darted out, clubbing him on the back of the head. The policeman slumped down to the ground, not moving, blood coming from a nasty gash.

Shaun ran to the house, hiding so anyone coming through from the front would not see him. In a few minutes the policewoman came through the side gate.

"John, where are you, what are you doing?" she asked, but wasn't shouting, but keeping her voice low.

By now, the policewoman had come along the side of the house to where Shaun was hiding. Shaun grabbed her, before she even realised what was happening, or had time to retaliate and fight him off. In seconds, in typical commando style, he'd snapped her neck, and she slumped soundlessly to the ground.

Liam joined him, looking down at the woman, obviously dead. "The other's dead as well, I've just seen to that. Let's get on."

Pushing the petrol can spout through the letter box of the house, Liam emptied nearly a gallon of petrol inside. Then pushing a petrol-soaked rag through, with one end touching the carpet inside, the other hanging out of the letter box, he lit it with his lighter and after waiting a minute to see the flames snake down to the carpet, which was already soaked in petrol, catching light, he ran back down into the garden. Both men didn't hang around, returning the way they came. Finally discarding their feet covers and gloves into a polythene bag, they set off back to their car, taking the bag and petrol can with them.

Once on the motorway, they headed back to London. Both were indifferent if the fire took hold, sufficient warning had been given with the loss of two policemen and almost certainly a warning to the family, with whatever damage the fire could now inflict.

***

Within an hour of Shaun and Liam leaving, the entire road was taken up with police vehicles and two fire engines.

Superintendent Jack Mathers had just arrived. He'd been joined by the fire chief and another police officer.

"Well, what happened?" Jack wanted to know.

"It's not good, Sir. We have two dead officers in the garden. As for the family, the firemen have only just managed to get into the house, but they hold out no hope. The fire was intense and had already got hold before a neighbour saw it and called the fire services."

"My god, we were supposed to be protecting this family."

***

The following morning, a meeting was taking place at the police station, chaired by the Chief Constable. Also included in the same meeting, by a video conference link, were Sir Peter and Karen. Both had been contacted urgently.

After introductions, Jack Mathers gave his report, which was listened to without comment by Sir Peter and Karen.

"This was expected, Superintendent, following the stories in the papers," Sir Peter told him.

Jack placed his papers on the table in front of him. "I am aware of the childish reporting, making out Ally as some female James Bond, Sir Peter. Although no one in this force realised just how dangerous these people can be, to kill indiscriminately, besides burn a house down, knowing a child and its parents were still asleep inside. We should have been briefed far more clearly on what we could expect from such people."

"Your liaison officer was briefed, both by myself and Commander Harris of Unit T, Superintendent," Sir Peter began. "Then and at Commander Harris's insistence, Ally was kept well away from her family, hopefully to reduce the risk to them. Except it does not help when the papers headline the abductors as jackasses and fools, with one even having a large photo on the front page of a clenched hand with one finger held up. What sort of mentality is that? Traffickers, abductors and pimps live in a world very few understand. It's ruled by fear, intimidation and death for those who don't conform, or who believe they can profit by informing. Ally's escape would be a slap in the face for them. The abductors would need to show they're still in control, because if others, held by them, became motivated by Ally's seemingly simple escape, they would be in trouble. Their answer to Ally, to the press as well as a warning to others believing they have a chance of escape, has been immediate on the basis that if they did not retaliate, they would lose respect from other traffickers."

"Can you confirm, Superintendent," Karen asked, changing the subject. "By your report, there was one officer halfway down the garden, the other up at the house?"

"That's correct," he answered.

"Then it would seem to me, the reason why your officers lost their lives was that the killer, or killers were already in the garden and were perhaps disturbed by your officers searching?"

"They had instructions to check the garden down to the bottom boundary. Is that significant?"

"Only that it indicates to me that both deaths suggest a trained soldier, not a civilian. I also don't believe there was any initial intention by Ally's abductors to kill your officers. I don't think the killer, or killers had an option."

"Why do you assume that, Commander?" he asked.

"If your officers remained around the house, then left, both would have survived. I think the officer, by going down the garden, stumbled on the attackers hiding. Then the killing of the female officer was inevitable, so as not to raise the alarm. By the initial description of how she died, it was professional, possibly carried out by an ex special forces soldier. She wouldn't have had a chance to retaliate, or even cry out."

"It's good of you to make up this scenario, Commander, but our forensics will find out just what transpired," the Chief Constable cut in after listening to the conversation. "As it is, this is a murder investigation and we will want to know what information and intelligence Unit T has about Ally's abductors, that may lead us to the perpetrator. Officers, it seems, by your assessment have been killed for no other reason than doing their job. We are determined to find their killer, or killers."

"That may be, Chief Constable. I've given you my expert opinion as to what may have transpired, and the type of killer, or killers you should be looking for, but we cannot help you beyond that," Karen replied. "We will officially request a report of your criminal investigation, so we can look at the overall picture against known facts. As for the loss of your colleagues, we don't involve ourselves in murder enquiries. We are after taking down a particularly vicious trafficking gang and will not be pursuing them on the basis of them having your officers and Ally's family killed. It is not our remit."

"That is not good enough, Commander. You and I work closely together, sharing information, or we will not work with your unit in the future," he retorted.

Karen shrugged slightly, indifferent to his threats. "It's foolish to talk like that. We have a far better understanding of the way these people work and could, by going deeper into their operation, stumble onto your killers. Withholding information from the murder scene, may mean us not having sufficient details to recognise the actual killer, or killers. So we may miss them completely."

The Chief Constable didn't like Karen, or what she stood for. He was determined to make his point. "I must warn you, Commander, it is a very serious offence, in this country, to withhold vital information that may lead us to the perpetrators of any crime committed in the UK. I do have the power, if you enter this country, to detain you, if I believe you're doing just that."

"May I request everyone leave the room now, apart from the Chief Constable, please?" Sir Peter suddenly cut in.

Everyone left, leaving just the Chief Constable.

"Malcolm," Sir Peter began. "We must not apportion blame, or even argue over who does what. Karen is correct. You may have an immediate local problem finding out who killed your officers and fired the house, but Karen operates under an EU mandate and Unit T investigations are directed to bring the gangs down, not waste time looking into crimes better investigated by the police. You should take her request seriously. Traffickers work internationally, Karen is far better placed to sort this out, than the local police, I can assure you.

Even my department doesn't have the intelligence databases Unit T can call on."

"That is my point, Peter. I believe Commander Harris knows far more about this than she's admitting. Her talk about suspicions is poppycock, she already knows who the killers are, or at least who sent them. To withhold that information can waste police time and I'll remind you, is a criminal offence. I've lost two good officers, one only twenty-one, three days back, who had just become engaged. The public outcry will be enormous, directed squarely at us, not her. I've a right to know what she knows, or I will make representation as to Unit T's conduct in this investigation at the highest level."

"You will fail, Malcolm, even if you go as high as the Prime Minister's office, they will also stonewall you," Sir Peter replied. "If Karen did know who had done this and passed across information, it would remain in my department, protected under the Official Secrets Act. At the risk of sounding callous about the murders of your two officers, neither the government, or the EU would be interested in finding their killers, if it meant compromising ongoing covert operations that affect not a few, but thousands of victims across Europe and beyond. Now I'm asking you in a polite way. You send everything you find directly to me and Unit T. It will be Unit T, or my department that will, ultimately, find your killer, or killers, not you. Try to go higher and all you'll do is risk your own position."

"I'll not be threatened or intimidated by you, Peter, or the EU with their illogical idea to form such a unit as Unit T, who can walk over the laws of a country."

"Then try, you've been warned, I can do no more. Karen and I will break transmission and leave you to it."

After he went offline, Karen remained on.

"You know who has done this, don't you, Karen?"

"I do, I'll also pursue them, but it will be difficult to prove in a court, even if I gave the information to the police. We don't work on their type of evidence. This is retaliation, a save-face exercise with no real direct thoughts as to who would get in the way. Like the two officers, if they had come five minutes earlier, they would still be alive. Five minutes later, and they would have seen the fire; the family may have survived, it would make no difference to the traffickers. The message had been sent."

"I agree with you. I believe your investigations in the UK surrounding Autumn and Ally's abductions, have now become far more important."

"Then you must leave it to me, Peter, we have it in hand. I'll also talk to Ally. I don't want her hearing about the deaths of her family off the television."

"I don't envy your task, Karen. Please keep in close touch, I'll make a few people aware of Malcolm's position, the stupid man could find he's out a job very quickly, if he tries to make waves."

"I will. When I'm back in London, we'll get together."

Chapter 31

Karen and Sherry, had returned to London, and making their way to the Carlton. On the Saturday that they were to go to Luca's private dinner and get-together before he left the country. This was after Sedrick had called and confirmed they were to be at his hotel by eight thirty, the time dinner would be finished.

As was expected, Ally had been devastated when told of the death of her family, requiring the doctor to step in and sedate the girl. By the end of the week, Ally had calmed and been moved into the camp, for protection while Karen and Sherry were away. She was staying with a family that had a daughter of her age. Karen had promised her she would be with her for the funerals. It was far too dangerous for Ally to return to the UK, and stay with her grandparents, while the abductors were still at large. During the week, the grandparents had flown out to be with Ally, but by the time Karen left for London, they had returned to the UK themselves, very happy at the way she was being looked after.

The press, in the meantime, had a field day. With police officers killed, as well as a family virtually wiped out, papers were sold in big numbers. Except the press, to keep interest, were already on another tack, in demanding answers from the government about what they intended to do over the trafficking industry, backed up by social media and politicians. Although the press avoided mentioning their responsibility in what had happened, comments on the social sites had painted a different picture. This had resulted in everyone blaming everyone else, so long as it wasn't them at fault. These arguments were even breaking out on the talk shows, as well as the politics programmes. The government, for their part, announced they had already been in touch with the EU to request help from the international police forces, and in particular Unit T. Now officially involved, the Chief Constable's complaint of having little cooperation from Unit T was discounted and as Sir Peter warned, he was told to keep his comments to himself in no uncertain terms. All this confusion left Karen with a free hand to carry on without having to answer to anyone.

***

It was close to eight in the evening when the two girls climbed into a taxi outside the Carlton, heading to Luca's gathering. Neither had said much today, Sherry had also been particularly upset over the death of Ally's family. Then to be in the same room as the man who had almost certainly ordered the hit, she wasn't sure how she'd cope.

"Tori, Charlie, it's good to see you're punctual in your appointments, please follow me," Sedrick said, as he opened the door of the hotel suite, seeing the two of them standing there.

They followed him in, the suite was empty, everyone was down in the dining room of the hotel.

"You're working separately tonight, one in each room. We've sixteen guests, you will each dance for them, except I want you finished by eleven and gone by quarter-past. There's no time for you to do extra services tonight, so don't offer anything to any guest. You're here to keep everyone relaxed. Your payment is five hundred pounds each."

"That's no good for us, we've cancelled all our work tonight and could have earned double that even without extras. You also told me we wouldn't be out of pocket," Tori complained.

"You can have another seven fifty each, if you work all night and entertain the two guests who are staying here in the hotel." Then he hesitated and grinned. "Oh, I forget, you're both lesbians, or are you when it comes to money?" he mocked.

Tori shrugged. "We'll do the dancing and that's it. But don't ask us again, we won't be available."

"Then get yourselves changed," he retorted, and left the room.

Tori glanced at Charlie, who ran to the door, opening it very slightly, looking out into the hotel corridor. She was in time to see Sedrick enter the lift. "He's gone," she said very softly.

Tori pulled out a number of thin tubes, pointed on one end. She pushed two into the settees, leaving just the very tip showing, but in such a position it couldn't be seen. Then going through to the two bedrooms, she did the same into each bedhead, before doing the bathrooms. "It's done, let's get changed before they come back," she said, coming into the main lounge.

**

The guests were partially drunk when they came from the dining room. Sedrick lost no time in selecting the first two for Tori and Charlie to take into the bedrooms. Then after their seven minute dance they had less than five minutes to dress again and be ready for the next.

Tori had done fifteen dances, some had even given her money and she'd over seventy pounds on the side table. Luca was her last. She did her usual dance, finishing astride his knees, clasping and releasing her buttocks a number of times to simulated intercourse before standing, turning away as she pulled her knickers on.

Just as she began to put her bra on Luca came up behind her, took hold of the clips, fastening it for her.

"Thank you," Tori said, as she picked up a top and turned to face him, pulling it on. "You wonder why they always fasten from the back, when it would be easier with a clip at the front."

"Designed by men I think, Tori, so we can take it off for you," he said with a hint of a smile. "As it is, you dance well and are naturally sexy. What are your plans from here, before you return to Spain?"

"We have one more week further up north, then Charlie goes to see her family. Why do you ask?"

"Where do you go?" he asked, ignoring her question.

"Back to Spain, I don't do families. We start our season there at the end of the month."

"So the week she's with family, how would you like to make some money?"

"Doing what?"

"What you do now, entertaining my guests. I'd fly you at no cost to my house in Belgium. You'd have your own room."

His offer was unexpected, except the opportunity to be in Luca's home could not be ignored. Even so, she had no intention of showing too much enthusiasm, so she gave a weak smile. "I've been ripped off by Musowa, with a payment far less than was promised. Like tonight, yes, you gave us work and it wasn't difficult, but with your start and finish time, it's wrecked the night for more work. We could have earned double if we'd not come here."

He nodded his head up and down slowly. "That is not

good business for you I think, but I didn't arrange tonight, Kenneth did, so I had no idea of the arrangements. What would be your fee, for a full seven days working just for me?"

Tori stood there. "How many hours would you want me to work each day?"

He shrugged. "Only in the evenings, from say eight to eleven, maybe twelve. We would also want at least two of your extras a night. The days are your own, maybe spend time looking around our city, you will not be bored."

"My fee, if I did the same number of dances, would be seven hundred. The extra I do with Charlie, so that would be a bit difficult on my own. In fact," she grinned, "they'd probably walk out on me."

He smiled. "Of course, but I will introduce you to Roos, she is a very beautiful and sexy girl who will take Charlie's place. She, like you, is a lesbian. You will fall in love with her, I can assure you. She is twenty-one and will be your guide to our city, your companion and lover. You will teach her how to lap dance, spend the nights with each other and show your intimacy with her in your performance. Then when you leave, I will have myself a dancer such as you. As for your fee, that is no problem, we will round it to five thousand."

Tori had gone cold inside. She'd at first suspected he wanted her in his house with the intention of taking her to his bed. If it had value to be there, she'd not have discounted the possibility, she'd done it before a number of times. But to be told she was to share her bed with a girl and be expected to perform with her in front of men, was completely different. Even so, at this stage, she wasn't going to refuse. The other guests here tonight could be important, maybe this was the entire trafficking group surrounding Parker. This had to be checked out before she rejected his proposal. In the meantime, it was time to revert to being a business woman. "If I agree, how will I be paid? Last time I was paid short. Told to take it or get nothing. I have costs, need to make money while I'm still in demand. I can't afford to work for nothing."

He smiled. "Saving for your pension are we? Very wise. Let me have a bank account number and I'll pay your fee before you come. I can't be fairer than that."

"You can't, and I appreciate it. Let me think, I was going to have a break, but your offer is very attractive. If you give me a number to call, I'll be in touch next week. But I have to leave on the following Sunday, to be back in Spain to meet Charlie. You won't mention this offer you have made to Charlie, will you? She could be a little put out, if she believed I was earning using another woman."

"I understand, so yes, our arrangement, if you accept, is between you and me. I will give you Yannick's number, call him and he will make all the arrangements. As for you leaving on Sunday, I'm leaving myself that day. I've a little business trip already arranged."

Chapter 32

It had been another half hour before Karen and Sherry left the hotel. Yannick had come out into the corridor and settled up with them. He returned to the hotel room, while Karen, with Sherry, entered the lift. Leaving the hotel, the two girls walked down the road, joining the crowds out for the night. However, they turned off, coming around the rear of the hotel and climbing into the back of a large van parked up with a number of other vehicles.

Inside the van was a lad with headphones on, and a computer in front of him. He looked up and nodded, removing his headphones.

"What's happening, Sam?" Karen asked.

"The guests are leaving, Colonel. Frank's out front, taking covert photos of each guest. We have surveillance at the taxi office and when Sam sends them a taxi number, they will request the destination for us. Do you have the pen cameras for me to transfer the photos?"

"Yes, but Sherry will go through them first, and separate out the ones suitable and add Christian names. Or at least, the names they gave us."

He smiled, understanding why. "She can use the laptop, it's in my bag," he said, nodding toward a bag in the corner, then handing Sherry a memory stick. "Just put the photos to be downloaded on there, Sherry, and I'll transfer them when you've finished." Then he replaced the headphones.

"That was pretty easy, Karen, what about you?" Sherry asked, at the same time going through the photos on the pen cameras, deleting some and keeping others, besides adding the names they had gleaned from the guests, when they came through to the bedrooms for their dance.

"Yes, it wasn't too bad, I even got a few tips, well, about seventy pounds."

"I did as well, besides an offer of a weekend away. He claimed he was a banker and gave me his number."

"You didn't refuse, did you Sherry?"

"No, of course not. Although I was wondering why a banker would be there, I don't think he was one of Luca's clients. Do you think Luca, or Parker, are bankrolled in some way?"

"It's possible, maybe when we put it all up on a board, with links, names and what they do for a living, we'll have a better picture of the operation."

Sam turned to Karen. "Parker and Luca are alone, do you want to listen to what they're talking about?"

"Yes, it may be interesting."

He handed her an extra pair of headphones. She took a seat at his side.

***

"We had a good night, Luca, the two lap dancers really made it. I think everyone went away happy."

"I agree, it did work out nicely. We've a couple of girls coming at midnight, they will stay overnight. I've also offered Tori a week's work back in Belgium, the other one's going home apparently."

"Since when did you want a lap dancer in your home?"

"It's good entertainment for my buyers, relaxing the meeting, besides, most prefer lighter entertainment to me providing prostitutes. I'm also using her to train Roos, then when I need a girl again to entertain my clients I'll use Roos.

You should have seen Tori's performance with Charlie, earlier in the week, it was good."

Kenneth grinned. "You may even get an offer for Tori?"

"Maybe. After all, she'd fetch sixty thou with ease. It wouldn't be bad considering I'm only paying five thou up front."

Kenneth laughed. "I agree there, if she was for sale. On another point, when can I expect my girls?"

"Yannick will be bringing them over in the usual way. Can you be at the usual pickup point this coming Tuesday, with the money of course?"

"I'll make arrangements. Do you think the bankers will play ball?"

"I've talked to Charles and Ronald, both have agreed to put up half a million. Ronald told me Griffin and Lennon will certainly match it, so we have the million. We just have to work on the others for the balance. As for your problem with Ally, I received some positive comments from the bankers. Although it couldn't have been more spectacular, even if you'd planned it, though I say it myself."

"Yes, Shaun and Liam are turning out to be money well spent. They've even pulled back money owed by the pimps. Unlike Musowa, who couldn't get some to pay up."

"Yes, if you have the right men, as I do with Yannick, you get less trouble."

They fell silent, both drinking brandy, then there was a knock on the door. Yannick opened it. Two girls were standing there. "Ladies, we've been waiting for you both, come on in," he told them.

***

Karen removed the headphones. "Seems like we may have stumbled onto something big. We need to keep observation until Luca leaves."

"That's not a problem, Colonel, I'll be here until the morning. Then I'll be relieved. Do you want the bugs retrieving?"

"Yes, remove all evidence we've been eavesdropping. We don't have permission to do this."

"We'll make sure that happens."

"Very well, I'm beat, so I'm going back to the hotel. Are you coming Sherry?"

"I am, just let this finish downloading."

Later, both Karen and Sherry walked down along the back of the buildings, coming out quite a way down. Then hailing a taxi, they returned to the Carlton.

"I'm glad this is going to be our last night here," Sherry said, coming through from the bathroom.

"Me too, you pinch too much of the bed and pull the blankets off," Karen mocked.

"No, I don't, it's you, you move around too much."

"Well, next time you do it, I'll wake you up and show you."

Soon they were lying together in the dark.

"Where do you go from here, Karen?"

"We go home, maybe we'll take Ally down to the coast for a couple of days. She needs to get out I think. Then the following two weeks you're on your delayed assessment."

"What about you?"

"I need to see Sir Peter, keep an eye on the surveillance, especially if Parker takes delivery of three girls. I've a mind to intercept next Tuesday and snatch them, including the money if possible, squeezing them financially."

Karen had not mentioned Luca's offer of work to

Sherry. However, after listening to the conversation between Luca and Parker she had already made up her mind that while Sherry was on the assessment, she would go. Although a little nervous about meeting the girl called Roos and what she'd be expected to do with her, she would have to put up with it. Even so, the appearance of Luca had opened up a completely new line of investigation. She had to see his house, plant listening devices if possible, whatever they had her doing.

Chapter 33

Returning to the camp the following morning, Karen caught Ally coming out of the school block. She was with another girl. But when the girl saw Karen, she left Ally.

"Would you walk with me, Ally?" Karen asked.

They walked in silence for a short time.

"So how are you bearing up, I see you're back in school."

"I had to, it was getting me down, sitting alone, with you and Sherry gone. How did you take the death of your parents?"

"Pretty hard, the same as you," Karen answered, although she was lying. At the time her memory had been in pieces, caused by a drug forced down her by traffickers. Even when she attended the funeral, with the knowledge her sister was in the hands of traffickers, Karen couldn't get emotional. She couldn't remember much about her family, her life. "You just have to pick up the pieces and carry on. Sherry was the same, she only had a mum, her dad she never knew. Sherry witnessed her mother's death, it tore her apart, which is why she's with me. We're both the same in lots of ways."

"I want to ask you something, Karen?"

"Anything, what is it you want?"

"After the funeral, can I come and stay with you? I've nothing to go home to any more and although gran said I can live with them, they're so old, I'd be rowing with them all the time, when they stop me doing what teenagers do."

"It's a bit hard on them, Ally, you're all they have. Although initially you will have to stay with us. Let's see how it works out, you may decide you really do want to go back, once it is safe for you to go. Anyway, on a lighter note, I thought we'd fly down to Cannes and sort you a smart outfit for the funeral, beside one you can use afterwards?"

Ally stopped and looked at her. "I'd love to, thank you. Not that I can believe I'm in a world where you take an aircraft to go shopping. At home, I'd be on the bus."

Karen laughed. "So would I have been, but here we don't have a bus service that will take us to Cannes. We could go by train to Paris if you don't want to fly. If we did, we'd be on it for hours."

"No way, I want to become one of the jet set. It was really cool to see all the spectators at the airport watching me get on a private plane. I felt dead important."

"So it's my jet, then. Anyway, I like flying, I may even give you your first lesson. So when you've made your fortune, you can have your own."

"Ha... some hope, unless I can find a really rich and cool lad who'll look after me. Have you time for a coke with me in the club?"

"Course I have, let's go, shall we?"

They turned into the social club. Karen was happy that Ally seemed to be bearing up, although she knew the hardest time was coming, when she buried her family.

Soon they were sitting at a small table with drinks.

"Don't you feel funny, when everyone stands as we come in?" Ally asked.

"Not any more. When you're the commanding officer their acknowledgment of your status is more a mark of respect. Then, Ally, the rank of colonel is even higher than what would be required for such a unit. Normally this unit would be run by a captain, maybe a major as the highest rank. Which means if you have a colonel as your commander, it indicates this unit has a very high status."

"Well, everyone seems to treat me very nicely, maybe it's because I'm staying with you?"

"Maybe, but only a tiny bit, you see, everyone in the camp lives and works with victims of trafficking. They don't look down on, or feel sorry for you. A victim doesn't want that, they want understanding, to be treated no differently to any other human being. Because you are no different. You may have been beaten, abused and forced into prostitution, but that's in the past. We offer the chance of a new life, restored dignity and self-respect. That's where my charity takes over, the same as it will to look after you. Added to all that, with a female running the unit, many victims are more relaxed, believe I can identify with them. Which I can, I've been where they have a number of times."

Ally sipped her coke, looking around. "Did you know the kids of the camp have their own places to hang out, even run their own entertainment? It's like a world within a world. I've been asked out a couple of times. I said no, I didn't want to live it up as if nothing had happened. My stupidity got me here to begin with. I've killed mum, dad and my little sister. I've got to live with that."

"I'll not lie to you, Ally, to make you feel better, you have got to live with what you've done. Your actions did kill your family. The same as mine did, the same as Sherry. You didn't do it on purpose, believed you were seeing your favourite band. Would you have gone if you'd even an inkling of what the consequences would be?"

She looked down, fiddling with her glass of coke. "I've thought about that a number of times."

"I bet I know the answer?"

Ally looked up at Karen. "What?"

"You wouldn't have believed it. Convinced yourself it was just words by someone trying to prevent you going."

She gave a slight shrug. "Wouldn't any teenager? Except my family would still be alive if I'd not escaped, wouldn't they?"

"Yes, they would. But on the other hand, you had a chance to escape and took it. No one gave you the choice of escaping and losing your sister and parents. If they had, you'd have thought twice. The woman only said they'd bring you back."

"I suppose."

"No 'suppose', Ally. Me, Sherry and yes, you, would have given up our freedom to save our family. Now you have to prove to them it was worth their sacrifice and make something of yourself, so they can be proud. Don't let them down."

"I won't, I owe them that at least. Neither will I ignore any advice given me again, believing I know it all. No one does."

Karen glanced at her watch. "Right, I'm due for a meeting. I'm not here, after tonight, for a couple of days, but Sherry is, then we will all go down to Cannes. If you give her a call, maybe she'll dig deep into her purse, fill her Porsche up with more than a litre of petrol and take you for a drive."

"So she really does have a Cayman?"

"She does, but hides it on the camp somewhere, so I can't use it. I'd only put on a couple of hundred miles, you'd think I'd worn it out when she saw the mileage."

"I've got to see this car, I'll call her," she said, then hesitated. "Thanks for talking to me, Karen. I'm glad you didn't try to patronise me, but told me straight. I needed that."

"No problems," she said, at the same time standing. "I'll see you at dinner later."

***

"The men at the dinner organised by Luca, Karen, are all financiers," Stanley told her, when she'd joined him in his office. "I'm of the same opinion as you, something big is going down. The sort of money being bandied about indicates drugs, rather than a trafficking operation."

"I have to agree with you there. So do we pass it on?"

"Pass what on, we have nothing to pass, apart from the names. I can't see any one them turning up at the handover of drugs, if that is what's happening."

"Yes, you have a point. It also means I've no option but take up Luca's offer to stay at his house and bug it."

"You believe his reasons why he wants you there?"

"Who knows Stanley, but it's an opportunity not to be missed. Even so, I'm not going in without a great deal of backup. We don't rely on local police, or anyone else for that matter. The unit protects me, like they did at the weekend party."

"I agree, that's essential. My only concern is we still have an informer in the camp. How do we do this without Luca or Parker from finding out?"

"You send a unit yourself, bound for Germany. Whoever is in charge, have him divert to Belgium, and you run the surveillance operation from my office at home. That is totally secure. With Sherry on assessment, Ally will be there on her own, so it's a good excuse for why you're staying."

"I'll look forward to that, Meg will enjoy the pool. You're still leaving for London later tonight?"

"Yes, I'm joining surveillance on Parker. With luck, he himself will meet Yannick to collect the girls coming in."

"So we have Parker then?"

"It's possible, but even if he is there, I've no intention of arresting him. He'll lose his girls and his money. I intend to hit them where it hurts and give him and Luca the need to have their backers provide more funds. If that's what they're there for."

Stanley was doubtful. "It would have been a good opportunity to take him down, Karen."

"I know, Stanley, but it does not mean we won't have an arrest warrant out on him. First, I want to see why all this money is required. So you're right, it's probably a pretty poor calculation of risk. But we do that all the time."

"We do. I'll have Lieutenant Ross prepare his surveillance and incursion unit and send him on his way by road. That way it won't attract much interest. They go out all the time."

Chapter 34

Kenneth Parker climbed into a waiting car outside a bank. He'd come from the safe deposit box area in the basement. Inside his briefcase were four kilo ingots of gold, with a combined value of just over a hundred and forty thousand pounds, along with bundles of currency in various denominations, which made up the balance Luca had asked to obtain his girls.

"This is our biggest payment to date, Kenneth, you're sure we can place them?" Sedrick asked, at the same time starting the engine and pulling into the afternoon traffic.

"No worries. The two Russian girls I placed this morning. The Scandinavian girl has attracted real interest from Sam Parsons. He's been after a girl for a while and was really taken with her photographs."

"So how much is he offering?"

Kenneth shrugged. "What we ask; he's worth millions anyway, but now spends most of his time in his country house in Scotland. Ideal for keeping a girl secure."

"Then it seems we'll have our share of the money for the deal with Luca?"

"We will, with plenty to spare. Anyway, call at my place will you. I've a few items I want to take with me. I'll also call the potential buyers, confirm they can and will take the girls, besides have the money available. With luck, when this is over, we'll be fifty grand better off."

***

It was after ten at night, on the same day Kenneth had picked up the gold and cash, when they passed through a village called Alderton, heading for the coast. This part of the coast, although popular for both walking and its beaches, was particularly desolate after dark. It was also very good for landing a small boat.

By eleven, they had parked up in a public car park and made their way down to the beach. Already Yannick had called to say he was now very close and would be coming in by dinghy.

"There he is," Sedrick said, pointing at a small dinghy in the moonlight.

Kenneth flashed his torch three times. There was a single flash back. Then Kenneth replied with two flashes to indicate it was safe to land.

As the dinghy hit the shale of the beach, Yannick jumped ashore, dragging the boat further up with the help of a rope. Kenneth and Sedrick joined him.

"You're on time. How are the girls?"

"They're all sedated, just guide them to your vehicle, they will be fine," Yannick said, shining a small torch on each of the girl's faces. "You have the payment?"

"I do, a mixture of bullion and currency," Keneth answered, handing him a large briefcase.

While Kenneth and Sedrick helped the girls out of the dinghy, Yannick checked the payment. Kenneth returned to the boat, once the girls were secure. "Okay?" he asked.

"Yes, I'll leave you with them," Yannick replied. Then, pushing his dinghy out, he jumped aboard and was soon rowing away towards a waiting cruiser.

Back aboard the cruiser, Yannick lifted the dinghy up at the stern with the help of two ropes tied either end, running through rollers hanging down either side of a cradle.

As he started the engine, he heard a sound behind him. Spinning around, he could now see two armed men standing there. Both carried M4 carbines. They must, he decided, have been hidden in the cabin area.

"Take a seat, Yannick, we've been waiting for you to come back," one told him. Then he raised a walkie-talkie to his mouth. Within minutes, a large high-speed launch came up alongside the cruiser.

One man took the briefcase.

Yannick glared at him. "Take that and you're both dead. We will hunt you down and you'll pay for it," he said slowly.

"Hunt all you want, you will never find us or your money. Mind you, I'd have liked to be there, when you try to explain to Luca what has happened. He'll want his pound of flesh," one replied. Then they climbed aboard the launch, before it pulled away and sped off.

Yannick tried to see the name of the launch, but it was blanked out.

***

Kenneth and Musowa had taken turns driving the two hundred miles to deliver the Russian girls. The journey had been without event. The roads quiet. The girls asleep.

After making their way up the private drive of a large house, Kenneth climbed out and rang the bell. Although it was gone four in the morning, he had telephoned ahead and was expected.

A man opened the door. "Kenneth, you've made good time. Come in."

He followed the man in.

"The girls are alright, aren't they?"

"Yes, they're fine, just a little groggy from the sedation. There is the small matter of a hundred and fifty, before you can have them."

The man handed him a bag. "It's all there."

Kenneth grinned. "I believe you, after all, I know where you live. Come and get them out, I've another to deliver."

Watching the car leave, with a short whip in his hand, the man sighed, then urged the two girls into the house.

Five minutes later there was a knock on the door. After locking the room he'd put the girls in, he came back down to the front door, pulling it open, half expecting Kenneth to be there, saying he'd forgotten something. But it wasn't him. Two men were standing outside, and both, as when Yannick was held up, were carrying M4 carbines. Except these were not in plain clothes. These were Dark Angel soldiers.

"We have come for the girls Kenneth Parker has delivered to you. You're under arrest for trafficking and abduction. Bad news for you, it's a mandatory ten years and all assets are confiscated."

The man just stood open-mouthed, convinced Kenneth had something to do with it.

***

It was another three hours' drive, after a short break in a service area where they had breakfast, before they finally arrived at Sam Parson's house.

All three of them entered the house this time, going through to the main lounge.

Sam looked the girl over. She was around five feet eight, very slim and had long blonde hair which cascaded down over her shoulders. Although the effect of the sedation had now worn off, the girl just stood there. She was tired, felt sick and just wanted to sleep.

"She's a nice looking girl, you did well, Kenneth. While Sedrick keeps an eye on her, we'll settle up in the office," Sam said, obviously very pleased.

In his office, Sam poured two glasses of whisky, while Kenneth counted the bundles of currency.

Satisfied, he put all the money into a holdall he'd brought with him from the car.

"We have more available in a month or so, Sam, if you want more."

"No, one's fine for me."

"Well, if you want to exchange her, give me a call. I'll be off now."

Again, they had not been gone long, before there was a knock on the door. Sam opened it. Karen was standing there, dressed in jeans and a bomber jacket.

"Mr Parsons?" she asked politely.

"Yes, what do you want, I'm busy?" he asked curtly.

"Commander Karen Harris, Unit T. I'm here to arrest you for trafficking and abduction. Shall we go in? Oh, if you think of running or resisting, I've six Dark Angel soldiers with me. All are armed and have orders to shoot to kill."

He didn't reply, just turned and went back inside, with Karen following. Behind her, soldiers spreading out.

Once in the lounge he sat down. "You're wrong about abduction or anything else. Kenneth called me and asked if I'd look after a friend of his, she'd been abused by her father. I agreed."

"I couldn't care less what excuses you make as to why she is here. We've tracked this girl since she was brought in from Europe and followed her since she was taken off a boat. Your friend Kenneth brought the girl to your door and left her here. With his departure you became party to the abduction and so will be prosecuted. Our mandate allows us to take all assets. You, Mr Parsons, have lost not only your liberty for ten years, but everything you own. It will all come to my charity, if it's a pound or a million pounds."

"I will fight you in court. You prove I knew she was abducted and I was not an innocent party in this."

"You can if you want. The final word will be from the girl. The court will want to know from her, if you'd asked her why she was there and where she came from. It's natural for any person being asked to look after a young girl, especially when the person who brought her and the one accepting her are both male. So let's cut the crap. You have one chance. I want to trap Kenneth Parker, he's not a nice man I can assure you, but you may know that. Agree to help and you keep your liberty. Believe you can fight me, then go ahead, we'll crush and bankrupt you, that's a certainty."

Sam knew deep down he'd never pull it off and would go down. "Very well, what is it you want me to do?"

"For the moment, nothing. Except, if Parker calls, you make out the girl is still with you. He's unlikely to travel hundreds of miles to check. If he does, you call me immediately and she'll be here when he comes. Later I may have another job for you, but that's not certain. Either way, do as I ask and we leave you alone. The girl is safe and unharmed, which for me is important."

***

Sedrick and Parker, after stopping at a service station, decided to book into the hotel next door. The journey had been long and tiring, and there was no real need to rush back to London, now the girls had been delivered. It was good to sit down with a drink, and have a leisurely dinner, before getting a good night's sleep. The business had been done and they were fifty thousand richer.

After splitting the money into two manageable bags, they kept them by their side all the time, not even risking the car or bedroom, while they drank and then ate.

They returned to the bedroom, where again they were staying in the same room, basically with Kenneth not wanting the money out of his sight for a minute and Sedrick looking to protect his share of the take.

It was three hours later that the door was opened using a key card, just enough to allow a bolt cutter through to cut the night chain. Both men were asleep. In seconds, the lights were switched on.

Sedrick was the first to wake; he sat up, rubbing his eyes, then just stared. Three men in balaclavas were standing there. All of them had handguns, with silencers fitted.

By now Kenneth had woken and was also looking at them. "What the fuck do you want?" Kenneth demanded.

"Carefully throw both bags toward us. Any attempt to stop us taking them, delay or object and you die. Either way we will take the bags," one man told him.

Neither men hesitated, you don't argue with gunmen if you want to live.

"That was sensible. Now both of you lie face down on the beds, hands behind your backs."

As soon as they did that, one gunman moved forward quickly, wrapping duck tape around each of the men's wrists. Seconds later, the gunmen were gone.

For the next few minutes they struggled to release each other, then ran out into the car park. But the gunmen were nowhere to be seen.

"Fuck, fuck, fuck," Kenneth shouted, punching the air with clenched hands. "Where did they come from, who were they?" was all he could say.

Chapter 35

Karen arrived at Brussels airport on a scheduled flight from London and come through to the arrivals area.

She had used the number Luca had given her earlier in the week, although it wasn't Yannick who answered but a girl. She'd actually answered in French, except Karen didn't intend to let Luca know she understood French and German, so she'd just spoken English and the girl instantly reverted, although she had a French accent. After a short conversation arrangements were made to meet at the airport on the Saturday.

Looking around the airport, she saw a girl holding a card up with the single name 'Tori'. She walked over to her.

"Hi, I'm Tori, you must be Roos?"

"Yes, if this is your only bag, we should go. The parking here is very expensive and I don't want to go into another hour. Luca might get annoyed with me," she said, looking at the bag Tori was pulling along.

"It is, shall we go then?"

As they walked, Tori weighed up Roos. She was her height, very slim and particularly attractive, her long, straight black hair falling halfway down her back. Then, the way she walked, she clearly knew how to show herself off. Tori felt positively plain alongside her.

The car was a BMW sports car, top of the range, again suiting the girl's image. Soon they were on the main road out of Brussels.

"I was expecting Yannick to answer the other day, is he ill?" Tori asked.

She shrugged. "I don't know, he's just not been around. But with Luca you learn not to ask questions that don't concern you. If I were you, I'd not even bring it up, you'd only be told to mind your own business."

"He didn't seem like that sort of man to me," Tori said.

"Yes, well, he has another side. Just do as you're told and no more, then they leave you alone."

"When you say, 'they'... do more people live in the house we are going to?"

"Two security guards in the day and two at night, a cook and cleaner. I'm not there, I live somewhere else. When we get to the house, you will be searched. Luca is paranoid about drugs; once he was caught in a hotel room with a girl carrying class A drugs. It cost him twenty grand to buy the police off that night, so if you take them, even the odd pill for yourself, we stop now and you dump them all. Walk into his house with some and he'll go berserk, you'll end up in the hospital."

Tori had expected to be searched, after the last two occasions, but she wasn't convinced it was for a little weed. "I nothing like that, I assure you. I went to one of his private parties and Yannick searched me then, with the same threat. But I don't do drugs anyway. I very nearly died in Spain, spending a week in intensive care, after someone spiked my drink - so now I'm really scared of them."

Tori could not ask anything more, they had turned into a drive that quickly came up to closed gates. Roos opened the car window, reaching out to press an intercom button. "It's Roos, I've got Tori with me," she said.

As the gates opened, a man came out from one side, watching as they drove through. He was carrying an AK47 assault rifle.

The house was large, the entrance a double doors, with an overhang in front held up by two pillars. It was, even to Tori, very impressive. Except she knew its purchase was more than likely paid for by human misery. A lady ran down to meet them.

"This is Tori, Roos?" she asked in French.

"Yes, she can't understand French, only English."

The woman looked directly at Tori. "Welcome, would you come with me please, also bring your bag," she said in perfect English.

They didn't go into the main entrance, but around the side and through a door at the back of the house. They entered a kitchen.

"Place your bag on the table and take everything out. Also, empty your handbag and your pockets."

Tori emptied her main bag, while the woman checked everything, then looked inside.

"You may pack it back up now," she told her, at the same time checking Tori's handbag. When she finished, she looked at Tori. "Stand with your arms out and legs apart?"

Again she checked very carefully. Tori was even more sure that this search was more than just for drugs. She suspected Luca was making sure she didn't carry a weapon, or maybe a listening device on her body, or in her luggage. He was a trafficker, so he'd be very careful that his conversations wouldn't be recorded, or someone hadn't come to kill him.

"Roos told you we don't allow drugs, I presume?"

"Yes, I don't do drugs."

"That's good. If you come with me, I'll show you your room." Tori followed her through into the main hall and upstairs. As she walked through it, she remembered being in a similar situation at a house she had once gone to. There she was searched, but then it was more intensive and intrusive. She was glad she'd not faced that sort of search this time.

Soon they were in a bedroom. It wasn't plush as she'd expected from the luxury of the house, more of a back room. There was a large double bed, a wardrobe and dressing table, with a small settee in front of the window. On the wall was a television. "That door leads to your bathroom. You're not a guest, but the entertainment, I understand. That means you only go into the main rooms downstairs when asked. You don't wander around. You can come down to the kitchen for a drink, and also your meals, otherwise you stay in here. If you want to go for a walk, keep away from the pool area. That is for the guests, unless Luca invites you himself. You cannot leave the grounds without permission, or it sets off all the alarms. We have armed guards, it's necessary. We don't want accidents, do we?"

"No, I suppose not. Luca did say the days would be my own time and I can go into Brussels."

"You can, of course, I'm only saying, security needs to know when you leave and come back. You will be searched whenever you return from outside, it's the rules, so be prepared." She looked at her watch. "Luca will see you at one, downstairs in the main lounge with Roos. Make sure you're on time, he's a busy man."

***

"Tori, I heard you'd decided to come," Luca said, when she came into the lounge. "Get Tori a drink, Roos."

"It's a lovely house, Luca. Living in hotels and the small flat I have in Spain, this looks like a palace," Tori said, taking a glass off Roos. She'd dressed in a short, slightly flared dress with high heels, not wanting to go in wearing jeans. She was glad she hadn't; Roos was also in a light summer dress.

"I'm happy you like it. Now to business. Roos, Tori's here as a lap dancer and she's very good. She will be entertaining our guests. You will, during the day, learn the dance, I want to see you performing it perfectly by Wednesday. The other part of Tori's act requires a partner, but she can't be with us, so you take her place."

Roos frowned. "Excuse me. You want me to learn to lap dance for you Luca, I can understand that, but what is this other act?"

He grinned. "You're not in the shop while Tori is staying with us, neither are you in your flat. Tori's a lesbian, she and her partner perform a sex act on the bed as entertainment, don't you Tori?" He didn't wait for Tori to reply, but answered for her. "Of course you do, and you Roos, will be her partner. So move into Tori's room and you stay there. You, Tori, teach my Roos your act, like you performed with Charlie."

Roos looked shocked. "Am I hearing this right? Apart from lap dancing for your guests, you want me to have sex with another woman in front of them?"

Luca glanced at Tori. "Excuse us for a moment," he said, grasping Roos's arm, urging her out of the room, leaving Tori standing there holding her drink.

Once out of earshot of Tori, Luca came up close to Roos, his voice low. "Why are you baulking, Roos? You're here because I want you to be around. For that to continue, you do as you're told, otherwise we fall out. If you have a problem with that, maybe you and I should discuss it in more depth down in the cellar?"

The terror in Roos's face was all too apparent when he mentioned the cellar. "I'm sorry, Luca. It would just have been nice if you'd warned me before Tori came. You know I'll do whatever you ask of me."

"No, I don't know, Roos. You seem to believe you're something special these days. You're not. You can be replaced tomorrow and put up for sale. In fact, the guests coming this week are in that business, would you like a new owner?"

She shook her head.

"Very well, one more outburst and you're out."

"I'll go to my flat and get my clothes," she answered meekly.

"You do that, and take Tori."

"I'll not let you down, Luca."

"You'd better not, because give us a pathetic performance and by the end of the week you really will have a new owner and be servicing up to twenty men a day, not just me. Keep that in your pea-brain."

Then he pushed her in front of him back into the lounge.

Tori had wandered around the room, while Luca and Roos were gone. Not expecting there would be restrictions on where she could go, meant she had to place listening devices at every opportunity. This was such an opportunity. She had seven electronic devices three millimeters in diameter and fifty millimeters in length, hidden in the edging of her suitcase inside the cord that surrounded the lid. They wouldn't be found unless you split the cord open with a knife, destroying the case. Except there was a way to remove the false cord from the case, with the original taking its place. She'd used similar devices successfully in many operations in the past, except these were more up to date, far more powerful and lasted longer. And the construction, with a microphone at one end and a spike at the other, allowed her to push them deep into upholstery, making them virtually invisible, unless you were really looking for them. The drawback was their

185

limited range, so to boost the signal required, Tori had to have her electric toothbrush charging up all the time. Then, as a secondary boost, her mobile telephone charger had to be kept powered. If both chargers were left unplugged, she had a final means of boosting the signal. That was the mobile phone itself, although the phone didn't need to be switched on. In fact, if it was off, the battery life would be that much greater. By the time Luca and Roos returned to the room, Tori had placed three of the devices, covering the big room completely.

"Sorry about that, Tori. Roos here seemed to have forgotten what we talked about last week. It's all sorted now. I want you to go with Roos to her flat, see if she's got anything suitable for her performances. If she hasn't, take her shopping."

"That's fine with me Luca, am I dancing tonight?"

"No, from tomorrow. Now leave me, I've work to do."

Chapter 36

Roos and Tori were back in her car, on their way to Roos's flat. They hadn't spoken, it was Tori who broke the silence.

"I couldn't help but notice that you and Luca didn't seem to see eye to eye, Roos. Have I caused a problem for you, coming?"

"No more than usual. He never tells me anything. But when you're told out of the blue you're to strip in front of other men, besides sleep with and be fucked by a prostitute, so you can perform the act in front of a load of men, how would you feel? I'm a shop girl and have only ever been with Luca."

"I'd be a bit pissed off. As it is I'm not a prostitute. I lap dance, which means I take my clothes off and at times mess about on a bed for the client with my partner, that's hardly prostitution. But if you're just a shop girl, why agree to it?"

"It's complicated."

"We've loads of time and I'd like to understand. After all, we've been thrown together, so to speak."

Roos sighed. "Maybe, but it's between Luca and me, not some stranger I've just collected from the airport."

They drew up outside a clothes shop. With very few garments in the windows, Tori could see this was a shop for the rich. She could understand now why Roos was well dressed. You'd not wear jeans working in this shop.

"Come on, we get in the flat round the side, not through the shop."

The flat was small, but tidy and had two bedrooms, apart from a single lounge with a tiny kitchenette off it.

"Don't you have a bathroom?" Tori asked, looking

around.

"No, we use the shop toilets. We've a shower in the basement. It's a bit messy and sometimes really cold when you have to run up from the basement with your hair wet and virtually nothing on, or need a pee in the middle of the night. Anyway, this is my bedroom, have a look inside the wardrobe and tell me what I should take."

All that was in the wardrobe was three dresses, a pair of jeans, and shoes - both high-heeled and flat. The drawers below had Roos's underwear and night clothes, with nothing else.

"Is this all you have?"

"Yes, I don't need much, anyway, besides the jeans, everything else is for wearing in the shop. I don't go out. The only place I go is Luca's house, to do his errands, unless he calls me like today, to pick you up. We buy our food at the local market."

"Right, you've got nothing here, we need to find a clothes shop. Then what about sex shops? Do you know of any around here?"

"We've a red light district, it's not very big and there's sex shops close by on the Rue de Brabant. It's best we go there, I think. I'll get some money out of the till. So long as I've a receipt, Luca will be all right with it. Make sure you remind me to get one, will you?"

***

They returned later the same day to Lucas house. Roos was in the shower. Tori had gone down to the kitchen. The housekeeper was nowhere to be seen. Out the back at the side of the pool, Luca had a sunken area, with a fire-pit in the centre. He was with five men, all were drinking.

Coming out into the hall, she looked around. Satisfied no one was in the house apart from her and Roos, Tori made her way to a door on the other side of the hall. Carefully, she tried the handle. It opened. Slipping inside, she was in a room that Luca called his office. Set up with a large desk and his thick leather chair behind it, there were three other chairs in front of the desk and two sofas facing each other by a fireplace. Tori didn't hang around, she assessed the room quickly and planted two listening devices into the soft covering of the settees. Going to the door, she pulled it open slightly, saw no one and re-entered the hall.

She was just in time, the housekeeper was coming down the stairs. "Don't stand around in the hall, it's the kitchen, or your room," she told her curtly.

"I came down for water and saw the pool, I love swimming."

"Then go to the public pool; now clear off, before they come inside."

Tori couldn't stand the woman and her demeaning attitude. She was no better than her in this house. "You don't have to talk to me like that, you're only an employee, the same as me."

The woman smirked. "That may be, but at least in my job, there's some dignity. You on the other hand, are as low as a woman can get and actually do it voluntarily. So don't dare align yourself with me, you're not fit to eat at the same table," she said, then walked away.

Tori stood there for a moment, a little stunned at the woman's outburst. While this was for her a covert operation, nonetheless it hurt her deeply. She wanted to tell her this was not what she did by choice, but would it be a lie? She was here by choice; however she wrapped it up, no one had told her to come, she had accepted an invitation knowing just

189

what would be expected. Returning to the room, she found Roos sitting on the side of the bed, drying her hair.

"So what do we do tonight?" Roos asked.

Tori sighed inwardly. "After I shower, we go to bed. Begin to get to know each other's bodies, maybe fuck, I don't know. Tomorrow you will learn your dance."

"How do we do that, the fucking bit?"

"How the hell do you think we do it?" Tori shouted at her, at the same time pulling a vibrator and a harness from her bag. "We stick these up each other's fannies and maybe the backside, that's how." Then she stormed through to the bathroom, slamming the door.

Roos looked at the items, then carried on drying her hair, seemingly indifferent to Tori's outburst.

Tori eventually came out of the bathroom. She was only wearing knickers and lay down on the bed. "Well, come on, I'm not lying on the bed undressed for nothing," she urged Roos.

Unplugging the hair drier and placing it on the dressing table, Roos dropped the towel wrapped around her body, slipped her knickers off and lay down beside Tori. "The housekeeper has opened her mouth, hasn't she?"

Tori looked at her. "How do you know?"

"She's always doing it, upset a few girls, believe me. Luca should do something."

Tori sighed. "I know what I do is not glamorous, Roos, but it's better than prostituting. I have to make a living somehow. She pulled me down to being no better than a slut."

Roos slipped her arm around Tori, leaning over and kissing her gently on the lips, running a hand over Tori's knickers. "Then, if you're a slut, I've been one for ages. Can you keep a secret?"

"Why not, I'm hardly likely to tell Luca, or even the

snobby housekeeper."

"Then I'll tell you. Because neither Mandy, my flatmate, or I can go out, we make our own fun. Most of the night we spend in bed together. Believe me Tori, there's nothing you can teach me that I haven't already done. Maybe I can teach you some things."

Their eyes met and Tori grinned. "I think you may just be right there. Charlie has a boyfriend, we only do the act to dissuade horny clients from believing we fuck after our dance."

Roos grinned. "Then let's have some fun, shall we? But I really can't lap dance. Why would you do that for another girl? I think on the dance side, you'll hold the edge."

Chapter 37

Luca was by the side of his pool. It was Wednesday afternoon. Yannick came round to the pool from the side of the house.

"Security said you'd be here," he told Luca, at the same time pouring himself a drink from a bottle on a trolly.

"So what news is there, do we know who hit us?"

"In a word, no. I've leaned on a number of associates, including the ones who supplied the boat, but not a thing. Parker is in the same situation, he's gone berserk and is threatening all manner of punishments when he finds out who they were. Then to make matters worse, the two Russian girls have been picked up by Unit T. Not the girl from Scandinavia, Parker told me he'd called the buyer and he confirms she's still there."

Luca lit a cigarette. "Unit T you say. Is it possible they have the money? You saw the gunmen, did they look or act military?"

"They certainly knew how to use their weapons. Then the pickup was very slick, so yes, it's possible. But many people in our business, the same as Parker, employ ex military?"

"He does. Which poses the question, has he staged the whole thing, to get his money back and still sell the girls. Even going as far as blowing the whistle on one of his customers to Unit T, to try to make it look as if they took the money. You notice he didn't tell them about his mate up in Scotland. He has to produce four hundred thou next month for our coming business venture. Did he say where he was going to get it from?"

"No, only that he would have the money. What about you?"

Luca gave a light shrug. "I'd have struggled, but I did a deal yesterday which will give me sufficient."

"That's good, do you want me to check out Parker in a little more depth?"

"I think you should. I'm a hundred and eighty grand down, someone has to pay."

Yannick left as the housekeeper came through from the house, accompanied by a man Luca knew only as Ikram.

"Alright, Ikram, come and sit down, would you like a drink? Perhaps tea, or coffee?" Luca asked.

"Coffee would be good," he replied, taking a seat opposite. Ikram was of Arab descent. He was a man of five foot ten, aged forty, with a stocky build and a beard that made him look a good ten years older than he really was.

"Well, what did you think of Roos, now that you've met her?"

"She's young, not very intelligent. Besides skinny," he replied somewhat indifferently.

"Roos is a good girl, I've had her since she was fourteen. She will make good entertainment for you and your friends. Tonight you'll see her in a different light. She'll be doing a lap dance, then a hot lesbian act, with the girl who danced for you last night."

Ikram sighed. "Listen, Luca, I know you want to sell her, but to tell you the truth she's not my sort. Even if you offered her for twenty grand, I'd not be that interested, apart from selling her on."

Inwardly, Luca was not happy, he needed the money from Roos's sale. Setting her price at sixty thousand would have helped him to replace the money taken from Yannick. As for him mentioning twenty, he'd get more selling to a brothel.

"Twenty's not nearly enough, Ikram. Why don't you

take her, try her out. She's a good kid, loyal and will work hard. Then, if you're really set on not keeping her, I'll take her back and find you one more suitable."

Ikram sipped his coffee, saying nothing. Then putting it down, he looked at Luca. "How much for the dancer last night? She's older, far more intelligent and my sort of girl. She's also got a good figure."

Luca threw his hands up. "She's not for sale, she's here for the entertainment and goes on Saturday. Then, even if you did take her, you'd need to keep her secure, not like Roos, who would go with you willingly and you could trust to stay with you wherever you travelled in the world."

Shrugging indifferently, Ikram leaned back. "Since when did it worry us if a woman's for sale or not? I've never known one to go willingly. So spin some story that will get her on my aircraft, complete with passport in the morning, and I'll give you what you're asking for Roos."

Luca, relieved he'd get his money, nodded his agreement. "If that's what you want, she means nothing to me, so long as she's kept secure and nothing gets back to me. But she's older, and by what I've seen of her, she's strong-willed, so you'll need to break her spirit."

"Believe me, Luca, I'll do that. When I get her home, I'll place her in a postion, within a day or so, for her to have a good thrashing, then be left to contemplate her new life with me. She'll soon come round to my thinking, even if I have to repeat the thrashing a number of times. Then, where I live she will have nowhere to go and quickly realise that."

***

Coming up to eleven, the same night. A bed without a headboard had been placed in the centre of the lounge. Already

Luca's guests were enjoying the nights entertainment. Most had had a lap dance by Tori, with a few asking for Roos, besides consuming plenty of drink. Now they were sitting around the bed, waiting for Roos and Tori to change.

The girls were brought in by Yannick, wearing nightdresses finishing at their hips, tiny knickers and high-heeled shoes to show off their long legs. Luca came up to them both, pulling Tori aside, telling Roos to go to the bed.

"When you're close to the end, I want to see my Roos get a good spanking; make her submit, then finish her off with the harness when I tell you. We have an understanding?" he asked her quietly.

"If that's what you want, but she won't be expecting it, that's not part of what we've practised."

"I couldn't care less what you've practised. I'm paying the bill, you do as I tell you. Roos is soon to have a change of lifestyle, she's wasted at the shop, that's why you're here."

Tori nodded and walked over to the bed. She was, like Roos, dreading the next quarter of an hour. But what future Luca have in mind for Roos, that he wanted her to do what she was doing with her, Roos had seemed to accept. She sighed to herself, the more she delved into this life, the more she found just how the traffickers played god to their victims and how little they thought of them, or their feelings. Since she was a child, Roos had been sold into a life that only had one outcome after Luca tired of her.

The two girls were urged on with shouts of appreciation over the way they had dressed, and clapping, as they climbed onto the bed, facing each other on their knees. Tori leaned forward to kiss Roos gently on the lips, that began a sequence they had learned, which had them undressing each other, followed by simulated lovemaking, which to the

195

watchers looked intense. Then Luca was shouting to Tori to put Roos over her knee and show her who was in charge, before she put the harness on. Tori did as she was told, but once she had the harness on, everyone was shouting at her to work Roos harder until she could take no more. Finally both girls fell back, completely spent. Luca came up to them, took their hands and helped them off the bed, parading them around like trophies, to everyone's delight.

Given bath towels to cover themselves, Yannick took them out of the lounge.

"I need a drink, Yannick, what about you, Tori?" Roos asked, turning to the kitchen, rather than going to their bedroom.

"I need the toilet first, I'll be with you in a few minutes," she answered, quickly going through to the downstairs toilet. Tori sat on the toilet lid, her head in her hands. The relationship with Roos in the privacy of the bedroom, Tori could cope with. The girl was loving, responsive and at times they'd had fun, with plenty of laughter. But with men watching this time, it was no longer between her and Roos, turning what they had into something dirty and disgusting. She had never felt so embarrassed, still unable to believe just what she'd done in front of everyone, and she was faced with two more nights of this. All she could hope was that the listening devices made it all worth it. Flushing the toilet, she went to the basin and rinsed her face, taking gulps of water from her cupped hands before spitting it out into the bowl, washing the lingering taste out of her mouth. Then sighing, she left the toilet, going into the kitchen. Roos was already sitting at the table, with a glass of coke in front of her.

"Sit down, Tori, you look knackered, I'll get your drink," Yannick said, filling a glass with coke from a half-empty bottle from the fridge.

"I was telling Roos, you did well, Tori. Luca was very happy," Yannick said while she drank.

Tori said nothing, she just wanted to walk out of this house. She had already placed the listening devices, maybe not in the pool area, but it was the best she could hope for, and time to close another chapter in her life, one she preferred to forget.

"Can you get us our clothes, Yannick, I'm freezing," Roos asked.

"Finish your drinks, while I check if you're on again," he replied, then left the room.

"They seemed to enjoy it, Tori?" Roos said when they were alone.

"Yes, they did, but men always enjoy seeing two women rolling around on a bed. I hope Yannick is not inferring they want a repeat tonight, I've had enough."

"So you didn't like being with me?" Roos asked, obviously disappointed.

"I didn't say that. In fact, I love being with you, it's just that out there I didn't."

"But you do it all the time with Charlie?"

"I do, but it doesn't mean I enjoy it and it's never as intense and aggressive as we had to do it out there."

They could say no more when Yannick came back into the kitchen. "You may as well go to the bedroom. Luca said you're finished for tonight.'

Once in the bedroom, Roos stood for a moment. "Would you prefer me to not sleep with you then? If you don't want me to, give me one of the blankets and I'll sleep on the floor."

Tori went up to Roos and gave her a hug. "I really want you to be with me Roos, I mean that. I've nothing against you in any way. Anyway, let's call it a night, I'm completely knackered, after twelve dances, and then, with what should have been a quarter of an hour turning into half an hour on the bed. I'm having a shower and calling it a day," Tory told her, breaking away and going to the bathroom.

Roos was relieved and smiled. "I'm with you on that."

Lying face up alongside each other in bed, Tori turned her head to look at Roos. "I'm sorry about hurting you. After what Luca said to me, I was really afraid they'd decide to gang rape us both if I didn't."

"I'm glad you did, what's a smacked bottom to the alternative? So I'm not mad at you." Then she hesitated. "But it did hurt, besides were aggressive with that harness, so you owe me."

"In what way?"

"Well, I should really have had the opportunity to do the same to you, it's only fair."

"Goodnight, Roos."

"That's charming, just go to sleep then, why don't you?"

Tori sat up, turned to face her, leaning on one elbow. "There's no way you're going to sleep is there?"

"No, not yet, I'm not tired. I'm younger than you."

"So now I'm old, I can't take the pressure by wanting to sleep?"

Roos smiled. She'd get her own back by the end of the week, she was certain. Roos kissed Karen on the lips. "Goodnight, mum."

***

Just after six the following morning. Tori turned to see Roos lying watching her.

"Hi, did you sleep well?" Roos asked.

"I did finally. What about you?"

"Okay, I suppose. I don't sleep well anyway." Then she snuggled up closer to Tori. "I like this time the best, when the bed is no longer cold and you feel cuddly and warm."

Tori didn't pull away, she just lay face up, gazing at the ceiling, thinking of nothing in particular.

"Can I ask you something, Tori?"

"Like what?"

"On Saturday you'll be gone, I'll be back in Luca's shop. But I've been so happy since being with you. I've never had anyone just for me, I've had to live my young life around Luca and his friends. We've become more than friends, we're lovers." She hesitated. "I don't want to lose you, Tori, can we meet again? Go out, have a good time and share a bed together because we want to, not like we are now?"

"I'd love to meet you again, Roos. As for sharing a bed, I presume you want me as your lover? I'd have to seriously think about that. Not that I wouldn't want to be with you, I would, it's just that it's a departure from what I always wanted out of life. I know I've not achieved it, maybe, perhaps it was never my destiny and my future is mapped differently?" Then she turned and kissed her gently on the lips. "We still have a couple of days, Roos, let's make the most of them, shall we? Then decide where to go from there."

Chapter 38

"Tori, when you finish your breakfast, Luca wants to see you out by the pool. Roos, you're to come with me to the market," the housekeeper told them, when they came through to the kitchen for breakfast.

Tori nodded and carried on eating. This for her was an opportunity to place her last listening device in an area Luca used a great deal, where she'd not had any opportunity to do so. Finishing her breakfast, she ran up the stairs to their room, cleaned her teeth and slipped the listening device out from her case's edging. Switching it on and slipping it into her jeans pocket, she left the room and made her way to the pool area. No one was there so she looked around quickly until she saw what she wanted. Behind the seating was an area she believed was the best location. This was built up in random stone, mortared together to form a back wall, but very loosely, leaving lots of gaps. On top of the low wall were hanging plants, most in bloom. Leaning over, as if to look at one of the plants, and selecting a suitable gap, she slipped the listening device in, then stood up, walking to another part, again looking at the flowers.

"I see you like flowers, Tori," Luca said as he came down towards the pool from the house.

She turned and smiled. "I do, but the place we have in Spain is an upstairs apartment, with a balcony and a couple of potted shrubs. I'd love a garden. Now the only plants I see are in the parks, you're very lucky to have such a nice well-kept garden."

"I never notice, it's just here. Anyway, thank you for being so prompt, shall we sit down?"

Tori sat and looked at him. "I'm a little worried

being asked here. Was my performance not good enough last night?"

"It was perfect, in fact, this is why you're here. My good friend Ikram, who watched you last night and you also gave him a private dance, has asked if you would perform at his get-together."

"When? If you'd forgotten I go on Saturday?"

"I haven't and you will be ready to go then as arranged. His get-together is Friday night. You will go with him today, settle yourself in and perform Friday night, leaving as arranged on Saturday. Roos has turned out to be a good dancer, she will carry on here for the rest of the week, before she goes back to the shop. It's worked out perfectly, and I'm grateful for what you have done with Roos."

Tori was glad to get out of this house, she'd been resigned to repeating her and Roos' performance tonight and Friday, something she didn't relish. As it was, her work here was done, with the last listening device installed. Then, who was this Ikram? Could he also be a trafficker? If he was, confident her support was close by, to go with him would be the right thing to do. She only wished she had more of the listening devices, so if necessary she could have installed them at Ikram's. "If that's what you want, after all, you have paid me up to Saturday," she heard herself saying.

"It is. Go and get packed and be at the front door in twenty minutes. Ikram is virtually ready to go and like me, he's a busy man."

Tori left Luca, going to the bedroom. Roos wasn't there, she'd already left with the housekeeper. Tori was sad, she wanted to say goodbye to Roos at least. Packing her small suitcase, she went down to the hall to find Ikram standing with Luca.

"Ah, there you are, Tori. Look after my good friend

here and get in touch after the Spanish season. I'll book you for a couple of weeks."

"Thank you, will you say goodbye to Roos for me?"

"Of course. She'll be upset missing you, she liked you a great deal. Anyway, off you go and dance well for him."

Tori, sitting in the taxi alongside Ikram, was looking out of the window when they turned into the airport, following the route to the area where private aircraft were parked. The car stopped close to a plane.

"We're flying?" Tori asked, somewhat alarmed.

"Did Luca not tell you? I live in Holland. The flight is very short, I have a private strip close to the house. You have your passport?"

"Yes, but where exactly?"

"A town called Arnhem. It is no distance. You have a problem? You will be taken to Amsterdam for your flight to Spain."

"No, I suppose not, but Luca could have told me."

As they climbed out of the car, a customs official checked her passport, then allowed her on the aircraft, with Ikram following. Ten minutes later they were on their way. Tori looked around the cabin more carefully, she knew her aircraft. This was a Gulfstream, probably a 550 and normally seating 13. But the seating had been reduced to make way for luxury seating and fittings. It was also an expensive aircraft. Far larger and more modern than hers, already she was jealous, like the driver of a Ford would envy a BMW man, but there again she didn't have over twenty million to splash out. She decided this man Ikram must be very wealthy, so it was important to find out just where he fitted into Luca's life.

Ikram had gone to the back, poured two coffees, and returning, placed one in front of her. "You want sugar?" he asked.

"No, I'm fine. This is a nice aircraft, is it yours?"

"Of course, only the best. You know about aircraft?"

She shook her head. "No, the only ones I go on are the budget airlines to Spain. There you're squeezed together. It makes a change to be able to sit in a seat which actually gives you leg room."

He didn't reply, sipping his coffee, watching her do the same. Shortly he stood. "More coffee?"

"No thank you."

He left her alone reading a magazine, going to the back and refilling his coffee cup, before walking through to the cockpit to talk to the pilot.

Tori placed the magazine back on the table and leaned back. She felt tired, having had little sleep last night, because of Roos, and soon she was closing her eyes. Minutes later Ikram was back. He leaned closer, slapped her face, lifting each of her eyelids, getting no reaction. Satisfied, he took a syringe from a drawer, filled it with liquid from a small bottle out of the same drawer and injected Tori, before taking the seat opposite. The short flight was not that short, by the time she woke they would be in Algeria, after a refuelling stopover. There she would stay until he tired of her, before being sold on.

Chapter 39

When Karen woke she was lying on a bed. The room was stiflingly hot, her head banged, she felt sick. Getting off the bed, and walking over to the window, she stood completely bemused. Wherever she was, this was not Europe as she knew it. This was more like desert, with no vegetation and an area that looked remote.

Looking in the wardrobe, she found her suitcase and nothing else. So she left the room, coming out on a long landing, with heavy wooden doors similar to hers, flagged floors and white painted walls. As she went down the stairs, Ikram was just coming out a room.

"Ah, you've finally woken. You must have been tired, the way you slept. Come, join me."

The lounge was large, with rugs scattered around, heavy furniture with two large settees. Karen sat down.

"Where the hell am I, this isn't Holland, I'm certain of that?" Karen demanded.

"No, it isn't. I just said that so as not to alarm you. As it is, I'm not one to go around in circles, so listen and listen good. The same as Luca, I traffic both children and adults. We often barter between ourselves and I'd gone to collect Roos. She wasn't suitable, unless I was moving her on, which wasn't my intention. Then I saw you. You've taken her place. For the time being, this is where you live. I have a cook and general workers. During the day you work with them, cleaning whatever. In the evenings you will entertain me in my bed, then at times, my friends."

"So you're telling me I'm stuck in this bloody place? I have a life at home."

"Then you should have listened to your mother

and not got into a vehicle, or in my case an aircraft, with a stranger. As it is, yes, you're stuck in this bloody place as you call it, until I no longer want you, or you decide you don't want to work or entertain. Then you still don't go home, I'll sell you on. What happens to you then, is not my problem."

"So how much do I get paid?" Karen asked, still acting the lap dancer.

He smiled at her seemingly stupid question. "Why would you need money? You get a roof over your head and fed, besides meaningful work, what more is there for a woman? So stop acting naive and listen. If you refuse to do as you're told, I'll string you up outside and beat you in front of the workers. If you believe you can escape, try it. We're over a hundred miles from any sort of large town. You'd either die, wandering in the desert, or you would be found and brought back. Do that and don't expect to stay here. There are many brothels that will take a woman like you, where you work fifteen hours a day. I can assure you they're not nice places. Any questions?"

"No."

"Then take that dress laid on the seat through to your room and put it on. I will allow you to keep your toiletries from the suitcase. The rest, along with what you're wearing, throw into the rubish tip behind the house. None of those clothes will be worn by any woman in my house. Now leave me and once dressed appropriately, go through to the kitchen. The cook will feed you, then you work."

***

As Ikram said, Karen worked during the day. The day's work began inside the house, cleaning, mostly caused by the constant sand being blown in. This was followed by working in an outhouse attached to the house. There she'd all his workers clothes taken to wash and sort out. Most were dirty from the fields, sometimes covered in human excrement and stank of urine. At night she would join Ikram in his bed. He was aggressive, hurt her a great deal. After he'd finished, he'd push her away, then she'd return to her own room. Already her confidence in Unit T collecting her was dented, she'd expected them to come by now and was concerned they hadn't.

Ikram's demand that she throw the suitcase and her clothes away, had to be carried out by her and not by the cook or one of the workers. While she'd every confidence that Unit T would soon effect a rescue, Karen needed to set up precautions in case that didn't quite happen to plan, or circumstances changed and she needed to make her own escape. Because of this, on the first day, after changing into the dress Ikram had given her and being shown her work by the cook, Karen had collected the case from her bedroom and taken it to the outhouse. Already her passport as Tori was gone, so too, her purse. Very carefully, she removed the case's top lining. Between the lining and the case was a passport in the name of Harris, money, credit card and a telephone SIM card. All were there in case her covert name of Tori was compromised and she needed an alternative way out. These items were packed in a vacuum-sealed polythene bag, making everything compressed into a very flat and tight package, as well as fully waterproof. On this occasion, the fact it was waterproof would be useful, as behind the outhouse, close to the wall, were old farm implements and an oil drum. The drum was very nearly full of stagnant water and like the implements, looked as if it had been there for years. Into this drum, she dropped the document package, watching it sink into the sludge at the bottom, confident it was in a place as secure as she could find, but easy to retrieve. However, Karen hadn't finished with her preparations, in case she had to get out quickly. Taking a complete set of clothing from the case, made up of knickers, jeans, top, socks and shoes, she found a plastic bag among the rubbish in the outhouse and packed it all in. Now happy, she stuffed this bag well out of sight, among a number of discarded items that must have been thrown in the back of the outhouse over the years and now been forgotten. The suitcase, as Ikram told her, was placed inside the rubbish skip. She had no intention of risking his displeasure by not doing as she was told.

***

On the second day, coming out of the outhouse late in the afternoon, Ikram was standing in the courtyard with two of his workers.

"Remove the dress and stand with your arms at your side," he demanded.

Karen took the dress off, standing there just in her knickers.

"I told you, you wear nothing but the dress, let's see if your failure to follow simple instructions extends to theft as well, shall we?" he nodded to a man who took the dress off Karen and handed it to Ikram.

He checked the tiny pocket, pulling out a small penknife. "What is this?" he asked, holding it up.

Karen looked at it in astonishment. She knew it wasn't there earlier, so he must have put it in the pocket of the dress himself. "I don't know, I've never seen it before," she gasped.

"This went missing out of my drawer this morning,

while you were cleaning the house, and it didn't just jump out into your pocket all on its own. Let's make sure you don't have anywhere to hide something in the future," he said, ripping the pocket off the dress. Then he changed his language and spoke to the men standing watching.

Immediately they ran forward; while one held her, the other bound her wrists together with one end of a piece of long rope, before dragging her to a tree. Then, the long rope was thrown over a branch and pulled, dragging her arms above her head, the tips of her feet just touching the ground.

Ikram followed; standing behind Karen, he pulled the knickers down to her feet. "I told you to wear only the dress, you do that from now on. I also told you you take nothing, or you would be punished. Do you remember that conversation?"

"I do and would never take anything. Please, I beg you, I don't know how it ended up in my dress pocket. I'm sorry about the knickers, I didn't realise I couldn't wear underclothes," she replied, very frightened, the fear apparent in her voice.

He stood back and was handed the whip. "Then you're not only a thief but a liar," he shouted, "you need to learn obedience and who owns you." Then he hit her across the back three times, once on the bottom and another time on the top of her legs.

Karen was screaming in pain.

Coming close, he showed her the whip. "Who owns you?"

"You do," she gasped.

"That's correct, remember that. Any more lies, more stealing, failure to wear what I tell you and next time it will be ten lashes. Understand?"

"Yes, I'll not take anything again," she stammered,

knowing it was pointless to claim she hadn't.

"That is good, you're also learning obedience. You will remain strung up here for the next hour. So you can contemplate your disobedience."

***

Over the next days, Karen was very down. She knew she'd been set up by Ikram to be punished and demeaned, in the way he'd left her to reinforce his threats over what would happen if she stepped out of line, besides keep her subservient.

Karen couldn't understand why Unit T hadn't come for her. She'd pressed the button on her watch, as usual, for them to track her when she left Lucas's house and again at the airport. Then, with her bugging his house, they must have heard the conversation she'd had with Lucas, when he told her she was moving on with Ikram.

With no sign of help, she spent her time studying all that went on, planning her escape. Each morning after breakfast, Ikram would leave the house, driving over to a number of long, single-storey buildings quite some distance away. Karen, during her constant cleaning, searched the house completely. She had, by chance, found a safe, after cleaning the frame of a picture from the sand blown in from outside. She decided that she must have caught a hidden button, or some sort of catch, because the picture swung open, revealing a safe. Beyond that discovery, she'd only found a few documents in a desk drawer, but little else. Already Karen was getting desperate, unable to form a plan as to a means of escape, beyond actually killing Ikram. Then, if she did, where did she go? However, this route was fast becoming the only option.

Chapter 40

Sitting in her bedroom, on the fourth night since arriving at Ikram's, Karen could hear plenty of voices downstairs. Vehicles had begun to arrive some time back; she'd helped the cook take food through to at least fifteen men. Karen had been nervous at the way some were looking at her, with comments in a language she couldn't understand, except she was certain they had been directed towards her. She'd had been in this sort of situation before with alcohol being consumed at the rate it was; the risk to her, as the night progressed, would become that much higher that she could be faced with multiple rape. This concern was very real as since her punishment, he'd become decidedly cold towards her, even as far as not taking her to his bed. He'd come through to her room, have her position herself on her hands and knees on top of the bed, her head down, her bottom up, while he stood at the side and took her from behind. Now she was seriously concerned, tonight could be her last and as he'd told her when she came, he would eventually move her on. Except she'd not expected him to reject her so soon.

Karen had dozed off, becoming alert once more when even more vehicles arrived, followed by shouts, then the sound of gunfire. She was relieved as the gunfire could only mean one thing. Unit T had come.

Climbing out of bed, she moved a chair behind the door, jamming the handle so it couldn't be opened. Concerned that Ikram might decide to use her as a hostage, she needed to make such ideas a little more difficult for him. She moved quickly off the bed and sat down on the floor in a corner of the room; she couldn't join in with the fight, having no weapon, left to sit it out, keeping clear of the window and perhaps stray bullets.

The gunfire went on for some time before it stopped, then she could hear people talking in the same language as Ikram's, not English as she'd expected. Karen stood, moving the chair from the door, undecided if she should go down. She decided not to, confident Unit T would soon come to find her. Now back on the bed, leaning on the headboard, Karen was watching the door, relieved that her time with this man had come to an end.

At that moment, three heavily armed men, none she recognised as being from around the house, burst into the bedroom. Seeing Karen, one pointed at her, speaking to one of the others. Immediately this man grabbed her, dragging her down the stairs and out of the house.

Karen's heart sank, who these people were, she'd no idea, but already had the belief they intended to rape, or execute her. Except they did neither. She was taken to the back of a lorry, where there were a number of women already on board. A man in the back helped her up, sat her down on a long bench seat, quickly attaching an ankle clamp. This was attached to a long chain. She could see other women were secured along the same chain, with similar ankle clamps. While she sat there, two more women were brought and attached to the chain. Much later, the lorry started up and left.

***

It was just becoming daylight when the lorry finally came to a halt. The women were helped down, but not released from the ankle irons and the coupling chain running between each of them. After the last woman was on the ground, they were led in a line to a small tent attached to a larger one. As they were taken to the tent, Karen looked around. They were out in the middle of nowhere, and yet there were a large number of vehicles parked haphazardly. The small tent they had been taken into was empty, at the far end was a curtain. There was no delay as one by one, the women in front of her were released of their ankle irons, stripped of their clothing, and pushed naked through the curtain. Soon it was Karen's turn. She too was stripped and pushed through. This large tent had been set out similar for a cattle sale. Men were standing either side of the roped-off narrow passage, that led from the small tent to a large roped circle in the middle of the large tent. Karen had already suspected what was intended for her, in the past she'd been sold this way before, so she was not surprised. Although she was scared of her future, every step of this operation was pulling her deeper into a world where there might be little chance of escape. The attack on Ikram's house must have been by people traffickers. Ikram had warned her, if she tried to leave the area, of marauding gangs who traded women, but never told her there was a risk they would attack the house. Already, from the little time she had been with them, she could see these were men obviously very experienced in confining women, giving little, if any, opportunities for escape. She could expect no sympathy if she was caught trying.

Once inside the large tent, Karen wasn't left to look around. A man using a stick, swiped her across the back, before poking her with the same stick, urging her along the narrow passageway out into the large circle. Once inside the large circle, he grasped her arm and led her to a set of scales in the centre. While she stood on them, he looked down at the reading, then she presumed, although she couldn't understand the language, he'd shouted her weight. Taken off the scales, he grabbed her arms, pushing them up above her head, at the same time kicking her legs apart, before placing his hand in the small of her back, arching her body to push out her breasts. He stood away from her, satisfied with the pose, which showed her off at her best. Then, with a few words from him, a number of men, Karen assumed to be potential buyers, approached. Their inspection of her was thorough and intrusive, as they looked for signs of infection, lice and mites. Some shook their heads and walked away, others commented to the man who had brought her into the ring. Karen, already aware that she was being sold with women, where the buyers suspected they'd already have infections or covered in lice, nevertheless felt demeaned and abused, to what they were subjecting her to, frustrated that she was unable to retaliate. When satisfied, the men left the circle, her arms were pulled down and with a swipe from a stick once more, she was made to walk around the outside of the circle. If she slowed at all, she received another swipe to urge her on. All the time she walked around, there was shouting from the buyers. Finally, she was sold and taken out by another exit of the tent. Already another woman was following her in.

Outside, Karen was given her dress back and allowed to put it on, then taken by two men to an uncovered Land Rover. She was helped into the back and immediately secured with ankle irons. By the time it left, there was another woman with her.

Karen was devastated. After the indignity of the sale, again, she was to be moved on. With her being moved around like this, she was already convinced Unit T would have even greater difficulty in tracking her down.

**

They travelled for most of the day, arriving at a long single-storey building set among a number of others. The man who'd brought them was small, fat and had a beard. He came around to the back of the vehicle, released the other woman and took her inside. Coming back, he offered Karen a bottle of water, which she drank gratefully, before they drove off again. Two hours later he stopped at another building, similar to the last, released Karen and took her inside.

For Karen, it was obviously a brothel, the smell unmistakable. The single room was large and long, at each end were curtains. A number of women were sitting around, some wearing old and very tatty underwear, with shirts that had the buttons removed, while others were naked. A man came up to them, looked at Karen, then nodded. She was left alone with him.

"You come," he told her in acceptable English, grabbing her arm.

They went through a door in the back wall, into a large kitchen with a number of tables. He went to the corner of the room. In the corner was a pile of clothes. Selecting knickers and a shirt handing them her. "In my brothel from now on you will wear these. There's food in the pan. Toilets through there," he said, nodding towards a door. "Eat, get yourself prepared, your work begins today. I will be back shortly for you, make sure you're ready." He left the room.

Karen was starving and went over to the large pan. All that was in it were a few dregs of what must have been stew, with burnt bits stuck to the bottom. She used a fork to scoop out what she could, eating it gratefully, finishing off with a drink of water from a tin mug she filled from a large tin jug alongside the pan of stew. Going through the far door to the toilet, she found it wasn't just a toilet, but a row of three toilets with no partitions between them. The shower area was three shower heads stuck out of the wall and a few old pieces of soap in holders. Below each shower head was one tap, which she presumed would mean only cold water. A number of toothbrushes, with a jar of salt rather than toothpaste, were left on a shelf fixed above a dirty handbasin. If you wanted to clean your teeth, there would be no option but to use one of them. Also on the shelf were two safety razors. Karen picked one up, it was dirty, the blade area still covered in pubic hair. She held it a moment undecided, but however much revulsion she had for this place, the reality was, she'd been sold into a brothel, not to one man, like Ikram, but to service an unknown number. She'd no illusions, this place was obviously the pits, the clients could well have lice and mites which would attach themselves to her pubic hair, before burrowing into her skin to lay their eggs while she slept. The hair had to go, even before she began work, then she needed to keep it that way. Unscrewing the razor, Karen cleaned all the parts, scraping the blade on the stone floor to sharpen it, then with the help of the soap, she began to shave. Every stroke made her stomach churn, as she hated herself in meekly accepting what was expected of her. Alongside the hand basin was a large tub of what looked to be animal fat. She pushed her fingers into the fat, first smearing her nipples, then between her legs and around her entrance, finally smearing plenty between her buttocks and up into her backside. Karen had been forced to prostitute many times. None of the places seemed as bad as this, but she knew what had to be done, to prepare her body and get through it.

Shortly the man returned. Karen was already dressed in what he'd given her and ready to work.

Until it closed, Karen stood around in the large room. Men would come, walk around looking at the women and take a woman to the curtained-off area. Behind the curtained area was a row of beds, with dirty and stained mattresses on top. Each bed was separated from the next with another curtain between them, effectively creating cubicles. Except, as she lay on her back, while the men took her, the beds were so close that she could hear women either side of her being taken as well; there was no privacy. Never had she felt so helpless and dirty.

***

Over the following days, Karen found out from women who could speak a little English, that the man running the brothel was called Nabil, and the one who had bought her at the sale was Zaki. As she suspected, when first coming here, this brothel was the pits. Here, like all the women, she was treated no better than an animal, often receiving the stroke of a whip on her back, if she'd not returned to the floor for the next client quickly enough, or didn't stand up straight when a client was making their selection. Like many of the other women, in the stifling temperature of the room, Karen preferred not to wear the dirty shirt and would stand around in knickers. Most clients were dirty, stank, and aggressive, with no thought for her. Taken in every position imaginable, and often up her backside, she was there for their pleasure, not hers. With the only consolation being that the sessions were short and she was expected to do nothing apart from open her legs, besides being available from when she woke until she went to bed, her one advantage was that she wasn't one of the preferred women, most men wanting the larger women with well endowed breasts. Even so, she could expect up to ten clients a day, with only two breaks of around half an hour, when she'd eat in the kitchen, otherwise she'd only be given enough time to clean herself after a client, before being available once again.

As the days passed, Karen was considering shaving her head, after finding lice in her hair. Most, if not all of the women had very short hair. She was the only one who still had a full head, resisting the inevitable in the belief that by taking that step, after already getting rid of her pubic hair, it would be like accepting she was here for the rest of her life and would never escape. Already she'd had her period, then she, with others on periods, would work in the kitchen, clean the bathroom and take the mattresses out to give them a good beating, leaving them out to dry the wet patches of body fluids and semen stains most would be covered in. At the end of the day, Nabil would bring into the shower area a bucket of warm water mixed with vinegar. Floating in the bucket were three vaginal douches. These were shared among the women who wanted to use them and the only contribution by the brothel to help prevent infection. After douching those women would wash themselves under the showers. Karen always joined the queue, anything, however primitive that would help control infection, she'd use.

The security was lax, in fact, she'd already found to her cost, security was not needed. After all, there was nowhere to run or hide. If you were lucky, you would get to use one of the mattresses behind the curtains to sleep, otherwise it was on the floor. Karen hadn't realised the shortage of beds until she tried to find a place the first night. But with two women to each bed already and no one wanting her near them, Karen always ended up on the floor. She could sleep outside if she wanted, but soon changed her mind after the second night, when she'd tried it. The other buildings around the brothel were occupied by men who worked the fields, and a woman sleeping outside risked being taken by the men from those buildings. Not knowing this, Karen had slept outside, as it was stifling in the brothel, but never again. She'd been asleep, wearing knickers and the shirt, when a man had rolled her over on her face, ripped her knickers down, forcing himself inside her, from behind, even before she'd fully woken.

It had also become obvious to Karen that with no sandals or shoes, you couldn't just walk away wearing an open shirt and knickers. If you did, you risked severe sunburn and dehydration. Then there was every chance you'd soon be picked up and brought back, or captured by one of the groups of bandits that roamed the area, raped, or taken to another brothel. So all she could come up with was a very weak plan of escape. But to actually implement the plan relied on Zaki returning. He hadn't, or if he had, she could have been with a client and not seen him. However, with Unit T not coming, she could only surmise they couldn't find her. It was now up to her to find a way out.

Chapter 41

It was around nine o clock at night. As usual, Nabil had greeted a client at the entrance, giving him the choice of the women on offer. Nabil on occasions and often with a new client, would have those women who weren't working line up, remove their shirts, stand straight, with their backs slightly arched, pushing their breasts forward. Then the client would wander down the line, at times grasping the breasts of a woman he fancied, or bringing his arms around her body, running his hands over her bottom, checking the firmness of the buttocks. Karen always felt degraded when she'd have to line up, as if she was an animal, not a human with feelings. Unfortunately for Karen, tonight she was in the line up and this particular client selected her, agreeing a price with Nabil. Grabbing her arm, he took her to a cubicle Nabil had told him was vacant. She stood there while he undressed, before she removed her knickers, ready to do as he wanted of her. He decided she should be on top, making her work by gripping her buttocks, not allowing her to slow down. She preferred it this way and responded well for him. This was a far better position than on her back, laid on a mattress, which by this time of the day was covered in wet patches and often infected with fleas, sometimes lice. Finally, with a few last thrusts he finished. Without a word he pushed her off, then left. Karen was glad he'd been quick and was gone; she had a stomach ache and her head thumped. Today had been the worst day she'd experienced so far. Every time she came out into the main room, rather than stand about as usual, Nabil had her joining the other women to be inspected by yet another client. With five women off the floor because of periods and illness, it had resulted in unusually high demand for her, leaving her bottom sore, her breasts bruised and vagina swollen.

Making her way to the bathroom, Karen knew at this time, for her, that client would be the last of the night, so rather than just wash herself down, she also cleaned herself internally both front and back before returning to the main room. Now she was leaning against the wall, with the night so hot, her body was already glistening with sweat and preferring to remain in her knickers and not put the shirt on. Although it would get cold later and she'd need it then. With only two clients left behind the curtains, soon the brothel would close for the night, allowing everyone to lie down and sleep. Tomorrow, at least three of the missing women would be back on the floor. It was only after today that Karen realised their value in giving her an easier time, compared to what she could have been faced with. This was a level she couldn't cope with and she knew she would be in serious trouble, healthwise, if it continued.

Already women not working had begun taking the empty cubicles. The women still with clients, would remain in the cubicle for the night, after the client left. Even foregoing cleaning themselves up, to guarantee them a bed. Tomorrow Karen had reluctantly decided to cut her hair very short, in an attempt to get rid of the lice making her head itch all the time. Every day was the same and to get through it, knowing there was no help coming, she was beginning to accept the fact this would be her life for the foreseeable future, so she had to make the most of it. This fact was strengthened by her being relieved when a man took her through to a cubicle after standing around, often for two or three hours, constantly rejected in preference to the other younger, more endowed women. These rejections upset her; she tried to attract the attention of a client, although she didn't relish going with man after man. Except, to be ignored made her nervous that Nabil would move her on, if she wasn't pulling her weight. By what she could understand, this brothel was good in comparison to other brothels in the area. Older women, or ones clients would not take, ended up in those brothels that had very few women, leaving no choice for the client, with each woman servicing at least twenty five clients a day, often many more.

**

While she was leaning against the wall, waiting for the brothel to close, Zaki, the man who had brought her to the brothel, came in. He had two women with him. Karen's heart was thumping. She'd waited so long for him to come, that now he was here, the plan she'd formed in her mind when she first arrived, of a possible way of escape, seemed unbelievably weak, with its reliance on what he did after dropping off the women, and being full of risks which might leave her injured, or even killed. Parts of her plan were also conjecture, as she could never be certain that what she had mapped out would fall into place. Since Zaki had left her with Nabil, she'd not seen him again, although she wouldn't have known if he had come while she was with a client. Her plan assumed he'd be earlier, so would he leave after Nabil took the delivery of new women, or remain here all night? With the way she was feeling, she wished it could have been any day but this one. In fact, Karen felt so bad, while she stood there watching, she decided not to go through with it and wait until the next time he came.

With the night unusually hot, making the stench of body odour in the room really bad Karen needed fresh air to clear her head, so she decided to go and stand outside until they were ready to lock up. For her plan to succeed, when she eventually made a break for freedom, the knowledge of his movements was important, so it was worth going outside just to observe what Zaki did when he left the brothel.

Walking round the room to the entrance, after slipping on her shirt, she went outside. Outside alone at this time of night was always a risk. But if she remained close to the door, Karen was confident she'd be safe. She'd done it quite a number of times before, with the knowledge she could run back inside if she suspected trouble. This was usually from the men living in the other buildings. If they saw a woman outside at night, they would often gang up and try to take her for free, rather than pay in the brothel. One woman outside alone and taken by them, was beaten up and raped by five men before Nabil had got them off her. She was so badly injured, she'd been taken away, but never returned to the brothel. Karen suspected the woman had been dumped in the desert to die. For Nabil, the cost of medical treatment would have been more than the cost of replacing her. Now with Zaki back, Karen decided another sale must have been held and the two women he'd brought were to replace the ones lost.

A number of women were standing around just outside the door, sharing a cigarette one of the women had been given. They completely ignored Karen, not wanting her to join them, and perhaps have to share the single cigarette with yet another person. The Land Rover, Karen had been brought to the brothel in originally, following the sale, was parked a short distance away. She looked at the vehicle, it was even in the position she'd hoped it would be for her plan to work. Facing the correct way, so the passenger door would be on the far side and unseen by people coming in and out of the buildings. Minutes before, she'd decided to put it off, preferring to wait until she felt better. This decision she was now questioning, as bits of her original plan were falling into place. Well, the vehicle was where she'd planned it to be at least. Already conditions in the brothel were affecting her health, which could only deteriorate, resulting in the determination and effort needed in making a break for freedom that much harder, maybe even impossible. Then, with the added risk of being moved on playing on her mind, it was important to weigh up all possibilities, even as far as making her break tonight.

At that moment, Zaki came out of the brothel with Nabil, going directly into another building. The lights outside the brothel had been switched off, now the only illumination was a small light over the entrance to each of the other buildings. These were kept lit by a generator, that only ran for another half hour or so before the brothel door would be locked and the generator shut down. This would extinguish the lights inside the brothel after the women had been given time to wash and settle for the night. Karen knew she had around fifteen minutes to get back to the brothel, if she didn't want to remain outside, with all the risks that entailed. Nabil wouldn't be interested in her remaining outside, in fact, he wouldn't know she was, short of counting the women asleep behind the curtains. Not that he would bother to do that. Where could she go, surrounded by desert and with no clothes? Providing she was back working in the morning, no one would think about her, or look for her until then. This aspect alone was very important for her plan, when she did implement it.

Deciding to at least take a closer look at the vehicle in the short time she had, Karen moved further from the safety of the brothel into the shadows.

Going around to the passenger side of the Land Rover,

parked facing away from the buildings and in the shadows, she tried the handle. It was open so she climbed in, first checking everywhere for anything that might be used as a weapon. If there was something, she'd take it to hide outside. All she could find was a flat-ended screwdriver around nine inches in length, but as far as Karen was concerned, it was better than nothing and could certainly be used as a weapon in close combat. Climbing out, she remained in the shadows, on the passenger side, looking through the vehicle towards the buildings, making sure there was no one around so she could return to the brothel safely after hiding the screwdriver.

Not feeling very well, Karen had not been as alert to danger as usual after moving away from the brothel. Unnoticed by her, a man had seen her leave and followed. He also kept to the shadows. He'd watched her climb inside the vehicle, taking the opportunity to move closer. Once she was out, he moved quickly and was up behind Karen, slamming her against the vehicle door, pushing her arms high above her head. It had been fast, taking her by surprise. He was also a big man and had no trouble in keeping her firmly wedged against the door and him, with the bulk of his body. Reaching down, he ripped her flimsy knickers off, followed by him pushing his own elasticated tracksuit bottom down. Already she could feel his hard penis in the crack of her buttocks, as he tried to work it up her back entry. Karen might at times be overwhelmed and unable to fight back, as when she was taken to be sold and only released from her restraints among a large number of men. But when she did have the opportunity to retaliate, she had the experience and the skills to take on even a combat-trained soldier.

Pushing her bottom towards him, as if she was assisting, he relaxed, convinced she was going to allow him to take her. He pulled back slightly, giving her more movement, as he reached down with one hand to guide his penis inside her. That was all she needed. Still holding the screwdriver, she brought her arm down, plunging the screwdriver directly into his leg. With the screwdriver not that sharp and also flat into a muscular leg, it did little damage, apart from break the skin slightly. All the same it was sufficiently painful for him to pull away from her completely, with the intention of taking off her, what she'd stabbed him with, or knocking her out. Karen had other ideas; now free, she spun around, grasped the screwdriver with her other hand as well, before ramming it with everything she could muster upwards, under the man's jaw and into his throat. Blunt or not, this time, going into soft skin and with real power behind the action, it sank deep into his throat. Blood spurted out everywhere, the loss of which sent him reeling, finally collapsing on the ground gurgling, trying to stem the blood from the vicious wound.

Karen stood watching, she knew he was dying, the screwdriver had burst a main artery. She had no compunction in killing the man. He had no respect for her, with only the intention of rape in his mind. As far as she was concerned, she was entitled to defend herself, which she would always do if possible. She also recognised the man, with most of their sessions like this attempt, finishing up her backside, leaving her in pain and distress. Karen had a quiet sense of satisfaction, that he had got his just reward in his attempt. But this action meant she had no option now but to go through with the plan she'd devised. To still be here in the morning when he was found, especially after she'd returned to the brothel tonight with her body covered in splattered blood, everyone would know it had been her who'd killed him and she'd pay for it with a beating, maybe even her life. Picking her knickers up, they'd been ripped apart and were no longer of any use to wear, so she wiped herself between the legs before discarding them. Kneeling down, she removed the man's sandals, followed by the tracksuit bottoms. To leave here in a shirt, without knickers, would be foolish. She had to wear the man's trousers, even though they were oversize, except with the elastic they were at least staying up, offering her a little dignity. Again, the sandals were too big, but she slipped them on anyway, not knowing if she would be faced with walking. If she did, the hard, stony ground would play havoc with the soles of her feet, with not being used to walking barefoot.

For Karen, it was lucky she had taken the man on. At that moment, Zaki came out of the building along with Nabil. They were talking while Nabil locked the brothel door, before they both returned to the building they'd come from. Karen watched and waited, expecting Zaki to come back out again, but he didn't. Then the generator died, everywhere was in darkness. She was in panic, it could be daylight before he left. She on the other hand, would not be able to hide, or take him by surprise as she intended.

Karen stood there at a loss as to what to do now. The brothel was locked up and she was stuck outside with a dead body. Making a decision, she dragged the man away from the Land Rover towards a pit that had been dug to throw rubbish in. This took her close to an hour, three times she had to rest. Her time in the brothel, with the poor food, had taken its toll. Pushing him in, she gathered the rubbish already in the pit to cover him as best she could. Then, with a short branch, broken off a bush, Karen swept the drag marks in the dust. All this was in virtual darkness, the only glimmer of light was from the moon, making it more difficult to see if her efforts had camouflaged him enough and the drag marks were gone. Returning to the Land Rover, Karen climbed inside, reaching under the dash for the wires attached to the key switch. Being an old Land Rover, there was only two wires and easy to pull off and wrap around to switch the ignition on, allowing the vehicle to be started. For Karen this was a last resort, she couldn't remain much longer than the break of dawn, which she knew would be around six in the morning. If Zaki had not come out by then, she would pinch the Land Rover. Where to go, she had no idea, after all, she didn't really know where she was. Her plan needed Zaki, without him she would be in serious trouble.

Chapter 42

The night, apart from being cold, was long. Karen was sitting on the ground, leaning against the passenger door of the Land Rover. Already she had dozed off a number of times, each time coming awake in panic, completely disoriented as to where she was. Now dawn was breaking and she could hear people talking as they came out of the buildings, on their way to work in the local fields.

Karen stood watching who came out the buildings through the windows of the Land Rover, at the same time remaining out of sight. The early starters had disappeared down the road; she knew if Zaki didn't come out in the next half hour, more workers would be leaving for the fields, climbing aboard the lorries. Then Nabil would be out to unlock the brothel. Then most women would sit around outside until it opened. The ones in the kitchen would begin the cooking and cleaning, walking over to throw rubbish into the pit. She couldn't be around when that happened, besides, by then, someone would notice she was missing.

It was at that moment that Zaki, along with Nabil, came out from the building they had spent the night in. Zaki was carrying a four-pack of beer. The two men embraced, Nabil headed for the brothel, Zaki the Land Rover.

Zaki never came around to the passenger side, but went directly to the drivers door. He pulled the door open and climbed in. Karen was relieved; if he had come to the passenger side, she'd have had no option but to kill him. That would have been a bad move on her part, she needed Zaki. Karen had been squatting down below the window of the passenger door; opening it quickly and inside before Zaki could react. Grasping the screwdriver, she pushed the tip up under Zaki's chin.

"You understand English?" she asked quietly.

"Yes," Zaki answered, nervous of a woman from the brothel holding a screwdriver to his throat and covered in blood.

"Then, shout out for assistance, or try to attack me and I'll ram this screwdriver up into your skull. You understand that?"

"Yes."

"Good, now drive."

He started the engine and set off, keeping his speed down as they travelled along the poor road.

"You're wasting your time," Zaki told her. "Look at yourself, dressed in rags, with no money. Then, you're covered in blood, what have you been up to? But whatever you've done, there isn't a hope of escape, no one will help you, and you'll be out in the sun, ending up badly burnt, maybe suffering heatstroke. If not that, there are many gangs in this area, you'll be raped, and then left for dead. Let me take you back, drop you off and I'll say nothing."

"You know the house of Ikram? The one where gunmen came for his women?" she asked, ignoring his assessment of her dilemma.

"I do, there's nothing there, the house is trashed. He's dead, his people were taken, his women sold, many men were killed."

"I know that, I was one of those women. How far is it?"

"Maybe three hours' drive."

"Why so close, it took a lot longer to get here?" Karen wanted to know.

"The auction is in the other direction and at least five hours' drive. You should give up this idea of escape. If you don't want to return to our brothel, I will take you to another. You will work hard, yes. But unlike ours, you'll have your own room, clean clothes and good food."

"It may sound good as far as you're concerned, but you're not the one locked up inside being shagged day after day. I don't even want to think about how many took me yesterday, except I was left with a blinding headache, and particularly sore. So you head towards Ikram's, when we get there you leave me. That way you get to live. Because refuse and I will kill you, that's how I feel about you, for taking me to that hellhole."

Zaki shrugged indifferently. "If that's what you want, but at Ikram's house, you're a hundred miles from Maghnia, in an area controlled by the people who killed Ikram. Soon it will be known you've escaped. You'll be found, have no doubt. When they do, following a good beating, you will go to a brothel that won't give you any freedom."

"That's my problem, not yours."

They travelled in silence for a time.

"Who were the men that came to Ikram's and why was he killed?" Karen finally asked. She really wanted to know what had happened. If she managed to escape and if Zaki knew where Ikram fitted in, it would be all to the good.

"He has a brother called Samir. They run the sales together. The one you were sold at was run by Samir. Ikram also dealt in petrol and drugs. Maghnia is very close to the border of Morocco. There, petrol would sell for ten times the price of what it is in Algeria. In many places you can just walk over the border, with no one to stop you. So it is easy to move both petrol and drugs. Ikram became a very important man, making a great deal of money. Samir didn't bother, he was a simple man, his income from women and child sales was sufficient for his needs. However, the police began to crack down on smuggling. They would impound tons of drugs, of all types, from cannabis to cocaine. They couldn't be corrupted, would arrest anyone travelling at night close to the border, believing them to be smugglers. It was affecting Ikram's income. He moved back into people trafficking, except rather than sell locally, he shipped women and children to more lucrative markets. The women in the sale apart from you, were local women who had been taken by Ikram to be sold that way. Samir considered these women belonged to him and Ikram was starving his sales, so he wanted them back. There was a fight, Ikram was killed, so Samir took his women and ransacked the house. Ikram was a fool. It had to happen one day. In that area Samir is king."

"Then Samir has all Ikram's money now?"

"No, Ikram never kept money in his house. He couldn't trust his people when he was away. But Samir would not have been bothered. Like I said, his life is simple, he has no need of large amounts of money. It would also be difficult for him to keep it, he has no bank accounts and would need to be constantly on his guard from those who would want his money."

***

It was, as Zaki suggested, just over three hours later that they arrived at Ikram's house. They had stopped only once, for the man to drink his beer. Karen even accepted one that he offered her. She needed it, although she was still tired; not sleeping much last night had taken its toll, but she didn't relax, giving Zaki no chance to overcome her.

"Get out, then start running," he told her.

"First, we both check the house. I want to be sure there is no one waiting for me."

231

"Why should they be waiting? No one knew you've escaped yet. But now they will."

"Just do as I tell you."

He shrugged. "If you want." Zaki climbed out and walked towards the house with Karen following him. It was obvious, before they even went inside, that no one was here, or had been around since that fateful night. She counted eight bodies decomposing around the front. Some of them she recognised from their clothes as Ikram's visitors. If someone had been here, or even taken the place over, they'd have removed the bodies.

Once inside the house, the smell, besides hordes of flies, was really bad. There were three more bodies, one being Ikram's, in the hall. Coming up behind Zaki, Karen rammed the screwdriver into his kidney. Zaki screamed in agony, collapsing to the ground.

"That's for putting me in a brothel to rot. Now you will soon answer for your crimes in front of your god, I don't envy you that," she told him calmly, as Zaki lay there on the floor, blood oozing out the injury.

"You bastard, you said I only had to leave you here."

She shrugged indifferently. "Like everyone around here, I lied. As it was, you made money out of me, lived a good life, indifferent to my suffering. So accept it's come to an end, you've lost and die like a man, not a wimp. Because you will die, that is certain."

Going through to the dining room, like Zaki said, the house had not only been trashed, but completely stripped of furniture, with just rubbish remaining on the floors. Taking the only item of furniture left, a dining room chair, with the back broken, she came out into the hall and sat down, looking down at him.

"Not dead yet? Not to worry, I can wait, or if you

232

want I'll put you out of your misery?"

"Who are you, why did Ikram bring you to this country?"

Karen shrugged. "I'm nobody. Sold by a man in Germany to Ikram. He too will die, believe me. I'll sit like this and watch as his life slips away as well."

Soon Zaki's eyes closed, he'd no longer any interest in her being there, or listening to her rambling. Karen now knew he was no threat. But after her time in the brothel, rather than kill him outright, she'd been determined to see him suffer just a little, because of what she'd endured. Karen stood and left the house, heading for the outhouse she had worked in.

It had obviously been searched for anything of value or usefulness. However, whoever had done it, hadn't gone as far as pulling the dirty and dusty rubbish from the corner. 'But why should they have done,' Karen thought, 'with such good quality goods in the house'. Carefully, she moved some of the rubbish, reaching underneath it. Her hands closed around the bag she'd hidden her clothes in. Karen sighed with relief, at least she could dress in clothing that would give her dignity once more.

Returning to the main house, she ran up to her old bedroom. Once in there, Karen was glad her clothes hadn't been left in the room. It was empty, even the bed and wardrobe had gone. Going into the bathroom, she locked the door. This room didn't seem to have been emptied completely, like the bedroom. There was still a half-used piece of soap in the shower and her toiletries, such as toothbrush, toothpaste and even a half-tube of antiseptic cream were still in the cupboard over the sink, although the bag she kept them in was missing, along with the perfume and make-up. Opening the window wide, so she could hear if a vehicle arrived, she turned on the shower. Karen was surprised it worked. Although when she thought about it, there wouldn't be a need for a pump as the water came from a tank on the roof, and being left unused, it had also warmed by the heat of the sun, coming out lukewarm, nothing like the bitterly cold water in the brothel - not that Karen would have been that bothered if it was cold, she wanted to wash away the dried blood, and the stench of the brothel, on her body and in her hair. In fact, since it was lukewarm, Karen spent a good ten minutes washing herself down, enjoying the cascading water, before using a little antiseptic cream from the half-used tube in the cupboard to relieve the soreness around her back passage and between her legs. With the towels missing and nothing to dry herself with, she decided not to bother to dress just yet, but to search the upper rooms first. By the time she'd done that, she'd be dry and could dress. Like her own room, they were empty, everything taken. Dressing and slipping her shoes on, she went downstairs.

Ikram's office was a mess. It was as if the contents of the filing cabinet and the drawers of the desk had been turned out onto the floor, before the items had been taken away, including the stapler, hole punch and pens. All that was left was paper. Most of the documents were written in Arabic, Karen had no idea if they would be of value. Even if they were, she'd not be able to take them all with her. But she decided to spend a little time to go through what was there, just in case she found something which she could read and may be of interest.

It was then, after putting what papers she'd looked through out of the way, that she saw the key. It must have been in one of the desk drawers on top of papers and been tipped out, covered over with papers underneath. Karen picked it up; it was no ordinary key, this was a multi-lever key used only for safes. Thinking back to when she was cleaning the house, she remembered the safe behind the picture.

Running into the dining room, the picture was still on the wall, although it looked as if the gunmen had used it for target practice, with many bullet holes in the picture. Finding the release on the frame, she hinged open the picture hiding the safe. Pushing the key into the lock, she couldn't believe her luck when it turned. Opening the safe, Karen smiled. There were documents, books and bundles of currency - although she was disappointed there was no weapon. Even so, maybe all the abuse she'd had to endure since coming to this country could be worth it, if the books held contact names with addresses? She hoped so, otherwise the last weeks would be for nothing. But for Karen there was something even more important. Both her passport, in the name of Tori, and her purse were in the safe as well. Thinking logically, this would be where Ikram would have put them. It would also enable her to leave this country, without the need to use her passport in the name of Karen Harris, which may have raised questions at the border. Now she could leave as Tori. This would not have happened without finding the key.

Karen was buoyant; closing the safe, she made her way to the back of the outhouse, now wondering if her suitcase could still be in the rubbish skip, besides money and documents in the oil drum. The suitcase was; although covered in more rubbish, it was unopened, with little damage. Not relishing putting her hand into the oil drum, Karen leaned on the wall, placed her feet on the drum and pushed it over. The water spilled out, releasing the polythene bag with all her documents from the sludge at the bottom. Rinsing the bag in the kitchen, she put it in the case.

Deciding further searching would reveal nothing of interest to her, Karen took her suitcase into the dining room and began filling it up with the contents of the safe. It was only then that Karen, believing the safe empty, found it wasn't. Stacked neatly in the very back were piles of gold Krugerrands. She estimated there had to be three, maybe four hundred of them. Not hesitating, she packed those into her suitcase.

Leaving the house, she drove the Land Rover over to the low outbuildings. Here again there were a number of bodies scattered around. The side doors were wide open, the rooms empty apart from rubbish strewn across the floor. But she found what she hoped might be here. There were a few drums of fuel, most were empty, but one still had a little in it. Opening the large double doors at the end of the building, she backed the Land Rover inside. Then screwing the hand pump off an empty drum, she fitted it to the drum with fuel in it still and began to pump the fuel into the Land Rover. She had no idea how far she'd have to drive, but the last thing she wanted was to run out, so every bit she could find would help.

Karen set off, heading in the direction she had come when Zaki was driving. She'd remained observant coming to Ikram's and was heading for a signpost on a wider road with the number N7 and the name of somewhere written in Arabic. She surmised that such a main road, with a number and a sign, must lead towards quite a large town.

***

On the road from Ikram's she never met, or passed a vehicle, until turning onto the N7; now it was far busier. She was also very hungry and seeing a bar with a few vehicles parked outside it, Karen stopped. She went inside, people already in there looked at her, then went back to their conversations. A man approached.

"Can you understand English, or French?" she asked.

"I speak English, you want food?"

"Yes, a sealed bottle, or can of beer and a salad?"

He nodded and walked away, quickly coming back with a can of beer.

Karen drank it, then the salad arrived with a hunk of obviously home-made bread. Half an hour later, after offering to pay him in dollars, which he virtually snatched out her hand, she was on her way, carrying a small plastic bottle of water. She'd also managed to get out of him that the road led to Maghnia, around two hours' drive away.

Coming into Maghnia on the N7, Karen still didn't feel safe, and she was tired. However, she saw a pharmacy that was open and stopped, going inside. There she bought shampoo to get rid of the lice in her hair and a more suitable ointment for use around her most intimate areas. She also found some dye to take her hair back to the brown it normally was. Already her roots were showing her original colour, so she had to either go blonde again or back to normal. Deciding finally to go brown, it was like taking the first step towards becoming Karen Harris once more, not Tori. The day was wearing on, she needed to eat and sleep and didn't want to be out on the street all night, alone and tired. Seeing a hotel with the name 'La Canta', she assumed it would be French-owned, and being able to speak French, decided to see if they had a vacancy.

Carrying the suitcase, Karen walked into the reception. But to protect who she really was, she had to be Tori just for a little longer. "You have a room for tonight?" she asked in French.

"We do," the man behind the counter said, handing her a sheet of paper. "Can you fill in the details? We also require to see your passport," he continued with a smile.

Karen nodded, filling in the form as Tori, showing him the passport. "I would also like to eat, can you provide food?"

"Of course, the dining room is open, it is through the far door."

After dinner, Karen went to her room. Took a long soak in the bath, followed by a shower to change her hair colour besides washing her hair with the new shampoo. Using the cream she'd bought at the pharmacy around her backside and between her legs, Karen finally lay down in bed wearing a T-shirt and knickers. Even though it was early for her to go to bed, to feel clean and not smell was like heaven, as she pulled the blankets tight around her. That was not before she'd moved a chair and jammed it under the door handle, placing an ornament on the chair. She'd made that mistake in the past, not securing the door and paying a dear price. She didn't intend to repeat that error, even going to the extent of locking the window shut. In minutes she was asleep.

Karen had not been asleep for long when there was a banging on the door, with the hotel owner shouting to her to open up.

She climbed out of bed, pulled her jeans on, then after moving the chair, she opened the door slightly.

"What do you want?" she asked.

"You must leave now, don't delay."

"Why?"

"I believe you're the woman sold into Zaki and Nabil's brothel by Samir and you've escaped. Samir is in Maghnia, checking all the hotels further down the road, looking for a European woman travelling on her own. If you stay here and he comes, other guests may tell him you're here. He will find you, take you back, put you in a brothel that will keep you chained up and you will never escape. I, my family, will not be safe for harbouring you. You must follow the N7 and turn onto the N99 to Ghazaouet. Take the ferry to Almera in Spain, it leaves tomorrow at two o'clock in the afternoon. Don't try to take the vehicle on board, without documents, otherwise they will arrest you for stealing. Until it goes, you hide out of the way, if you value your life and your freedom. He has many friends in Maghnia, not so many in Ghazaouet. Either way, until you get on that ferry, you will not be safe."

She nodded. "Thank you for the warning. I don't want you risking your life for me. Five minutes and I'll be gone."

"Then leave by the back way, I'll open the door. Good luck, you will need it."

Chapter 43

Nabil was told by one of the women that Tori was missing when he opened up. A search was instigated, culminating in finding the dead man later that day. Nabil was convinced Tori had done this and he wanted her back, as well as punished.

Nabil had called Samir. "The European woman is missing," he told Samir when he answered. "We've found a man dead and done a search. She's nowhere to be found. All I can think of is that she's overcome Zaki and is with him in his Land Rover. Samir, the woman has probably forced Zaki to take her to the nearest town. There's only Maghnia. If your contacts see Zaki, or the vehicle, can you check it out?"

"You want her alive?" Samir had asked.

"Yes, I want her alive, she has value. But I've decided I don't want her back. You are to sell her on to a more secure brothel for us. You will receive your usual commission."

"Very well, I will find her. If Zaki contacts you and tells you where he's dropped her off, call me. I'll make a few calls to find out if anyone has seen his vehicle," he'd told him.

One of those calls had been to the owner of the cafe where Karen had eaten. He told him a European woman had eaten there and was driving Zaki's Land Rover. He also said she was alone and heading for Maghnia.

***

"Slow down, you watch the left side for Zaki's Land Rover, I'll watch the right. We'll also check the hotels, just in case she's booked in," Samir said, as he and his partner Malik, headed for Maghnia on the same road Tori had.

Stopping at the first hotel, Samir went inside. Five minutes later, he was out, and they were on their way to the next hotel.

Eventually they were outside La Canta, where Karen had stayed. Going into the hotel, he walked up to the reception along with Malik. "Have you had a woman check in today, European and on her own?" he asked the owner.

"No, we have no such guest."

"What about the one who came earlier?" A guest, sitting reading a paper asked, hearing the conversation.

Samir turned to the guest. "What did she look like, this woman?"

"Blonde hair, tall, slim, carried a smallish suitcase and wearing jeans."

He looked back at the hotel owner. "You lied, maybe she paid you not to talk. Where is she?"

"We have no such woman. At times we have people who decide not to stay for various reasons. There was a woman who enquired, but she didn't like the room and went."

"When did she leave?"

"She stopped for food, then left around five, I think it was."

Samir didn't believe him. "Let me look at your guest list?"

The hotelier showed him the forms. He'd removed the one Karen had filled in and destroyed it.

"Malik, go with the owner here and look in all the so-called empty bedrooms."

"Excuse me, this is a hotel, not one of your brothel's. If I tell you the person you're looking for is not staying here, then she's not."

Samir shrugged, somewhat indifferently. "You have

a choice, I'll burn the place down and watch your guests leave, or you show Malik she's not here. Either way we will find out. That woman cost a great deal of money, she's killed to escape and we want her back."

The hotel owner frowned. "You say she's killed? Who has she killed?"

"An innocent man and probably Nabil's brother Zaki as well. This woman must pay for her actions."

"That is different and you're correct, she must pay. If the woman who had dinner here, is the same woman you're looking for, she is on her way to catch the ferry in Ghazaouet, heading to Spain. I know this, because she asked the way, following her dinner." While the hotel owner wanted to tell Samir her name, he was afraid that would show he'd been lying, that she had actually been booked in and stayed there. Samir would then want to know why she'd suddenly left. He decided that by giving Samir the destination of the ferry, she'd be found before boarding, leaving him in the clear. They would never believe any explanation by her, or even be interested, once they had her.

"It makes sense. We will go to the ferry terminal and collect her. You have done well to be able to tell us this," Samir told him after some thought.

Chapter 44

Karen was on the road to Ghazauoet, finding it was less than fifty minutes' drive away. Leaving the vehicle as the hotel owner told her, she wandered round the area close to the ferry terminal. Finding a hotel, she went in, booked a room for two nights and settled down. Again she took the precaution of trapping the door with a chair, but she didn't expect a visit. The Land Rover was well hidden from the main road, it was dark and the vehicle would be difficult to find.

After breakfast, she wandered around the local shops, purchased a backpack, baseball cap, leather bomber jacket and a cheap watch, before returning to the hotel. She had the intention of pretending to be backpacking, if asked, so she needed to discard the suitcase. Carefully, she removed the base of the backpack, and in it put all the gold coins, laid out between layers of the currency, to prevent them rattling against each other, before refitting the base on top. Packing all her underwear in, followed by the rest of her clothes, the backpack was practically full.

Karen's decision not to be outside until close to the departure of the ferry, was why she had booked two nights. It would enable her to remain in the room the following day watching television, besides plan a good explanation of where she had come from, in case any officials asked when she boarded the ferry.

***

It was noon when she finally left the hotel, heading for the ferry terminal. Two hours before it sailed, already there was a queue at the ticket office.

Karen stopped dead. She recognized a man hanging around the office as the one who had hit her with a stick in the tent, when she'd been sold. She suspected this must be Samir, the one the hotel owner said was looking for her. Had the hotelier told Samir where she was heading, or was he here on the off-chance, in case she decided to leave the country by this route? She had no idea, but it left her in a quandary as to what to do next. He'd only seen her for a short time, then she'd had blonde hair and was naked. Could she walk past him and book a ticket, or would he be interested in any young woman approaching the ticket office alone?

Karen decided she must wait till the last moment to board the ferry, just in case he recognised her. She began to walk away, but suddenly a man was behind, poking something into her back. It was Malik.

"Down the alley and through the open door. I've a gun with a silencer fitted and will use it if you try to run," he told her in perfect English.

Karen had no option but to do as he said. Soon they were in what looked like an old workshop, which seemed not to have been used for years. She looked him over. He was small, with a beard and wearing Arab clothing. He was also carrying a plastic bag, similar to what was used by supermarkets.

"Take the backpack off, then put your arms behind your head, your hands clasped together," Malik demanded.

"I've got a little money, if that's what you're after, you're welcome to take it," she said, at the same time doing as he told her.

"I'm not interested in your money. You're the property of Nabil."

"I've never heard of the man. As it is I'm the property

244

of no one, I'm a student backpacking from Morocco and heading to Spain," Karen answered indignantly.

He stood for a moment, looking at her, was it possible she was telling the truth? She was alone and apart from the hair colour, fitted the description Nabil had given them. "If you're coming from Morocco, why are you in Algeria?"

"I'd got as far as Afihr. There I was told the ferry from here is cheaper to Almera, than the one from Melilla. So I thumbed a lift. A lorry dropped me off only an hour back."

Malik was confused. She was right, the ferry from Ghazauoet to Spain was cheaper. Could he be wasting his time with her and maybe allowing Nabil's woman to board the ferry? Then he had an idea.

"If what you say is true, you'll have a passport, money?" he said, convinced if she did belong to Nabil, she'd not have anything like that.

However, Karen had prepared for such questions, although she'd expected it from the officials at the ferry, if they had doubts about her. "I have both, do you want to see them?"

"Yes, show me."

Karen dropped her arms, opening her backpack, pulling out the passport, not in the name of Tori, but Karen Harris, and a bundle of both local and Moroccan currencies. She'd avoided showing him her passport as Tori, in case he knew that name. Even so, it was still a risk, not knowing if he had heard of Karen Harris.

"It seems you may be telling the truth, we shall see. My partner Samir will know if you're the woman he sold in his sale. If you're not, you can go on your way," he said, handing the passport and money back.

Karen sighed inwardly with relief, it seemed he

hadn't taken much notice of her name, or didn't know it. "Can I leave my arms down while we wait for him. He'll soon confirm I'm not the person you are looking for. Besides, I'm hardly going to make a run for it, or even attack someone with a gun?" she asked, looking up, while she put the passport and money back into her backpack.

"Yes, stand still, don't move." Malik removed a mobile telephone from his pocket and keyed in a few digits, talking to someone in a language Karen couldn't understand, all the time watching her. "I've found a woman on her own, Samir. Her hair colour is different and she claims she's come from Afihr to take the ferry to Spain. She has Moroccan money and a passport, the one from Nabil would have had neither. Have you seen anyone yourself?"

"No, but maybe the woman you've found really is Nabil's and has obtained money and a passport somehow?"

"I believed she was, that's why I took her. Dying her hair in an effort to avoid us. Now I'm not so sure."

"If she isn't, could we still sell this woman?"

"She's good looking for a European, so yes, she'd sell."

"Then you have done well, we'll take her as a bonus, even if we find Nabil's woman later. Where are you?"

"In the old printer's workshop, off the main road."

"I'll collect the car and be there as soon as I can. Have you the bag with you?"

"Yes."

"Then get her ready to leave immediately I arrive. Remember, if this is the woman, she's already killed and maybe still carrying a weapon. So have her strip. You must be sure she's not hiding anything when she gets in the car."

"I understand, she will be ready when you arrive."

He looked at Karen, after putting his telephone

back into his pocket. Deciding to follow the route of her belonging to Nabil, even if she wasn't. "You're lying, you are the woman we sold to Nabil's brothel. It was very foolish escaping from him, because you are now available to be sold at our next auction in two days' time. Believe me, in Nabil's brothel you had it easy, the next one will be very different," he said aggressively, at the same time pulling a dress out of the bag he was carrying, similar to the one Karen had worn in Ikram's house, dropping it to the floor. Then he took out a set of ankle irons, which he kept hold of. "I'm also told you have killed, which means I need to be sure you're hiding nothing, so strip, you wear only this dress when you leave here," he told her curtly.

"I'm not undressing for anyone," Karen retorted indignantly.

Malik didn't hesitate, raising his gun he fired at the floor in front of her. "The next shots will be into your feet. Injured or not, you are coming with us. So make up your mind - walk out, or crawl out. I couldn't care less, so long as you're still able to shag, someone will purchase you."

Karen felt sick inside. This shouldn't be happening to her, she'd escaped once, only to be taken so easily again. But whatever happens, she must be in a position to make an escape, particularly not crippled. There was no option but to do as he asked. Saying nothing more, she began to undress. Now, standing in front of this man naked, she felt as if she'd never left Nabil's brothel. It seemed like she was destined to remain as a prostitute and was already dreading being taken back into the sale ring. Very aware the next brothel could be much worse, to what she'd already been through.

"Put these ankle irons on and snap them shut," he demanded, throwing them at her feet. "After you've done that, place the discarded clothes into the backpack, then stand up straight, with your arms out in front of you, your hands palm side up, the fingers open."

She did as he asked and Malik looked at her hands. "Drop your arms and clasp your hands together, then turn round," he told her. Once she'd turned round, Malik came up to her, running his fingers through Karen's hair, removing her hair clips. Satisfied, he stood back, already relieved she was secure and couldn't run, only shuffle, with nothing on her that could injure him or Samir, although he still kept his distance from Karen, watching her every move. "Put the dress on, we leave shortly," he said.

For the next few minutes, neither said anything. Then they both heard the noise of a vehicle outside, followed by the quick sound of its horn.

"Samir is here, pick up your backpack, we go."

Karen took hold of one of the backpack straps and began shuffling forward, her movements restricted by the very short chain between the ankle irons. Malik turned towards the door, in order to pull it open, taking his eyes off Karen for only seconds. For Karen that was enough, it was time to make a break, or allow these men to take her. The alternative, once secured in the vehicle outside, didn't bear thinking about, particularly if they went through her backpack and found out who she really was. Close behind him, she swung the backpack at Malik, landing a blow to the small of his back. Normally, a few clothes in a backpack would have just sent him reeling, before he retaliated, maybe even using his gun to protect himself. However, with over ten kilos of coins in the bottom, for Malik, it was like being hit in the back with a brick. It knocked the wind out of him and sent him completely off balance, the gun going one way, he the other. Karen followed him, again hitting him with the backpack, but this time across the head. Now, with him completely disorientated, she'd picked his gun up.

By the time Malik recovered, Karen was standing looking down at him, his gun in her hand. "You have the bloody nerve to calmly tell me I can't go home and have me strip, because a piece of shit like you believes you can just take a woman off the street and put them up for sale? If that's your belief, then you're more stupid than you look. As it is, I'm now in control and holding your gun with a silencer fitted. Where's the keys to the ankle irons?"

He pulled a key from his pocket and threw it at her. "Samir will never let you leave. He will bring more men. You should give up, I'll not tell Samir you tried to escape, otherwise he'll whip you," he told her.

Karen picked the key up and released the irons. She looked up at him. "Give up? In your dreams, little man. Get over to the far wall and sit down, your hands under your bottom. We'll wait for this man called Samir to realise you are not coming out. I warn you though. I'm of a military background, trained in the use of weapons. Don't for one moment believe you can take me on, I will shoot to kill, have no doubt. So when Samir comes in, you keep your mouth shut, or I will kill you."

When Samir did come in, minutes later, Karen was standing a short distance from the door, leaning against the wall, the gun in her hand, but hanging down out of sight.

He glanced at Karen, who was still wearing the dress, then at Malik, sitting on the floor. "I've been waiting outside, didn't you hear me? We should leave immediately," he said, talking in their own language that Karen couldn't understand.

Malik said nothing, apart from moving his head very slightly, his eyes glancing towards Karen, then back to Samir.

However, whether Samir understood or not, Karen

cut in. "Whatever you said to your partner here, Samir, you'll find he has a problem. He cannot talk to you, because if he does, he's dead," Karen said quietly.

"What are you talking about, I recognise you as the woman I took from my brother's house, who was purchased by Zaki. You will be put up for sale again, so put those irons on, before I whip you into submission," Samir replied in English.

Karen just shook her head slowly. "You don't get it, do you? I'm owned by no one. In fact, I'm in charge here, not you, or your partner."

He looked at her for a moment, not understanding her arrogance. "We'll soon see about that, " Samir came back at her, at the same time reaching into his pocket to pull out a gun.

The next moment Karen raised her gun and fired at Samir, directly into the top of one of his legs. He screamed and fell to the floor rolling about in agony.

"Bit bloody stupid that, Samir, shouldn't you have asked the simple question as to why he might die, or do you think so little of women that they can never be a threat? Now take the weapon out of your pocket very carefully, using only two fingers, then throw it towards me. Any attempt to try using it and you will find I'm a very good shot, the next bullet will kill you."

He did what she asked, holding his leg and glaring at her. "Kill me and you will never leave the country. My people will hunt you down, no matter where you go," he mocked.

"Oh! I'm really scared now. I think that would make it over a hundred different groups chasing me across the world, with the same thoughts. But to do that, wouldn't they need to know who to look for, in particular who I really am?"

"What are you talking about?" Malik cut in.

She shrugged. "Ikram, Nabil and maybe you too, would have known me as Tori. It isn't my actual name. I'm part of a military unit called Unit T and I often go covert. Unfortunately, you've got yourself mixed up in one of my covert operations."

Samir laughed. "You're military, what fantasy world do you live in? You were a whore living in my brother's house. Besides, Unit T would never be in Algeria. So get out and start running, we'll even give you a head start, before we come after you."

"It's good you believe that I'm not part of Unit T, so will others in this country." Then she glanced at her watch. "It's time I left to board the ferry. I'm glad you had the decency to come and see me off before I leave, I'd have been really pissed off just killing Zaki for taking me to the brothel and missing the sellers. As it is you owe me, it's time to pay," Karen said indifferently as she raised the gun and shot him through the heart. Then picking Samir's gun up, she shot Malik.

Discarding the dress and stuffing it into her backpack, Karen quickly changed into her own clothes. Finally pulling her hair back, she put her baseball cap on, threading her hair through the opening in the back. Once ready, she cleaned her fingerprints off Malik's gun and put it in his hand. Then fired it once, to leave powder residue on his hand. Doing the same with Samir, she was now satisfied that from a cursory inspection it would seem the two had shot each other. Leaving the room, Karen pulled the door firmly shut, wiping the handle to remove any fingerprints. Returning to the ferry terminal, she purchased a ticket. Keeping among others with backpacks, who were already queuing to board, it was soon Karen's turn for the official to look at her ticket and check the passport in the name of Tori. He seemed satisfied and let her through.

Finding a window seat in the main lounge, Karen settled down with a can of coke. Her relief was all too apparent when the ferry finally sailed. The last weeks had been the worst she'd ever experienced. Although she had a quiet satisfaction that many of the perpetrators were dead.

"Are these seats taken?" a lad asked.

She looked up at him, he was around twenty-five, by his side was another lad of similar age and a younger girl.

"No, they're empty," she replied, then turned to look out of the window. Karen was more than happy they had joined her. She no longer felt out of place.

The girl was sitting at her side. "You don't know when we arrive, do you?" she asked Karen.

"Ten tonight, according to the timetable. Are you on holiday then?"

"Yes, we've been doing a bit of backpacking, it's been fun, except people are not very nice. I think they believe we're vagrants. We're not, just taking a year out after university before we all look for work. What about you?"

"The same."

"God, on your own, I wouldn't. They don't think much of women in that country. You have to be unseen and not heard."

Karen smiled. "You could be right there."

The three of them carried on talking, leaving Karen out. She was happy with that and closed her eyes.

***

After an hour, Karen stood. "Will you keep my place, I'll be back soon?" she asked.

"Yes, no problem," the girl replied.

Karen went through to the purser's office, joining a small queue. "I need to make a telephone call, do you have any facilities?" she asked when it was her turn.

The woman pointed to a booth. "You may use that. It uses standard telephone credit cards, would you like to purchase one?"

Karen purchased a card, went to the booth and pulled the door shut. She called Unit T, giving her access code number.

"Karen, we were getting worried, you've been missing a long time, where are you?" Stanley asked, once she had been put through to him.

"I'm on a ferry due into Almera in Spain at ten tonight. I need an aircraft to pick me up at Almera airport."

"I can send yours with Sherry, Karen?"

"That's fine, have Sherry meet me at the ferry terminal. I'm on the ferry from Ghazauoet in Algeria."

"No problems. Is there a reason why you're on that ferry?"

"A bloody good reason and the surveillance teams have some explaining to do. I'll talk when I get back."

Karen didn't at first return to her seat, collecting a sandwich and cake for later. Already, after talking to the unit, she felt better and not so alone.

***

Sherry flung her arms around Karen and hugged her tight. "God I've missed you. Where have you been Karen, you've been gone ages?"

"In a bloody brothel. Let's get out of here shall we?"

They said little in the taxi, but once on board the

aircraft and on their way, with Karen at the controls, they had time to talk. Both girls had large paper cups of hot coffee which they'd brought on board. Sherry had also brought sandwiches in case Karen had not eaten.

"Do you want to tell me about it?" Sherry asked.

"Not really, it was so demeaning, but I need to tell someone. It goes no further Sherry and will never show up in a report. I couldn't live with myself if it got out."

"It won't come from me, Karen, believe me. But I would like to know just what happened and what you went through."

For the next hour, between munching on the sandwiches, Karen went through from when she left Luca to the ferry crossing. Karen fell silent, then looked at Sherry. "Would you believe I was at the point of actually accepting I'd never escape, prepared to just settle down and work as a prostitute, besides actually looking forward to my next client?"

She reached over and touched Karen on the hand. "I know what you went through Karen. Twice now I've been in a brothel, servicing client after client for weeks, so I know what goes through your mind. To believe you're the same as the other girls while you are there makes it easier, except the reality is, you were like me, surviving in the only way you knew how under the circumstances, so whatever your thoughts while there, it was gang rape. Although the conditions in the brothel you ended up in, sound a thousand times worse than what I ever endured."

Karen sighed. "I suppose it served as a wake-up call for me, Sherry. I need reminding sometimes why we do what we do. The only consolation is that a least Ikram is dead and maybe because of that a number of women will avoid what I went through." Karen had not admitted to Sherry how many she killed to escape.

"He deserved that. What of the documents from Ikram's safe, do you think they will have value?" Sherry asked.

"I hope so, I'd hate it to have all been for nothing," Karen replied. "Most of the documents I can't understand, because of the language. There is a number of bank statements from a bank in Germany, with a German the address at the top. They could have value. Then Ikram dealt a lot with Luca, so I'm hoping we'll get mileage out of that business relationship. That's before I kill Luca."

"You're that mad with him then?"

"Just a little, but believe this, if we don't pull him down and he doesn't go away for ten years, I will kill him."

She smiled. "I'd do the same. What of the money you brought back?"

Karen had only mentioned the currency bundles and not the gold coins, wanting to play down just how much she had come out with. "I earned every cent of it, Sherry. No compensation award would ever cover that experience, believe me. Although it will all go to my charity." Then she grasped Sherry by the hand. "Will you come to Paris with me? I'll have to go and be checked out medically, I'm not talking to the doctor in the camp."

"Course I will. We should go sooner, rather than later."

"I know, once Stanley has all the documents, we'll go. If anyone asks, it's a clothes trip."

Sherry laughed. "Who's going to ask?"

Chapter 45

When Karen entered Stanley's office, she was obviously annoyed. "So where the hell was my back-up, Stanley. Have you any idea what I've had to go through in that godforsaken country?"

"I haven't unless you're prepared to tell me, Karen. But for a start, please sit down and calm yourself. We were fully aware of where you had been taken. In fact, two of our lads were in Algeria after we had tracked Ikram's aircraft to an airport in the country. It then left a couple of days later and is in Germany. Once we'd confirmed you were not on the aircraft, when it left Algeria for Germany, it took a week and a lot of bribing in Algeria to find where Ikram actually lived and another day to get to the house. According to the lads, once they arrived, they found there had been a massacre. The place had been stripped of its contents, there were bodies everywhere and everyone had left. We were at a loss as to what had happened to you, then more importantly if you were still alive. We still believed you were, because we couldn't find your body among the dead at Ikram's. The only lead we had was that Ikram had a brother called Samir, who trafficked. He apparently ran auctions out in the desert, selling the women he'd brought in. We suspected maybe Ikram had already sold you to his brother for sale in his auction. By him doing that, you'd avoided the massacre, but we could get no leads as to who purchased you."

"So did they give up and go home?" Karen asked.

"We never gave up, Karen. We looked for this Samir, but he was elusive and we had difficulty in finding people to talk about him. We did find out Samir ran auctions every three to four weeks. It was our intention to go to one of them and snatch this man, then beat out of him what happened to you. Only yesterday did the lads call to say they had the date of one of his auctions and where it was being held. They intended to go to that auction."

Karen sighed, already embarrassed for blowing up as she had. "I'm sorry for getting upset, Stanley, it seems you were trying to find me. Thank you for that. In fact, I did escape the brothel I was sold to and returned to Ikram's house." This admission was in line with how Karen had intended to report, again as with Sherry,with no intention of admitting she killed the man at the brothel, or Zaki. Neither did she intend to admit to the killing of Samir and his partner. "I, like the lads, found it had been stripped. Fortunately, I'd hidden my documents before I was taken from the house, so that's why I went back. I also found among the rubbish left, a key to his safe. I've a book and a number of documents I took from the safe," she said, handing the bundle to him. "It's all in Arabic, apart from some of the loose documents, one I believe is the bill of sale for his aircraft, including its title document. I want to know if we can take it? There are also statements from a German bank with an address in Germany. I'd like to know what that property is. As for the rest, I've no idea how important it all is. Can you get it translated and reviewed. I think I'll go home, get myself cleaned up and changed into something more in keeping and just chill out."

"I agree, we'll talk tomorrow."

"No, I'm in Paris with Sherry, we'll be back the following day."

He didn't comment. He knew she had a doctor in Paris, often preferring to use her rather than the camp doctor. That would mean she'd had a bad time, not that she would ever tell him how bad it had been.

***

Walking into her house, Karen went directly to her office, dropping the backpack containing the rest of the contents of Ikram's safe, while she went up to shower and change. The sun was out, so soon she was in the pool doing her usual twenty lengths. She failed, the weeks had taken their tole and managed only twelve. After her swim, she flopped down on a sunlounger.

Twenty minutes later Sherry arrived with Ally, running round the house to the pool area. "Hi, have you eaten?" Sherry asked.

"No, I've been waiting for you two. Early night tonight. We need to be up at half four, we leave at six in the morning, it's the only slot I could get into Paris."

"That's fine."

"Am I going as well?" Ally asked.

"Sorry, Ally, not this time, it's business," Karen said. "We'll be back the following morning. But I will take you for a very long weekend soon."

"No problems. I'd not want to be sitting around while you two are in meetings, I'll wait for when we can blitz the shops. Have I time for a swim before dinner?"

"If you get your skates on, you have," Sherry told her.

Ally ran back to the house.

"How's she doing?"

"She's good and has settled down well. Talks to her grandparents a lot and the school headmaster said she's really bright for her age."

"They all seem to be these days."

"Yes, not like I was. Anyway, while we're in Paris, Karen, my clothes are looking a bit dated so a couple of dresses wouldn't go amiss. Do you think we will have time to look around?"

Karen looked at her. "You spend money?" she hesitated. "Oh, I see it now, you're still going out with James."

Sherry sat down on the sunlounger alongside her. "I am seeing him, not often, but he wants us to go to the coast for a weekend, so I just wanted something better than wearing jeans all the time. You're not mad at me are you?"

"In what way?"

"Me going out with a lad and not going to the coast with you."

"No, why should I be? I've told you lots of times to get out with others your own age in the camp and enjoy yourself."

Sherry had fallen silent for a moment. Karen lay back and closed her eyes.

"What's happening with Parker and this man Luca?" Sherry asked.

"I've a meeting on Wednesday to assess the information coming out from the listening devices I planted. While I can pull Luca in for trafficking, I'm more interested at the moment in what deal those two are cooking up, but with me being away so long, they could already have done the deal by now."

"So we won't be doing the Tori, Charlie bit again?"

"No, they're dead, Sherry."

"Thank god, I really didn't like it, Karen. I felt so vulnerable and out on a limb."

"We were, it was too far out."

"Right, I'm off for a shower, I'll see you in the dining room in half an hour," Sherry said, at the same time standing.

At that moment, Ally came running through from the

house in her bikini, taking a dive directly into the pool.

Karen and Sherry looked at each other.

"Were we like that at Ally's age?" Sherry asked.

Karen laughed. "I would have been, if we'd had a swimming pool at home. In the local baths you'd have got thrown out arriving in a bikini as brief as that."

"I think you're right there, I'd have been thrown out as well. I'll see you at dinner."

While Ally was swimming, Karen slipped a dress on and went through to her office. Emptying the backpack, she pulled the bottom out and removed the currency and gold. Taking it through to her inner room, she pulled open the safe. Standing there she looked inside. It was obviously getting out of hand; it contained stacks of currency, a considerable number of gold bars and packets of diamonds. Now she was putting even more gold and currency in there. Except for Karen, this was not all she had, she had also aquired more from previous operations. In London there was a safe deposit box with nearly a million pounds in value. While she wanted to funnel a large amount into her charity - after all, most of the money was earned on the backs of the people who had been trafficked - she couldn't see a way she could actually pay it in. Maybe a few hundred thousand, but millions, that was a real problem, as first the gold and the diamonds would need to be sold. Closing the safe, she went through to the office, collected her backpack, refilled it again with her clothes and took it through to the kitchen.

The housekeeper looked up from her preparations. "Are they for washing, Lady Harris?"

"Yes, if you don't mind? Check them carefully, any that are ripped or not worth washing, throw away." Then she placed the backpack in a corner and pulled out her lap dancing skirt and jacket. "Will you treat these very specially for me please? Maybe we should send them for dry cleaning?"

She took them off Karen and looked at the labels. "I agree with you, it is advisable. I must say the style is not what I've come across before. Except together they look very smart, daring and I might say, sexy. Did you wear them for a fancy dress party?"

"Sort of, and they hold a lot of memories for me, so I don't want to damage them."

She just smiled. "I understand."

Karen nodded and left the room.

Chapter 46

"I can't believe it, you're telling me we have nothing?" Karen asked, after listening to Stanley's reports.

"You know the bugs only last around thirty hours, Karen," Stanley reminded her. "Then, you have been missing for nearly four weeks. After you left the house with Ikram, Luca was there until the Sunday. Then he left for Holland, before heading to London and meeting Parker. Following that meeting, both he and Parker effectively dropped off the radar, surveillance lost contact with them. This big deal they were setting up, may or may not have already gone ahead. The listening devices are just not good enough for a protracted surveillance operation. They were good to find out where you had gone, not that we could do much for you. Then in hindsight, you should never have got on the aircraft, knowing the real problems we would have in keeping track of you."

"That may be, but this was a new lead to follow and I did believe I was heading to Holland, not Algeria."

"With respect, Karen, it was the height of stupidity. Since when in the past would you have fallen for that? I also believe you've paid very heavily for that mistake, because of the time you were incarcerated and by the way you're playing it down."

Karen couldn't argue with Stanley's assessment. She'd been a fool and knew that. But she tried to put a brave face on it. "You're right, I wasn't thinking. I'd been drugged and didn't come around until we'd arrived. Anyway, still staying with my abduction, did you at least get the discussion between Luca and Ikram agreeing to take me? That would allow us to tie Luca in with it?"

"No, we didn't. I suspect they'd already discussed your fate, before you were able to plant a listening device in the sunken outside pool area. Our first confirmed indication of your leaving was your discussion with Luca, who was asking if you'd go to Ikram's get-together, when you agreed to go. The next indication was when you pressed the button of your watch indicating you were on the move. But you didn't press three times to send out a distress signal. If you had, we'd have come for you, so it was assumed you had it under control."

"What about the documents I've brought back? Don't tell me those are useless as well?"

"Truthfully?" he asked.

"Of course."

"Then they're a waste of time for us. The book lists dealings in Algeria, are mainly with buyers across in Morocco. I would suggest the Algerians and maybe the Moroccan governments would be interested in them, for use by their intelligence units, not us. The German connection has possibilities as to the impounding of assets in Europe. The address is an apartment in an expensive area. We will, if we go down the correct route legally, be able to obtain the bank account details and impound on your behalf. You're the only person we know he trafficked, unless others come forward. With Ikram dead, we will get no opposition from him. Unless a member of his family object, but that will be unlikely. According to what we found out, while tracking your whereabouts, as I told you, he had a brother called Samir, except this Samir has been accused by the Algerian government of trafficking and is under investigation himself. The aircraft would be the same. We have, as you know, its bill of sale and ownership documents. Again through the legal process, we could take the aircraft."

Karen sat quietly for a moment. It seemed it hadn't been reported that Samir was dead. She was now wondering how long it would be before the bodies were discovered in the disused building. "Can you get me an appointment with the correct officials at the Algerian embassy? Don't tell them what we have at this stage, I'll play that side of things by ear. If the documents have value and can help in their own investigations, I'd like that to happen at least. My end seems a complete disaster."

"I'll do that. Will you be going to Germany and looking into the apartment and the other leads you originally had?"

"I will. I want back-up, but low key and not obvious. Also, can you talk to the technical boffins, see if there's better surveillance equipment available for future operations. As for Ikram's aircraft, can you talk to legal and have them obtain an official release? Have him do it on the basis it's evidence and will be kept secure, pending our investigation? I'll take two pilots to Germany, they can bring it back."

"You think there will be a claim?"

"I don't know, but if there is, I want to know all about it. If we hold the asset, whoever claims, or their legal team will have to come through us. Then the very fact Unit T is holding it will send out alarm bells that Ikram must be under investigation for trafficking. Many will keep away from getting involved and admitting they're something to do with Ikram."

Stanley smiled to himself. Karen was angling to keep the aircraft for herself. He doubted she'd pull it off, but she could well do if no claim was made. Although he suspected the Algerian government might make a claim, if they could prove it was acquired through Ikram's smuggling and trafficking operation outside the EU border.

"What are your plans for Ally, Karen?"

Karen smiled. "You mean short of adopting her?"

"It's a thought, she's really settled here. But seriously, both her grandparents, on her mother's and father's sides, are already making noises, wanting their granddaughter home."

"I can understand to a degree, with both Musowa and Ricky dead. However, Kenneth Parker is still active and so is his sidekick Sedrick Main and we know Musowa or Ricky were not responsible for firing the house." She fell silent for a moment. "In a couple of months she'll be at an age to choose where to live. I agree though, she'd be far better with relatives. On the downside, do I believe she's still at risk? I do, even if Parker may feel he's made the point of destroying her home, her family. The man is psychotic enough to snatch her again, if it became common knowledge she was back home."

"So you're going to say no?"

Karen shrugged. "Not if she wants to go, I won't. Except both her and her relatives must understand how we view the current risks. Is our legal department sorting out the insurance claims and other legal matters?"

"We offered, but the grandparents have got a solicitor and have virtually taken over. The parents died intestate, so they have all registered independent claims, believing substantial compensation may be forthcoming."

Karen sighed and shook her head slowly. "It figures, where money is concerned, the child no longer matters. So I presume they really want her back to show they're supporting her?"

"In a nutshell."

"I'll look into it, in the meantime, I'll talk to her. What else have we got?"

He smiled. "You mean apart from all the reports

backing up in need of your signature, soldiers waiting for you to agree their entry into Dark Angel, and a hundred other day-to-day decisions?"

"Yes."

"Then no, it's now mundane hour, Karen."

***

Karen wandered into the camp's main dining hall. It was crowded, except when she entered all the soldiers came to attention. Their commanding officer didn't usually come in here. If the officer's club was closed, which it was during the day, there was a private dining room in the command suite.

She just nodded to them to carry on, before going across the dining room to join Sherry. Two other girls were with Sherry. They quickly moved, leaving Sherry alone.

The chef in charge of the dining room came across. "Will you be dining, Commander?" he asked.

"Yes please, whatever the special is will be fine, and a soft drink," she replied, sitting down.

Sherry smiled. "You're really spooking everyone, Karen, keeping turning up unannounced."

"It's my camp, well, as the commander it is. But forget that, we need to talk."

"What about?"

"Algeria was a disaster as far as intelligence was concerned. I spent time in that brothel for nothing. The banker who asked you out, are you still in touch?"

"Yes, you told me to be. He mails me often, wanting to know when I'm back in London. You want me to make contact?"

"I do. I've got to pick up the pieces and hope what I can find leads me to Luca and Parker again."

266

They fell silent when Karen's dinner was brought across by the chef. She thanked him and they were left alone.

"I'll mail him, say I'm back for the weekend and see if he's free."

Karen said nothing for a moment, while she tucked into her dinner, then looked up at her. "You realise he'll be expecting to see Charlie? I know I said Tori and Charlie were dead, but I'm really at my wits' end on this. I also know you're going out with James. If you don't want to do this, tell me, don't think you need to go under duress."

"I know that, Karen. He'll also be expecting a lap dancer, very used to taking her clothes off. Like I've said many times, it's what we do, so I'm no prude. Anyway, James and I aren't serious, we just go out and have fun. So where are you off to?"

"Belgium. There's a girl there named Roos. She works for Luca and we got on well. I'm going to look her up."

"You're taking back-up aren't you?"

"I am. So will you. There's no way I'm risking you being taken, Sherry."

Carrying on eating, Karen finally pushed the plate away. "You know, I'd forgotten how good the food was in here. I should come more often."

Sherry grinned. "Rubbish, it's the crap you've been fed on in the brothel, anything will taste good after that. Mind you, yours looked far better than what was on my plate. Do you have some sort of pull around here I don't have?" she mocked.

Karen looked at Sherry for a moment as if in thought, then shook her head. "No, what pull do I have? How about you collect us both a pudding, then see if mine's different?"

Chapter 47

Sherry, with her hair styled differently, her make-up heavier around the eyes and red lips, was back to being Charlie. Wearing a light coat, with a short, slightly flared dress underneath six-inch high heels, she entered an upmarket restaurant in Chelsea.

The head waiter approached. "Good evening, Miss, you have a reservation?"

"I'm meeting a Mr Aizenburg, has he arrived?"

The man gave a hint of a smile. "He has, would you like to follow me?"

They went through the main restaurant and into an open corridor. Halfway down, the head waiter knocked on a door and went in, Sherry following.

"Your guest has arrived, Mr Aizenberg," the head waiter announced, then left the room, pulling the door shut.

Sherry looked round the small, intimate dining room, the table laid out for two. In the corner were a settee and easy chair, with a small coffee table between them. Another door led off the room. The man she'd arranged to meet was Meir Aizenburg, a banker, aged forty-six, tall, thin, with a rugged complexion. For lots of women he would be handsome, but to Sherry, no matter how good-looking, he was far too old for her, so she wasn't interested beyond her assignment.

He immediately came up to Sherry and embraced her, kissing her on each cheek. "Charlie, it's good to see you again, thank you for agreeing to join me for dinner," he said, at the same time helping her out of her coat.

"It's good to see you again, Meir, isn't this a little over the top, a private room? I'd be quite happy eating with other diners."

"No, this is perfect, I rarely go into the main dining area these days, preferring more intimate dinners."

Collecting two drinks, already poured, off the small table, he handed her one. "So have you been very busy in Spain?"

"I would have been if Tori had come, but she didn't, so it's been really hard. That's why I'm back in London. I'm thinking of looking for work in the clubs here."

"Yes, I heard she decided to go and stay with a man called Ikram, he lives in Algeria I believe. But you don't want to mess around in the clubs around Soho, they're not your class, Charlie."

"That may be, but I still have to eat, pay for somewhere to live."

"Let me think about it, in the meantime, let's enjoy the evening."

***

The dinner went well, the talk general. Now they were both sitting together on the settee with coffee and a glass of brandy.

"Perhaps a little dancing would be in order for the remainder of the night, Charlie?"

She smiled. "I'm always up for dancing."

"That's good, where are you staying?"

"I've borrowed a flat in Mayfair. It belongs to the family I met in Spain, I got on really well with their daughter. They're still there for the next month, so when I said I was going to London, they insisted I use the flat, rather than waste my money, while I found somewhere. It's really upmarket I can tell you. I feel like a millionaire just walking up to the door."

"Mayfair, that is upmarket."

"So how are you doing? Is the banking business really busy then?"

"It has its ups and downs, like any business. I myself don't do the sharp end of banking, I invest money for discerning clients."

"So if I had money, I'd give it to you and you'd invest it?"

He shook his head. "Not really that low level, Charlie. I invest minimum blocks of a million, although sometimes clients will get together and each put in, say, a quarter million and I will place the total."

"Then people want that sort of money? Like to buy a house or something?"

"No, that would be a mortgage. The people I broker money for are short-term, maybe a month or even up to a year, then they will be payed back with interest."

Sherry tried to look confused. "Is it in cash, where you take a big bag round like they do in the movies?"

"Hardly, most, if not all, is just shifted around interbank. Do you know how heavy a million pounds is in cash?"

Sherry frowned. "I can imagine, a thousand pounds can be a big bundle. So when we last met and Tori and I were entertaining you all, the guy Luca, running it, was using us to soft soap you all and was after all those millions?"

He laughed. "Something like that, but we don't discuss our clients."

"No, I wasn't asking you to, I was just trying to get my head around so much money and what you'd actually do with it."

"You'd be surprised why people want what you call such large sums. Anyway, it's time we hit the town, don't you think?"

As he helped Sherry on with her coat, she was in deep thought. If Meir was lending money to Luca, by what he said, he only dealt in the short term, so maybe Luca wasn't buying property or similar, he was being bankrolled short term, meaning it could be a drugs buy. Then, understanding what Meir's role was, Karen with her contacts, should be able to find where the money was going. Maybe even freeze the funds and place them all in real trouble.

***

Meir hadn't taken Sherry back to her flat, which in reality belonged to Karen, but to his own house. This turned out to be a mews house in Kensington. When she went inside, it was obviously expensively furnished.

"Drink, Charlie?" he asked.

"Yes, please."

He filled two glasses and came back to her. "I've had a good night, you can certainly dance, I could hardly keep up."

Sherry smiled. "I am only twenty-two, you know? So in this really posh house, have you any nibbles?"

"I think I can find something, take a seat, I'll be back."

As soon as he left the room, Sherry dropped a very small tablet into his drink. The tablet began disintegrating and by the time he returned with a plate of biscuits, there was no indication the drink had been spiked.

Meir switched some music on using a remote control, a took a seat by her side. Slipping his arm around her, he pulled Sherry close, kissing her long and hard. Sherry didn't pull back, this was why she was here. Finally, he broke away, picking up his drink.

"You really are a very attractive and intelligent girl, Charlie. Rather than work in the clubs, why not join me on my yacht next week? It's lying in Cannes at the moment. The film festival is beginning next week and it's the place to be seen."

"That sounds good to me, Meir, but I lap dance, would you really want to be seen with me in public?"

"If you were a prostitute, no I wouldn't. But a girl doing a little lap dancing in Spain, why not? We all have to live. Not that I'd like you to make it generally known among my friends there."

"Then yes, I'd love to go. Anyway, come on, drink up, I'm finished and want another."

By the time he had refilled the glasses and returned to sit at her side, his eyes were drooping. In a few minutes he was completely gone. Sherry pressed the button of her watch three times and walked over to the door, pulling it open. In less than a minute four lads were in the house with her. No one spoke, just went about their business, bugging every room. In an office where there was a safe, they fitted a tiny surveillance camera looking directly at it. This was in such a position that with anyone using the lock dial, the camera would record the combination. In addition, they took his mobile apart, scanned the contents and downloaded a programme via his SIM card. Now every call, every text would be monitored by Unit T. They would even be able to tell exactly where he was at any time.

"It's all done Sherry, what now?"

"I'll sort him from now on."

After they left she called the emergency services for an ambulance.

***

"We suspect he's had a mild heart attack, miss," the paramedic told her. "We'll need to take him to hospital."

"That's fine, can I come in the ambulance?"

"Yes, no problem."

Later in the hospital, Meir opened his eyes.

"Hi, how are you feeling?" Sherry asked.

"Where am I?" was all he could say.

"In the hospital, it was a good job I was there. One minute you were talking, the next moment you grasped your chest and just passed out, your body jerking, like really weird. They believe you've had a mild heart attack. Probably couldn't keep up with me."

"Then you saved my life?"

"I wouldn't go that far, you could have just woken up and called an ambulance yourself. I don't know. Anyway, you have to stay for twenty-four hours, then if everything pans out, you can go home. Do you have anyone I can call to collect you, or would you like me to come?"

"I have a sister, she will come for me. I can't thank you enough, Charlie. Can I call you about Cannes?"

"Of course, it sounds cool. Except I'll only hang on your arm, if you get the all-clear. I don't want you dying on me in bed. I'd not know how to explain that away to the police."

He smiled. "We'll see about that. Did you bring my mobile?"

"Yes, everything's in your drawer. Keys, wallet and phone and I locked the house up, before I left. Not the alarm, I didn't know how to do that."

"That's really good of you, thank you."

"No probs. I'll get off now, I'm knackered and need

sleep." She leaned over and kissed him on the lips. "Call me," she said, then walked away.

Minutes after Meir had got off the phone to his sister, when a nurse came in along with a doctor. "How are you feeling? Has Charlie left?" the doctor asked. "You're very lucky your daughter was with you, her quick thinking in realising what had happened probably saved your life."

"Yes, it seems that way," he answered, not correcting the doctor's assumption as to who Charlie was.

Chapter 48

While Sherry had been in London, Karen had flown to Brussels. Hiring a car at the airport, she made her way to the shop where Roos worked. It was after seven on Saturday night, so she knew the shop would be closed. Then, if Luca hadn't had her go around to his house, she would be in.

Parking, Karen walked round to the side door which she used last time, when Roos took her to the flat. Ringing the bell, she waited.

Soon she heard movement, then the door opened. "Hallo, kann ich wissen, oder?" Roos asked.

"Ich spreche wenig Deutsch können wir in Englisch sprechen?" Karen replied.

"Of course I can talk in English. But don't I know you?" Roos asked.

"You should, we did spend time together. Although I've changed my hair colour, it's Tori,"

Roos's mouth dropped open, then she flung her arms around Karen, hugging her tight. "I'm sorry, I really didn't recognise you. Your look is so different, come on up."

Karen followed her upstairs. "I've not come at a bad time, have I?"

"No, I closed the shop about half an hour ago."

By now they were in Roos's flat. Roos pushed the door to, and again pulled Karen close, this time kissing her gently on the lips, then more intensely, when she didn't pull back. "I've really missed you, Tori. I was shocked when Luca told me Ikram had booked you for the rest of the week. Then when he said you'd already gone, so I couldn't even say goodbye, or exchange numbers, it was really hard."

"That was the same for me, Roos. Luca told me after

breakfast that I was to collect my clothes and go with Ikram."

Roos broke away. "Then you must tell me all about it," she answered, walking over to her small stove. "Would you like to join me for dinner? It's only soup, but I've loads and won't eat it all."

"I'd love to," Karen replied. "But what about your flatmate, won't she want any?"

Roos shrugged. "She's not here any more. Luca opened another shop in Amsterdam and she's working there. He said it wasn't necessary to have two girls in his shops. I agree, we don't have the work, but she was company. Now all I do is wait till he calls for me to go round. That doesn't happen much. Anyway, take your coat off, make it look as if you're staying, soup's ready, pull a chair out for yourself."

Sitting opposite each other at a very small, round table, eating the soup with huge chunks of bread, Roos was urging Karen to tell her all about Spain.

"I never went to Spain, Roos. Luca sold me to Ikram, he took me to Algeria and held me hostage. I had to work during the day and entertain him in his bed at night."

She stared at Karen, obviously shocked. "The bastard. Don't get me wrong, I do know he has prostitutes working for him, but I always thought they were with him voluntarily, and he was their pimp. But to actually sell someone, who'd just come to entertain his guests, that's sick. Have you told the police?"

Karen shook her head. "They'd not be interested. I've only just managed to get out and back here."

"I don't believe what I'm hearing. Luca owes you big time for what he's done. Are you going to see him?"

"I'm not sure. When I was at Ikram's, he told me Luca needed the money he got for me. Apparently Luca, with a man called Parker, had a big deal going down and he had to come up with a lot of money. Do you know what it was and if they have actually done the deal? If they have, then maybe Luca won't be short and be willing to pay me what he owes?"

Roos thought for a short time, taking the opportunity to finish her soup. "I know this man, Kenneth Parker. He's a horrible person, treats you like shit, no matter how much you try to be sociable with him. Luca says he prefers very young girls, like eleven, even younger, so I shouldn't worry. He'd not be interested in me. But I think you may be right, they were working on something together. I was at the house to help out, the housekeeper was off. Anyway, I'd taken coffee into the room for them, Luca was worked up over something and was really rude to me. I wouldn't mind, but he'd asked for coffee, I hadn't done it off my own bat."

"Then you overheard what they were talking about?"

"No, but they had a pile of plans on the table. I'd asked if they could move them to one side, or if I should fetch a small table from the other room. Like I said, Luca took his frustration out on me. Then had me stand there while they clear the table."

"So you never found out what he was doing?"

She shrugged. "No, but the next week he told me there was a shop opening in Amsterdam, and that's where my flatmate went. So it must be something to do with that, I suppose."

"How is he now, Luca I mean?"

"He's okay, in fact, I think whatever it was all about, must have been sorted. He had me over to dinner last night." She shrugged. "I was there only to make up the numbers. He often does that, when he has friends over. I wasn't allowed to stay overnight, I was sent home around twelve."

Karen decided this was as far as she could go for the

moment, without Roos getting suspicious. While she liked the girl, she didn't trust her. Roos's life and so her allegiance must rest solely with Luca, she had no one else.

Roos collected the empty dishes, taking them over to the sink and rinsing them. "You've not got any other plans, have you, and you're going to stay tonight?" Roos asked.

"I'd not planned to stay, Roos. After all, I thought you lived here with your flatmate. I'm booked into a hotel and all my clothes are there," she answered, at the same time pushing the chair back under the table, then sitting on the settee.

Roos turned, dried her hands on a towel, before joining Karen on the settee. "Please stay, Tori," she urged, grasping her hand. "I've got a new toothbrush you can use. I'm so alone these days, not allowed out on my own. Not that I could go, if I wanted to, Luca doesn't give me enough to even eat properly. Then I belong to him so I can't accept dates."

Karen frowned. "How long should the soup have lasted, Roos?"

"Two days... but it really doesn't matter, I'll sort something, the traders on the market often give me extra. But if you stay, you'll have to buy the croissants for breakfast."

"You can't go on like this. It's time you broke away, maybe came with me."

She shook her head. "I can't do what you do. I had to lap dance the next two nights after you went. With you it was okay, I suppose, but alone I was so embarrassed and afraid Luca would finally push me away, perhaps sell me on. Even the housekeeper has stopped talking to me."

"Thanks, Roos, you really know how to make a girl feel bad."

Roos looked embarrassed. "I didn't mean it that

way. You've got a fantastic body and know how to show it off, even deal with the clients. I've lived a life completely different to yours. I've only ever had one man, worked in this shop and wouldn't know how to survive on my own. To stand naked in front of men, besides simulate intercourse, was so alien, I threw up once I was back in the bathroom...." she hesitated. "I suppose by you turning up here, you hoped I'd come with you, become a lap dancer? Now you know I won't, you'll not want to be my friend, or stay around?"

While Karen had no intention of forming a relationship with Roos, she still believed she needed her to break further into Lucas's operation. With this in mind, the last thing she wanted was to alienate the girl. "If you're happy here that's fine, I'm not making it a condition of our friendship that you come with me. Except I won't be able to come round much, it's expensive to get here from Spain, or London. But I do want us to remain friends, I really do."

"Great, we should celebrate. I've a bottle of wine I've had for ages, given me by a regular to the shop. We'll open it and get a little drunk."

"No, you keep it, I'll go and buy a couple of bottles that will get us really drunk, shall I? I can't remember the last time I was drunk."

She grinned. "I like that idea even better, come on, let's go."

Chapter 49

It was the morning after Karen had come to Roos's flat. She was asleep, as someone began shaking her.

Karen stirred and opened her eyes. Roos was standing at the side of the bed, holding a cup; another cup she'd brought was on the table by the bed.

"Come on sleepyhead, I've made coffee, move up, it's bloody cold standing around like this."

Karen took the cup gratefully and moved over. "God, I've not been as drunk as that for a long time."

"I'm with you there," she answered, sliding in alongside Karen and picking up her own cup, sipping the coffee slowly.

"I don't remember much of last night, how about you?" Karen asked.

"Not a great deal, apart from helping you into bed. Then I woke up this morning, bloody freezing, with you hogging the duvet."

"Sorry about that, I'm not used to sharing a bed, particularly when out of my mind on alcohol. Anyway, I need the toilet and a shower."

"Then use my robe hanging on the back of the door, it can be cold in the shop once the heating goes off, besides, there are cameras that keep recording. You don't want to be caught on one of those just in your knickers, they monitor it back at Luca's house. The shower's down the next flight of steps, in the cellar. You'll find a towel and soap, but run the water, it's one of those instant ones, so it does eventually get hot. There's a new toothbrush in a packet above the sink. The other girl forgot to take it, when she left. There's no cameras in the cellar, so you're all right there."

Once down in the shop and after using the toilet, Karen wanted to look around. But like Roos had said, as soon as she came into the shop area, she saw the cameras, positioned to look at the counter and the general area. Deciding not to go near the counter, she made her way down into the cellar. It was full of sealed boxes stacked alongside a passageway down the centre, ending up in a smaller room converted into a shower room, with a handbasin.

By the time Karen had come out of the shower, Roos was already cleaning her teeth over the basin. "So what do you think of my spread-out flat, with the toilet on one floor and the shower on another?"

"It's different, Roos, I'll give you that." At the same time rubbing herself dry with a large towel.

"You can say that again. If you leave the robe and keep hold of the bath towel, I can use the toilet. When you're dressed, we should go out for breakfast and maybe a walk in the park. If you don't mind paying, that is?"

"No, that's fine, I'll also need to go to the hotel, if you remember, all my clothes are there?"

Roos looked at Karen. "Will you be staying with me, or do you want to stay at the hotel? We won't be able to drink like last night, I couldn't afford it and I won't let you pay for everything. And then, I need to work the next day and not smell of drink."

While Karen had enough of men to last a lifetime, she wasn't sure about getting emotionally involved with a woman. However, Karen didn't want to bail just yet; if it meant sharing a bed with Roos, with the implications that came with that, she would. After all, she'd come to Brussels in order to take Luca down. Roos might well have information to help her do that, particularly after she told her a few more home truths about Luca.

"I'm only here for a couple of days, I need to work as well, Roos. But I'd love to stay with you. In return, I'll buy the food and whatever we both need. It'll be cheaper than paying for a room in a hotel anyway, so no arguments."

"Who's arguing, let's get dressed and make the most of my time off, shall we?"

*　*　*

The day had been good; following a simple breakfast, they walked, like Roos wanted, in the park. Then after going to the hotel and collecting her bag, besides checking out, they were now in a restaurant for dinner.

"I was surprised, Roos, you were still in the flat, I'd only come on the off-chance," Karen told her, now wanting to push the girl further.

"Why do you say that?"

"Luca told me, before I went with Ikram, that he wanted me to work you hard during our lesbian act, because you were having a change of lifestyle. At the time, I thought it was possibly marriage he was talking about, although marrying a girl after she'd stripped so many times in front of men, besides performing with another woman, seemed strange. But after he sold me, Ikram mentioned that Luca had offered you to him, but he rejected you, saying you were too young, that's why he took me. I suspected then that Luca still had every intention of doing the same to you and the real reason he had you dancing was he wanted you to show yourself off, so he could get a top price."

Karen saw a noticeable change in Roos. It was as if she'd hit a sore point. Except she suddenly just smiled. "He's always threatening me with such things. But deep down I have to believe he likes me and would do nothing to hurt me, provided I toe the line. I'm still here, Tori, even weeks after you were taken. I'd have gone by now if that had been the case."

"You are, but like I said, I didn't expect you to still be in the flat. Anyway, let's forget it and find a bar. Just one drink, as you said, you're working in the morning."

***

Later, Karen was lying in the bed, she had already been to the bathroom, Roos was still downstairs. While she was gone, Karen had taken the opportunity to read her mail using her smart phone. Stanley wanted her to call, it wasn't urgent, but he had more information on Ikram and wanted her to be aware of it. Then Sherry had mailed to say she'd written a report and needed to know where to go from there. Karen decided to call tomorrow while Roos was working.

Roos came in and hung the robe up before joining her in bed. Seeing Karen looking at her phone, she asked, "Anything interesting in your texts then?"

"Nothing that can't wait. Charlie's in London and wants to know if I'm going to join her."

"Are you?"

"No, not for a while."

She snuggled up to Karen. "You're really warm," she muttered.

"Yes and you're bloody cold."

"What do you expect, I've just come from the cellar? I'll soon warm, anyway, you still owe me."

"How do I owe you?"

"You bailed at Luca's, before I got my own back for your slapping my bottom as hard as you did, besides using that harness."

Karen looked at her. "That was ages ago and it wasn't intended; you can't still hold a grudge? But if you do, what will be my punishment?"

She gave a mischievous smile. "I could do the same to you, I'm entitled. But I'll think about that, now you accept you still owe me," she said, at the same time leaning over and kissing Karen. "In the meantime, can you still remember our time together, or am I just a blurred memory?"

Karen turned to face her, slipping her arm around Roos's back, then down to her bottom, pulling the girl closer. "If I'd really forgotten you Roos, would I have travelled hundreds of miles to come and see you?"

She shook her head.

"Then shut up and show me what you remember of our routine."

For the next twenty minutes, they made love. It was intense, demanding on their bodies, Karen more so, as she released her frustrations built up over the time she spent in the brothel. She was with someone she at least wanted to be with and who wanted her. Karen was also surprised at herself, that she could be bisexual and not feel uncomfortable with it. Finally they lay back, both exhausted. Roos as usual snuggled close to Karen.

"I'm really glad you looked me up."

"I am as well, Roos, we're good together, don't you think?"

"We are. I never want it to end, Tori."

"Me neither, Roos." Karen had lied, she knew it would end. Particularly when she had to finally leave Roos's world and return to Unit T and her own world. She closed her eyes, slowly drifting into a deep sleep.

***

The following morning, both girls were up early. Roos was finishing off her cereal and orange juice, while Karen made the coffee and buttered the toast.

When she brought both to the table, Roos looked up at her, she seemed worried. "I've been thinking, Tori, about what you said at dinner yesterday."

"We talked about loads, what in particular?"

"About Luca wanting to get rid of me, it's made me realise you could be right."

"Why do you say that? Like you said, you're still in the shop and now the other girl has gone, he needs someone here," Karen asked, confused.

"I know, but this Wednesday I'm to close the shop and go to the house. He said he'd people arriving from London. When I took the takings last Friday, he even gave me a dress to wear. If you saw it on me, you'd see it's really short, slightly flared, besides pushing my breasts up. He's not had me wear such a dress in front of visitors before, he's usually very fussy about what I wear. These visitors are pimps, and each run a number of girls. After what he said to you, besides the way he's treated me over the last week or so, I think he intends to sell me this Wednesday." She hesitated, obviously very worried. "I'm scared, Tori. Any one of these men would put me to work, not keep me to themselves like Luca has."

"So what do you want to do? I did say you could come with me."

She sighed. "I don't know. Let me think and we'll talk later. What are you doing today?"

"Probably a bit of shopping, do you want anything?"

"No, I close at four, will you be back then? Maybe you can pick up a pizza or something for dinner?"

***

After Roos had gone down to the shop, Karen left and, sitting in her car, she called Stanley.

"How's it going, Karen," he asked.

"It's interesting Stanley, I've met a girl called Roos, she was with me at Luca's. I'll send a full report, but on Wednesday, she's supposed to close the shop she runs for Luca and go to his place. Apparently he has a number of pimps over from London. She also has the feeling that Luca has a mind to offer her for sale. There's two points here. First, I want to know who these pimps are, which means we will need close surveillance. Second, if he really intends to sell her, then I'll have him for trafficking and we can move in. To that end, I'm putting a tracker on her dress. She won't know, but it will be there. Once I know which handbag she's using, I'll slide one of our surveillance devices in it somehow. I'd like to listen to the conversation, if feasible."

"I understand, I've talked to the surveillance team already there and will increase their presence. Will you be coordinating the operation?"

"No, I want to stand off for the present. Roos knows me as Tori, I don't want to change that belief. Unless she doesn't return to open the shop on Thursday morning, that is."

"I see, then you're more interested in the pimps, at this stage?"

"Precisely. They can't be small operators, to come over to see Luca. Which means we want to know who they are and where they operate from. What updates do you have on Ikram's affairs?"

"As you know we brought his aircraft back to the unit. We had to pay the outstanding parking fee and refuel

286

costs, to the airport. They were glad to get shut of it and had already taken steps in trying to get in touch with Ikram, with no success, after the pilot had told them he'd quit, as no money had been paid into his bank for his wages. Our legal team is about to place adverts announcing the impounding of the aircraft, based on Ikram's suspected involvement in trafficking, inviting interested parties to contact Unit T within ninety days. It will be interesting if anyone actually does, don't you think?"

"It will, have our legal people put in a claim against Ikram by me personally, via my charity? Also, can you find out about the pilot and where he lives. I've a mind to go and see him. He'll need money and if he knows Ikram's dead, he may be very receptive to talking to me."

Stanley smiled to himself, he'd suspected she would impound the aircraft. "I will find the pilot's address for you, Karen. We have also made an urgent application to suspend Ikram's bank account, in Germany, will you be visiting the address in Germany attached to the account?"

"Yes, later this week. How did Sherry do?"

"She did a good job. The house is bugged, so too is his phone. He's asked her to Cannes, on his yacht. She wants to know if she should accept?"

"For the moment, yes. Let's see what, if anything, the surveillance throws up, shall we?"

"I agree."

"I'll call Wednesday morning, once Roos is on her way to Luca's."

Chapter 50

"Roos, you look stunning love," Luca told her, at the same time kissing her on the lips.

She gave a weak smile. "I'm glad you like the dress, Luca, but it's not really me."

"Nonsense, you're the sort of girl, with the figure and looks, that can get away with wearing anything. Now come and join me for coffee, then we can talk about what I want from you, when my guests arrive."

They went through to the main lounge and sat down, after Roos had filled two cups from a coffee pot on a side table.

"So what have you been up to, Roos? I called you on Sunday, but you didn't answer."

"I went out for the day. I was on my mobile all the time. Was it important?"

"No, not important, I was going to have you over for the afternoon. So who did you go out with, not a man I hope?"

"God, no, I'd never do that, Luca. Well, not without asking you. You remember Tori, who taught me to lap dance, it was her."

Luca had just lifted his coffee cup, but froze, staring at her. "You've met Tori?" he gasped.

"Yes, she came Saturday night."

"Is she working around here?"

"No, she just came to see me, we got on well. You know she's a lesbian, so I think she has a thing about me. In fact, she wanted me to go with her to Spain. I don't think Charlie's with her any more. But I refused, I'm with you."

"Then you took her to your bed?"

Roos nodded.

"Where is Tori now?"

"Left this morning."

"You should have called me, Roos. You know you shouldn't have anyone staying at the flat without me knowing?"

"I'm sorry, I just didn't think."

"No you didn't, so if anyone else comes knocking at your door, you tell me. Did Tori mention Ikram, or me?"

"Yes, she said you owed her money and she intended to collect. Maybe she's coming here?"

"Why do I owe her money, did she tell you?"

Roos shrugged. "She told me some weird story that you'd sold her to Ikram and he wouldn't let her go for ages. When she escaped and with Ikram not paying for the time she was with him, she decided you owed the money, because you told her to go with Ikram."

"Bloody cheek, she'll soon learn I don't. Anyway the guests arrive at twelve. Help the housekeeper to lay the table and make sure the bar is well stocked. I don't want you in the kitchen getting your dress dirty. You will look after all their needs, besides keep the glasses well filled. There's one man in particular, Jason Main. He saw you at the New Year's Eve party, since then he's asked a number of times if you're available."

"And you said I was?"

"I said you don't have a boyfriend, so he's asked if I'd let you visit London with him. I think it would be a good thing, you've never been there and there's plenty to see. It'll do you good to get out of the shop for a month or so."

Roos looked down, sucking her lower lip, already she was nervous. "I want to stay with you. You are, and always have been my life, I don't want to go with another man."

"I'd believe that Roos if you had remained loyal, but it's sounding a bit hollow after spending the last few nights being fucked by Tori."

"You told me to go to bed with her."

"Yes, to learn a routine, not every time you two got together. So are you seeing her again?"

Roos nodded. "She said she'd call me when she was back in the area."

"So you're prepared to carry on a relationship with another woman, but are baulking because I've found you a man to be fucked by? You've not gone lesbian on me have you?"

"No, I'm just so lonely and I didn't think you'd object, with Tori and me being together before."

"Well, I do, so it's a good job I've come to your rescue. No more arguments, you go and don't you let me down by having one of your little paddies or anything else. Unless you want a reminder in the cellar before they come?"

She shook her head. "If you want me to go I will. Don't I need a passport, money, clothes and a suitcase?" she asked, clutching at straws, in the hope he'd forgotten she had nothing like that.

He smiled. "I will finance your trip, you can go in jeans and once there take time shopping for a simple wardrobe to suit your needs. As for a passport, you have one. If you remember, when you were nineteen and you did a photo shoot, for the shop, the photographer wanted you to stand for a more serious photo? That was used to apply for a passport. It's in my safe."

"When do I leave?"

"Tomorrow, Yannick will take you to the flat, so you can collect your personal items, such as toothbrush, whatever, then you go directly to the airport to join Jason on the eleven o'clock flight to London. Now clear off, find the housekeeper and sort the dining room out. Also, have Yannick come and see me."

Roos left the room, she knew it was pointless arguing. If that was what Luca wanted, she couldn't argue, it would only get him annoyed if she did. All she could hope was that the trip was what he said it it would be and not for her to be set to work with Jason as her pimp. How she now wished she'd accepted Tori's offer.

"Roos said you wanted me?" Yannick said, coming into the lounge.

"Yes, shut the door."

He did and took the seat opposite Luca.

"Roos has just told me Tori came to see her. How's that possible, Yannick?"

"It isn't, no one has ever escaped, if they did, Ikram would have been on the phone telling us. I'll call him."

Yannick pulled his mobile out of his pocket, selecting Ikram's number. With no response, he tried Samir, Ikram's brother. That rang for a short time, then someone answered in Arabic. Unlike Luca, Yannick could speak the language fluently. He talked for some time, then cut the call.

"Well, what did Samir say?" Luca asked, returning to his seat, after collecting a refill of his coffee from the coffee pot on the side table.

"It wasn't Samir, but Mohammed. Apparently Samir killed Ikram over some long-running dispute. He also said Tori was taken, along with Ikram's other women, by Samir and sold by him, some time back. Now it gets interesting. Nabil along with his brother Zaki purchased Tori for their brothel. She disappeared and a worker has been found with his head bashed in with a stone. Samir and his partner Malik were found dead yesterday, they'd been shot. Zaki, since leaving the brothel, has been missing and he's also presumed dead."

Luca lit a cigar and leaned back in thought. "Thinking aloud, Yannick, by what's being said, it seems to be pointing to the possibility that Tori killed them all, apart from Ikram?"

Yannick shook his head. "Tori! You met her, you tell me if she's a killer? Maybe the worker, particularly if he was fucking her against her will and she hit him with a stone. But Samir, Zaki, both well used to handling women, no matter how violent they are? She would have little or no chance."

"Then do we assume it's a set of coincidences and Tori escaped in the mayhem? Personally, I don't like coincidence. I'm moving closer to the idea she's a spy. So the reality is, she never shot her way out, or killed the worker, whoever planted her got her out. That I could accept, but it begs the question, who planted her and for what reason?"

"Such a scenario certainly begs the question, if she is a spy, plant, whatever you want to call her. She originally went to your meetings as entertainment, came to your house. Ikram wasn't in the picture. They, whoever they are, are after you, Luca. Then, with her being back in Brussels talking to Roos, it would seem you're still the target."

Luca stood and began pacing the room, then he stopped and banged the side table the coffee pot was on in annoyance, before walking over to the door, pulling it open. "Roos..." he shouted into the hall. "Fucking get in here quick..." he shouted once more.

Roos hurried through from the dining room. "You want me?" she asked, obviously scared by the way he'd shouted.

"Get your fucking clothes off," he screamed at her.
"Why?" she gasped.

"You don't fucking question me, get them off, or I'll rip them off you," he shouted.

Roos removed the dress.

"The fucking lot, I want you standing here naked," he demanded, snatching her dress from her and beginning to rip it apart.

By now Yannick had stood, he, unlike Luca, was far more calm. Walking over to the coffee table, he pulled open a drawer and removed a small electronic device, switching it on. With Roos standing naked, holding her underwear, he took it off her and quickly scanned it using the device. Then he ran the detector over her body. Luca, by now, had given up and thrown the dress to the floor. However, Yannick also began to scan the dress. Immediately the electronic device started to bleep.

Luca looked at the dress as Yannick lifted it up and soon found the tracker pushed into the lining. "Where's your handbag?" Yannick asked Roos quietly.

"In the dining room."

"Get it."

She hesitated, trying to decide if she should at least take her knickers, decided against it and ran out of the room, soon to be back with the handbag, handing it to Yannick. Immediately the electronic device began to bleep.

Luca grabbed Roos's arm and dragged her out into the hall. The housekeeper was just coming out of the dining room, she looked at Luca with Roos, but said nothing. In this house, whatever you saw, you kept your mouth shut.

"Take her to the kitchen and sit her down. Find her something to wear." Then he went back into his lounge, slamming the door.

"What have you done, Roos?" she asked her quietly.

"I don't know, he just had me strip and began

checking my clothes. But he'd given them me to begin with," she answered, tears already running down her face.

"Come on, let's find something for you to put on, shall we?" she said, taking Roos's hand.

Back in the lounge, Yannick was looking at the devices, after finding a way to shut them both down. "At least you know why Tori came to see Roos. She's bugged the girl, so whoever she works for is after you, Luca. These devices are also pretty sophisticated, pointing to a government department, rather than a competitor."

"Fuck. And we've got a load of pimps in later. How far would you say these items could transmit?"

"Only local, which means whoever it is, is already close by."

"Then increase the guards around the perimeter and see our escape route is unlocked. We can't stop the visitors now, but at least whoever was listening won't be able to hear any more."

"I'll sort it, what are you going to do about Roos?"

"Leave her to me."

***

A short time later, Luca went through to the kitchen. The housekeeper was busily cooking, Roos was sitting at the table, a glass of water in front of her, wearing a coat used by the cleaner.

Roos looked at Luca when he came in, she was obviously terrified, her hands shaking.

"Come with me," he demanded.

Roos followed him out of the kitchen, then Luca grabbed her hair and dragged her across towards the cellar door. She began to hold back, knowing what was about to happen. "Please Luca, tell me what I've done," she begged.

"You'll know soon enough, in the meantime shut up, or I'll gag you," he demanded, at the same time pushing the cellar door open and dragging her down the stone steps.

Soon they were in a room off the passage. Luca pulled her coat off and slammed her face down over the edge of a table in the centre of the small room. "Don't dare move, or I'll tie you down and add to your punishment."

Roos, bent over, her feet on the floor, she was resigned to a beating. Not that she could understand why.

Luca stood back, looked at her for a moment, before walking over to the corner, picking up a multi-strand whip leaning against the wall. Coming back to her, he got hold of her hair once more, turning her head to face him. "Your lover, Tori, planted listening devices on your clothing and in your bag, to spy on my affairs. Why would she do that, Roos? Could it be you opened your mouth and told her of my visitors due today? Maybe you've made a deal and are ready to bail? Maybe you're in love with her and agreed to do anything she wanted?"

"I don't know what you're talking about, what's a listening device, all I had in my bag was my make-up. I've got nothing else, Luca. As for going with Tori, I turned her down, I wanted to stay with you."

"You lie, let's see if we can loosen that tongue of yours?" Then he let go of her hair and hit her across the back with his whip.

Roos screamed in pain, tears streaming down her face, already wetting herself.

"Please I beg you, I would never lie to you, or do anything to hurt you. You're my life, Luca, I know no other."

Again he hit her, this time across her bottom. Again Roos was screaming. She wasn't a strong girl, and was now close to passing out.

He moved closer to her. "I can no longer trust you, Roos. You will go to London, while I decide your fate. Now, get yourself upstairs, tidy yourself up and find clothes to wear. Make sure you're down to meet my guests."

Roos stood, then turned to face him. "I don't understand what I've done, Luca. But if I'm not to be with you any more, then kill me. You owe that much to me for all my years of loyalty," she said quietly.

"I owe you nothing. Bringing Tori to your bed, you could have lost me this house, maybe my freedom, if I'd not found what Tori was up to. Death is an easy way out, Roos, but for you that is too easy. So unless you want more punishment, get out of my sight and do as you're told."

Roos said nothing more, just picked up the coat and left the room.

Chapter 51

Karen, after leaving Roos, flew to Berlin in her own aircraft. For the time being she could do nothing but wait until the pimps from the UK arrived at Luca's. She had set up surveillance, and with Roos's tracker along with the listening device, she hoped to be able to collect useful information. After arriving in Berlin, she changed from jeans to a smart, black trouser suit and white blouse, before leaving the aircraft.

Coming out of the airport, Sherry, along with Sergeant John West, who controlled a surveillance group for Unit T, were waiting. Sergeant West was five feet ten, twenty-seven, well built and married with two children. He'd been with Karen for six years.

Karen gave each one of them a hug. Out of uniform, there was never any formality, their greetings always as friends. Quickly they made their way to the car park.

"Well, what do we know, John?" Karen asked as they left the airport, with John driving, Karen in the passenger seat.

"The address, on the German bank statement, turns out to be an apartment on the eighth floor of a shopping and residential complex. It's rented by Ikram and occupied."

"When you say occupied, by whom?"

"Two girls around twenty. We have followed them a number of times. At first we thought they were meeting boyfriends, but they're not. The girls are escorts, pretty expensive ones at that, judging by the venues where they meet their clients."

"Well, it would have been expected of Ikram. I can't see him renting, or owning property in Germany, unless it was earning. How do they get their clients, have you found that out?"

"We have their mobile phone details from the provider and it turns out to be an agency. The agency employs two people with a registered address in Algeria."

Karen sighed to herself, why was it every lead they followed opened up more avenues? How she wished sometimes they could just come to a dead end and know they had closed an operation? "So if there are employees, it must be quite busy?"

"It is, Stanley has obtained the appropriate documents to allow us to tap their telephones. They send clients to around sixty escorts, across Germany, France and the Netherlands. They regularly advertise the services for both male and female escorts. On the face of it, they seem to be legitimate. The two girls in Ikram's flat are German citizens, both have the correct documents and even pay taxes."

"What about names? Who runs it?"

"Arif Fenton is the name listed as running the agency, the two employees are local women." John glanced at the car clock. "Stanley confirmed to me an appointment for you with the manager of the bank where Ikram had his account. It's in half an hour, but they would change the time if your aircraft had been delayed. We're only fifteen minutes away. Do you want to keep the appointment, or set it for another time?"

"No, I'll go now."

"That's fine. Sherry, can you pass the file to Karen please?"

She passed it forward and Karen spent the next ten minutes reading the report. Nothing was said while she read. Then she closed the file. "After you park up, wait for me in a bar. Depending on my meeting, I'll decide where we go from here."

***

"Colonel Harris, my name is Günther Apel," the bank manager said, at the same time holding his hand out, when Karen was shown into his office. "Please, may I arrange tea, coffee for you?"

"Coffee would be most welcome Mr Apel, I've come directly from the airport," Karen replied, shaking his hand.

Mr Apel nodded to the lady who had brought Karen into his office, she quickly left.

"Perhaps Colonel, we would be more comfortable on the settees?"

She didn't reply, but sat down, in seconds the lady was back with a tray containing two cups, a jug of coffee, with a plate of biscuits.

He poured the coffees, leaving Karen to add her own milk and sugar.

"I must say, Colonel, I was very surprised to receive the account suspension notice from our legal department, our client has conducted his affairs with us completely above board and never given any rise for concern."

"The world, Mr Apel, is not as people often perceive it. Law-abiding citizens to murderers, we all share the same planet. Neither you, nor I, standing alongside a murderer, abuser of children, model citizens, would be able to tell the difference as to which one was which. As it is, Ikram made his money by drugs and people trafficking, besides smuggling. He wasn't a nice man and in fact was particularly violent towards his victims. We can only fight back and hit a trafficker where it hurts, that is in his wallet. Any other punishment, including incarceration, is only temporary, eventually they're allowed out and will go on to reap the rewards of the suffering they caused."

"You're correct of course, most of us live in our own bubbles, never seeing the complete picture. I feel sad that a person of your age has been forced, since childhood, to live in such a world. Now, rather than waste your precious time, how we can I help?"

"Do you have the current status of the account?"

"I do. It is in credit to nine hundred and eighty six thousand euros. Payments are still coming in at the rate of around sixty thousand euros a week. However, we've already had a local business contact us asking why outgoing payments are not being made. Also, the landlord of an apartment here in Berlin has called to ask why the rent has not been paid."

"This local business, are you talking about the 'After Midnight Agency'?"

"We are, a Mr Fenton is the proprietor."

"I will see this man later today. I'll also arrange his banking to be under the control of Unit T, until the situation is sorted out. Have you had anyone contact the bank in regard to this account beyond the agency and landlord?"

He shook his head slightly. "No person has come forward with regard to the affairs of the account."

"I'm not really surprised, apart from the agency, those in the know about Ikram and his operations will stand well away if they suspect Unit T's involvement. They risk Unit T picking up their names and investigating their affairs, most would prefer we didn't, no matter how much money may be involved. I also understand there's a safe deposit box. You have received the official documentation for me to open the box?"

"I have and it is all in order. The courier from

head office has arrived and is waiting for you to sign for the package containing the client's spare key. We of course cannot accept the package, only you can."

"Then I should see him, without delay. I've a great deal to do today."

"Very well, if you would come with me, I'll take you to the safe deposit area. I also have the transfer papers ready for you to sign to transfer the funds out our client's account to Unit T's. Personally, in view of what this man has been up to, I'll be happy to see the account closed in its present form and your unit take control."

"I can understand that, Mr Apel, I live with it every day."

***

Karen was sitting in a small private room with the safe deposit box belonging to Ikram. In the box she found a considerable amount of share holding certificates, with not hundreds of shares held, but tens of thousands. She was beginning to understand just how much money Ikram was making in his illegal business. Along with these certificates was the lease for the apartment, and the agency building and partnership agreement. It would seem Unit T now owned seventy-five per cent of an escort agency. She smiled at the thought. In lots of ways she was disappointed that there was nothing else which could have directed her deeper into Ikram's activities, yet she'd have been surprised if there had been any. After all, he ran most of his operation from Algeria. If she could get at the bank account Ikram had in Algeria and maybe a safe deposit box there as well, perhaps they would have had more value in understanding what he was up to. Although her legal people were working on securing that bank account, she didn't hold out much hope.

***

A girl in her early twenties looked up from her desk when Karen entered the reception of 'After Midnight Agency'.

"Guten Tag, kann ich Ihnen helfen?" she said to Karen.

"Ich spreche etwas Deutsch, sind Sie Englisch oder Französisch understand?" Karen replied.

"I wished you a good afternoon, asking if I can help," the girl replied in perfect English.

"I was hoping the proprietor, Arif Fenton, was available, if not, how can I get hold of him?"

"Arif only sees ladies by appointment, I can make one if you want?"

"I think you should tell him. I'm here on official business. The name's Colonel Karen Harris of Unit T. "

Her mouth dropped open slightly. While she knew the name, she had never seen Karen's face, but wasn't going to risk the fact she wasn't who she said she was. Picking up the telephone, the girl talked for a minute in German. Replacing the handset, she gave Karen a smile. "If you'd like to go through the far door, Arif will see you," she said weakly.

Arif was a big man, at least six foot three, he was broad and obviously worked out, with his bulging muscles under a thin T-shirt. He didn't get up, but looked at her for a moment. "Helena tells me you are Karen Harris, from Unit T. If you're not and it's a con to get to see me, then clear off. Where's your ID?"

Karen pulled out her warrant card and showed it him.

"It would seem you are who you claim. I presume

302

then you're the people who have been fucking about with my bank account. Start to do things like that, girl, and I'd advise you to watch your back."

Karen took the seat opposite him on the other side of the desk. Their eyes met, hers were cold, lifeless, with no hint of fear. "I've lived with such threats since I was eighteen, many from some of the most powerful cartels in the world. They, like you, don't worry me. If you want to go down that route so be it, but you will lose everything, including your freedom, have no doubt. As it is, Ikram is dead, and so is his brother Samir. Ikram was involved in people trafficking; under EEC law I have impounded all assets within the EU, and this business is part of his assets. So you talk to me civilly, or you and the girl sitting outside can go home, I'll close you down immediately."

Arif was in some ways nervous of Karen, her was one of intimidation, often coupled with violence, and she would not have come alone. Her heavies would be outside awaiting her orders, although, that side didn't worry him - she'd have little chance in taking him on. Except if she persisted in stopping him using the bank, he'd have real difficulties. "Maybe I was a little upset, after all, we spent the last two weeks trying to find out what had happened to the banking arrangements. Lots of my girls rely on their income to live and are desperate. But it was good of you to come and tell me about Ikram's demise. He was a minor partner anyway, I'll make other banking arrangements, if you return the money belonging to the agency."

"No Arif, I have the legal agreement signed by you both, he owned seventy per cent, you are the minor partner. If you want to continue, that is okay with me. We will value the assets and you can buy me out, or I'll allow you to carry on trading, using one of our accounts. Either way I will send in auditors to check the accounts, and also check the business is operating legally. There is no negotiation, you accept what I say, or like I said, you and the girl can walk out now and I will close the business down."

"This is a legal operation, it is also my income," he said, hesitating. "I'll accept your conditions, but I will engage a lawyer to look into your claims."

She shrugged indifferently. "That's your right of course, you will be contacted later today with new banking arrangements. Expect auditors tomorrow and have all your books available. We have all the past banking details, so don't try to deceive us, otherwise you and I will fall out. I wouldn't advise that if you still want to work here," she said, then stood and looked down at him. "Normally I'd close everything, we're not here to run businesses, but I have a requirement under our charter to maximise the assets for Ikram's victims. On the face of it, this seems a well-run business, keep it that way. Once we have a value, buy us out, find another partner, if you wish, and you will have no problems with us."

Arif watched Karen leave, then lifted the telephone handset, dialling a number. He waited until there was an answer. "This is Arif, we need to talk urgently. Ikram is dead and Unit T has come."

***

Karen joined John and Sherry, waiting in the car. "Right, Arif has agreed to our auditor going in tomorrow. I want you with them this week, John. Report back to me if you have any issues. I don't think you will, he seems to have accepted Ikram's demise and perhaps sees an opportunity to take over."

"No problems there, do you want to return to the airport?"

"Yes, I'm finished here for the moment."

"What about me?" Sherry asked.

"You're off to the film festival in Cannes, with Meir, although, he'll also have a little more company by way of me, not that he knows it yet. But first we go to London."

Sherry grinned. "That's great, I'm already looking forward to it."

Chapter 52

Roos was sitting in the window seat, on a scheduled flight to London from Brussels. Alongside her was Jason. She felt very down, having been deceived by Tori. It wasn't because of the punishment off Luca, it was because she'd really believed Tori liked her. Roos had no other friends.

The flight was short; soon they were leaving the airport on the shuttle bus to the long-stay car park. Jason had said very little until they finally left the bus and were in his car, turning onto the motorway and heading for London. "You've been to London before then?" he asked suddenly.

"No, never, is it a long way?"

"Around forty minutes in this traffic."

"Luca told me I was staying with you and I'm to buy suitable clothes. Did he give you any money?"

Jason huffed. "He never told me that. But I have plenty of clothes for you to wear." He said no more and soon they arrived in Westminster, came to a halt outside a large Victorian house, set among a number of others.

"Right, out of the car," he ordered, at the same time climbing out himself.

She followed him up to the entrance, where he pressed the doorbell. Soon a woman opened up.

"Hilda, this is Roos. Look after her, sort her clothes, I'll be back later," he said, then returned to his car.

"Come this way, have you eaten?" Hilda asked.

"Only breakfast and coffee on the plane."

"No problem, I'll show you your room, then you can come down to the kitchen, it's the door behind the stairs."

Soon they were in a very nicely appointed bedroom.

"This is nice, better than my little flat back at the

shop," Roos said with obvious admiration.

"Our clients are from the city and expect this level of décor. You're about the same size as Suzy, who used to be here before you, sort something nice to wear from the wardrobe and I'll see you downstairs."

Roos stared at her. "Clients, excuse me, what are you talking about?"

Hilda looked at her. "Did Jason not tell you? This is a brothel, and you, girl, will be working tonight. So get yourself sorted out and we'll talk about the house rules downstairs." Then she left the room, not allowing Ross to object or comment.

Roos, on her part, just stared at the door. Tori had been right, Luca had every intention of selling her. She just didn't believe it. With tears coming to her eyes, she opened the wardrobe. Inside were short skimpy dresses, with high-heeled shoes. There were knickers with matching suspender sets in trays.

***

"There you are, come and sit down, I've made sandwiches for you, Roos," Hilda said, when Roos came into the kitchen, wearing one of the dresses from the wardrobe.

"I think there has been a mistake. I'm not a prostitute," Roos said quietly, sitting down opposite her.

"Nonsense, you wouldn't be here otherwise. Anyway, we have a very select clientele. We work until three in the morning, usually from six. They will be with you for around thirty minutes each. After servicing one, tidy yourself up for the next. Use condoms at all times, lubrication is in your bathroom. After getting yourself ready, you come down to the front lounge; there you mingle with the clients, until one picks you, then you take him to your room. Around ten, you will have time to eat."

"I can't do it. I've only ever been with Luca. Beat me all you want, but I'll not prostitute for anyone."

Hilda smiled. "You know, every girl who comes here tells me that. If I were you, Roos, I'd give it a try. You're an attractive girl, most will be regulars and you'll get to know them. Believe me, they will be just like boyfriends, so you will cope here very easily. Jason has other places which are a hundred times worse than this. He won't beat you, just fill you with cocaine, there you'll work fifteen hours a day, begging for your next fix. But you won't get it till you've serviced at least thirty men off the street. They're the drunks, the ones up in London, out for a good time, looking to shag something. If that's what you want, then go back to your bedroom and wait until he comes for you. Believe me, by the end of the week you'll be so addicted to coke, you'll be prepared to do anything he wants of you."

Roos said nothing, she was frightened, but realistic. She'd seen so many in the park, close to her flat, out of their minds on drugs; she didn't want that. Picking up the sandwich, she began to eat.

"Well, what is it to be?" Hilda asked.

"I don't have a choice," she replied softly. "I'll do as you ask."

"There is always a choice, Roos. But you have taken the sensible one, believe me."

Chapter 53

"Charlie, over here!" came a voice behind her.

Sherry turned to see Meir waving and began to walk over to him. She had arrived in Cannes on a scheduled flight, after contacting Meir. "Hi, how are you?" she asked, giving him a kiss on either cheek.

"I'm fine, how was the flight?"

"It was good, is it far into Cannes?"

"No, thirty minutes. Let me take your bag."

"No way, I don't want you collapsing on me," she mocked.

"Just give me the bag, Charlie."

***

The boat the taxi drew up alongside was obviously expensive. Large, sleek, with all its brass shining.

"God, you must be loaded to have a boat like this," Sherry said, standing looking at it.

"I think you misunderstood. I don't own it, nor do we have it to ourselves, the owner's son is aboard. His name is Pier Demont, the family's in oil, or similar. Please don't mention the lap dancing, just that we met at a club and took it from there."

"No problems, I'll be on my best behaviour," Sherry answered with a smile.

They went up the gangplank and into the main lounge. Again the fit-out was of the best quality - the carpets you sank into.

"You're back soon, Meir, and I presume this very attractive young lady is Charlie?" a man asked, approaching them both. He was in his early thirties, around six foot in height, with dark hair, obviously very fit, with bulging biceps under his T-shirt.

"Yes, this is Charlie. Charlie, meet Pier."

Pier embraced Sherry, kissing her on each cheek. "So, Charlie, you're here to mingle with the celebrities of the film industry, are you?"

"I'm not sure, but if Meir is expecting me to do that with him, I suppose I am. Not that I know much about the industry, all I ever do is pay loads to see their movies."

"Well, we'll have to enlighten you, won't we, Meir? In fact, tonight we're at a reception to open the festival. I hope you have appropriate clothes?"

"Yes, Meir told me I needed at least three dresses for such events. I'm cool with that."

"Then you should both join me in a light lunch, then you can tell me all about yourself, Charlie."

***

Later the same night, they all arrived at the reception, in a large limousine. Where Pier had spirited it from, Sherry had no idea, but it had been waiting to take them after she'd dressed.

Once inside the room where the reception was being held, Meir had left Sherry and Pier alone to collect the drinks.

"Have you been to this type of event before, Charlie?"

"Sort of, but not with so many recognisable celebs, although I've been to a few reception and charity events. What about you?"

He shrugged. "It's my life, what's expected of me. The family likes to be seen at all events, often to make nice fat donations, at times to show how much we care for the environment and of course, people not so lucky as us. You see, oil is often looked on as polluting, what with the many major spills that have happened. Without it though, the world would come to a standstill."

Sherry grinned. "That's very deep, me, I just go with the flow."

By now Meir had rejoined them and already Sherry was being introduced to a number of guests.

At that moment her mobile vibrated a little. She knew what she must do. "Oh my god, that's Lady Harris, she's dead famous don't you know? I wonder if she'll recognise me."

Meir looked at her. "Why should she?"

"We've spoken a few times at different events in London. Well, not spoken in depth, more like casually, although once in the Ladies, when I broke my nail and was trying to find someone with a pair of scissors, she saved my life."

"Then let's see if she remembers you," Pier urged. "This is a woman I've always wanted to meet."

Sherry had in actual fact, texted Karen with the venue she was attending tonight. She had arranged to meet her at the event. Karen would be escorted by one of her soldiers, but he would leave once the text arrived. She was to invite Karen to join them.

"Lady Harris," Sherry said.

Karen turned, trying to look confused.

"I recognised you immediately. It's ages since we last met. Do you remember helping me out with scissors?" Sherry asked.

Karen looked at her, as if she was thinking, then smiled. "Of course, isn't your name Charlie? I didn't know you came to Cannes."

"First time, I'm here with Meir, we're guests of Pier's and staying on his boat, aren't we, Pier?"

"You are indeed. It's an honour to meet you, Lady Harris," he said, kissing her on each cheek. "I've read so much about you, except the pictures don't do you justice."

"It's nice of you to say so, Pier. Tell me, are you in the film industry?"

"No, the family's in oil. I just dabble in investments."

"Are you alone, Lady Harris?" Sherry asked. "If you are, why not join us?"

"I wasn't until five minutes back, when Oliver had to shoot off, after an urgent phone call. But I wouldn't dream of intruding, I'm on my way out as well. I was only here for Oliver and to show my face."

"You wouldn't be intruding, I assure you, Lady Harris. Please join us?" Pier urged.

"Yes, come on, you can't leave yet, can she, Meirs?" Sherry urged.

"Of course you can't, besides, we're leaving ourselves shortly and going on to a club. You must come."

Karen smiled. "Very well, thank you. But I insist you all call me Karen."

Pier was in his element, introducing Karen to many of the people he knew. He was convinced his family would almost certainly approve, because she was so famous. They in turn were inviting her to so many events she'd lost count. Such was her popularity besides the need to have high profile names at their event. Soon they left for the nightclub. Once inside, Sherry and Karen went to the ladies.

"We think we know what Meirs has bought with Luca, Sherry. There's a hotel in Amsterdam that is used solely by prostitutes, with another owned by the same man in Berlin. It's ostensibly above board and cost close to two and

312

a half million euro. Except if Parker and Luca are involved, I've a feeling they have plans beyond what is legal for such an investment."

"So is there any value in me continuing with Meirs?"

"Not that I can see now. Except the bugging of his apartment put us in the right direction to find out what they were up to, so the operation wasn't wasted. You can still see out the week if you want to. It's an interesting event if nothing else."

"I'd have to think about that, Karen. He'll be expecting me to go to bed with him for certain. I'm not overjoyed about doing that with Meirs and would only carry on if you wanted me to stay around."

"We can get nothing more out of Meirs. Whether this Pier has an interest in what's going on, I'm not sure, but remaining with Meirs wouldn't tell you that." She hesitated. "As for myself, I've agreed to attend a few preview events representing my charity, which doesn't compromise me with Pier, so I'll need to hang around for those at least, but it's up to you if you want to stay."

"Then I'll bail and leave you to it. I really don't want to be around Meirs."

"That's fine; you go to London and wait for me there. Anyway, we'd better get back."

***

Eventually, Pier accompanied Karen to the entrance of the club they were in, while she waited for her car to arrive.

"I've really enjoyed your company, Karen. Would you like to join us on the boat tomorrow? We could have a lunch, then maybe you'd agree to join me for dinner later?"

Karen shook her head. "I can't do lunch, Pier, I've

lots on. I may be free for dinner." She gave him a card with her number on it. "Call me late afternoon and we'll try to arrange something."

***

Karen contacted Stanley the following morning. She was in her hotel suite.

"This Pier is an interesting man, Karen. As you know, Meirs didn't have the money, he raised it from a man he called Pier. You and Sherry, by chance, have put a face to the name. We're looking into his past and I'll be back to you later when we know more."

"That's good, how about Luca?"

"He of course found the tracker and listening device we suspected he would discover, leaving the more sophisticated one that shut itself down while he scanned the room. With Yannick believing he'd shut the bugs down, it strengthened our surveillance. We now have the evidence that Roos was sold to Jason and have since tracked her to a house in Knightsbridge. According to Sir Peter, this house has been long suspected of being a high-class brothel. He wants to go in; already he has good intelligence on the operation and the sale of Roos now gives him evidence of Jason trafficking."

"I'll call him. What of the other pimps at Luca's?" Karen asked with interest.

"We're already profiling them and their operations. Their time is very short, before we take them down. Are you ready to take on Luca yet?"

"I wish, I've not got enough to make it a watertight case as yet."

"Then I'll leave you with that problem."

"Yes, I'll call later today and see what you've dug up on Pier, shall I? He's asked me to dinner and I'm still considering if there is any advantage to going."

"That's fine, Karen, leave it as late as you can, will you?"

Once Karen broke the call with Stanley, she called Sir Peter.

"Good to hear your voice, Karen, is everything okay with you?"

"It is, thank you. I've called about Jason. Stanley said you wanted to go in?"

"I do - with this girl called Roos turning up, we believe it is a good time to move."

"I'm not sure, Peter. Roos has a very strong allegiance to Luca. If she says she's there voluntarily and not selling herself, what then?"

"She'd do that?"

"I believe she would."

"Then your recording of Jason's conversation with Luca may not be good enough to take him down for trafficking - just running a brothel."

"That's what I suspect. You will need to wait for me to return to London. But put a very close surveillance team on Jason and see what he leads you to."

"I'll do that. When are you due back?"

"That depends on Stanley and what he can find out about a certain man here in Cannes. Either way, I'll be back at the end of the week."

"Then I'll look forward to seeing you. In the meantime, I'll do as you ask."

Chapter 54

Pier was waiting for Karen in the foyer of her hotel. This was not just any hotel, this was a five star, thousand-euro-plus per night hotel for just a basic room, except Karen was in a suite. Pier didn't fail to note this when he had reception call up to her room to say he was there. From what he'd heard and read in the papers, he'd understood Karen was wealthy; but not so wealthy he'd have expected her to be staying here. This wouldn't be a girl you'd impress by taking her to a top restaurant to mingle with celebrities, since she was one in her own right.

Karen had selected a short, figure-hugging, blue satin dress, six-inch heels to show off her long legs, and she'd put her hair up. Coming out the lift, she walked over to him, giving him a nice smile, kissing him on each cheek. "Hi, I've not kept you waiting too long, have I?" she asked.

"No, I'm early, but I must say Karen, you look stunning. I love the dress," he replied with obvious admiration. "Anyway, the car's outside, shall we go?"

However, even before she left the hotel, photographers were taking her photo. Karen hesitated, allowing them to do that, before climbing into the car. While she was in Cannes a great deal, she'd expected increased attention, particularly this week, with so many well-known names in attendance, being seen like this at times was good for her charity's profile.

Once in the car, it sped off.

"You seem to take the attention of the press in your stride, Karen. I like to shy away as much as I can."

She gave a slight shrug. "It happens all the time, and besides, it keeps my charity's name in the public eye, so I'm cool with it. Where are we going?"

"I hope I've not been too presumptuous, but this week most of the best restaurants are fully booked and always very crowded. I have a very good chef on my boat, so tonight I decided to show you just how good he is, besides giving us the best and only table in the restaurant."

Karen smiled. "I must say it's different, although I'm more than happy to dine on your boat. I'd love to see it anyway." Then she frowned. "But aren't Meirs and Charlie on board?"

Pier looked a little put out. "They have left, Charlie's gone home. I got the impression Pier believed that with Charlie coming to Cannes, she'd join him in his bed. Maybe that was her intention, but she was quite upset at not being given the choice, finding her bags had been moved this morning, from the original room she had last night into his bedroom. I can't blame her, he'd never even asked, just presumed. Charlie has a right to her privacy and to make her own decision to join him in his bed. I'd never compromise a girl in that way. Although to be fair, my parents are due tomorrow, so she would have had no option if she'd wanted to remain aboard, we only have three bedrooms, besides the crew quarters."

"That was the worst mistake he could have made there, without asking her; I'd have done the same. It'd be different if it had been an ongoing relationship, but a casual one… I'd want my own room as well."

"Well, let's forget them, shall we? Although secretly, I'm more than pleased to have the boat all to myself tonight."

"That's fine with me, except I had the impression you and Meirs were very close?"

Pier shook his head slightly. "No way. Meirs brokered a recent deal on my behalf and for a number of other investors. Basically, he was working for me. But the deal was a good one, so I wasn't averse to him joining me in Cannes, as a small token of appreciation on my part. Besides, there was also another small investment to be discussed."

"That sounds very interesting, is Meirs on the ball when it comes to good deals? I'm always looking to invest."

"It offered a twelve per cent return on capital, with security, so yes, it was a very good deal, except the minimum was half a million. Is that the sort of level you'd be interested in?"

She smiled. "I might have had a problem producing five million in cash, without moving it out of existing investments, if that answers your question?"

"It does indeed. As it is, the investor is asking for a second input totalling three million. I know for a fact three of the investors will not meet that sort of amount. What if I could find a way for you to invest up to a million?"

She shrugged indifferently. "If it's offering anything upwards of six per cent, count me in," she said, then touched his arm. "I'd be a sleeping partner; in fact, you would hold the investment. I'd not want my name known to the client."

"No problem. I'll get you a complete proposal, how it's supported, in fact everything, for you to look over."

"Do that Pier, and also cover what you've already invested in, I'd need to understand it all."

"Of course, that goes without saying, but tonight we talk nothing more of money, it's time to just enjoy the night."

"I'm okay with that," Karen answered, at the same time looking out of the window. She was glad she'd accepted his invitation, it would seem she could well obtain the complete picture of what they were up to. As for producing funds for the investment, that would be no problem if it became necessary, not that she thought it would go ahead, she was already close to impounding both Luca's and Parker's assets. She could also expect panic setting in with Pier, if he lost his money. Although to be fair, she quite liked him so far. He was pleasant, thoughtful and not at all bad-looking, besides being more her age compared to who she normally ended up with on a date. With those final thoughts, she sighed inwardly that every man she felt attracted to turned out to be tied up with, or actually the opposition!

"You're very quiet," Pier said suddenly, bringing Karen out of her thoughts.

"Sorry, I was just enjoying the drive down the marina, looking at all the boats. They all look fantastic, with their lights on and reflecting across the water. I don't do boats myself, I have an aircraft."

"Interesting, do you fly yourself?"

"Yes, I've had a licence for ten years now." She smiled. "My first aircraft was a Cessna Apache, with a single propeller. It used to bounce about the sky, but I loved it."

"So you no longer have it?"

"Sadly no. I needed a jet, with a longer range, so I reluctantly replaced it with a Mustang, although I may have the chance of a Gulfstream 450, but that deal's up in the air at the moment, so to speak."

"You don't do things by half then? Our family has a Gulfstream, they are fabulous planes," he commented, knowing such an aircraft could cost anything between three to thirty million dollars.

The car came to a halt by the side of Pier's boat. When Karen climbed out of the car, she looked at it for a moment. "I must say this is a very smart restaurant you've brought me to, Pier."

"Exclusive, Karen, and like I promised, serving some of the finest food in Cannes."

***

Following dinner they were sitting with drinks out on the deck.

"Will you be attending a number of the previews this week?" Pier asked.

"Not all week, I've work to do. But I'll be here for the next three days, why do you want to know?"

"I was hoping this was not going to be a one-off dinner and we could see each other again?"

"I'm not averse to that, Pier. I'd be happy if you'd join me at times."

"Then it's settled, we should plan the days. In fact, you should be a guest on my boat. Your own room, of course, and no strings in any way. My parents will be arriving tomorrow, they'd love to meet you, I'm sure."

Karen would have jumped at the chance, if circumstances had been different and he'd no association with Parker or Luca, but he was a target at this moment and she didn't intend to be compromised publicly by staying on his boat.

"It is a lovely thought, Pier, but I must say no. Nothing personal, I like you a great deal, but you forget, beside being here on behalf of my charity, I'm also the commander of Unit T. That means the places I stay in need to be protected. For me to just up and move, would not make my security very happy."

His mouth dropped a little. "You're telling me you have armed protection?"

"Of course. We've had a tail since leaving the hotel. I can also call for armed assistance at a moment's notice."

"Oh! It didn't enter my head, but I can understand the need for it. I'd forgotten your military role, you just don't

320

look the type of girl to be in the armed services."

She smiled. "So how should I look then? Maybe have short cropped hair and in fatigues?" she mocked.

He laughed. "Not at all. Although I bet you'd look just as feminine and sexy dressed that way. The enemy wouldn't know what to do with you."

"They would, you can be sure of that. So now you know, do you want to get rid of me?"

"Of course not. In fact, I'm relieved that you're so well looked after. When my parents arrive, they'll also come with armed protection. It's the way they live. Anyway, the night is still young. Would you like to go to a nightclub and we'll dance the night away?"

"Very much, besides, the restaurant will want us to leave, so they can tidy up."

"They will - shall we go?"

Chapter 55

Luca, along with Kenneth Parker, was in Amsterdam. They had come to the brothel purchased by them and other investors. A lady opened the door, she was small and in her twenties, with blonde hair and a petite figure. She knew Luca, he'd been there a number of times to talk to the previous owners.

"Good morning, Luca."

"Good morning, Noa. This is Kenneth Parker, my partner. Is Wouter in?"

"He is, and waiting for you in the office. Can I fetch you coffee?"

"Later, I want to see what has been done upstairs first."

Wouter, a man in his thirties, tall, with blond hair and very fit, came out of the office on hearing Luca's voice.

"Ah, Wouter, this is Kenneth Parker, you'll be seeing a great deal of him in future. We both want to see what has been achieved upstairs."

"Of course, Luca, it is all finished and ready to operate. If you'll follow me..."

They went into a lift and Wouter put a key into a lock above the floor buttons. "The lift only takes clients to the third floor, this key takes a client on to the fourth. You'll notice the indicator still shows it to be the third."

When the doors opened, they came out onto a large, square, carpeted landing. Settees were set out around a central pole, set up on a circular platform. Off the landing were a number of doors, each with a name on. In a corner was a desk with a single chair in front of it and one behind.

"As you can see, we are ready to take clients. Each

room has a super king-sized bed and an en suite, except the special room where, if you follow me, you can see what has been achieved."

The special room had been fitted out as a torture chamber, complete with various punishment tables, chains, axes and whips on hooks hung around the room. It was also windowless, and painted black with powerful spotlights over the top of the various punishment contraptions.

Kenneth picked up a few of the torture implements, then checked the main table, its adjustments and drainage system to direct the blood into a bucket below.

"Where is the lift?" Kenneth asked.

Wouter went over to the far wall and pressed a button. A small door opened. "Once the body is bagged, it is slid in here and the lift takes it to the basement. There the two furnaces used to heat the building will incinerate whatever is placed in them. We also have special filters on the chimney stacks that will filter out any possible smell from the burning. The room is like a wet room with drainage and can be power washed as you requested. It is also soundproofed. This room off it, which has an entry code, is the master changing room." He keyed in a code and the door opened. Although the room was small, it had a shower, lounge chairs and hooks around the room to hang regalia upon, besides a large mirror. "This is alright for you?"

Parker nodded. "Perfect. Do I have a separate way out, if required?"

"You do, the exit is behind this curtain," he said, grabbing the curtain and pulling it away. "Push the panel and it will release and hinge open. It leads into the attic of the house next door. As you know, that is made up of flats so you just make your way down to the communal area and out of the front door."

"Where are my subjects kept?"

They will be kept sedated in another room off the other side of the chamber. They can be prepared in there, either before clients enter the chamber, or as part of the act. The room can accommodate up to two."

"And the underage girls?" Luca cut in. "How are they brought up to this floor?"

"They come by van from the house. The main lift has doors front and back, the back doors open onto a passage into the rear courtyard of the hotel. We have a covered area the van goes under and the girls are brought out and put directly into the lift. That happens at around four, while all the working girls are eating. They work until two in the morning, then they are taken back."

"Very well, shall we go back down and have coffee now?" Luca said, more than satisfied with the top floor conversion.

***

Sitting in the office with Kenneth, who was going through the earnings of the last weeks, Luca was reading the paper. Turning to page five, he stared at a picture of Karen coming out of a nightclub with Pier, with the paper asking if Karen had a new boyfriend.

"Isn't Pier Demont Meir's investor, and the one prepared to put up another million for the second hotel here?"

"He is, why do you ask?"

"I thought it was, look who he's with in Cannes," he said, passing the paper to Kenneth..

Kenneth looked at the photo in silence, then at Luca. "Could it be just a coincidence?"

"That woman doesn't do coincidences. She's had a

girl called Tori infiltrate us already. Now she's with Pier. She's getting too close for comfort. I'm calling Meirs," he reacted, at the same time pulling his mobile out and looking up Meirs in his directory, before dialing and switching the sound on to speakerphone so Kenneth could hear the conversation.

"Meirs here," came a voice after a few rings.

"Meirs, Luca, can you talk?"

"Yes, I'm at home. What can I do for you?"

"The investor, Pier. Did you know he's with Karen Harris?"

"Yes, Charlie introduced him to her. I think he fancies her and has already taken her out for dinner."

Luca looked at Kenneth. "You say Charlie introduced them; not the Charlie who was with Tori?"

"The very same girl. I'd taken her to Cannes for the week, but after the first night she bailed on me and returned home."

"And that was after she'd introduced Pier to Karen?"

"Yes."

"Do you have Charlie's address?"

"No, she lives in Spain and was staying at a local hotel. I have her mobile number, but when I called it this morning to try to patch things up, all I got was a disconnect tone. It's as if she doesn't exist."

"Well, if she calls, or you hear from Tori, let me know, will you. I've some work coming up which will suit them both."

"Will do."

Luca cut the call and looked at Kenneth. "It's a set-up. Charlie and Tori were sent in to gather information initially, now Karen Harris has used Charlie to get an intro to Pier. It also confirms my suspicion that Tori did have help to get out of Algeria. Unit T must have gone in. Pier is a risk to us now."

"You're right, Pier needs to be shut up, before he blabs to her. I'll send Shaun and Liam to take him out. I've already had a number of clients wanting to attend one of my special shows. I'm not delaying indefinitely because of her."

"I agree. If she gets in the way, have them take her out as well."

Chapter 56

Pier's parents entered the lounge of the boat. Pier stood and embraced them both.

"So why are you here, Dad?" he asked.

"Your mother and I decided we'd like a break. With you being here, we thought it would be nice if we were all together. But I read in the paper you went out with Karen Harris last night," his father answered.

"I did, she's a fantastic girl, Dad. Even flies her own aircraft."

"Yes, I know, in fact, I know a great deal about her. Most is not good, son. Karen may seem a nice girl, but she's not and is particularly dangerous. Your mother and I have talked and decided you should have nothing more to do with her."

His attitude changed to one of annoyance. "You've decided? Since when do you tell me who I do or don't go out with? She's here tonight for dinner, to meet you both. I expect you to be civil to her."

"Son," his mother cut in. "Karen has no boyfriend because most, if not all, have been killed in one way or another. She brings with her dangers you can't even imagine. According to sources, she prostitutes and lap dances besides spending time in brothels. We as a family cannot be associated with such a woman."

Pier smirked. "Since when does a multimillionaire need to prostitute? That's ridiculous. The girl's in a hotel suite of a five star hotel. Besides, they don't give titles to prostitutes in England."

His father shook his head slowly. "She's from a working class family; does it not seem odd she has gone from that, to being a millionaire, when only a few years back, she was just a lieutenant in the army, which she's still in? Even when her parents were killed and the will was made public, their estate, besides the value of the house, was less than a hundred thousand. For her, that's petty cash. No, Son, she's made her money by taking it from traffickers. Her charity's worth millions. It has also been rumoured for some time that she took five million off the Russians. But even before that she had substantial funds. A reporter I know personally has spent five years in painstaking research, trying to find out if her accumulated funds are backhanders off the cartels, in exchange for keeping away from them. He estimates she has over twenty million in a Swiss bank, besides substantial property assets across four countries."

Pier thought back to Karen's offer of going in with him on an investment and her request that her name was kept secret. Could his father be right? "Well, she's here tonight for dinner. I can't put it off now. Then I'll do as you ask and bring our relationship down to a very low-key level. Are you happy with that?"

"Very sensible, Pier," his mother cut in. "Don't get us wrong, we'd love you to meet a girl and settle, but not with Karen Harris. She will bring you down by just being around her. As for tonight, we will be the perfect hosts for you."

***

Karen stepped onto the boat in the early evening after Pier had collected her from the hotel. She felt he seemed a little cold tonight, but put it down to his parents being on board. She'd decided on wearing a long dress, not expecting to be going out later to a club. With Pier's parents around, a short dress would not have been appropriate.

Both his mother and father were standing when she came into the lounge. "Lady Harris, it's a pleasure to meet you," Pier's father said, embracing her and kissing her on each cheek. "I'm Carlos and this is my wife Vivien," he finished, allowing her to embrace his wife.

"It's very nice of you to invite me to dinner, but please would you call me Karen? I use my title very little, apart from events for my charity. And then, being out of uniform, my military title would not be appropriate."

"Then Karen it is. Please come and sit down, may I offer you an aperitif before dinner?" Carlos asked.

"Just tonic water with a twist of lemon, please. May I open the bottle myself?"

Carlos looked at her for a moment, but decided not to ask why, just nodded to the waiter, who left the room. By the time he returned they'd all sat down. He held a small bottle of tonic and a glass containing a slice of lemon. Karen thanked him, opened the bottle and poured the drink, handing him the bottle back.

However, Vivien was intrigued, no one had ever done that before. "May I ask you, Karen, why did you ask for a sealed bottle?"

She smiled. "No reflection on you, I did the same at the Russian Embassy. But I had a drink spiked once and ended up in intensive care. In my job, you don't take risks; I was foolish and didn't take simple precautions, nearly paying for it with my life. It makes you nervous for a while, now it's just habit."

"You seem to live in a fascinating world, Karen. I've read a great deal about you in the papers over the years. Do they exaggerate?" Carlos asked.

"They know little about my life. I live in a very

dangerous world. I believe there's a hundred- thousand-pound contract out on me, dead or alive. Does it worry me, of course not. If it did, I'd not be able to live any sort of life. I have told Pier, to be with me is not without personal risk, but like you, I have protection that can be with me in minutes. Although that would not prevent a determined assassin from getting close, before help arrived. But you ask, do they exaggerate," she replied, hesitating. "The press believes I spend most of my time in combat clothes, or on a beach wearing as little as possible. I don't do either, nor do I act like a female James Bond. Most of my life is mundane, writing reports, following up leads. There are times when it is dangerous, perhaps even exciting, if you believe it exciting to see a child raped and abused, or young girls spaced out on drugs that keep them working ten to twelve hours a day, as they are taken by a hundred men a week?"

"Does it not make your vision of life very tainted?" Vivien asked.

She shrugged. "It used to, these days for me, it's the norm, so I'm not phased any more. I just accept it as part of the job. Mind you," she said more pointedly, "since the new EEC laws over people trafficking and the liability of getting involved, even investors need to be very careful. If it's proved even a penny of an investment goes towards trafficking, or on using the trafficked in any way, they stand to lose everything, plus get ten years in prison."

"But how would an investor know?" Pier asked.

Karen smiled. "It's the old adage, if the investment seems too good to be true, the investor should look deeper. So, the investor should beware what they invest in. There is no appeal, I take the lot."

Carlos frowned. "When you say you take the lot, in what way?"

"All retrievable funds from perpetrators go to the victims, which can often be in the millions. My charity is the only charity in the EU able to receive such funds. This was decided on so as to prevent bogus charities starting up and trying to get at substantial funds, besides not allowing the locations of the victims to be known beyond our control. I've helped thousands of victims, now settled in new lives. We fund their education, give them a place to live, pay them wages until they can support themselves, besides negotiating compensation on their behalf. We are with them until they no longer need us. I myself was paid compensation. For the trafficker, the pimp, the abuser, it hits where it hurts most, they come out of prison with nothing to show for their activities."

"I really didn't realize just how extensive your involvement is, Karen, " Carlos said, a little taken aback. "You should be congratulated."

Karen shook her head a little. "I don't want, or expect, thanks. It was getting out of hand and needed someone to step in and fight for the victims. What better than a victim who was also a photogenic and able to sell papers just with her story and photos taken of her scantily dressed? I started my charity at eighteen with nothing, funded everything myself out my salary and the fees received for my story, because nobody was interested in the victims, believing they were just prostitutes and deserved all they got. I fought for the change of law and eventually embarrassed the UK government into doing something. Now taken up by the EU the ball is rolling and it cannot be stopped."

At that moment the waiter came in to tell them dinner was ready. They all went through to the dining room.

***

Shaun and Liam had watched Karen arrive at the boat with Pier. They had initially begun to follow Pier when he left the boat to collect Karen. Of course they were surprised when he didn't take her to a restaurant, or one of the many events on in Cannes, but returned to the boat.

"That's a turnup for the books, to get them both together, we should take them both down," Liam commented.

"Well, remember what Kenneth told us, she won't be alone; somewhere she will have Dark Angel Soldiers. I'm not unduly worried about them, but she's not the primary target, Pier is. We will take her down if an opportunity arises after Pier," Shaun replied.

"You're right, we should do that and add to the confusion. But this is France, with the largest concentration of her soldiers, we might take her out, but could we escape afterwards?"

"Then you take the time to plan such an escape, I'll use the sniper gun. Now we wait, if she's just there for dinner, he'll take her back to the hotel. Then either stay with her or return."

"Why wouldn't she just stay on board?" Leam asked.

"She's no overnight bag, just a purse. No, she's definitely going back to the hotel. Whatever happens, the first opportunity to take him out, we do it."

"And if we don't get him before he leaves to take her back to the hotel, then stays overnight with her, what then?"

"We wait, he's bound to return to the boat sometime tomorrow. But then, we'd need to go on board."

***

It was after eleven at night when Pier's parents retired. Karen had gone out on the deck with Pier.

"Have you had a good night, Karen?" he asked, pouring her a drink, before handing it to her.

"Yes, it's been interesting. Your father has certainly done a great deal in his life. Although both of them seem very protective of you."

He smiled. "It shows, does it?"

"Just a little, well, a lot really," she said, then changed her tone. "They don't like me, do they?"

"They don't dislike you, Karen. It's what you stand for that they can't get to grips with. They, like you, came from nothing; just sheer hard work, long hours and a dogged determination to succeed gave them what they have. When dad looks at you, he asks the same question on everyone's lips. Why are you so wealthy? Where did the money come from? Are you as bad as the people you hunt?"

"It was an inheritance and all legal, I can assure you, besides being cleared by the British government many years ago."

"I would assume it must be, you'd never get away with it otherwise. The truth is, Karen, I like you a great deal. I'd also like to see more of you."

"I'd would as well, but your parents don't want that, I assume?"

"No, they believe you're trouble and my life would be at risk." Then he gave a huff. "Since when did that prevent two people getting together? Most parents have the belief their son, or daughter, could do better."

She smiled. "Well, I didn't bother about what my parents said. Although if they had found out who I'd selected to marry and have children with, they'd have flipped."

"Who was he then?"

"I fell in love with the original man who purchased me, despite our first encounters, when at those times I'd have killed him. You may think that strange, but I found, by him purchasing me, he saved me from the brothels and he was my type. For me he was everything I ever wanted in a man. In fact, if I'd known him before I escaped, I'd never have tried and my life would have been very different."

"So what happened?"

"His partner killed him, to take over his business. I was to be sent to a brothel. It didn't happen."

They both fell silent, looking out across the water. It was Karen who broke the silence. "So do you still want to take a chance with me?"

"I do, if you can take the flak from my parents?"

She laughed. "In my line of work you get indifferent to insults and people trying to pull you down all the time. So yes, I can if you can?"

He stood and walked over to her, grasping her hand. Karen also stood and he embraced her, kissing her long and hard. Then breaking away, they moved to the side of the deck, looking across to the town. "I think I should take you back to your hotel, not that I want to, Karen."

"You should, it's best not to upset your parents just yet. We've plenty of time."

It was at that moment that a red laser light flashed across Karen's eyes. Immediately she knew it was emitted from a sniper-type gun. Her reaction was to drop down onto the deck, reduce herself as a target. As she fell, she shouted at Pier. "Get down, Pier, now! There's a gun trained on us," she shouted at him, grabbing at his arm to pull him to the deck.

But it was too late, his head shattered above her. Almost simultaneously there followed the unmistakable sound of a rifle shot. Karen pressed her watch button three times, already in a position where Pier's inert body protected her to a degree from the direction the shots came from. Opening her purse, she pulled out a gun. All she could do was wait, although against a rifle, which would be quite a distance away, her handgun would be no protection. Its only advantage was if that the bullet had been intended for her, the assassin could decide to come closer, to ensure she was dead, and she could engage then.

All was quiet; then two Unit T Range Rovers screamed to a halt at the base of the gangplank, soldiers spilled out and took up defensive positions, and two came aboard.

"I'm on the top deck," Karen called down to them, "there's at least one sniper, maybe more. I'm unhurt and not exposed."

"Remain where you are, Colonel, until we secure the area," came the reply.

By now, with the vehicles arriving, Odile, accompanied by two other security men, both armed, had come out on the lower deck. They came face to face with two Dark Angel soldiers, already with visors down, M4 carbines at the ready. "What the fuck's going on?" Odile demanded.

"Drop your guns, get face down on the deck," one of the Dark Angel soldiers shouted at him aggressively.

Neither Odile or the other two men intended going up against soldiers with carbines, so they dropped their guns and lay face down.

By now the police had also arrived, brought by calls from people on other boats who had seen the goings-on. They too were held back, after warnings given to them that there could possibly be an active sniper.

It was over fifteen minutes before the area was declared safe. Lieutenant Soyer of Unit T came up to Karen with another soldier.

Karen stood, she was covered in Pier's blood.

"The area is secure, Colonel, we found no one."

"I didn't think you would, it was a professional hit, although I'm not certain if it was directed at me."

"I don't think it was, otherwise, looking towards this deck from the land, they couldn't have missed; you'd be an easy target."

She sighed. "I think you're right, Lieutenant. I need to clean up, what have you got in the Range Rover?"

"A shirt, nothing else."

She pulled out the room card for the hotel she was staying in from her purse. "I'll need to talk to the police, can you have someone go to my hotel room and collect whatever they can find for me to wear, please?"

The soldier accompanying the lieutenant took the key card and left.

"Have the owners been woken?" Karen asked.

"Their security man, called Odile, is waking them. The police want this deck secured, so they are not allowed up here."

"Then they don't know their son has been killed?"

"They don't know anything as yet, Colonel. But you need to leave this deck, it's too exposed."

She followed him, meeting Odile at the entrance to the cabins.

"Do you have a cabin where I can get cleaned up, my people are fetching something for me to wear?" she asked.

"This way," he said, turning back inside.

She followed him into a small cabin.

"What of Pier?" Odile asked.

She shook her head. "He had no chance, it seemed they wanted him not me, both of us were targets," she said quietly.

He nodded. "I'll have your clean clothes sent to you when they arrive. I'll also have a plastic bag brought for your dress, the police will probably need it for the investigation."

***

"You, you killed our son, get off our boat," Vivien screamed at Karen when she came into the main lounge, before beginning to sob uncontrollably in Carlos's arms.

Karen hesitated for a moment. She'd already showered and was now dressed in jeans and a jumper, with her hair tied back. "If you mean that by my being here, Pier died, maybe, maybe not. We shall never know, unless the perpetrators are found. As it is, I've also lost someone I liked a great deal and I will leave the boat as soon as the police allow."

"Why do you say you've lost someone?" Carlos demanded.

"Why can't I? Pier and I got on well, he'd asked me out and I'd said yes. On the deck we'd agreed to carry on our relationship despite your objections." She hesitated. "I feel his loss a great deal. But I don't feel responsible. The assassin wanted your son dead, not me. If they had, I'd have been just as easy a target as he was. The point is, why, and it's certainly not because I was with him, I'm confident of that."

Vivien spat at her. "You lie, they wanted you, Harris, not my son. What did you do when you saw the gunmen, did you push him in front of you? Cower in a corner? As it is, you're a bloody whore, more at home in a brothel, and have the audacity to stand there and say he wanted you, when you aren't even good enough to lick his boots. Oh yes, we know all about you Harris. Hide behind your titles, your money, but never believe it will hide the fact of what you really are. So tell me, how many times have you prostituted? How's a pauper got herself millions of pounds? Taken it as backhanders off the traffickers you've allowed to walk away? Just how many people have died because of you? Many questions about you and your past remain unanswered. Then, you even managed to get your own parents killed. You're a tramp, Harris, and always will be. Get out my sight, wait in the servants' quarters, it's your level."

Her words hit Karen hard, with not only the police, but a number of her soldiers listening to her. Karen was all too aware of what her job had forced her into. But to be reminded in public, then be blamed for the death of her parents, she was close to tears. "You believe my world is what the papers tell you then? It isn't and never has been. I've lived with it since I was seventeen. Stood in front of the world and admitted, and described my rape. Not for myself, but to receive payment and help others in the same position," she said, hesitating before continuing: "It's cost me dearly, my health, my family and yes, the chance to be happy, often my past is thrown in my face by people like you, who believe they're better than me. Maybe you are? Only you know that, but you'll never know just how much I wanted that bullet, rather than your son. I'm tired and pray all the time for my nightmare to end, but God won't let it, he hasn't finished with me." She turned and left the room.

"Go on Harris, crawl back down your hole. Your words won't change my mind. You're a whore and always will be," Vivian shouted after her.

Lieutenant Soyer looked at the woman. "I can understand your need to blame someone for your son's death, madam, but that was uncalled for. Colonel Harris holds more bravery awards than any other serving soldier and is respected by every soldier under her command. She has brought out hundreds, no thousands of victims of trafficking, besides sent down a large number of traffickers, mostly at some personal cost to herself. But I'll tell you this, you'd best hope your son was not mixed up with traffickers who, believing Unit T was closing in, killed him to shut him up. If that is found, you will see another side of our colonel, have no doubt." Then he left the room.

***

Finding Karen on the deck, on the opposite side looking out across the bay, Lieutenant Soyer joined her, leaning on the same rail and looking out himself. "Forget her, Karen. Often grief can make people say very hurtful words, as they try to come to terms with their loss. The people who really matter in your life understand just what you go through at times to infiltrate these organisations, and they respect you. There isn't a soldier in the camp who wouldn't stand at your side, during any of your covert operations, if they could, I think you know that?"

She sighed. "I know and I'm proud of you all. It's just at times I get so lonely. I try to do my best then get slapped in the face. It hurts, Derik, believe me."

He slipped his arm around her, pulling her close. "Come on, let's go shall we? The police have just told me they don't need you tonight. Someone will call at the hotel tomorrow for a statement."

Chapter 57

Luca replaced the telephone handset after speaking to Kenneth. He looked at Yannick. "Seems like Pier was taken out last night. The ironical part was the Harris girl was standing at his side. They should have taken her out first before she realised. As it was, her reactions were quick and she protected herself with Pier, before they could get a shot at her. But no matter, the loophole has been closed, Meir will need to find a new investor."

"What happens to Pier's investment?"

"Good point. I think, following the funeral, I'll make a visit to his parents. They're not short of money and could jump at the chance to get Pier's money back, as well as add to his investment."

Yannick glanced at his watch. "I'll get off to the airport and collect Nabil. Will you want me around while he's here, I should really be in Germany to finalise the conversion of the brothel we bought?"

"No, you shouldn't delay, our new brothel's more important. In fact, I'll drive, then collect Nabil after dropping you off at the station."

With this agreed, Luca was standing in the arrivals area of the airport, waiting for Nabil. When he came through, they embraced and were soon on their way back to Luca's house.

"Good flight, Nabil?" Luca asked.

"It was pleasant and good to get away from my work for a change."

"So you're busy then?"

"I am always busy; now with Zaki dead, I've needed to engage people to look after the brothel while I provide a regular supply of new women."

Luca was always interested when brothel owners said they needed more women. "So you have a turnover?"

"Unfortunately, due to the nature of the work and the harsh conditions, the women don't last much more than a year. Samir was very useful in making up my shortfall, but since his demise, I've not been able to obtain suitable stock."

"Well, I've no such problems. I also hear you've come to Europe for other reasons?"

"I have. My brother Zaki was married to Ikram's sister. She's made a claim to Ikram's assets. I am here as her representative and will be joining her in Germany tomorrow. I understand he'd a share in an agency supplying escorts, besides substantial funds in a German bank and I'm told, an aircraft."

"I didn't know he had so much. But you say you want women, what nationality?"

"Samir, in the past, sold us an English woman. Can you supply them?"

"I can of course, but wasn't the last one a problem?"

"She was and I admit I totally underestimated her."

"In what way?"

"It would seem such women have a different attitude, believe they're special, having the idea they shouldn't be there. I did not consider this attitude as a risk, thinking that with the high demands of the women in my brothel, she'd have had little time to ponder her dilemma. Also, while I provide only knickers and a loose shirt for use in the brothel, in the desert a woman would quickly dehydrate if she left the brothel wearing such items, and be very easily caught. So I treated her like my other women, gave her the same freedom and she took advantage. Any future ones will be kept more securely at night and watched. None will escape again."

"We all learn the hard way at times. So you found her a good worker?"

"She was fair and even building up a client list of repeats. Of course, many of the clients wouldn't use her, with some having hostile that a European woman should be in my brothel; the ones that did use her were more than happy, coming back many times to take her again."

"You know such a woman cost Ikram sixty thousand?"

"I didn't, Zaki only paid twenty at auction. I'll go to forty, but no more."

"We can deal at forty. After all, the woman for Ikram was very special, could speak a number of languages and was intelligent. For you, such women would be of no value. You need an eighteen- year-old, fit and already broken in, so she can go to work immediately."

"So have you such women for me to look over?"

"I do, we will go later today and you can see what I have in. Maybe you'd like to try one out for yourself, you'll be more than satisfied, believe me?"

***

After staying with Luca for the night Nabil had gone on to Germany with his sister in law Sarah. He intended to sort out Ikram's accounts.

The manager of the German bank, Günther Apel, stood when Nabil, accompanied by Zaki's wife Sarah, entered his office. They all sat down.

"I must say, I was surprised receiving the call from your lawyers. We were not aware Ikram had relatives," Günther said.

"Well, you know now, we want details of his accounts and access to his private box?" Nabil said curtly.

Günther shrugged. "It is not possible, did your lawyer make you aware of the position?"

"He said something about the account being temporarily suspended pending claims. We, or rather my brother's wife is here to make such a claim."

"I'm sorry, for us it is too late. The account was not suspended as your legal team told you. People suspected of trafficking in the EU have their assets impounded pending investigation. All assets of this lady's brother are held by Unit T. You will need to speak to their legal department and then meet with Unit T's commanding officer, showing her proof of your entitlement. Their legal team will make a note of the claim and if it is found this lady's brother was not involved in people trafficking, their commander will sanction the release the funds."

Nabil was obviously annoyed. "You're telling me that we have to prove that the funds did not come from trafficking? That they can just walk in and take all a man's assets without any proof?"

"I can assure you, sir, if Unit T has impounded, they will have proof. They don't waste their time otherwise. The legal department of the bank has seen the documents and has agreed there was sufficient justification to allow them to take over the assets."

"How do we see this so-called commander?"

"I'd advise you not to believe for one moment that you're dealing with a tin-pot organisation controlled by a 'so-called commander'. Colonel Harris is a highly decorated and well-connected throughout the EU. Her position and her unit have been ratified by all EU member states and hold a unique status. Try to treat her as a fool and you can say goodbye to any claim you think you might have, she will just ignore you."

Nabil didn't like being talked to this way, but decided to tone down his manner. "Perhaps I was a little abrupt? How can I arrange this meeting, while I am still in Europe?"

"I can contact them, inform them you are here about the account and safe deposit box and wish to have a meeting. It will be Colonel Harris's decision if she wants to meet you. I suggest you leave it to your legal people, they will know EU law and what you can, or cannot do."

"No, I'm not prepared to wait around for months while bills from such people are mounting. In my country, we deal face to face, I want the same. Tell Unit T that, will you?"

***

Karen was in the office of her house when the bank manager called Unit T. While she didn't talk to him directly, her legal man, Nigel Summers called her, after his conversation with Nabil.

"You're telling me Samir's sister is in Germany with a man called Nabil?" Karen asked, astonished, at the same time experiencing a cold shiver down her back at the actual mention of his name.

"That's correct. He and his brother's wife want a meeting."

"Where do they want this meeting?"

"They're prepared to meet you anywhere. After all, including the value of the aircraft, we're talking about an estate valued in millions of euros."

Karen leaned back in thought, then made a decision. "They must come to Paris. I normally stay at the Champs-Elysees, we can set up a meeting there. Let's pencil in this Friday; have Stanley book in for me and arrange a flight

344

plan, will you?"

"I'll pass on the arrangement. Do you need legal there?"

"Not initially, but we'll forward a transcript for you."

Chapter 58

It was Friday. Karen had flown to Paris the night before and gone directly to the hotel. Although she had a suite, Karen had booked a private meeting room. Sherry was also with her, as well as two other Dark Angel soldiers, for her protection. While none of them would be at the meeting, they would be in the hotel and could be with her in less than a minute.

Nabil looked at his watch. They had arrived at the hotel nearly twenty minutes before and been shown to the private room, but Karen hadn't joined them as yet.

"She's late, the arrogance of these people. In my country she'd have been taken outside and flogged in public, keeping a man waiting," Nabil commented, sipping a coffee that Saura had poured.

"Perhaps she's busy, or hasn't arrived at the hotel yet, held up in traffic," Saura suggested.

"That's not my problem, she should have allowed sufficient time, or called. When she comes keep your mouth shut. This money belongs to the family, not you. You have sufficient for your needs."

"I know my place, Nabil. Although I cannot understand English too well, if you speak fast."

"As far as that's concerned, you can't understand English, that will avoid her questioning you."

At that moment Karen came into the room, carrying a document bag. She was dressed in a black trouser suit, with a white blouse and wore five-inch heeled shoes.

"I'm sorry I'm late, I was delayed by an important telephone call," she began. She glanced at the side table and walked over, to pour herself coffee, then sat down opposite them at the table.

"Well, now you're here, let's not waste any more time. This lady is Saura, the sister of Ikram. She cannot speak English, which is why I'm with her, besides having my own own claim as Zaki's brother. You may call me Nabil. We believe you're holding assets of Ikram's and we want them back," he said, without even a hello.

Karen sipped her coffee, relieved Nabil didn't recognise her, although he might do soon. "Yes, my legal people have looked at Saura's documents and confirmed she is indeed Ikram's sister. I presume you both know what Unit T is and their role in the European community?"

"We have been made aware. I'm surprised that a military unit can operate in the way it does. In Algeria it wouldn't happen. But Ikram was Algerian and not of the EU, you have no authority over him."

"You're correct, and if Ikram had conducted his illegal operation from Algeria, as he had done in the past, we couldn't touch him, but he didn't. He came to the EU and abducted a woman to take back with him. EU law is very clear. Abduction of a person for whatever use, beyond being taken for ransom, is classed as human trafficking. This crime in the EU is punishable by a custodial sentence and all assets, within EU borders, held by that person will be confiscated. We have clear documentation of Ikram taking a woman from the EU, via his own private aircraft, then imprisoning her. Following his demise, by the hand of his brother Samir, the woman was not handed to the authorities, as she should have been, but sold by Samir to a man we know as Zaki. He in turn used the woman in a brothel run by his brother. That person was you, Nabil."

"Rubbish, Ikram had no need to take a woman from the EU and imprison her. He has any amount of women at his disposal, back in Algeria. As for me using a European in my business, that would not happen. She would be rejected. Also, if such a thing had happened, why hasn't the Algerian authorities done something about it? It is true that I do operate a brothel, although all the women working in the brothel are there of their own free will. I don't keep women against their will, nor are any sold to me."

Karen nodded her head up and down slowly. "I agree the Algerian government has been a little slow in responding to our information, mainly because the woman who was taken had been unable to give them a true location of the brothel. However, when we talked to them about you and your brother Zaki, they knew the location immediately. They're prepared to go to your brothel, if we request it. If they do and confirm to their own satisfaction by both inspection and photographs that the brothel is as described by the woman, you will be charged under their own laws for trafficking. You see, Nabil, for a victim to describe the location as well as she has, down to the number of toothbrushes, the size and number of cubicles and extra toilets, it could only mean she was there. Then, if the other women are questioned, further confirmation that she was there would be forthcoming, besides which, many may also claim they too were sold in a trafficker's sale and forced to work in the brothel. It would seem your greed in trying to take Ikram's assets may be your downfall."

Nabil stood to leave. "I am not listening to any more lies, in an effort to keep Ikram's money. I can also assure you, the word of a European woman against a man's word in my country would be ignored by the authorities. So you return Ikram's assets, or you will hear from our legal people."

"You're not going anywhere until I've finished with you, Nabil," Karen told him curtly. "Outside this room are two armed Dark Angel soldiers from Unit T, who will ensure that. So sit down and listen."

He spun round. "You dare to threaten me? You should remember your place."

Karen smiled. "I don't dare, Nabil, I am threatening you. In fact, I'm happy to go even further and personally put a bullet in your head. The same as I killed one of the workers outside your brothel, your brother Zaki, Samar and his partner. It's what I do and it's something I'm very good at."

He stared at Karen for some time. You, you were the women in my brothel? Rubbish." Even though he had said that, for her to know that a man was killed, she'd at least be in touch with the woman who was really there and escaped.

Karen continued. "You seem to have doubts. Why is that and why was I there? An operation went wrong, I was taken and you eventually purchased me. That was a bad choice. I kill for a living, so anyone who gets in my way, or prevents me leaving is likely to get themselves killed."

Nabil looked at Saura. "Leave us, wait outside."

Saura did as she was told.

Once she closed the door, Nabil turned back to look at Karen. "So the great Karen Harris is really a prostitute, are you sure you want to admit that to the world? You see the woman who came to my brothel, was no stranger to prostitution and immediately prepared herself as soon as she arrived, was comfortable with her body and I watched that woman many times with her clients. She was hard working, a natural pleaser for her clients, obviously enjoying her craft and unlike other women in the brothel, knew many ways to please a man."

Karen was wishing now she'd not had to admit it was her. She felt her skin crawl as he described her time in his brothel, while she tried to cope and avoid any injury which could prevent her escaping when an opportunity came.

Nabil by now had the feeling Karen was not as confident as she'd portrayed and determined to take advantage. "I see you are not prepared to comment. So if you are who you claim, stand up, let me look at you more closely," he demanded aggressively at her.

Karen stood, although he posed no physical threat to her away from his brothel, she wanted him to have no doubts as to who she was.

Nabil pushed her long hair off her shoulders, gripped her face, forcing her to look into his eyes before pushing her away, shrugging indifferently. "It is possible you are the woman from my brothel, but your admission that you worked in my brothel is your downfall. Because you will know I lock no woman up; if you believed you shouldn't have been there, you could have just walked away. As it is you were with Ikram before you offered yourself for sale, in exchange for a roof over your head and food, the same as every other woman in my brothel. Why you were with Ikram, then sold yourself into prostitution, rather than go home, is not my concern. Maybe the money Zaci paid Samar was to pay a debt, help others, such as your family. Most of the women are there for their families. Because I paid money for you, you're still in debt to me, until you buy your freedom; I am entitled to put you back to work in any way I see fit. Your price to release you of this burden? All of Ikram's assets you're holding, then you get your freedom. Otherwise, you work your debt off here, or in Algeria."

"I like your assessment," Karen replied, with just a hint of a smile. "Your belief as to why I was there, it is academic and as for carrying on working for you, or buying my so-called freedom with Ikram's assets, worth millions, that is not going to happen. So you sit down and we talk."

He sat down again. "Then, I presume the reason we are at a hotel and not a police station, or even a more remote location so you can kill me, is because you want something from me?"

"You're correct. No matter what happens, I've sufficient evidence to complete my claim for the EU assets of Ikram to be paid out in compensation to victims, such as me, so a meeting would have had little value. As for Saura, I understand there is a bank account in Algeria belonging to Ikram. While I currently have it on hold, we won't be pursuing that account, so I will release it, once we have an agreement. She may then make her own claim for whatever is in the account. As for you, I should kill you for what you put me through. But I'm a realist, which means for you there is a choice. You work with me and you get to return to Algeria, or you die. There is no middle road."

He looked at her for a moment. The mention of the Algerian account was interesting. "After your time in Algeria, I can accept you are capable of murder. So what is this so-called work, that keeps me alive?"

"I want Luca. He was the one who sold me and many more besides. It is time for him to pay. I already know you have come directly from him. I presume you were there with the purpose of making arrangements for the delivery of more EU women to your brothel?"

"We may have talked about such an arrangement."

"I'm not messing about listening to your elusive words. He's a trafficker, you would only have gone to him because Ikram and Samir are out the picture. As it is, I intend to take him down, with or without your help. But you help me and you get to live, it's as simple as that."

"Why should I believe you will not kill me, after I give you Luca?"

"Because in Algeria, I was in your world. Forced to prostitute, or be punished, maybe even killed, or sold on to ever more violent people if I'd refused. So I had a right to fight, or even kill for my freedom. The roles have now reversed. You do as you're told and you live, refuse and you die. Believe me, after what I went through in your brothel, that would be very easy. Is my word good? Unlike you lot, it is, when I say you walk free if you help me, you walk free. If I say you die, you die."

He went over to the side table and poured more coffee, before returning. Her offer of releasing the bank account in Algeria was good. Saura wouldn't get the money, he would, and there was a considerable amount. "Luca has offered me three European women. I've seen them and come to an arrangement and will pay him tomorrow. He intends to deliver them as far as the Algerian border. Will that be sufficient to take him down and for me to return to Algeria?"

"It will, if we add all the rest of our intelligence on him."

"Then I will do it. But you must also take the holding notice off Ikram's account in Algeria."

Karen pulled a document from her case and placed it onto the table. "This document releases any claim to Ikram's assets in the EU by the family, allowing me to complete our claim. Once that is signed by you and Saura, I will release the account in Algeria. After you pay for the women tomorrow, you will be held in a safe house. Communication to Luca will be as usual, except if he tries to track where you are calling from, it will show as a location in Algeria. Following his arrest, you will be free to go."

"What of the money I need to pay him for the women?"

"How much do you want?"

"A hundred and twenty thousand."

"I will see you get that money."

"So what happens now?"

Karen smiled. "You will be our guests. When you leave here, you'll be taken to a safe house. Tomorrow you will return to Brussels to meet Luca. If he asks how you got on, tell him we have accepted your claim and it's going through."

***

Sherry listened to Karen as she told her of the meeting with Nabil. "I don't know how you could sit in the same room, Karen. I'd have killed the bastard. Then to have him say to you what he did... how did you feel?"

"Scared, Sherry. It was as if I was back in the brothel, my skin was crawling, I was actually shaking, even though I knew he couldn't touch me."

"I can understand that, I was the same in the brothels I was taken to. Your world is so closed up from reality, anything beyond the floor has no relevance. So moving on, what do you want me to do?"

"I want you to relocate to Brussels with the lads. Although I trust Nabil not to run, it's best to have the option to pull him in. I suspect Ikram's account in Algeria holds a substantial amount of money and he wants it, so I can't see him rocking the boat, though. It will be down to you to keep very close to him."

"I can do that."

"I know you can. While that is going on, I'll fly to London. I've a little unfinished business to take care of."

Chapter 59

It was just after eight in the morning. Roos was in her bed, staring up at the ceiling. The last week had been a nightmare. Already she was being taken by different men five times a day, but Hilda wasn't satisfied. From today, she was to work the lunchtime session as well as at night, increasing her clients to at least ten a day. She had no idea how she was going to cope. But cope, she had to, with the constant threat of being sent to work the streets.

The door suddenly opened. "Come on, get yourself up and down for breakfast. The main room's a tip. You will clean it before the lunchtime clients begin to arrive," Hilda demanded.

***

Roos spent the morning cleaning. By now more girls had arrived and they, like her, were in the main lounge. By now, a number of clients had turned up and girls were being taken.

A man in his fifties called Roos over. "Give yourself a complete turn for me?" he asked.

Hilda had also joined them. "She is a very nice girl, our Roos here, Frank. A little thin yes, but works hard to please."

"I like her, have her taken to the room and prepared."

"Very good choice. Roos, get yourself prepared."

Hilda walked away, very satisfied with the demand at lunchtimes. It had only started the week before as an experiment, when some clients had suggested they would prefer this time rather than early evening.

With every girl working, Hilda went through to

the kitchen, joining the minder, who'd poured two cups of coffee. She sat down and began to read the paper. Ten minutes later the front door bell rang. Hilda looked across to a CCTV monitor, but the camera on the front door was only showing a blank screen.

"I thought you'd sorted that, it's always going off. How can I watch who comes and goes?"

"It was working earlier, do you want me to go?" the minder asked.

"No, it'll only be a client who's early for the next session. You stay here, I'll sort him."

Walking through to the front door, she pulled it open. It wasn't a client, but a woman.

"Yes?" Hilda asked curtly.

"Hi, I've come to see Roos," Karen said with a smile.

"Excuse me, you've come to see who?"

"Roos. I know she's here."

"You have the wrong house, this is a private men's club," she said, then made to close the door.

However, Karen placed her foot in the way and pulled out a gun, raising it until it was inches from Hilda's face. "I won't say it again, just blow your fucking head off. Take me to Roos."

Hilda was terrified, even afraid of shouting out for help from the minder. All she could do was let go of the door to allow it to open fully. "This way," she said meekly.

Karen followed her in, along with three soldiers, who had been hidden out of view to anyone opening the door.

"You have minders, security people?" Karen asked.

"Only one man, he's in the kitchen."

Karen nodded to one soldier, who immediately went ahead and through to the kitchen.

"Now Roos, if you please," Karen said.

Hilda went across to the cellar door.

"Why is she in the cellar, don't you have bedrooms?"

"We have a special room, some members prefer it. She's down there with one."

Karen sighed. "You lot are sick. I hope this man with her likes publicity, because he's going to get it, believe me," she said, at the same time taking out her camera.

"You can't do that, the girl is there voluntary, this is not a brothel. And then, the member is the CEO of a large company and expects discretion."

"He can expect it, but he won't get it. Hold her while I go and see what he's up to," she ordered one of the soldiers.

Karen walked into a room in the cellar converted into a mock torture chamber. Immediately it reminded her of the time when she had been taken, then used in a pornographic movie. The room, although small, was very similar. In the room and bent over a central table was Roos, her hands tied up above her head, the bonds wrapped around a steel ring at the top of the table. Behind her, a naked man was holding a whip, at the same time taking her up her backside. Roos was screaming.

He didn't hear Karen enter, only stopping, and pulling out of Roos, to spin round and see why a camera was flashing behind him.

"Who the bloody hell are you? Get out of here, the session hasn't finished and give me that camera," Frank demanded.

"Well, if it isn't Sir Frank Sage, so this is what you get up to in your lunchtime. Your daughter and of course, your wife, along with the media, will be more than interested in the lunchtime activities one of our largest bank board members. Now release Roos and give her something to cover her body. Delay and I'll blow your fucking penis away, so you can never use it again," Karen ordered, raising her gun, so he could see she wasn't bluffing.

Frank now recognised Karen. She was a woman he knew better as Lady Harris. Except he also knew she commanded Unit T. Quickly he released Roos.

Roos on her part, with a blanket covering her naked body, was staring aghast at Karen. "Tori! You must go, they have a man, he's got a gun," she blurted out.

Karen smiled. "Have no worries on that score Roos, I've one as well and also, a few others with me are carrying guns. You're perfectly safe. Have you any clothes apart from what's used in this brothel?"

She nodded. "I've jeans and a jumper."

"Go and get yourself dressed, you're leaving with me. Neither the woman, or the man with a gun, are in a position to prevent it."

Roos left the room.

"What are you going to do with me?" Frank asked.

"You've a choice. You pay Roos compensation, or you take the consequences. I can assure you, using a trafficked girl carries a ten-year sentence with all assets taken. But I know your family very well, I wouldn't like to see them out on the street."

"How much?"

"Two hundred thousand, by bank transfer."

"You're mad. The girl's not worth a few pounds. She can have ten thousand and think herself lucky. "

"That's big of you. After you got yourself a bonus in the millions last year. If you agree to pay and don't I'll double it every day until you do. Then, if it's not paid by the end of the week, these pictures will be across all the social media sites. You will also have the police knocking on your door, with an arrest warrant."

"That's blackmail. You're supposed to uphold the law, I could get you sacked."

Karen sighed. "You can try and go down that route, but I left out the third option. With a bullet in your head, it's going to be a bit difficult standing up in court claiming I asked you for compensation. You see, Frank, the world you dipped your penis in, is not how you imagine. It is a world of violence and intimidation. A world where people get killed and maimed. If I followed the law all the time, many would walk away. People like you would use fancy solicitors to get themselves off. I'm giving you the chance to walk away, with your reputation intact, your wife and daughter not on the street, besides having set up a trafficked girl for life. I can take the long route, of course. Have you sent down, claim your assets and pay her out from my charity. It makes no difference to me, but your daughter Caroline and I get on well, I wouldn't like her to see what her dad really is. I can also have you killed; there again, my mandate allows me to shoot to kill, in order to protect myself, or a victim from a machete-wielding madman down in a torture cellar. So are you going to pay, end up in prison, or die in this mock dungeon? You have until I leave the room to decide. But hear this. Agree to pay and fail, and you will be in a police cell by the end of this week, or dead."

"How do you want me to pay?"

"A donation to my charity, all legal and above board, for at least what I ask and you'll even get tax relief. You will also send a covering letter to say how impressed with our work you are along with the donation. Do that and you are forgotten. However, if I catch you at it again, I will not be so lenient."

By now he was dressed. "Get me out of this house now. You will have the money by close of business today.

Don't think I will forget this, Harris, you will pay, believe me."

"Yes, I get that a lot, Frank. But think on; believe you can start a war with me and you fight under my rules. I use street law; that, my friend, is far more violent and often leaves the perpetrators dead."

***

Karen left Unit T soldiers, along with the police, to sort out the brothel. However, before the police arrived, Frank had been taken through the cellar and out the back. With only Roos having been trafficked and the other girls being regular prostitutes, Karen knew her case to pursue Luca's assets would be weak and very much rely on Roos. Except, Karen had no confidence that Roos would go through with it. She'd lived under the shadow of Luca for too long and would always be frightened of him. So her deal with Frank would be the best outcome she could expect, apart from the house owners being prosecuted for operating a brothel. Because of this, she'd had Roos taken out with Frank. Now she and Roos were in her flat above the charity offices.

Roos flung her arms around Karen and kissed her on the lips. "You don't know how relieved I was to see you standing there, Tori. On the Wednesday after you left, Luca had me sent there. I've had to prostitute since then. It's been a nightmare."

"Yes, I've known you were there ever since you arrived. As it is, let's get things straight, Roos. My name is Karen Harris, I used the name Tori for a covert mission against Luca, which is still going on."

By now Roos had pulled away. "So you've allowed me to be raped day after day, doing nothing about it, when you could have? How could you have done that to me, Karen?"

Karen didn't answer, but went through to the kitchen and made two coffees using her coffee machine. She brought them through. By now Roos had sat down.

"I'm waiting for an answer," Roos said, when Karen placed the cups on the coffee table.

"For a start, although you told me that pimps were going to Luca's house, it doesn't follow that just because you came to London with one, he had the intention of using you as a prostitute. You entered the country by a scheduled flight, never alerting anyone at the airport there could be a problem, so we had to assume you were there by choice and not against your will. Only when we looked into the actions of the man who took you to the house you were staying in did we begin to suspect it was a brothel and there could be a problem. That was confirmed after we placed surveillance on it to see who came and how regularly. Believe me, Roos, most of the women we pull out are in those places weeks, months and often years. So, why didn't you just walk out, go to the police station, or refuse to prostitute?" Karen of course knew why, but wanted Roos to answer.

"I couldn't. They threatened me all the time with beatings, or being put to work on the streets with a pimp, pumped full of drugs. What could I do? I've seen how drugs affect people in the park, when I used to go for a walk. I didn't want that to happen to me."

"Then, Roos, you took the sensible route. Remained uninjured and ready to run, if and when the opportunity arose and it would have. You forget that Luca intended Ikram to take you, not me. As it was, I could have coped, the same as you, servicing one man. But after his brother killed him, I was sold to a brothel servicing up to twenty a

360

day in appalling conditions, sharing toilets with fifteen other women. If I was too slow back from cleaning myself up for the next man, I was whipped. You had a bed, your own room, men who weren't covered in lice, or diseased. I had the floor. I came very close to shaving all my hair off, in an effort to get rid of the lice crawling about in it, besides suffering the indignity of dousing myself every day with disinfectant and having to wash myself out internally. So think yourself lucky you didn't end up with Ikram. We would never have found you then."

Roos looked decidedly embarrassed. "You're right, I'm sorry. I needed the wake-up call. What do I do now? Can I stay here with you? I've nowhere else to go."

"You can for the time being. To earn your keep, you work in my charity offices downstairs. It will open your eyes, believe me, besides telling you what I do beyond my military work. The charity will also talk to you about your future, where you want to live; whether it is accommodation shared with another girl, or having a place of your own,that will be your choice. It does not have to be in this country, we have a number of properties in many parts of the world. I've already set compensation for you in motion. That means you will have money to fall back on, until you get settled."

Her mouth dropped slightly. "You'd do all that for me?"

"I do it for every victim, Roos. It's what we do. You're among others who understand, you won't be demeaned, pulled down, looked on as some tramp. We're all the same, believe me. But we don't talk about it, just get on with our lives. Many are now happily married, have children and a new life away from the streets and the traffickers."

"You haven't taken that route."

Karen looked down. "You're right, I didn't settle

into a new life away from the dangers. You see, I can't have children, Roos, drugs damaged my reproductive organs. Like you, I lost my family, and most, if not all the men I've cared about are dead, or have walked away from our relationship, unable to accept the way I live. So this is my life and what I do. There are good times as well as down times, so I'm cool with it."

Roos grinned. "Well, that will all change, you've got me now; so what have you got to eat inside this really cool flat? I'll make a late lunch for us. I'm starving."

"I've no idea. I usually eat out, or have it sent in."

Roos stood and made her way to the kitchen. "Then it's a good thing I came when I did, at least with me here, you will eat," she called back from the kitchen, looking into the fridge. "God Karen, one ready meal, is that all there is?"

Karen came to the door. "I've just told you, I don't often eat in. Do you want to go out? I know a cafe that does specials, he'll feed us up?"

"Yes, I'm starving. We'll also go to a supermarket. Even in Brussels I had food in the house, not a lot I agree, but I fed you."

***

Karen was in bed after showering. There was a low knock on her door, then Roos pushed it open, standing there silhouetted in the doorway, wearing a set of silk pyjamas Karen had lent her. "Do you mind if I join you? I don't want to be alone, Karen?"

"Come on then, but you keep your cold feet off me."

Roos grinned and ran across the room, slipping in beside her, immediately putting her arm around Karen and pulling her close. "I've missed you, I really have. Although

362

I should be mad at you," Roos whispered in her ear.

"Why, what have I done now?"

"You bugged me, which got me a good strapping off Luca when he found them. So now you don't only owe me a good spanking of your bottom, for when we performed together, you owe me another to make up for what I got off Luca."

Karen sat up. "God, Roos, don't you ever forget anything? I've rescued you, I should get points for that?"

"Why? Like you said, it's what you do."

"Bloody hell, you're worse than me. Okay, let's at least get one over with, shall we? Sit yourself down on the side of the bed."

"No, I've no intention of getting out of bed, I'm nice and warm now. You'll have to wait."

Karen flopped back down. "It's a good job I like you, otherwise I'd have you go back to your own room."

Roos moved closer, kissing Karen hard and long. Karen didn't pull back.

"You wouldn't let me go. Anyway, I'm no longer tired, so are you going to help me sleep then?" Roos asked, beginning to unfasten the buttons of her pyjama top.

"Why not, you've woken me up now," Karen said, pulling her own nightie over her head.

Soon both girls were naked, their lovemaking intense, happy to be with each other again.

Chapter 60

Nabil was back in Belgium. He'd just left Karen's soldiers and was in a taxi heading for Luca's house. Happy he was going to get access to Ikram's bank account in Algeria, he had no compunctions about helping Karen out - after all, this money would negate the need to be hands-on with the brothel. He could live the good life and want for nothing. As for Luca, he had no allegiance to him, he could take his chances the same as him.

The taxi dropped him off outside Luca's house, where he was met by Yannick and taken through to the pool area.

"Ah, Nabil. I trust it was a successful meeting?"

"It was, they had nothing on Ikram. I think they were hoping no one would come forward and question their actions."

"You met the Harris women then?"

"I did."

"What is she like?"

"Nervous, very naive. But a good-looking woman all the same. I'd like to put her to work."

Luca smiled. "Many have said that. Anyway, the girls are ready for your final inspection before they leave, we should go?"

***

They had been travelling for over an hour when the car turned down a side road, coming out in a clearing.

"Where are we, Luca?"

"The car will be here soon. I like to be in a place that

cannot be set up for surveillance. Shall we get out?"

However, when Nabil climbed out, Yannick, who had been driving, grabbed his arm and propelled him a distance from the car, forcing him down on his knees.

Luca came up, standing in front of him. "It would seem, Nabil, you have decided to join forces with the Harris woman. Don't tell me you haven't, I've had a call from an informer at Unit T's camp about the document you signed and also seen the transcript of your conversation. You must think we're stupid in Europe? We are not and we have a code of conduct. We don't sell others down the river."

"You have me wrong. I agree I made a deal, you would with a gun at your head. But I was going to tell you, plus an alternative route Harris believes we are taking."

"Yes, I suspected you'd come up with such an excuse. But we also know Harris. You tell me she's a naive girl that portrays nervousness, but she is neither. Karen Haris has survived since she was seventeen under conditions that would tax the hardest of men. She's done that because she's not only a born killer, but very astute, capable and extremely dangerous. For you to believe you had one up on her makes you a fool, to even attempt to move girls across a border with her breathing down my neck. As it is, she needs a calling card, to remind her I'm not a fool as well. Besides being one step ahead of her." Luca nodded to Yannick.

Yannick pulled a gun from his pocket and shot Nabil in the back of the head. Then he took a detector from his pocket, which had found Karen's location device on Roos, and scanned Nabil's body. It suddenly came alive with a continuous buzz. "He has a locator fitted."

"That's good, it means they will come here. Give me the locator and put his body in the car boot." Taking an envelope from his pocket, Luca placed it on the ground with the locator on top. Then he and Yannick left in their car.

**

"Karen, Sherry."

"What is it, Sherry?"

"Nabil didn't keep his appointment with us. According to the tracker we placed on him, he's not moved from a location about five miles from here. Do you want us to investigate?"

Karen sighed, she'd a feeling it had gone wrong. "Yes, do that and come back to me as soon as you have information."

Sherry was back in twenty minutes.

"All we've found is the locator we put on Nabil. There's also an envelope with your name on it. Do you want me to open it?"

"Yes, make sure you're alone, then read it out to me."

Sherry left the others soldiers and walked over to the Range Rover. After climbing inside, she shut the door and began to read.

'So you believe I am a fool, Karen Harris? I was onto you and your deal with Nabil, hours back. Take the death of first Pier, and now Nabil, as a reminder of how easy it would have been for me to take you down on that deck. But I decided to spare your life, to show you how vulnerable you really are. It's time you retired Karen. Look after Roos for me. I know you have her and that you two are lovers. She'll be perfect, loyal in your retirement, you couldn't have a better going away present. I was just surprised how long you left her in the brothel. I couldn't have made the clues of her demise more obvious for you.'

"That's it, Karen."

366

"Thanks, Sherry, keep hold of the note for me. Show it no one else."

"No problem. When will I see you back in France?"

"I'll be there tomorrow."

Sherry shut down the call and leaned back. Luca's words about Roos made her feel sick inside. Karen should have told her there was more between her and Roos than she'd admitted. As it was, she had always been there for her, but it seemed she wasn't good enough.

Chapter 61

Karen was back in France. She'd arrived an hour earlier, grabbing lunch in the camp restaurant. As usual, it was crowded, but when she entered in her uniform everyone came to attention. She just nodded for them to carry on and selected a seat by the window.

The chef approached. "Good afternoon, Colonel. Can I tell you what's on today?"

She shook her head. "No thank you, I'm happy to eat whatever the special is, with coffee."

He nodded and left her. Stanley came into the room, looked around and came over. "Can I join you Karen?"

"Yes, no problem. Are you eating?"

"I only want coffee, I had my sandwiches earlier. Are you sure we need to talk now, you should at least have your dinner in peace?"

"Yes, it's fine. But I've a feeling we may have the informer."

He looked a little taken aback. "What makes you believe that?"

Before she could answer, the chef approached with her food. It was lasagne and chips. "Are you sure this is alright for you, Colonel?" he asked, placing the plate down in front of her.

"Perfect, believe me. Can you bring an extra coffee for Stanley, please?"

When he left, Karen began to eat. "Sorry, Stanley, I am starving. I missed breakfast and arrived at the airport with no time to collect even a sandwich, otherwise I'd have missed my take-off slot. Anyway, as I was saying, we might have the informer."

"Just finish your dinner, Karen, I'm happy to wait. Whoever you suspect is going nowhere in the next few minutes."

As she finished, both coffee and rhubarb and custard arrived.

Stanley smiled. "You should eat here all the time, Karen. This way we can see you're being fed properly."

"You wouldn't need to, you'd notice soon enough after I put on a few stone. But it was good for a change. Anyway, I was saying. After the meeting with Nabil, I sent you and Nigel a summary. No one else."

"You did, and with such a heavy workload yesterday, I've still not copied the relevant information to interested parties. It's not like me, Karen, and I apologize."

"It was a good job you didn't this time, Stanley, because it meant only you and Nigel knew what had transpired."

Stanley looked at her as she finished the sweet. "Are you suggesting Nigel may be the informer?"

She put her spoon down. "We know whoever it is has access to highly classified information, yes?"

"That's correct."

"Well, Luca knew all about my meeting with Nabil. I think Luca killed him."

"How do you know that?"

"There was a letter addressed to me by the side of the tracker. In it, Luca claimed he already knew what Nabil and I had agreed. I told Sherry, who found it, not to tell anyone what was inside. But she has read it out to me."

"You seem to be suggesting, because only me and Nigel had sight of the transcript, it could only be he, or I, who talked to Luca."

"Exactly. Although I believe it is more complicated

than that. If we look back at the times we suspected there was an informer at work, Luca wasn't part of it. So the informer could hardly peddle information around to each criminal we investigate. I believe Nigel is selling it to one man. It is that man who is in contact with interested parties in the criminal fraternity."

"That makes sense, but it could well mean Nigel is not his only informer."

She sipped her coffee. "I'd not thought of that, but it's possible. After all, Nigel is not party to all our operations, especially the covert ones that have also gone wrong."

"So what do you want me to do?"

"We tie him down so tight, he won't be able to breathe without us knowing about it. We also feed information that seems to have value through him and see what happens. I'm not bothered if it takes us six months, Stanley, to finally nail him and who he's reporting to. Provided when we move, we are sure he was the only one, or we have them all."

"I'll set it up. Anyway, what is your next move towards Luca and Parker, now it's gone pear-shaped?"

"Parker worries me. The man is a psychopath and I can't honestly believe he's invested a considerable amount of money in what are legitimate businesses for nothing. What better way to hide illegal activities than legal ones? I'm of the mind to go to Holland and look over this brothel he and Luca run."

"Is this going to be covert?"

"To get inside the brothel, yes. Even if I put clients in, they wouldn't get behind the scenes. The point is Stanley, this can only be between you and me. I'm not risking my life by an informer tipping Luca off."

"I understand, Karen. But I'm not happy you being there without any sort of backup."

"I'll be fine, Stanley. This is just a quick look-around, that's all."

***

Sherry was by the side of the pool when Karen arrived home later that day.

"Hi, had a good day?" Sherry asked.

"It's been a long day and more than a little stressful. How about you?"

"I actually went for a drive when you weren't home for lunch. I took Ally, we had a good time."

"Where's Ally now?"

"She's in her room catching up with her homework. Dinner's at half seven, are you joining us?"

"Why shouldn't I be? Anyway, I'm getting changed and having a swim, how about you joining me?" Karen asked, walking over to the small changing cubicle attached to the house.

"No, I've washed my hair so I don't want to wreck it."

Karen came out in a single-piece costume. She liked to wear a single piece when she intended to do her twenty lengths. "So if you've done your hair, you're out with James tonight then?"

"No, I was staying in. I often wash my hair without going out, not that you'd notice."

Karen looked at Sherry for a moment, sighed, then dived into the pool. Then she bobbed up. "Time my strokes per minute Sherry, at the start of my second length after I've warmed up. Then I'll do my twenty."

By the time Karen was on her fifteenth length, Ally had come through, wearing shorts and a T-shirt.

"Karen's back then, when did she arrive?"

"Half an hour ago. I hope you're going to change for dinner. You know Karen won't have you in the dining room wearing shorts at night?"

"What's up with you? Give me a grain of sense."

Suddenly Karen came to a halt, she was breathing hard. "Well, what am I at?"

"I'm getting around ten strokes in 8 seconds. That's rubbish, Karen. You're down to around seventy five a minute, you used to do ninety. Now you'd struggle to keep up with me, when six months back you'd have left me in your wake."

Karen climbed out, nodding to Ally. "It's no use, I'll have to get back in the gym. The last weeks have taken their toll. I'll get ready for dinner, see you both in there."

"So what's she been up to over the last weeks then?" Ally asked, after Karen left.

"You know better than to ask, Ally. I'm going in as well."

***

It was getting on for half-eleven, and Ally was in her room. Karen and Sherry were sitting by the pool, both had drinks. The night was warm, the pool shimmering in the lights from the patio.

"Come on, spill it, Sherry. You've been off all night. Has James left you?"

"We're not going out any longer, if that's what you mean, but it was mutual. He told me he felt uncomfortable with me living here. Feeling you'd come around the corner at any moment. So to continue our relationship he wanted us to live together. I wasn't interested in moving out and living with a man, this is my home."

"I'm sorry, Sherry, I really am. How about we go to the coast for a couple of days. From next week, I'm away again."

"Where? Back to London and Roos?"

Karen smiled. "Oh, so this is what it's all about is it? Roos and the letter from Luca. It goes to show you shouldn't read other people's letters."

"You told me to read it and yes, it is. We've been together for a long time Karen. If you wanted to go that way, why not with me? You know I'd do anything you want. I've had more than my fill of men, so if you wanted me to join you in bed, I'd have done that. It just hurts to be pushed out."

Karen reached out and touched Sherry's hand. "I've not pushed you out, Sherry. Roos and I were forced to do a sex act together on the bed, the same as you and I, in Luca's effort to sell her. I admit I've been close to her, she's very fragile, living her life with a trafficker that treated her like shit since she was fourteen. The girl was very insecure, gaining a little security from the girl she shared a flat with, replacing that lost security with me after the girl left. Roos doesn't look at having sex with another woman as strange, it's just that being close to a woman gave her much-needed comfort. As it is, she now works in the charity, the girls there will take her out, give her confidence in herself, and she will be moving to one of my houses in Spain very shortly. There was and never will be a relationship, except a need for the girl to not feel as alone as she's been."

"Then we're still friends?"

"We've never not been, Sherry. I love you a great deal. We owe our lives to each other. I'll never turn my back on you. But a sexual relationship? Even with the abuse I've put up with in my life, I still flipped when I was with Pier. I wanted to be held, loved and feel safe in a man's arms," she said, then hesitated. "Even though deep down I know it can never happen. I'm not ready yet to turn my back on my dreams. When and if I am and you're still with me and feel the same, maybe that's our future."

Sherry grinned. "I'll be here, Karen, believe me. In the meantime, let's go to the coast and flirt, shall we? Should we take Ally?"

Karen smiled to herself, Sherry only needed a boost to her confidence and was already back to being the girl she knew and loved. "We'll have to, otherwise she'll mope around for days complaining."

Chapter 62

With her hair dyed black and permed into ringlets, a spray tan that darkened her skin, and a dress that finished well below the knees, Karen no longer looked like Karen or Tori. She was Martine, a French girl from Paris and a cleaner. She had also deliberately dressed in such a way as to look plain and like a woman in her thirties.

Karen had flown from Paris to Amsterdam on a scheduled flight and booked into a low-cost hotel, after finding out that the brothel Luca and Parker owned was advertising for a live-in cleaner. After calling the agency advertising the vacancy and furnishing them with false references, they had arranged an interview with Wouter for her.

The following day, Karen rang the bell of the brothel. Noa answered the door.

"Je suis de l'agence à propos de la vacance de nettoyage," Karen asked in French.

"Ik kan niet begrijpen Frans, kun je niet nederlands spreken?" Noa replied in Dutch.

"Ik kan spreken Engels," Karen answered in Dutch, using a phrase book she'd pulled from her pocket.

Noa smiled. "Then we will speak English. What is it you want?"

"I'm from the agency about the cleaning vacancy."

"Ah yes, then you must be Martine, please come in."

Karen followed her through to the office. Wouter was sitting at a desk with a computer on.

"This is Martine, she's from the agency," Noa told Wouter.

He looked at Karen, then smiled. "The agency told

me you were working in a brothel before your current job and looking to live and work in Amsterdam. The references they sent, from your current employer, speak very highly of you."

Karen gave a weak smile. "It was nice of them to say that. When you work in a brothel the job required a cleaner to be discreet, besides honest, because I was at times around clients. I'd often find items on the floors, or in the beds that belonged to clients, sometimes of a personal nature. I would always hand them in, I'm not a thief. You will also find I work hard and keep well out of the way."

"We like your honesty and it is true, clients mislay items at times. It is a six day a week job, you live in and will begin at six in the morning, working until eleven when we open. Then it's four hours off before you help the cook in the kitchen. Our girls have a break at half-past four for food. After you clean up and wash the dishes the night is your own. Although occasionally, if you're in your room you may be asked to tidy up after a spillage, or if a client has drunk too much and makes a mess. You have no objections to that?"

"No, it's what I'd be here for. Do girls stay overnight?"

"They're all gone by three in the morning. We have a security guard who looks after the building. No one else, besides you, remains on the premises. Your room is a bedsit in the cellar. There is a way into the bedsit from the service road behind the building. You can come and go when you are not working. The door from your bedsit into the house will be locked after the last girl leaves and will be opened at six in the morning. That's for security."

"How much would I be paid, and can I eat when the girls have their tea, or would you expect me to make my own?"

"We will pay you five hundred euros per week,

with fifty euro taken off for your accommodation. You may eat with the girls in the afternoon, but we don't provide breakfast. You must buy that. There is a single ring and a fridge in your room."

"If you decide to offer me the job, when can I start? I'm in a cheap hotel at the moment, while I look for work."

"We have more interviews, then we will decide. If you are to be offered the job, we will call you later today. You can begin immediately. Do you have any more questions?"

"No, it's what I enjoy doing, so you will have no complaints about my work. Would my lack of the Dutch language be a problem for me?"

"It won't, but by having knowledge of German, you will pick it up quickly. Although most, if not all the girls, including the cook and security, can speak either English or German."

***

Karen returned to the hotel she'd booked into and was sitting on the bed, looking at plans Stanley had given her before she left the unit. These plans were of the brothel, obtained from the local authority. It showed four floors and a basement. With a total of six rooms on each floor, she'd be faced with cleaning eighteen rooms and three small lounges. Karen didn't relish the work, but it was better than going into the house as a prostitute. They would have far less freedom to wander than she would have.

It was just after six when her mobile telephone rang. "Hi, this is Martine," Karen answered in French.

"Martine, Noa. Wouter has asked me to call you," she said in English. "We are prepared to give you a month's trial. You would begin Wednesday. You can move in tomorrow, if you still want the job?"

"Thank you, yes, I would love the job. I'll bring my bag in the morning."

"Very well, we will see you then."

Chapter 63

Karen had been in the brothel for over a week. Her room, in the basement, was large and being next to the boiler room was nice and warm. It was sparse, with only a bed, an old settee, wardrobe, besides a kitchenette. Also fitted to the wall was a modern flat screen television. The toilet and bathroom were in another room of the basement. The only other room was a store, where all her cleaning materials were kept. Stone steps took her up through a door into a large hall, with three small lounges coming off it and the office. This door from the hall into the basement was the door that was locked at night. However, following closer inspection, the mortice lock was actually fitted on the basement side of the door and she suspected if she carefully unscrewed it, she could go through. Karen decided, once she had the lie of the building, she might need to do just that.

Karen was also confused. The plans she had of the building showed four floors, including the ground floor, but she only cleaned three and there were no steps to the top floor; even the lift only showed three floors and the basement. Another interesting part was that the lift opened front and back. This allowed her to load the lift with cleaning goods and food delivered around the back of the building. For her this was useful and saved carrying anything through the front door and downstairs.

With never really having come to Amsterdam before, she'd spent time looking around. She'd found a bar the locals used and had already made a few acquaintances. Karen didn't need to eat out, the dinner for the girls was good and there was plenty of it. So with her cereals and toast in the morning, that was sufficient.

The brothel operated very differently to what she had been used to. The front door was discrete, among a number of other houses. A client would be taken to one of the lounges and shown the girls available that night. If he decided on one she'd take him to a room, otherwise he would leave. Very rarely did clients meet each other and never would they be in the same lounge together. The client could also have a drink in his lounge, often with the girl. But it was part of the arranged session time and the drinks could be very expensive. The bedrooms just had a bed and a shower room. The client always had to shower, if he paid extra the girl would join him. As for cleaning, Karen found it very easy. A quick wipe around in the shower rooms, cleaning the toilets, besides changing the linen and vacuuming, was all that they required.

Karen, by now, was beginning to wonder if she was wasting her time. However, she did have a number of anomalies to clear up before she called it a day. The help she gave to the cook to prepare dinner also included sandwiches. The sandwiches were put on five plates, including a slice of cake. Then the plates were stacked with plate spacers between, ready to be taken away. She never saw what happened to them, assuming they were for clients. But no plate was ever left in a room. Then when she tidied up the kitchen in the morning, the plates were always back to be washed. The night before had also rung alarm bells that she was missing something. When cleaning a spillage in the hall, three clients came through and were taken directly to the lift and not into a lounge. With the missing floor, the extra food and now, these clients not being accompanied by a girl to a room, she figured it was essential she got to the top floor. But how, she'd no idea. Twice, cleaning the inside of the lift, she'd looked around the interior, trying to work out how to get up there. She'd tried button combinations, but never got above the third floor. She'd even been out the back and although the emergency fire escape did go to a door which she suspected was on the fourth floor, when she went up one night after everyone had gone, she found the door could only be opened from the inside, telling her there had to be an inside entrance. Finally Karen came to the conclusion, that the lock set into the button panel inside the lift and used to take the lift out of service, had to be the key to getting to the floor. That meant, when she was alone in the morning doing her cleaning, she'd need to sort out how to bypass the lock.

***

Karen wasn't one to sit watching television every night and would go to a local bar she'd found. A man of thirty-three had taken a great deal of interest in her when she was in the bar and they'd played pool at the table in the back room one night. His name was Bram and he worked in a hotel. She liked him; at over six foot tall, he obviously worked out and looked after himself, and he was good looking, so why wouldn't she?

"Would you like to eat?" he asked after they finished a game and handed the table over to others waiting.

"A burger or similar, not a full meal. The place I work in gives me with dinner."

"A burger sounds good. I'll also show you a good dancing club later, if you dance?"

She smiled. "I dance, lead on, Bram."

Soon they were sitting in a small cafe, the burgers were huge and Karen was glad she'd said no to chips and salad.

"You enjoy where you work?" he asked.

"It's okay, as cleaning jobs go. Not like a hotel, so long as it's clean they're happy. What about your job?"

"I do thirteen hours, four, sometimes five days a week. Serving breakfast, lunch and afternoon teas. They wanted me to do the evenings as well, but I drew the line at that."

"Well, at least you can get out at night."

"I can, you also."

"Yes, I'm on at six in the mornings as well. Tomorrow, though, we are closed, so it's my day off." Karen looked around the cafe. Most girls, it was obvious from the way they were dressed, were prostitutes. "It's really busy this place," she commented.

"At this time, yes. The working girls use it before they begin again. I've a confession to make. When I first saw you I thought you were a working girl. Not that your clothes are what they would wear around here, but you're a good-looking woman and very desirable. Although, I'm glad you're not."

Karen gave a hint of a smile. "I'm not sure if I should be flattered, or annoyed, Bram. But it's nice of you to say I still look attractive at my age. Especially when around me there are eighteen-year-olds, particularly attractive and I might add, very sexy in the way they dress."

"They are, but I'd rather be with you, then take one of them out for the night. Anyway, if you've finished, let's go and see if you can dance as well, shall we?"

***

It was coming up to quarter to three in the morning. Karen was walking back to the brothel with Bram. They'd had a good night and he was gripping her hand tightly. Already she was wondering if he expected her to ask him in. If he was, he'd have a nasty shock. She'd never been to bed with a man on the first date and had no intention of starting, even if he was good-looking, muscular and she was very much attracted to him. Karen never considered the times when she was taken against her will as any sort of relationship, such actions were nothing short of rape and formed no part of her actual life. So anyone asking her out would need to follow her rules, particularly if they wished to continue the relationship. Not that she told someone asking her out that, except they wouldn't get very far with her, if that was all they wanted from the relationship.

As they rounded the bend coming onto the back street, where the outside entrance to her bedsit was located, a van was parked close to the back entrance of the brothel. The back doors were open and a man was standing there smoking. Karen suddenly grabbed Bram and kissed him with real passion. He of course reacted and they moved closer to the wall and into the shadows, continuing their embrace. All the time, Karen had moved herself into a position to watch the van.

Bram had taken her actions as wanting more intimacy and had already lowered his hands down, gently rubbing her bottom, pulling her tighter to his body. She on her part could already feel his hardness as she arched herself up, virtually on her tiptoes, to carry on kissing him.

It was at that point that the back door of the brothel opened, the light inside spilling out. Four girls, obviously very young, were being urged out by Wouter and into the back of the van. Then the doors were closed and it drove away. Wouter went back inside the brothel and pulled the door shut.

Karen, so interested in this, had not really taken

much notice of Bram, who by now had moved his hands around and released her jeans. She pushed him away. "I'm not fucking in the street," she told him curtly, at the same time re-fastening her jeans.

"So where do you live, we should go there, Martine. You know I want you and you're the same?"

She just shrugged. "Maybe, but I don't fuck on a first date. So get lost, I'm going home." Then she turned and began to walk away.

He made a grab at her, stopping her in her tracks. "What was all the kissing about? If you don't want to be fucked?" he demanded.

Karen turned and looked at him. "I'm not averse to kissing, anything more, you wait until we get to know each other. That's the difference between me and the prostitutes, otherwise I might as well be one of them, and you pay for it." She shook his hand off her and this time she did walk away.

"Fucking bitch," he shouted after her.

But Karen didn't respond. Already she was deep in thought. At least she had an idea as to what was going on. Where the clients were going, the sandwiches she'd make and the floor with no obvious entry.

Chapter 64

During her day off, Karen had taken the opportunity to look round Amsterdam and even went on a boat ride. It had been a good day, however, later in the afternoon, with a plan already forming in her mind, she'd hired a small car, parking it up a short distance from the brothel.

***

It was coming up to seven in the morning the next day. Karen had been up as usual at six, when the door from the basement to the house was unlocked, and she'd begun her cleaning. Already the security night man had left and she'd be alone in the house until Noa arrived at half past eight. The woman never arrived before that time, having to first take her child to a nursery before coming to work. Using a screwdriver she'd purchased locally, Karen began unscrewing the panel in the lift. Pulling it away to get behind it, she used the screwdriver tip to short the two wires fitted to the key switch. There was a spark, then the lift door closed and it began to rise, eventually stopping. Karen looked at the floor level, disappointed she was still on the third floor, until the door opened; then she knew she wasn't. This was different and certainly the elusive fourth floor. With the foresight to jamb the doors of the lift in case it closed on her, and she couldn't get back down, Karen stepped out onto the landing. She began to check each door, finding they led to bedrooms similar to the floors below, until she entered Parker's special room. Standing there, she stared at the table; this was a cleverly disguised autopsy table, the slops underneath leading to a drain. She knew that to use such a table for autopsy, a bucket would be placed under the drain hole, to funnel off bodily fluids. There were a number of high chairs set around the room and a large television screen attached to one wall. Hanging on hooks around the walls, were instruments of torture, besides a machete and an axe. Karen went cold inside, her body was literally shaking at the thought of what went on in here. Her thoughts went back to what Samuel French had told her Parker was up to. This was why they purchased the brothel; this was his new torture chamber. Going through to the far door which was open was his dressing room. Coming back into the chamber, Karen walked across to the other side and into another room. Inside were two steel tables on castors, long enough to lay a person on. In a corner, ankle shackles. Karen had seen enough, so after taking photographs of the rooms, she returned to the lift, selecting the third floor. It went down and opened. She screwed the panel back and began cleaning the rooms. This had now turned into something far more sinister; she had to think. If she got it wrong, delayed too long, Parker could kill more victims, or escape.

***

It was quarter to three in the morning, and Karen had been sitting in the little car she'd hired for nearly half an hour. Dressed in black jeans, black T-shirt and bomber jacket, she also had a gun and a camera on her.

A few minutes later the same van that had been there two nights before turned down the back street, reversing to the doors of the brothel. Karen was out of the car quickly, moving up to the same position she and Bram had occupied, backing into the shadows. Using the camera, after setting it on movies, Karen filmed the man who was driving the van and Wouter coming out the back of the brothel with the girls. Then she ran back to her car and waited. Soon the van turned out onto the road, joining what little traffic was around. Karen followed, keeping her distance.

They travelled for over twenty minutes, she was getting worried the driver may notice he was being followed, with only her and him on the road. But he didn't seem to and turned into the drive of a house. Karen carried on past, stopping quite a distance away. Zipping her jacket up, after pulling her gun out and checking it was operational, Karen left the car. Keeping in the shadows as much as she could, she soon arrived at the driveway the van had turned into. Without hesitation she made her way down, coming out into a large parking area. The van was parked up beside a number of other vehicles. The only lights on were in the hallway and two rooms at the top of the house.

Moving around the house, Karen began checking the widows, but all were locked. Deciding she needed help, Karen took all the registration numbers and left. Soon she was back in her bedsit. Pulling out her mobile, she called Unit T.

After giving her access codes she was put through to the duty officer. "What can I do for you, Colonel?" he asked.

"Patch me through to Lieutenant Foster, please."

With everyone asleep, it took a little time before the lieutenant came to the phone. "Colonel, Foster here."

"Colonel Harris, Lieutenant. I'm mobilizing Dark Angel. Wake everyone up and I want that camp shut down as tight as a barrel. Nothing in, nothing out and all communications shut down or blocked. Anyone not following my orders, arrest them. Civilian or military. Have we an understanding?"

"If that is your order, Colonel, it will be implemented. Can you give me the reason for such tight security?"

"Not at this moment, but I can assure you it's necessary."

"I understand, Colonel. Where is Dark Angel's target location?"

"Amsterdam. Once there, you wait for me to contact you. I'll need Sergeant Malloy, so have a security detail collect her from home please."

***

Stanley turned over to answer his telephone. He glanced at the time, it was just after four in the morning. "Hello, Stanley here," he said sleepily.

"Sorry Stanley. Lieutenant Foster. Karen's ordered mobilisation. But it's even more serious. She's had the whole camp awakened and shut the place down completely from the outside world. Nothing is allowed to move in or out apart from security collecting Sergeant Malloy. People are going to their allocated locations, knowing she's mobilised, but not why."

"Has she given a target location?"

"Amsterdam. The first C4 is already warming up and will leave in the next half hour."

"I understand. I'll be there as quick as I can. Has all communication been blocked?"

"It has, that was the first thing I did."

"Very well. I understand where Karen is coming from so you must do exactly as she's ordered."

***

Sherry very nearly fell out of bed when the telephone at her bedside began to ring. She'd turned the sound up for when she was in the shower earlier and forgotten to turn it back down.

"Hello," she said sleepily.

"Sergeant Malloy?" came a curt voice.

"Yes."

"We're outside, Unit T has mobilised, don't bother to dress, just get yourself down here now, you're wanted."

Sherry was out of bed in seconds, grabbed her dressing gown, pulling it on, before taking a small bag out of the wardrobe. This was her mobilisation bag, containing essentials for just such an event. It was always packed ready to go. Running downstairs, she came outside to find a Land Rover with two MPs waiting.

"You have no mobile or any other means of communication, Sergeant?" one asked, having her stand while he patted her down, as the other opened her bag to check through.

"No, nothing," she answered, expecting to be searched, with her being outside the camp when mobilisation was actioned. Normally she'd have to remain outside, but it seemed they, or maybe Karen, wanted her.

"Then get in."

Sherry gasped as they approached the camp, it looked like the entire camp was awake, the perimeter had far more guards than normal. Whatever had happened was serious, if Karen is mobilizing in the middle of the night and securing the camp as she had done. Only once had she seen this level before, when she first arrived at Unit T. Then, there was an imminent attack by mercenaries.

Once in the guardhouse, she was taken into a back room with two female soldiers, where she handed over the dressing gown and nightdress, before being allowed to dress in her combat clothes. Soon she was on the way to the second of the C4s waiting to leave. The first one was already roaring down the runway, shaking the camp as it took off.

***

Nigel Summers, like everyone else in the camp, were awake. While he'd not been woken directly, the noise outside from vehicles on the move, the tannoy announcements, followed by the taking off of the C4s, would wake anyone. He was annoyed, he didn't want his base to be here, his job was only legal and it required him to spend most of his time travelling. But Karen would have no one who worked for her based outside the camp. You had to be here, or not at all.

His wife came up behind him, slipping her arms around his waist. "So what are they up to now?" she asked.

"This must be one of their so called mobilisations. I ask you, at bloody four in the morning, the woman is mad. What difference would it make, to wait until a more reasonable time, when everyone is up?"

"They're soldiers, love, not solicitors. You're far more laid-back, this lot play at soldiers like children, believing they're important."

At that moment there was a low knock on the door.

"I'll see to it love, you go back to bed, now the aircraft have left, at least we'll have peace," Nigel told her.

Once she returned to bed, Nigel went outside. There was no one there so he made his way around the side of the house. From the shadows a woman stepped out.

"Can you get a call out?" she asked quietly.

"Possibly, is it important?"

"The destination is Amsterdam. The conversations I'm hearing between Stanley and Lieutenant Soyer running the task force indicate the target to be Luca's brothel. He needs to know. I checked Karen's mobile call to mobilise and its location. She's in Amsterdam and must be covert, there are no records of her going there, but by the way Stanley's acting he knew she was there. Her aircraft is in Paris and has been there for over a week. So she either took a train, or a scheduled flight, and has never reported back to control, unless she's talking to Stanley off the record."

"She could be, but often even Stanley has no idea where she is. I'll see what I can do, I think I've a way to get the information out."

The woman put her arms around Nigel and kissed him gently. "Be careful Nigel. Karen is no fool and for some reason she tightened the camp up beyond anything I've seen in the past. She must suspect something."

"We're fine and bulletproof, believe me. She can't know, otherwise she'd have made her move before mobilising."

"I hope so. When do we leave? I'm fed up with meeting you in the forest and playing second fiddle to your wife all the time?"

"Soon, very soon, I promise. For us this is the big one, it's worth a considerable amount of money, believe me."

"I must go, before I'm missed. Be in the restaurant at half twelve, table three. I'll leave a SIM card on the floor, close to my seat. I'll vacate the table as soon as I see you carrying a tray, so take my place. It will have all the details of the operation."

"I'll be there," he said, kissing her once more.

Chapter 65

Luca replaced the telephone and leaned back in thought. Then he shouted for Yannick. "Unit T has mobilised, according to Padjent's contact in the camp."

"Is that important?"

"Normally no, but he's also told me the Harris woman hasn't been seen for over a week, left her aircraft in Paris, but has popped up in Amsterdam. I don't like it, Yannick. We cannot afford to underestimate her."

Yannick shrugged. "It's a large place with many brothels and escort services. The odds of her targeting you are slim."

Luca drummed his fingers on the desk, then picked the telephone handset up, beginning to dial.

"Hello," came a voice on the other end of the phone.

"Wouter, Luca. Can you talk?"

"I can. Kenneth is in with me, do you want it on speaker?"

"Yes, but shut the door."

Luca heard a door bang. "It's closed, how can I help."

"Harris is in Amsterdam. She's covert, which means she's sussing something out. Now I've just heard Unit T has mobilised. Have you had any new girls starting recently?"

"No, apart from a cleaner. She's come from an agency and had good references."

Luca looked at Yanick. "Do you think she'd be a cleaner?"

"Possibly, for a short duration."

"How old is the cleaner and what does she look like, Wouter?"

"Mid-thirties, five eight with black curly hair. Could

be attractive if she didn't wear sloppy jeans and jumpers with flat shoes. She works hard and frequents a local bar on her time off, then tidies herself up a bit, but puts too much make-up on. If she is the woman you're looking for, she'll not find anything. She works only the bedroom floors and lounges, besides helping in the kitchen."

"Is she ever alone?" Luca wanted to know.

"Only for an hour or so in the mornings, when she cleans the bedrooms. Noa is in at half eight. Then, as you know, there is no access to the top floor."

"What have you on this week, Kenneth?"

"Two specials, tonight and Friday, why?" Kenneth answered.

"Can you put them off?"

"Bit difficult, Luca. The four tonight have paid for an hour session with an underage, followed by a show. At five grand a head, that's a lot of money, besides, it could put off the clients in the future if we delayed."

"Mail me her application and photo, Wouter. If she checks out, go ahead. If she doesn't, you could have a new victim to use in your entertainment. I'll also push my contact who has informers in Unit T and try to find their target."

Chapter 66

After finishing her cleaning, Karen left the brothel, taking bus 22 and getting off at Kadijksplein, close to the Nemo Science Centre. A short distance from the bus stop, she entered a car park and was soon sitting in the back of a Unit T Range Rover. Also inside was Lieutenant Soyer.

"I must say I wouldn't have recognised you, if I'd passed you on the street, Colonel."

"Thanks, I'm not sure which way to take that. As it is, we have a problem with timing on this one. Stanley has given you the two locations has he?"

"He has and we've already set-up surveillance at the house where the youngsters are being kept, so we will know when they leave for the brothel. As instructed, we have kept away from the brothel itself."

"Who's going in as clients?"

"Mathers and Holden."

She nodded. "They're good lads. The brothel has cameras inside the house, but they aren't attached to recording devices. The manager, Wouter, uses them to keep a cursory eye on what's going on from his office. I'm off work after the girls finish their break and I've tidied up. That's about half- five. Parker arrived this morning, I saw him when I was cleaning the lounges on the ground floor. If he's here, then something's going down. My problem is, I'm not sure how often the children are used, so we may not go in tonight. Only you will know that, when they leave the house for the brothel. This is important, Lieutenant. We can only go in when we're certain the underage children are being used. To go in before leaves us with nothing. I know it means further abuse, but it can't be avoided if we want to take this operation down completely." Karen pulled out her camera and showed the lieutenant photos she had taken of the entrance hall of the brothel, the lift, with the button panel intact and removed, and the rooms on the top floor, including the torture chamber. "You can see how the chamber is set up, there's even a drain for the blood from the victim." She changed the picture. "This is what I believe is a preparation room." Again she changed the picture. "This is the changing room for Parker. How the hell we are going to prevent Parker doing what he intends, having no indication as to what is happening, I don't know. I wish I'd had surveillance equipment I could have placed, but I didn't, so we're going in blind."

Lieutenant Soyer looked at the photos. He, like Karen, was very experienced in incursion operations. "Tell me, Colonel, would you be able to give us the heads up, after we let you know the children have been delivered and you saw clients getting directly into the lift?"

Karen thought. "The only way I could do that would be if I was on the ground floor. When the children arrive, send in either Mathers or Holden. Have whoever you send throw up in a lounge. Odds are, if I'm in my room, they'd call me to come and clean it up, they wouldn't want to do it themselves if I was there. That way I could hang around to watch the lift. I can't see them leaving the children for long without their first clients."

"We could arrange that. The other thing is communication between the rest of the house and the top floor. It must logically be from the office. If we secure the office, maybe the soldiers going up in the lift, could effectively arrive on the top floor without anyone on that floor knowing we were coming."

She smiled. "I like your thinking. Do you want me to

hold the office and then you come in?"

He shook his head. "No, Colonel, you've done your part. We will work better if you are out of the way. We cannot afford to have you taken hostage. You remain a worker there and don't interfere. My team will be well briefed in their objectives."

Karen didn't argue. This was the lieutenant's area of expertise, not hers. "Very well, is Sergeant Malloy with you? Because with children involved, we do need a female, otherwise they could panic or go into hysterics."

"She is, and will come in with us as support. I'm thinking out of uniform and only wearing a bulletproof vest, so as not to frighten them."

"Then you seem to have the operation well in hand. What I'm going to tell you now is top secret and must remain so. We know Unit T has at least one high-ranking informer. Because of certain things that have happened in the past, I don't believe he's working alone. This is why Unit T is locked down as hard as it is. Stanley is aware, but even so, they could still get information out of the camp. If it does get out, then Luca, or Parker could pull back and do nothing. They could even look more at who has recently been employed there. If they did and picked me up as a possible informer, that may leave us out on a limb, me in particular."

"I see, I'm glad you've shared this information, Colonel, it could make the operation that more difficult if your cover is blown. These are not nice people and your life could be at risk. So in view of what you've told me, your safety, even beyond the victims', is paramount. I'm asking you, no, in fact, as the lieutenant in control of the operation, ordering you. If your cover is blown and you can get at your watch, you press your watch button three times. Children there or not, we will come in, Parker may decide to try to get information out of you in his chamber. The thought of you being in Parker's hands in that chamber, does not bear thinking about. As for the children's fate, we know where they are and can pull them out, stuff the brothel. But that is not all, every ten minutes, you press the watch button once. That will tell us you're safe and your location in the house. If we don't get that constant assurance, we will come in anyway."

"I understand."

"No, not understand. I want you to promise me. No heroics, no single-handed attempts to take them on, you follow my orders to the letter, Karen. You and I know there will always be another day, if we miss them."

"I know how to take orders, Lieutenant, and will do as you tell me. This is not about rank, it's about working together, besides trusting each other to follow the brief. I'll not try to act the heroine and go it alone, it would be pointless us all being here if we can't work as a team."

He put his arms around Karen, pulling her close, giving her a hug. She didn't try to pull away, these were her friends, people who were prepared to place their lives on the line for her, as she would for them. Karen owed them respect. "We all love you, Karen, always believe that. You have done your part, it is now our turn to finish what you have already done alone and at great risk to yourself."

Chapter 67

Karen spent the rest of her time off looking around the Nemo Science Centre. Now back in the brothel, she had just finished helping the cook with dinners for the girls, made sandwiches as usual and gone back to her room. On her mobile was a text message advertising Viagra. However, this was a hoax and was really from Lieutenant Soyer to confirm that the children were inside the brothel. From the time she'd arrived back there, she had been sending a signal via her watch every ten minutes, as arranged. She was nervous of actually being in the house now Parker had arrived, and the press of the button gave her a real sense of confidence that she wasn't alone.

There was a knock on her bedsit door and Noa walked in. "Sorry, Martine, we've had a little accident upstairs in one of the lounges, can you tidy it up for us?"

"Yes, it's what I'm here for."

They went upstairs, Karen following Noa through to the lounge with her mop and bucket. As arranged, one of the soldiers had made a mess; thankfully for Karen he'd not been sick, but dropped a litre tankard of beer, leaving broken glass and spilt drink.

"I'll need to get a dustpan and brush for the broken glass, I'll be back in a moment," Karen said, leaving the room.

Karen took her time cleaning the mess made by the dropped tankard, leaving the lounge door open so she could see the lift. Now she couldn't delay any longer, so after pressing her watch button once to say she was okay, she left the lounge carrying her bucket.

Wouter had come out of his office with a security

man she knew was called Sem. They both walked up to her and grasped an arm each. "You come with us," he demanded, propelling her through to the office.

Parker was in the office, in his hand was a gun with a silencer screwed on. "Drop the bucket, place your hands flat down on the desk," he demanded.

"Why, what have I done?" she asked, putting the bucket on the floor and placing her hands on the desk as he'd asked.

He never answered, but Wouter had come up behind Karen and frisked her. "She's clean." he told Parker.

"Hold out your hands," Parker demanded of Karen.

She held out her hands, then after Wouter removed her watch, she was handcuffed. With Parker following, Karen was marched out the office by Wouter and Sem and into the lift. Parker placed a key in the key lock and turned it. Immediately the lift began to operate, opening when it reached the top floor.

Taken Karen through to the torture room, Wouter and Sem stood her in front of the table and moved away, while Parker slammed the door shut. "I must say, Harris, you make a good cleaner. You lost your vocation in life. I'd have put you down to be more of a prostitute myself. Don't waste my time in claiming you're not she, we've already had confirmation from people in your unit that says you are. Now it is time for you to pay for that mistake and also, give us information as to what you've been up to," he said, at the same time walking up to her.

"I'll give you nothing, kill me if you want, your time is short anyway, before they come for you."

He nodded his head up and down slowly. "I expected you'd not volunteer to provide information, but it gives me an excuse, not that I need one, to show you just what we do in this room as entertainment for our clients. Of course, it means the victim suffers intense pain for our clients' entertainment, but that cannot be helped. You see, I'm a past master at skinning, having done this many times. With a woman I've even had the skin of her breasts turned into little bags as a memento for clients to bid for and remember their time in the chamber. Just for you, Harris, I intend to do this while you're awake, showing you your breasts before they're taken away. The pain, believe me, is excruciating, you will be begging me to kill you, as the first sheet of your skin is peeled off, exposing your life-giving heart still beating, your lungs working hard, as you gasp in shortened breaths. Except I won't be killing you, or allowing you to die. Before I have that pleasure, you will have told me everything. Maybe perhaps, even lost both fingers and toes, stuffed one at a time into your mouth as you try to suck even your own blood, in place of water you will so desperately need, as I dismember the rest of your body. I promise you, all the time you will be alive, feel every cut, the saw going through your bones. Then you will see the nail in front of your eye as I push it in, experiencing the liquid inside the eyeball spurt out, before you go blind. Even if you pass out and at times you will, I'll waken you, so you miss nothing of your demise." While he'd talked, he'd been shuffling his instruments on a tray left on the torture table. He'd already picked up a saw, making sure she saw it, as he ran his finger down the blade. Placing that back, he shuffled his sharp scalpels. "Works of art, don't you think, and only appreciated by the surgeon who uses them, as I will? Perfect to slice the skin into strips, before I grip the strips by my pliers and pull them away gently, to give my victim the maximum pain."

Karen just stood there, already the fear of any of those items touching her body made her skin crawl. Her only consolation, while he enthused on about his instruments, was that time was ticking, soon the time would come for her to signal that all was well, and when it didn't come, they would not delay, but enter the brothel.

He had now taken a thick rod off the tray. It was eight inches long, rounded at one end, a flat round disk on the other end. Parker brought it up to her face, a sickly grin spreading across his. "You know what this is? Of course you don't, but soon you will. It is my favourite and for every victim the beginning of their experience on my table. You see most, if not all my victims, the experience of pain makes them piss themselves, even shit. Shit's not nice for the clients, don't you think? The smell can be particularly unpleasant. Except this little device, designed by me, rammed up your backside and prevented from coming out with a little duck tape across your bottom, sorts it out."

She looked at the rod, it made her shudder involuntarily at the very thought. This man knew how to dig deep into a person's fear and she wasn't immune. "I knew you were sick, a psychopath, now with admitting you've done it before, a gun to your head is too easy for you. One in the gut, to watch you die in agony, would be far more preferable," Karen came back, in an attempt to hide her real fear of him.

He gave a forced laugh. "Such arrogance, Harris, even when you're about to meet your maker and condemned to an everlasting hell, this is appropriate punishment after your time on this earth." Then he changed his tone. "I'm tired of talking to the woman, we should begin, take her to the preparation room and get her ready, before securing her."

Karen was beginning to panic. How long it had been since she'd pressed the 'all is well' signal, she had no idea. But time had run out, Parker would soon have her on his table and she'd be helpless. But handcuffed with three men in with her, she couldn't see a way to escape, or delay him any longer.

She was taken into the room, where she'd found two trolleys last time she was here. Karen looked at the two trolleys in horror. She wasn't the only one tonight. Already a little boy was laid out on one of the trolleys a white cloth covering his naked body. He was secured down with leather straps and gazing up at the ceiling. A large strip of tape was stuck over his mouth. Next to him on the other table was a girl. She too was secured, the same as the boy. Neither could have been over fourteen. Both of them had turned their heads to see who had come in.

Parker came up to the boy, looked carefully into his eyes. "Perfect, he's just coming out of the medication I used to calm him," he commented, then looked across at Karen. "You seem a little shocked, Harris. You weren't so full of your own self-importance as to believe you were to be the only one tonight? Sorry to disappoint, you're number three. While you're chained up waiting for your turn on my table, you can listen to their screams of terror as I work on them. All the time knowing you'll soon be taking their place."

Karen couldn't let the children die. Aware of the delay between her being taken and the possible rescue, she could save them if she took their place. "Use me for your show, let the children live," she suddenly blurted out.

Parker began to laugh. "What do you think lads, we've got ourselves a hero, offering her life for the children? Is that what you really want, Harris, to take their place?"

"We all have to die sometime, including me. I'm prepared to take their place, without any objections or struggling," she replied softly.

"Then you're very brave, or stupid. I suspect the

latter. But if that's what you want, so be it. Release her handcuffs. Forget about trying to escape Harris, the door's locked and my men here will bring you down. Then get yourself undressed, before placing your hands flat on the wall," Parker ordered.

Wouter released her handcuffs.

Karen was shaking inside as she removed her clothes. Already she had begun to pray, terrified at what was going to happen. Her only comfort was that her unit wouldn't let her down and the two children would survive. Soon she was standing facing the wall as he'd told her.

Chain her up, refit the handcuffs, then sit her down," Parker told Wouter. He looked at Sen. "Get rid of her clothes down the chute, she'll not be needing them."

Wouter chained her ankles, handcuffed her once more and pushed her to the floor, while Sen took her clothes away.

Parker looked down at her. "I lied, you're not going first. Except you've conveniently stripped for me, so I now know you're carrying nothing, which you could use as a weapon, or self harm to spoil my fun. As it is, my clients didn't pay good money to see a woman of your age taken apart, they, like me, prefer to see a child on the table. They're so much more fun to watch the innocence in their face turn to sheer terror, as the knife slides through their skin and I rip the first slice from their body. As for you, your dismemberment, that will be very private, between you and me. Slow, particularly painful, while you give me the information I want. You will die with the screams in your head of the children that went before you."

Karen felt physically sick at Parker's words. "You bastard, but it's you that's the fool, delay in attempting to force me to talk and it could be too late for you. I've not come here alone," she came back at him, in a desperate attempt to change his mind about taking the children before her.

"Ah, yes, I was told you'd mobilised your unit. Perhaps you have the belief they would find you up here, while I'm cutting you up, before I'd started on the children? Or maybe you believe you could hang on to life long enough on my table, even partially dismembered, in the hope of rescue?" he hesitated, allowing what he said to sink in. "I promise you this, if they do find the chamber and manage to break in, you and the children will be dead, I'd have killed you all and be long gone."

Karen felt deflated, her efforts to save the children had come to nothing, apart from delay him starting.

He smiled. "Lost your tongue have you? No more cards to play?"

She didn't reply, to antagonise him would gain her nothing.

"I'll let you think about that, Harris. Take the boy through."

All she could do was stand there helpless as they wheeled the trolley with the little boy on through to Parker's torture table.

In the chamber, Parker laid out the items he intended to use on a small tray by the side of the table as the little boy was lifted on, before Sem brought the trolley back into the room Karen was in.

She'd known Sem since she began working here. They had talked, even sat together and drank coffee. "So you're going to stand by and watch that psychopath murder a child? What sort of man are you, Sem?"

He shrugged. "The child's worthless, picked up from the streets. A beggar, a thief, who will only get worse as he grows up. We are doing the world a favour, by ridding it of vermin."

"And the little girl, what has she done to deserve to die?"

"She, again, at fourteen is already prostituting, to feed her habit. The world, like the boy, doesn't want drug-dependent prostitutes. Amsterdam can do without that sort on its streets."

"I beg you, Sem, help me and I'll take them off the streets, give them a real life, they're just children struggling to live, that's all."

"Help you? All you've done is lie to me, pretend you were something you were not. Maybe even laugh at my naivety? Tonight I'll be the one laughing, when Parker puts you on the table."

Before she could reply, Wouter shouted through. "Sem, we want you now?"

He left the room, slamming the door behind him.

"Sorry, Martine was trying to get me to help her."

"I've told you, she isn't Martine, she's Karen Harris. So don't listen to her. She's only interested in saving herself by telling you a pack of lies and would kill you given the chance," Parker told him. "Anyway, you should be downstairs to take over from Noa, she finishes in ten minutes."

Sem said no more, and left.

"When do you want to begin?" Wouter asked.

Parker glanced at his watch. "The clients should be finished fucking the kids by now, bring them through, I'll get ready, we start immediately."

Minutes later, four clients were in the chamber. All were sitting on high stools around the table. Above the table was a camera, relaying an overhead view of the child to a large screen, so they would be able to see better what Parker was doing. Wouter slipped the large sliding-bar lock across the door and took a seat himself.

Parker came out of his room, dressed in a long, black robe, a high head dress and a mask.

"Gentlemen, welcome to the chamber. Tonight, for your entertainment, we have provided you a boy, then a girl, both ripe for skinning, before they're taken apart. I pride myself that all the time I work with them, they will remain alive, watching as you will, their own beating heart before they die. Two of you will also have the opportunity to snuff their life out, when I am finished. Please use the buckets provided, if you have the need. Drinks are on the side table. Shall we begin?"

***

Karen's mind was racing. She knew she couldn't help the boy, but confident that Unit T would soon come, she must try to save the girl. To do that she had to prevent them getting into this room. Lying down flat on the floor, stretching out, she grasped the trolley with the girl on, pulling it towards her, pushing it to one side. Then, with that trolley out of the way, she lay down again and caught hold of the empty trolley the boy had been on. Manoeuvring the trolley, she aligned it in front of the door to the room, which opened inwards. Standing, she shook the girl, who had dozed off again, as a result of the drug Parker had given her. The girl opened her eyes.

"You can understand English?" she whispered.

"A little, where am I, who are you?"

"No questions, you and I are in danger, you must keep as quiet as you can, there are people in the other room who want to kill us," she said, at the same time beginning to unfasten the leather restraining straps. It was difficult, with her hands handcuffed, but soon she had the girl's arms released, enabling the girl to do the rest. "I'll help you off the trolley. Then we need to stand it on one end and jam it behind the other and back wall."

The girl nodded, so with Karen's help and somewhat unsteadily, climbed off the trolley.

With the trolley empty, Karen and the girl stood it up on one end, sliding it behind the other. It was very tight, but with the help of the girl, using their joint body weight against the back one, the trolley was finally in position. Karen, now very confident she had protected them both, as best she could, by making it practically impossible to open the door, when they tried to come for the girl.

"We need to wait, help is coming, but it could take a little time," Karen told the girl. "Whatever happens, we must make sure the trolleys can't move; if they do, the door can be opened."

"I understand," she answered quietly.

They both sat on the floor, their backs against the rear trolley, relying on their weight to prevent it coming out, once Parker, or others, tried to open the door. Both had wrapped their naked bodies in the sheets that were on the trolleys. Karen's sheet was the discarded one that had covered the boy. Already Parker had begun. Both of them were soon reduced to tears, their hands up over their ears, trying to block the screams coming from the other room. All Karen could do now was pray Unit T would come, before they could break into the room and take her, or the girl.

Chapter 68

"The colonel has not sent her usual ten-minute signal, Lieutenant. It's now three minutes overdue," a soldier monitoring Karen's watch signals told him.

"Very well, it is pointless to delay any longer. We know the children are inside. Send a text to Sergeant Mathers and Corporal Holden to secure the office. Let's go."

Inside the brothel, Mathers and Holden left the rooms they were in, with a prostitute each, and ran down the stairs to the main reception hall. Mathers, gun in hand, burst into the office. Sem was sitting at the desk, reading. He looked up, his mouth dropping open slightly, seeing the gun.

"Lie face down on the floor, delay and I will shoot to kill," Sergeant Mathers shouted at him.

Corporal Holden meanwhile, had run to the front door, unlocking it and pulling it open. Seconds later, Unit T soldiers headed by Lieutenant Soyer burst in.

Lieutenant Soyer shouted for the lift to be brought down, then went into the office. "You, the key to get to the top floor now, or I'll blow your head off," he demanded of Sem.

"It's on the desk, with the blue tag on," he said, obviously terrified of what was happening and how they knew there was another floor. But he had no intention of not cooperating and giving them an excuse to kill him.

A soldier took the key, others outside were waiting for the lift to come down.

"Where's Martine?" Lieutenant Soyer asked Sem.

"She's locked up on the top floor,"

"Is she injured?"

"No, chained up and ready for the table. Parker

intends to kill her later, after the children."

"There are children to be used on his table up there as well?" Lieutenant Soyer asked, obviously shocked.

"Yes, a girl and a boy, before Martine is to go on his table."

Lieutenant Soyer exited the office. "Where's that bloody lift?" he asked.

"Nearly here, Sir, it was on the third floor and very slow coming down."

"Call an ambulance, tell them we want paramedics as well," he ordered another soldier, who was guarding the front door.

At that moment the lift opened, five of them, including Sherry, piled inside, turning the key lock with the key brought from the office. Immediately it began to move.

As the doors opened, they burst out onto the landing, each had a task, with two heading for the torture chamber.

***

Parker looked towards the door. Already banging was coming from outside, as someone tried to get in. He glanced at a CCTV monitor of the landing in a corner, seeing the uniforms of Unit T.

"They've got to this floor somehow. Wouter, kill Harris and the girl, then we get out of here."

Wouter ran to the door and tried to open it. "Help me, she must have jammed it shut somehow."

He came over, but even with both of them pushing on the door with their shoulders, it was only giving a little and not nearly enough to get inside.

Outside, the attempt to get through into the chamber had stopped. Parker suspected they had gone for a battering ram.

"I'll sort her out," he told Wouter. Then he turned to the clients, who had realised something was wrong and were in a panic. "You all follow Wouter, there is a way out, none of you will be caught."

As they left through the secret escape door, Parker plunged a knife into the boy's heart and went to his room, coming back out with an early M1 carbine, its barrel sawn off. Looking at the monitor, he discharged a number of rounds at the torture room door, grinning as he downed at least one soldier.

Inside the preparation room, when Karen heard the gunfire, she knew immediately by the sound it was not an M4 carbine. Parker, she decided, must have a gun.

"We must both squeeze between the upturned trolley and the wall, quickly," she told the girl, at the same time urging her to move. Karen had a feeling that he might try to kill them both, but unable to open the door, he could well shoot directly through. It wasn't a minute too soon. Parker did discharge the rest of the magazine contents through the closed door. The bullets embedded themselves in the back wall, some hitting the top of the trolley facing the door, they were hiding behind, ricocheting around the room.

Parker was laughing, as he made his way to the escape door, closing it after he went through. He knew with Unit T believing there was a gunman inside, they would be cautious, slowing them down. Which would give him plenty of time to escape.

***

On the landing, Lieutenant Soyer had called for a battering ram to open the door. Then when Parker shot through it and a soldier was hit, everyone was moved well away from the door.

"Get me a surveillance camera pushed through one of the bullet holes, let's see what's going on inside," Lieutenant Soyer ordered.

A soldier with the equipment, keeping flat to the wall and not standing in front of the door, worked the tiny camera, fixed to a flexible rod, through a hole made by one of Parker's bullets. Lieutenant Soyer looked at the screen with another soldier.

"The room seems empty, Sir. There's someone on the central table, but that's all."

Lieutenant Soyer raised his radio, calling surveillance behind the building. "Has anyone come out, perhaps down a fire escape?"

"No, Sir, it's all quiet."

"Bloody strange, has the enforcer arrived yet?" he asked a soldier at his side.

"On its way up, Sir."

At that moment the lift opened. Another soldier came out carrying a short steel tube, welded blank at one end, with two handles, one each side. Commonly known as the enforcer, it was able to apply more than three tonnes of impact force, while being less than half a metre long. Very few doors would resist such a tool.

"Break the door down, two soldiers stand behind it, with your guns primed," Lieutenant Soyer ordered.

In minutes the door was open, soldiers spilling inside, two going through to Parker's changing room. Another tried to open the door that Karen and the child were behind.

Inside the room, Karen had heard the soldiers batter the door down and the all-clear shouts, before someone tried their door.

"Just a moment, I'll let you in," Karen shouted.

She and the girl dragged the back trolley from its position. "It's open."

Two soldiers came in, seeing Karen with the girl. "Are either of you injured, Colonel?" one asked.

"No, we are fine, we both need clothes, and keys to release my ankles and the handcuffs?"

He went away to look for a key and find clothes for them both. Lieutenant Soyer entered.

"You did well to jam the door. It would seem, looking at the holes in the door, Parker intended to kill you both before he left."

"I think he did, fortunately when I heard him firing at the other door, I suspected he might do that, so we hid behind the upturned trolley, which protected us a little with its steel top. It was pretty frightening, the bullets were flying everywhere, god knows how none hit us. Have you got him, and the others in the room?"

He shook his head. "There's no one here, they have all escaped. We've found an escape door into the next building. With him delaying us, by firing through the door, we were slowed until we could be certain he wasn't inside, perhaps using a child, or even you, as a human shield."

"And the little boy?"

"He killed him before he left."

Karen sighed. "I'll get that bastard, believe me," she said quietly.

"We will, you can be sure of that. Now we need to get the children to hospital."

Chapter 69

Karen, along with Sherry, had flown to Paris, where they collected her aircraft and flown on to the camp. After calling home, to wash the dye out her hair and change into her uniform, Karen was in her office and had been joined by Stanley.

"You did a good job, Karen. It now gives you a way to take the brothel off Luca, leaving him and his backers out of pocket."

"I could have done better, Stanley. A little boy died because of my determination to catch them in the act. His screams will live with me for a long time."

"No Karen, at the time you'd no idea he had children up in his room... If you'd gone in too soon, there may have been nothing to find. After we'd left, Parker would be up to his old tricks and how many would die before we went back? We live in a cruel and vicious world and can only do our best. But I think you should take a break, recharge your batteries. It won't be possible for Sherry to go with you, she is tied up in refresher training. So why not take Ally? Just go as tourists, maybe on a cruise ship. But no fancy hotels and restaurants. Show her Egypt, or maybe Greece, and their history. The girl needs to be away from here, the same as you."

She looked at him aghast. "Do you have any concept what it's like to take a teenager away, be with her twenty-four hours a day? She already runs me ragged, besides being so cocky and self-confident. We'd end up fighting."

"No you wouldn't. She's a good kid, you know that and she misses her family. You're all she has at this moment, besides elderly relatives that can't relate to her. As it is, if you can't handle a young girl, what chance do you have commanding the unit?"

Karen sighed. "You're right, I suppose. Tell you what, find me a ship with sails, which will give her the experience of working as a team and me a break from trying to keep her interested and I'll take her."

"You're on, we will find such a ship, Karen, so you'd better pack. Now to more serious and mundane work, what do we do about Nigel Summers? We already have the evidence to convict him and we know how he got the information out about your operation."

Karen's mood changed. "That man's actions, by giving me away, killed the little boy as if he'd put the gun to his head himself. Our problem, Stanley, is he could not have given the information without help. That now means we have at least two people working together, we need the other one."

"I agree, but this time we can narrow it down to only three people who had the information about your covert action, once you'd mobilised. Two women and one man, all I'm afraid, in my intelligence unit. With your permission, I intend to feed each with certain information, that on the face of it will sound very valuable and important, to see if we can flush the informer out."

"Then you do it, Stanley. They're risking lives, and more importantly, my covert operations, which yield real results. I'm not going out on a limb to be taken down by one of my own. I'd rather get rid of them all. However, doing that allows the informant to walk away. Lives have been lost, they must pay for it."

"Leave it to me, Karen. Take the holiday and I guarantee I will find this other person."

"Come on Karen, you've had me pack very little in my backpack, fly to Athens with you, take the bus rather than a taxi, now we're walking down to the docks. What gives?" Ally asked, catching up with Karen, after she'd had to stop and re-fasten her shoe.

Karen was waiting for her by now, sitting on a low wall. Ally sat at her side. "You and I are having a holiday together. It's a little different, because we're on a sailing ship, along with a few other singles around our ages."

"That's cool, will I get to sail this ship?"

"Sail, clean, cook, lie in the sun besides swim in the sea, you'll get the lot, Ally. I try to stay low-key on holiday, so we don't talk about where I live, just say we both come from the north of England, if anyone asks. Never discuss the actual town, the street or your school. You're on holiday and not here to give your life story. I work in an office, you've left school and are waiting to go to college. Can you do that for me?"

"I can and thank you."

"For what?"

"Bringing me on holiday with you. I know we have our arguments, but I am a teenager, so it's got to be expected, I'm growing up."

"You are, but arguments apart, when we are away, you live by my standards. I was your age once and know how warm skies, walking around in skimpy clothes, along with having a little more drink than usual, with lads telling you how beautiful you are and how they'd like to get to know you better, makes you feel."

She grinned. "So you're a prude?"

"No, I like a man's company, even sex at times, but

415

I don't go to bed on the first date, or even the first week, sometimes. I have my pride and it's been a rule since I was your age and I keep to it."

"Well, I've no intention of going that far. So we'll just have a great holiday together and end up with a killer sun tan."

"Come on then, that's the ship over there, let's go shall we?" Karen said, standing and nodding towards a sailing ship, with a number of people already aboard.

Ally looked at it, then frowned. "It's a bit small, don't you think, is this holiday on the cheap?"

"I don't do cheap, Ally, in fact it's bloody expensive for what you get. But if you had the belief I'd take you on a full-size cruise ship to lounge around, you've another thing coming. So get used to it, you'll be living on board for the next ten days."

"God you're so easy to wind-up, Karen, I'm going to enjoy this," she mocked.

Karen sighed inwardly, a large cruise ship might have been a better bet, she'd at least lose Ally sometimes, this one, as she had commented on, was very small, they'd be living in each other's pockets.

By now, Ally had linked her arm with Karen's. "Let's go and meet our shipmates, shall we?"

Chapter 70

"Welcome aboard girls, my name is Crios and I'm your captain, your guide for our little cruise."

Ally looked at this man, not much more than thirty, muscular, bronze and good-looking in a rugged sort of way. She went weak at the knees.

"We expected something a little larger, Crios, how many people will be aboard?" Karen asked.

"Six guests, two crew. I can assure you there's plenty of room."

"And our privacy?"

"That goes without saying. Do you have your tickets?"

The cabin was tiny, Karen stood looking around, not sure if this was what she really wanted. "It's really small, Ally. In fact, one of us would have to sit on the bed, or even go out of the cabin, while the other dressed."

However, Ally's enthusiasm prevented her from deciding not to stay. "It's fun Karen, besides, we'll be out on deck most of the time, we wouldn't need to get dressed up that often. Look at it as a tent, you went camping didn't you, the same as I used to?"

Karen sighed. "I did and I agree most tents I went in were a great deal smaller than this. But you take the top bunk."

"Okay, I'm cool with that," she said, then lowered her voice. "Did you notice the rest of the guests are male and looked like real sailor types?"

"I did, not that I can see why you say they're sailor types? As it is, none are even close to thirty. I'm already feeling very old," Karen sighed.

Ally gave her an impromptu hug. "I'll stick with you, they may be young for you, but they look dead old for me," she mocked.

"Thanks, Ally, that's all I need. I may as well get a deck chair out and settle down with a shawl and start knitting."

Ally stood back. "You knit?"

"No, I don't bloody knit, let's just unpack, change, and get out of this excuse for a room, shall we?"

A little later, Crios and his brother Nilus, who was two years younger than him, watched the guests assemble for the safety training. Karen and Ally emerged last, both wearing shorts and T-shirts.

"We have two attractive girls on their own for a change, Crios, is the older one the mother?" his brother commented.

"She looks old enough, but I don't think so, they have different names, not that it means much these days. Maybe you should ask her."

***

It was the third day of the holiday. Both girls had settled into the routine and were now relaxed. The cabin wasn't such a problem, as Ally said, they spent all their time on deck, lying in the sun, helping to sail the boat, with plenty of stops where they could swim. Ally had thrown herself into the holiday, joining in everything that was going on. She loved the attention, then being able to swim, like Karen, and with most of the games devised around swimming, she was very popular. Karen was happy to stand back and watch the young girl really let herself go, she needed this.

Tonight they arrived at the island of Spetses and

had anchored out in the bay close to the main town of the same name, with the intention of staying overnight. It gave everyone the opportunity to go into the town and visit the many bars and clubs. It was very different to where they had been anchoring up to today.

One of the other holidaymakers on board, called Talos, aged nineteen, had asked Ally if she'd like to go to a dance club that night, and she'd jumped at the chance.

"Why don't you come with us tonight?" Ally asked, as she and Karen walked into the town.

"No way, did you know Crios had the bloody nerve to ask me if I was your mother? I was mortified, I can tell you. I don't look that old, do I?"

"You mean you're not old enough, or you don't like to admit your age? As it is, I'd love to have you as my mum, she was only two years older than you."

"Thanks, Ally, I'm flattered, but you go out with the younger lads tonight and have some fun, I'll find a bar with a pool table, perhaps take a few locals on."

Karen, even though she was on holiday, couldn't take risks, and would wear her ankle knife, if she had jeans on, besides always carrying a gun in her small handbag. On their first night aboard, she'd made Ally aware of the gun and told her that if anything happened and she needed to defend them both, she was to hit the floor and stay down.

"You sound really worried about being away from the unit, Karen? Do you really want this holiday?" Ally had asked, after being told about the gun.

"Of course, I still need a life you know. It's probably overkill and I'm a bit paranoid these days, but I don't take unnecessary risks. If it ever becomes necessary, and I hope it never will, you mustn't be in their, or my line of fire. Your life may depend on you doing as I ask."

"I understand, I had a little taste of it, nothing like you, mind, but I won't mess up and I'll not get drunk."

Karen gave her a hug. "We'll still have a good time, Ally. Just be aware, that's all."

Leaving the sea front, they were soon among all the shops before sitting down in a small bar in a side street. "I need a new bikini, Karen. Mine's really too small for me, particularly the top, and I feel self-conscious, can I buy one?"

Karen pushed fifty euros into her hand. "I should have given you spending money earlier, Ally, not that we needed it then. Don't go mad, buy what you need and if you run out let me know. Remember, I just work, you don't, so we can't go back to the boat with loads of expensive items. Staying under the radar, so to speak, it's about remaining in character, even if you fancy something, so you can't buy an item that's so expensive it would give the game away as you not being who you're purporting to be."

"Is this how you operate when you go covert?"

"That's different. Then I really am someone else, often in very high risk situations. Sometimes down to wearing costume jewellery and a five-pound watch. I've even stayed in hotels that are so downmarket, you could see the fleas jumping about on your bed and the carpet. In that place I slept on the chair."

"But you do the millionaire bit as well don't you?"

Karen smiled. "I do, in Cannes I was in a three thousand euro a day hotel suite, taken to dinner on a posh boat, so it swings around."

"I was going to talk to you about my money. While you were away last week, I got a letter from a solicitor. Apparently everyone like relatives, even distant ones have made a claim on what inheritance I had coming. I'll even lose the family home and have to live with relatives. Grandma

Jessop has rung, told me I should agree for him to act for me, but I've never heard of the man, he was arranged by them. What should I do?"

"We have legal people in the charity, Ally. I'll have them look it all over, make sure you're not being cheated. We don't charge you, it's all free on our side, so you'd be financially better off letting the charity sort it out. Even if you don't, we'll still look after you. You should ask Sherry, she left it to us and she's set up. She now looks after her affairs herself, with very little help."

Ally grinned. "Looks after it! That's an understatement, she's like a magpie, once she has it, you can't prise it out of her. She even measures the fuel in her car and never really opens it up in case she wastes it. The complaints I got from her, when you borrowed it and hadn't filled it back up to how much was in it."

Karen smiled. "It's understandable. Sherry was brought up with nothing, always had second- hand clothes, most not even fitting her. Then, there'd only be food on the table when her mother was sober enough to earn money as a prostitute, often there would be no food in the house for days, with only the school dinner, if her mother was on a bender during the week. Sherry had a very hard life, Ally, and was determined never to be in that position herself, when she was older. Although she'll not admit it, she loved her mother, saw what she went through to keep her, rather than place her in social care, and would never put her down."

"I didn't know, she never told me."

"She wouldn't, the girl has her pride and hates to talk about her past. But don't mock her for doing what she does. Sherry is very wealthy in her own right, but that makes no difference in her eyes, she'll not spend it, or even tell you she has money."

While they were talking, neither girl noticed a man was taking a more than casual interest in them both, in fact, he'd already taken a few photos, before he left.

Chapter 71

That evening, Ally was dressed in the only dress she had with her. It was short, slightly flared and wearing high heels, she looked and felt very feminine. Karen also had a dress on for a change.

Ally had laughed, watching Karen attach two narrow straps around the top of her right thigh before fitting her knife in them, upside down. "You really don't know how sexy that looks, Karen, we could be in a movie, and later, you'll lift the dress, pull it out and take on an aggressor like all heroines do."

"Yes, well, it has its downside, it's bloody uncomfortable to wear this way, when I sit down," Karen mumbled. "Sometimes I wish I was born a man, they have it so much easier."

Ally grinned. "Come off it, you love flirting and being chatted up, I can see it in your eyes."

"I suppose I would miss out on a lot, let's go, shall we?"

***

"Aren't you the lucky one, Talos?" Nilus said, when Ally came up on deck. "You're out with one of the most beautiful girls in the town tonight."

Karen looked at Ally, who remembered their talk on the dock. Ally burst into laughter. Not that the lads could understand why.

Karen, on the other hand, was more down to earth, moving closer to Talos, grasping his arm, after Ally ran ahead and down the gangplank. "Look after her well, Talos and don't get her drunk. She's only fifteen, remember that, or you'll answer to me."

He looked at her for a moment. Her tone, the coldness in her eyes and the way she spoke made him shudder a little, this was no longer the fun-loving girl joining in all the games. "I'll look after her, Karen, you can be very certain."

She just nodded, letting go of his arm.

Five minutes later, Karen left the boat on her own. Entering a bar on a side street, she bought a drink and sat down outside. Minutes later, a man who'd followed her into the bar bought himself a drink, before joining her.

She looked at him. "Ally's being watched isn't she?"

"Hanson and Mitchell are very close to her. She'll be fine no matter what she gets up to."

The man who joined Karen was, in fact, Paul Broker, one of Karen's specialist surveillance soldiers. He, along with his team, had been tasked with looking after Karen and Ally.

"Have you noticed anything unusual?" she asked.

Paul pulled out a photo and handed it her. "We watched this man taking more than an interest in you and Ally earlier today. He also took photos. I've sent his picture and the car he got into back to Stanley for identification. At this stage we're not sure if it's the paparazzi, or something more sinister."

"God, they pop up everywhere, don't they?"

He smiled. "They do, one of the hazards of being so photogenic and of interest to the public, Karen. We do know the informer has made it known you're on holiday in this area, so if the picture finds its way into a paper, we'll increase surveillance, just in case Luca or Parker decides to make a move towards you. Anyway, was Stanley's choice of holiday good, are you enjoying it?"

"It's different I can tell you; and then, sharing a cabin with a teenager, who lives in a completely different world to the one you live in, that, Paul, is hard. As it is, I bet you've got a far more comfortable and larger bed than I have, if I move even slightly, I'd fall out of bed. Tonight, I had to stand outside while Ally got ready to go out, there just wasn't the room, short of sitting in your bunk bed. Even then you have to keep your head bent, or lie down."

"I think the break is showing value, Karen, you look your old self, have even got your colour back and are no longer look tired. But if you're complaining about where you sleep, perhaps you should come on a few Dark Angel training exercises. It sounds like you need hardening up again. Got yourself too soft in that big house of yours," he ribbed.

Karen's thoughts went back to Algeria and the brothel. To be out with the lads in sleeping bags was better than that, but she just smiled. "You're right, I have. I might just do that when I get a little time. Also, thank you for the compliment, it feels good coming from one of the team. Do you want another drink?"

He shook his head. "I'm on duty, but I'll fetch you one and make sure it's poured correctly."

Karen watched him go to the bar. She liked Paul, he was her type and a man you could rely on.

***

Ally was really enjoying herself. Her life in England was nothing like this, even when the family had gone abroad for holidays, it was just sitting in a bar of the hotel at night with all the other families. Now she felt she was the centre of attention, was well aware of her sexuality and milking it for all she was worth. Already she had been dragged onto the dance floor not only by Talos, but the other lads from the boat. Talos was put out, with others pushing in and Ally going with them. Deciding he'd had enough, he wandered away. For a time Ally didn't notice; when she did, she left the dance floor to find the toilet. Joining a queue, another girl got chatting with her.

"You're English?" she asked, with a German accent.

"Yes, and you?"

"German, are you here alone?"

"I'm not supposed to be, but the lad I was with seems to have disappeared."

"Then you join us, I am here with six girls. You will have a good time."

It was coming up to eleven, Ally had never drunk so much. Every time she finished one, another was pushed into her hand. She was feeling decidedly drunk. A number of German lads had joined the girls, with one taking Ally onto the dance floor holding her tight, otherwise she'd have fallen down.

Eventually she pushed him away. "I need some fresh air," she told him, walking away and outside. Minutes later, down a narrow passage, Ally threw up. When she came out, she felt a lot better, but still lightheaded and unsteady, not really knowing where she was and what she should do now.

At that moment two men approached. "I think you've had enough, Ally, it's time you returned to the boat," one said quietly.

Ally was looking at them. "Who are you and how do you know my name?" she asked, already trying to decide if she should run, or scream for help.

"We're part of Unit T and here to look after you and Karen. The name's Hanson, this is Mitchell," one of them said, at the same time showing his warrant card.

The relief on her face was obvious. "You mean Karen sent you?"

"No, we've been with you all night. You were perfectly safe, but we decided to step in when it was obvious you were drinking too much and out here alone. Karen's down in a bar on the front, we'll take you." He pulled out a small packet of wet wipes. "But first of all, let's get the streaks of eye make-up off your face, shall we, then you can comb your hair," he told her, wiping her face.

Finally, after he cleaned her up and she'd combed her hair, Ally gave them a weak smile. "Thank you. You've saved my life, I was really worried about what I should do now."

"Not really, Ally, you weren't in any danger. But you look your old self again, let's go, shall we?" Hanson told her.

As they walked Ally sobered up even more. "Karen's going to be mad. I've made a right fool of myself drinking as much as I have."

"Then don't admit it. We're not here to decide if you drink or not, even if you let your hair down and party, we're just here to keep you safe," Hanson answered.

"So have you been with us since the start of the holiday? Does Karen know?"

"Yes to both. It's what we do, we look after our commander, as much as we can, or as much as she lets us."

"So she can be a bit of a rebel at times?"

They both laughed. "You might say that, she was worse when she was seven years younger, then we had our work cut out."

"Is it because you were watching me, that she allowed me to go out alone then?"

"Probably, we don't know that. But she'd not have

been comfortable in leaving a fifteen-year- old out at this time, in a strange town, unless she knew we were around. It's your holiday as well you know."

"So if I'd found a lad, what would you have done then?" Ally asked with interest.

"Nothing, just made sure he got you back to the boat safely. Whatever time you left him, we don't nurse you, Ally, we protect you." Hanson stopped. "Right, Karen's sitting outside the bar, we'll leave you. Remember, Unit T was never here, if anyone on board saw you with us, you just asked the way to the seafront. As we were going that way, we showed you. Although you don't need to mention to Karen you had a little too much drink, she will eventually receive a report, we have no option. She is the commanding officer. But it will only say that you left the club alone and we made sure you got back to the seafront."

"Thank you, see you around maybe?"

"Hopefully not. Just enjoy your holiday, Ally," Hanson said, then they walked away.

"Hi," Alley said sheepishly, as she approached Karen.

"Where's Talos?" Karen asked.

"I think I upset him, he didn't like me dancing with other lads from the boat. So he bailed."

"You should have called me, Ally."

"I know, but I've a confession to make. After Talos bailed, I met some German girls, I drank a little too much, drinks just kept coming and I didn't realise how it was affecting me. I went outside alone and threw up. Two men from Unit T brought me back. I'm sorry, but I don't intend to lie about how stupid I've been."

"We've all done the same, Ally, believe me. So long as you learn from the experience, it's fine. But Talos shouldn't have left you, whatever you did. Not that I can see dancing with others is a big deal on his part. I don't suppose you want another drink then?"

She shook her head. "I'm fine, I'll just sit here with you."

"Thanks, that blows my chance of being picked up then, I may as well get another drink and drown my sorrows," Karen ribbed.

Ally grinned. "Then it's a good job I came. I can't have my new mum being picked up by a stranger, you never know where it would lead."

Chapter 72

Kenneth Parker was looking on the page of a paper that reported on the famous and what they're up to, who they're going out with and the functions they attend. He had sent Shaun out to collect a paper after receiving a call from a man called Padjent, who sold information to the criminal underworld. The call had come after Parker, incensed at losing the Amsterdam brothel and Karen's escape, had contacted him to find out where she was. He was determined to take her down once and for all. Indifferent to who replaced her, she owed him big-time and she would pay with her life.

"The bloody nerve. Walks around as large as life, as if she is invincible," he commented.

"Who are you talking about?" Shaun asked.

"Karen Harris, photographed in Greece on holiday with that girl Ally we snatched some time back."

Shaun looked at the photos."It could be her, but Ally is recognisable."

"It's her, believe me. The hair's even back to its own colour. Last time I saw her, she had black curly hair. Anyway, according to this article she's with Adventure Sailing, look them up on the internet, will you?"

Keying in the name, Shaun soon had the website. "They sailed from Athens on the seventh for a ten day cruise. According to the holiday dates they're back in Athens next Saturday."

"Is she now. Then we go to Athens and meet her. This time she will die. I want you and Liam with a few lads."

"Why do we want so many? I'll take her out getting off the boat."

"No way, she got away from me last time, this time

I'll complete my promise and skin her alive. That's after she witnesses Ally being skinned before her. You just get the lads together."

"What about weapons?"

"I'll arrange to pick them up in Greece. Luca has contacts there."

***

By the Saturday, Kenneth Parker was in Athens, along with five ex-military soldiers, including Shaun and Liam. They were standing around in an industrial unit, checking over a number of weapons that had arrived in the back of a van.

"Some of this stuff is crap, Kenneth," Shaun told him. "Look into the barrels, you can see rust."

"Then get the fuckers to clean them. We've two hours before the boat arrives. So you and Liam get yourselves down to the dock, pick a location and snatch them both as they leave."

"You definitely want them taken to the abandoned Heliniko Olympic site then?"

"I do, it's a fitting end for her to die in such a place. After they're skinned, we'll string the bodies up from the Olympic diving board for the world to see."

***

Shaun pointed to the sailing ship as it came into sight. "That's it, once it docks we should bring the car closer to the jetty."

Nearly an hour later, Karen and Ally, after having given everyone on the boat a hug, were walking up the jetty, carrying their backpacks, dressed in jeans and T-shirts.

Liam had manoeuvred the car closer to the beginning

of the jetty. In this position the girls would have to pass them. Shaun had already climbed out of the car and was leaning on the sea wall looking out into the bay, having seen them come off the boat. As the girls passed him, he suddenly spun around, grabbed Ally's long hair, pulling a gun from his pocket, he put it up to her head.

"Both of you, in the back of the car. Delay and she dies," he demanded.

Karen climbed into the back. Shaun pushed Ally in after her, slamming the door shut, then climbed into the front alongside Liam. He twisted round watching them both, the gun raised and directed at Ally as the car sped away.

"Where are you taking us?" Karen asked.

"You're going to be a star, in fact, because you both like swimming so much, we're going to hang you both off the old Olympic swimming pool. No medals of course, we don't do medals," he mocked.

"Let Ally go, she's done nothing, I presume it's me you want?" Karen said quietly.

Shaun gave a hint of a smile. "Think a lot of yourself do you, believe you're that important? You're not, Parker wants you both. You, Ally, for escaping and losing him money from your sale. You, Harris, for interfering with his venture in Amsterdam. In fact, he intends to carry on from when he was so rudely interrupted, last time you were with him. He intends to skin you both alive."

"Parker is with you then? That's handy, last time I saw him, I told him I'd put a bullet in his gut. I still intend to do that," Karen said, with obvious hate in her voice.

"Can you believe the arrogance of this woman, Liam? She has some sort of belief she's going to escape. Well, Harris, unlike the last inept efforts to keep hold of you, we're ex special forces, with a further three gunmen waiting for us, just in case we get company. You're going nowhere this time, except to your death. We don't mess about, as the police found out in Manchester."

"So it was you two who killed the policeman in the UK?" Karen asked.

"They got in the way, after Parker decided to teach Ally here a lesson she wouldn't forget. As it is, if you'd not taken her to France, she would have been back with us, working her butt off in a brothel. So blame yourself, not us, her family died."

Ally stared in horror at Shaun. "You killed my family?" she gasped.

He sniggered. "Burned them alive, didn't we Liam? We even listened to their screams," he mocked, embellishing on their actions. "Soon you'll be joining them. "

What happened next, no one expected, not even Karen. Ally had been told they died peacefully, but it was a lie, they died in agony. This sent her berserk. She suddenly started lashing out at him, scratching her long nails down his face, no longer afraid of the gun, screaming abuse, tears streaming down her face, such was her distress. Shaun was taken by surprise, then, to have her fingernails embed themselves in his face, he tried to fight her off, but dropped the gun down between the front seats, in his efforts. Realising his error and in his haste to retrieve it, he pushed Liam to one side out of the way. He in turn temporarily lost control of the car as it veered all over the road, narrowly avoiding hitting vehicles in the busy traffic as he struggled to bring it back under control.

Karen, in all this panic, calmly reached down and opened her bag, pulling her gun out, shooting directly through the front seat, knowing she'd hit Shaun somewhere.

He screamed in pain as the bullet ripped through

him, before slumping down.

"Don't stop, keep on driving," Karen said curtly, with the gun now raised and touching the back of Liam's head.

They came out of the traffic to a quieter area.

"Pull in at the side of the road," Karen demanded.

He stopped. "You should both piss off, think yourselves lucky that Parker hasn't got hold of you," he said.

"I decide what I do, not you," Karen came back at him. "So, very carefully, with two of your fingers, reach into your pocket and take your own gun out, holding it up in the air. Believe you can turn it on me, think again. I'm no amateur, no naive girl trying to escape. I've lived with guns since I was eighteen, know how to use and handle them."

"I know what you are," he said, at the same time doing as she wanted.

Karen took the gun. "That's good, I also want the other gun, so do the same, reach down between the seats, pulling it out with your two fingers."

Again he did as she told him. Liam was realistic, very aware that Karen would shoot, he was certain of that. "So you've got the guns, what now?" he asked, after she'd taken the second gun from him.

"Drive to the Olympic site, where Parker is waiting for us."

"You want me to take you to Parker? Are you some sort of fool, Shaun's already told you he has three gunmen."

"You don't question, you do as you're told, or die. Now shut up and drive."

"If you want. But it will be you who will die," he said, pulling out into the traffic once more.

Ally by this time had quietened, scrunching her knees up to her body, her arms around her legs, on the back seat, staring ahead vacantly, tears still running down her face. The girl was in obvious shock, no longer aware of what was going on around her. All she could hear were the screams of her mum, dad and sister in her head, knowing it was she that had killed them.

Karen glanced at her. "Pull yourself together Ally. Shaun lied to you, the smoke would have overcome them while they slept. They would have died well before the flames reached them, believe me."

"It doesn't matter who I believe, I killed them, that's all that matters," she came back.

"You can think that way, I did about my own family. But it can't be undone. You now owe it to them to show that their deaths weren't in vain, as you're their only daughter left. Only you can show them that, by living the life they always wanted you to live."

Ally looked at the man driving, the other possibly dead at his side. "What do you want me to do?"

"For a start you can sit up properly, wipe your face and tidy yourself up. I don't want a blubbering child sitting at my side. Then you can take my mobile out of the bag and send a text for me."

Soon they arrived at the Olympic Park, Liam pulling up alongside a fence that was down in many places.

Karen looked out of the window. "My god, the bloody place is derelict," she said, completely shocked at what she was looking at.

"What did you expect, Parker is hardly waiting in the centre of a modern shopping complex?" Liam mocked. "So are you going to run now?"

Karen said nothing as at that moment a car drew up behind them. Paul, along with Hanson and Mitchell, climbed out, all carrying guns.

He opened Karen's door. "We got your text, Karen, you seem to have things under control."

"I have, Hanson, can you and Mitchell sort these two here, while Paul and I talk? Ally, out of the car and into the one behind please."

Karen and Paul walked a short distance away.

"I must admit, I never expected Parker to go to these lengths to find me and try to take me down, Paul. He must have been really pissed off. As it is, we have a choice. Do we walk away, or go in and flush him out? He has three others with him."

"Three gunmen and Parker. We've M4s in the boot, I can't see them being much of a problem. There will be three of us. You should remain here and look after the prisoner."

"I'm going in, that man owes me," Karen came back at him.

"That's not recommended, Karen. You're emotionally involved and would go in with the real intention of killing Parker. I'm not prepared to assist you in that, leaving you open for a premeditated murder charge. No matter what he's done, the law must punish him, not us."

She shrugged, but wasn't prepared to admit to Paul just how many times in her covert operations she'd acted both as judge and executioner. "It's not about emotion and the need to kill the bastard. As far as I'm concerned, providing he's captured and only killed if he resists, I'll follow the law."

"In that case, you have no bulletproof jacket, or suitable weapons, so you remain here. This is not about who is in command, it's about who is suitably equipped, and not putting others at risk if they are vulnerable."

She knew he'd got her and was determined she wouldn't be let anywhere near Parker; he was convinced in his mind that she would kill him. "Very well, I'll stay here. Just make sure you get him for me, will you?"

"If he's there, we will. You look after Ally and the prisoner."

Chapter 73

Kenneth Parker was pacing. He was with a man called Vinny, who for five years had been in special forces. Both were by the outdoor pool close to the changing rooms. "Where the fuck are they, it's not that far away and the boat docked over two hours ago?" Kenneth commented obviously uptight with the delay.

"The Harris women, from what I've read, is pretty astute." Vinny answered. "Unless the traffic is holding them up, which from what I've seen is pretty bad, we should take up defensive positions in case they have failed. If Harris has got Dark Angel soldiers around here, they will quickly box us in."

"How the fuck can she bring in soldiers that quick? The woman's on holiday and I've had no information about a Unit T mobilisation. No, it's the traffic, send the other two to look around for anything unusual. I'm not weakening my position on a hunch."

At that moment one of the men ran out of the changing room area across towards Vinny. "There's at least two, maybe three soldiers approaching from behind the buildings. We can't see any more, but that doesn't mean there aren't any."

"How are they dressed?" Vinny asked.

"All black, combat clothes, bullet proof jackets and helmets. Probably special forces."

Vinny looked at Parker. "No Unit T you say. Dressed that way, they will be troops belonging to Harris's Dark Angel unit. So you can be certain she's already captured Shaun and Liam. Then, if they are forward surveillance, she'll have at least one unit backing up, that's twenty-five men."

"Rubbish, I'd know if Unit T had moved that number of troops to Greece. I can assure you she hasn't. So we call her bluff and take the three on, show her we're not messing about," Parker told him.

The man who'd just brought the information cut in. "Excuse me, have you seen the weapons you provided? There are trained soldiers out there, with the firepower they carry, you can forget it. I'll fight anyone on equal terms, with decent weapons, but I'm not going up against possible sniper fire and M4's."

"It's what you're being paid for, besides, we have a commanding position, they have little cover," Parker retorted.

"Maybe, but if they have sniper rifles, they can pin us down while they bring in more troops, or wait for nightfall, then using night vision glasses move in. This is not good," Vinny added.

"Stop whining," Parker told him. "If you can't take out a few soldiers, what am I paying you for? We meet Harris head-on and send her to hell. Now do as I tell you to do, before she can bring in more troops, or get any closer."

***

Paul's first objective was the difficult task of getting into the complex of changing and restroom areas behind the pool. He suspected, after seeing odd flashes of binoculars in the building, that they had already been seen, not that he was certain it was any of Parker's men. Except it made it all the more critical to find suitable cover. The uncertainty was soon clarified after spurts of gunfire came from the complex. He suspected the shooting was designed to hold him back, rather than have any hope of hitting any of them. However, the gunfire made the situation more confusing, because a number of people actually using the complex, for somewhere to live, began running out from all directions, believing the authorities were on one of their regular operations to clear the area. It all contributed to a difficult position on Paul's side, and risked the killing of innocent people.

Soon everything was quiet, but the confusion had allowed Paul and the other two soldiers to actually gain enough ground that they were now inside the complex. What they found was a rabbit warren of rooms, virtually impossible to search and particularly dangerous, not knowing who or what was round the next corner.

He called Karen. "We need more troops, Karen, it will take us far too long to clear each area, even then, they could double back and we'd not know. There are also civilians, most have left, but we can't be certain. It is far too dangerous and risky to go on with just three of us."

"Very well, hold your position. I'll get help."

Karen, using her security code, called the International Police Cooperation Division of Greece's Hellenic Police force. After hearing her situation, they dispatched armed police units. Like every other country in the EU, they were aware that a call for assistance from Unit T, must be acted upon.

***

Parker had been left alone, while Vinny, with the other lads, assessed the situation. Soon Parker could hear gunfire; he decided that no matter what, the chance of taking Karen or Ally was lost. It was time to get out, before there was no place to run.

Taking the opportunity, when the initial gunfire

caused chaos, Parker began to move through the passageways of the complex. To blend in with the people running from the complex, he grabbed an abandoned jacket, dirty and ripped, quickly slipping it on. Now he was running out of the building along with others, towards the high fencing that surrounded the Olympic village. As far as he was concerned, Vinny and the other two could do what they wanted, die, surrender, whatever, he couldn't care less.

The gunfire had stopped as he walked around the perimeter. He was heading for a parked hire car left outside. In five hours he was due to fly out anyway, considering by then he'd have killed Karen and would need to get out of Greece fast. It was then when he saw the car, Shaun had hired with another vehicle behind it.'

He came to a halt, staring at it and the person standing alongside. It was Karen, she was obviously on the telephone and not looking his way, but across towards the derelict swimming pool.

'So, she's not had the guts to go in herself, has she?' he thought. 'Maybe we should get acquainted once more?'

Pulling his gun out, he walked towards her, confident she would not recognise him, dressed as he was in the old jacket. She didn't, and he was only feet from her before she turned in his direction to see who was approaching.

"Don't make a move to your pockets, Harris, otherwise I'll stop you with a bullet," he told her curtly.

If Karen was nervous, she didn't show it. "Well, if it isn't Parker, I didn't know you were here on holiday as well."

"Sit on the ground, at the side of the car, hands under your bottom," he told her, at the same time looking into Shaun's car. He could see Liam inside, sitting on the back seat, one of his wrists secured to a safety belt anchor point.

"Where's the key to release Liam?"

"In my pocket."

"Throw it to me, but be very careful how, a wrong move and I'll put a bullet in you."

Karen moved a hand into a pocket, pulling out a handcuff key.

"Let me see it, before you throw it," he demanded.

She held it up in the air.

"Throw it."

She threw it, perhaps a little too hard, but intentionally so that the key would land behind him. Cursing her under his breath, he bent down to pick it up, for just a second taking his eyes off her.

That was all Karen needed. Moving her free hand quickly, she pulled the ankle knife from its sheath. The next moment she'd thrown it directly at Parker. Her throw, with the accuracy of a person very experienced in using a knife, which she'd had since she was eighteen, was on-target: the knife embedded itself into Parker's side. The shock of it finding its mark was immediate, at first Parker believed it was an insect that had bit him, but he soon realised it wasn't. By then Karen was on the move; she'd literally rolled herself away from the side of the car, pushed herself up and threw herself at Parker, grasping his arm that held the gun and ripping it from him, throwing it away. But Parker was fighting back, he hit her across the side of the head, sending her reeling. He pulled the knife from his side, with every intention in using it himself to kill her.

Ally had seen all this, sitting in the back of the car. Then when they had actually begun fighting, she'd opened the door and climbed out, remaining still watching, not sure how she could help. That was before the gun ended up at her feet. She bent down, picked it up and like she'd seen so many times on television, aimed it at Parker. "Leave my friend alone, otherwise I will shoot," she screamed at him.

Parker, ignoring Karen, who was only just recovering from his blow, looked at Ally and smiled. "So, Ally, you believe you can shoot a man? Just give it to me, little girl, and I'll let you walk away."

"You killed my family," she replied, tears running down her face. "Go to hell," she said, then squeezed the trigger. Not once, but time after time until it was just clicking.

The first bullet hit him in the chest, the following ones missed as he was thrown back. But the first shot was sufficient to prevent him retaliating in any way.

Karen stood and took the gun off her. "That was a very brave thing to do, Ally," she said, putting her arms around her and pulling her tight.

"Have I killed him?" she whispered.

"No, just wounded him, but he's going nowhere now and the police are on their way."

Chapter 74

The day after returning from Greece, in the afternoon, Karen was overseeing the weekly meeting. Stanley had opened his folder to give her and the others in the room an update.

"The Greek police have confirmed the capture of the gunmen who were with Parker. They finally gave up when dusk came. They were out of ammunition and were talked out. Our men are unharmed and on their way back as we speak. Parker is under guard at the hospital and will survive to stand trial. A warrant has been issued against Luca, the other man, who owned the brothel in Amsterdam. He's disappeared, the police are looking for him." He hesitated, looking around the room. "None of you know, but Unit T had an informer. Their actions have caused a great many problems in the operations we've conducted. We knew the identity of one, but suspected there was another. We were right and this morning Sharon Mercer, from my intelligence unit and Nigel Summers of legal, has been arrested. They have caused the deaths of many and their information has allowed violent criminals go free. They will be charged, among other things, with conspiracy to murder."

The meeting went on for some time as operations were brought up to date, with many speaking. Now they had all left, leaving Karen and Stanley alone in the room.

"I haven't had time to ask, Karen. Did you have a good holiday?" Stanley asked, as she re-filled her cup with coffee.

"Eventful, Stanley, as always."

"Yes, it made interesting reading. Looks like this rebel teenager, who you dreaded taking on holiday, turned out to be very competent. Maybe you even owe her your life?"

Karen sighed. "There's a great many people I owe my life to, Stanley. I'm not a one-person army and do need help at times. But you're right, Ally deserves to be congratulated on what she's done. Although, to be fair, her actions were those of a girl facing her family's killers, who had gone into hysterics. Even so, her presence of mind in picking that gun up was very brave of her, if just to hand it to me. I'd rather she had done that than use it, a young girl holding a gun with the intention of killing anyone no matter what the provocation is not good. Look where it's landed me."

"I can understand your concern and you're right, it would be dangerous for her to have the belief she could mete out her own justice, to anyone who has done her harm. You know she's asked to stay on at the camp? She doesn't consider there is a life in the UK to return to?"

"Yes, I do. I'm not sure if we can do that, Stanley. This is more of a job for my charity, to find her a home and settle her in, not me directly. I can't keep collecting people, I've already got Sherry."

He looked directly at her. "I wasn't considering for one moment that you should look after her. You and Sherry can't even look after yourselves, let alone have the responsibility of bringing up a teenager, even if it's just for a few years before she's of age."

He could see the indignation on her face.

"Excuse me, I am perfectly capable of looking after Ally, thank you. In fact..." Karen hesitated. "Ally can live with me. I'll give her a home, until she's eighteen and can make her own decisions."

"You, with Sherry, are going to take Ally on? I've got to see this," he said, hiding a smile of satisfaction. The young girl would do Karen good, maybe it would even curtail her high-risk operations if she knew she had a responsibility back home. He hoped so, the three girls really did need each other.

CPSIA information can be obtained at www.ICGtesting.com
Printed in the USA
BVOW08s2220050715

407360BV00001B/1/P

9 781908 090454